MW01172261

ACCIPITER WAR

Fort Brazos: Book One

Patrick & Blake Seaman

6276 KM

LENGTH: 6,270 KM
RADIUS: 1,448 KM

SA: 70,274,160 SQ KM
ORIGIN: UNKNOWN
AGE: UNKNOWN
LOCATION: UNKNOWN
INHABITANTS: UNKNOWN
PURPOSE: UKNOWN
ENVIRONMENT: EARTHLIKE
OTHER LIFE: HOSTILE

ACCIPITER WAR

MILSTAR BOOKS

ACCIPITER WAR

by Patrick Seaman & Blake Seaman

Third Edition
January 2023

Printed in the United States of America
EBook Edition: ISBN-13: 979-8-9873243-2-5

First Paperback Printing: June 2018
Paperback Edition Original: ISBN-13: 9781983041853
Paperback 2023 3rd Edition: ISBN-13: 9798987324318
First Hardback Printing: May 2021
Hardcover Edition Original ISBN-13: 9798503357974
Hardcover Revised Edition ISBN-13: 9798987324301

Blake Seaman original theme music is available on Spotify, iTunes, Amazon, CDBaby, etc.

Cover Art by Ron Miller

MilStar Books
MILSTARBOOKS.COM

This work is dedicated to the men and women who selflessly defend freedom and civilization every day.

- Patrick and Blake Seaman

Search & Rescue

Outskirts of Fort Brazos
Day 2. Noon

Fort Brazos Sheriff's Deputy Grayson Miles' tan and brown Sheriff's Department SUV turned off the Interstate and led the way down Farm to Market Road 21, followed by Lt. David Garreth's Humvee, towing a small trailer. The day was bright and clear, and they had already made many stops at homes and businesses in their Search and Rescue designated area of responsibility.

All four men in the Humvee were Army Recon veterans of multiple Middle East deployments together. They were all still in shock from the events of the last day and a half and rode in uncharacteristic silence, without their usual banter and music. The driver, tall and lanky, with jet-black hair, leaned forward, again, looking up, out the windshield.

From the passenger seat, Lt. Garreth glanced at the driver, Specialist Simmons, and fought the urge to sigh. "Eyes on the road, Simmons," he admonished. His tone was firm but understanding. Lt. Garreth was lean and compact, with worry lines earned in dark and dangerous places. Specialist Simmons wasn't the only one who had been preoccupied with the sky. Corpsman Mendez and even Sargent Washington had also been looking up.

Specialist Simmons blinked and swallowed, "Sorry, LT."

Lt. Garreth sighed. After all that had happened, he could not bring himself to be too hard on them. He'd caught himself doing the same thing. "Look, I get it. Everyone just stay sharp. We don't want to miss anyone who needs help."

Corpsman Mendez, usually the most ebullient of the group, looked drawn and haggard instead of his normal lady-killer poster-boy devil-may-care persona. His chocolate eyes and brilliant smile were haunted. He'd faced horrific medical trauma countless times, but this was different. They had encountered a few people with minor injuries, but there were a great many dead. So many that they had stopped reporting in, except to periodically update the death list to schedule someone to come and collect the bodies.

The situation today was different than the battlefield. There were no bombs or destruction or gunshots echoing. There was no smell of burning cordite or the stench of mangled death. There was no battlefield. The dead were civilians who should have been safe from harm, at home in their beds.

The Sheriff's Department SUV turned down an unmarked tree-lined dirt road, and they followed it to a small, unpainted wood-frame house, repeating their pattern for the day. They had figured out early on that having a crowd of soldiers at someone's door might not send the right message. They waited for Deputy Miles to knock on the door and inquire if anyone needed help. The deputy had a heavyweight boxer's build and a shaved head underneath his Sheriff's Department-issued Stetson hat. Something about him made Lt. Garreth make a mental note to ask if he had served. Marines?

A slim old man answered the door. They spoke quietly. The old man worriedly ran his hand through his thinning grey hair while glancing up through the trees at the sky and back again. After a few minutes, he smiled weakly, and they shook hands before he retreated inside. Deputy Miles walked over to the Humvee.

"That was Mr. Collins. His wife is visiting their daughter in San Antonio."

Corpsman Mendez groaned, and Sargent Washington closed his eyes and shook his head. Specialist Simmons simply swallowed and turned to look away.

Lt. Garreth pursed his lips. "Does he know?"

"I think so, yeah. He's in denial. I'll put him on my follow-up list. I'm afraid he may decide to, well…."

Lt. Garreth cleared his throat. No one was surprised. The scale of the crisis was such that each of them knew some people would decide to end things. "O.K. Deputy, where to next?"

"The Hoffman dairy farm is up the road. They're a big family, and Barrett Hoffman is a City Council member."

"Okay, lead the way."

Minutes later, they were back on FM 21, paralleling a long and well-maintained and recently painted white double-bar fence line. The field beyond was dotted with large round hay bales and a great many dairy cows. Some of the cows were lying on their side like toppled toys, clearly dead.

It was a familiar sight now, and they were already becoming numb to it.

Deputy Miles' SUV slowed and crossed a large in-ground cattle guard – rows of stainless-steel metal bars in the ground that cattle cannot walk over. Specialist Simmons followed, and they slowly wound their way up the hill towards a large rambling farmhouse with its own separate fence and circle driveway.

No one came out from the house to greet them. The wind gusted dust and leaves for a moment, but it was quiet except for the mooing of the cows.

Deputy Miles got out and walked to the front door, and paused. The door was slightly ajar. He knocked and called out, hand resting on the butt of his service pistol, "Councilman Barrett? Margaret? Is anyone home?"

He repeated the call and waited a full minute before slowly walking out toward the Humvee. It was freakishly cool for August, and he pulled his jacket close.

Lt. Garreth and the others got out to meet him.

"Lieutenant? Would you and your men help me look around? I know Barrett, and he's not the kind who leaves his front door open like that. Something's not right."

"Of course, Deputy." He turned to his men. "Mendez, go with the Deputy and help him check things out. There might be some injured people like at the first house we stopped at. Washington, scout around the house but stay close. Simons, remain here with me."

Sargent Washington nodded, "Yes, Sir," and shared a worried look with Lt. Garreth before leaving. They had no radios with them except for the long-range unit in the Humvee. Sargent Washington was the oldest of the group. Black with very dark skin, he was happy sticking with doing exactly what he was best at and had "avoided" attempts to promote him to Officer Candidate School. He turned and walked away before furtively looking up at the sky again.

Carrying his medical ruck, Corpsman Mendez followed Deputy Miles to the house, where the Deputy banged loudly on the door, "Sheriff's Office! We're coming inside. Anyone home?"

At the Humvee, Lt. Garreth put his hand on Specialist Simmons's shoulder, looked him in the eyes, and spoke quietly, "Simmons, get your M4 out and stand watch. I don't like this." Although there were M4 rifles secured in the back of the Humvee, only Lt. Garreth wore a sidearm. General Marcus had been concerned that citizens might not react well to seeing armed soldiers show up on their doorstep. However, he'd ordered that the teams carry rifles in their vehicles, just in case something changed.

Specialist Simmons swallowed grimly and nodded, "Yes, Sir, I don't like it either. This is creeping me out too."

Deputy Miles and Corpsman Mendez returned a few minutes later.

Deputy Miles began, "Nobody's inside except grandma Abigail, and since nobody is here, I asked your man Mendez to get a body bag for her. I'd like your help to search the rest of the farm to see where everyone else is."

Sargent Washington rounded the corner of the house in an urgent trot, grim-faced, and shouted, "Lieutenant! I found signs of a struggle, blood and shell casings on the ground, and, well, something strange you've got to see for yourself."

Sight & Sound

Highway
36 Hours Earlier
Day 0. 0 Hour

Twenty miles outside of Fort Brazos, Texas, the interstate highway was a cold black ribbon, disappearing into a stygian night. An 18-wheel semi-truck sat on the pavement, surrounded by a motionless fog like some lifeless insect in amber. The road split a vast open prairie that disappeared into the darkness. There was no sound, smell, or movement of any kind.

Then, in the distance, a sound grew as though the world were new to the idea. A moving wall of soft white light backlit the fog, racing closer and closer. The sound swelled into a deafening, smothering hiss as the ethereal wave of cold, pale light swept across the fields and highway and then over and through the truck and disappeared into the fog beyond.

In its wake, the grass in the field swayed, and the fog shimmied and swirled free from its freeze-frame stillness. Water droplets danced in Brownian motion. There was sound everywhere, from wind through the grass to other sounds of an almost living world. Condensation beads began to form on the truck's cold metal and glass.

Another wave of light approached. The fog glowed green and came alive with electric crackling and pops. An actinic tsunami of rippling electric St. Elmo's fire thundered and dopplered across the plains, licking everything in its path, flashing over the road and truck before racing off into the distance. In its wake, a Promethean wail split the world asunder, and the landscape heaved with acrid ozone.

Wayne Blanchard sat inside the truck cabin as though frozen with his head leaned back and his eyes closed. His long wavy chestnut hair framed a face both innocent and world-weary. Pinky, his Chihuahua, lay in his lap looking like a stuffed animal. The cabin was carefully decorated with Oriental rug pieces, earth-toned fabrics, and hardwood accents.

As the green St. Elmo's fire splashed through the cabin, Wayne and Pinky spasmed to life as though shocked by defibrillator paddles. Wayne gasped for air, and his eyes bulged open. Pinky screamed and yipped in terror and burrowed into the bulky safety of his master, while Wayne shuddered, shook, and blinked in pain and terror. His thick muscled arms reflexively braced against the steering wheel for an impact that didn't come.

Without warning, the truck's diesel engine coughed to life, and the cockpit gauges, lights, and computer screens flickered on. The exterior running lights and headlights flared on as well, reflecting back from the fog.

Wayne's chest heaved, and sweat poured off his brow. Looking around desperately, he cried out, "Wha... Wha... What the hell! What happened?!"

Behind him, in the sleeper berth cabin, his wife Sybil sat cross-legged, silent, trembling and pale, clutching a forest-green linen blanket. Rich fabrics and pillows surrounded her in the sleeping cabin that Wayne sometimes joked looked like the inside of a Genie's bottle. Her long, dark, curly hair was awry, framing a face more comfortable with smile-lines and mirth. Her red and black silk pajamas seemed a size too big, as though she'd somehow shrunk inside them. Her lips were slightly parted, and her watery brown eyes stared into the distance.

Sybil opened her mouth wider to speak, but nothing came out. She blinked hard and swallowed, trying again. Her voice was weak and small. "W-Wayne?"

Suddenly sweating profusely, Wayne desperately looked around him, clutching his heaving stomach. "Uh..." There was nothing in the rear-view mirrors or camera displays. "Uh... are you okay? I... I don't think we crashed. I think... Uh... What happened?" He swallowed hard.

Sybil pulled the blanket up to her chin. "Are... we... are we dead?"

Shaking and breathing hard, Wayne decided, "Uhm, we seem to be in one piece, baby."

Her eyes focused on something not there, and she shuddered. "I think I was."

Wayne turned around to look at her. "Uhm, you're okay, we're okay, baby. I think."

Sybil whispered. "Wayne, I don't understand. It's been so long. We were… I was… I can't explain it. I was there… and… and the stars fell."

Wayne turned a shade of green. "Just a nightmare, baby… I think we both must have dozed off, but I don't remember parking… God, we're lucky. I don't understand. I wasn't even tired! I've never fallen asleep at the wheel before, never! Wait, what did you say?"

Outside, the headlights shone through a break in the fog. Glancing out the windshield, Wayne exclaimed, "Jesus! We're in the middle of the road!" He quickly put the truck in gear and pulled over to the side of the road. He hit buttons and, outside, the hazard lights joined the standard running lights.

Shaking and sweating, he unbuckled his seat belt and put Pinky in the passenger seat. "Baby, I'm going to check the rig over… make sure everything is okay." He had the presence of mind to grab a flashlight from its charger before he climbed down out of the truck. Looking back at his wife as he did so, he smiled weakly, "We're all right, baby. It's going to be okay."

He opened the door and climbed shakily down to the pavement, where he collapsed to his knees, unable to contain it any longer. He vomited onto the asphalt. He muttered under his breath, "Get it together, Wayne… Get it together. What's wrong with you?"

Breathing deep, he slowly got back to his feet. His legs felt wobbly and uncertain. He swallowed and looked around. Everything glistened with moisture. Faint steam rose from the ground, but other than the truck's gentle rumble, everything was quiet and still. Wayne took a few tentative steps, inhaled, and started working his way around the truck, checking tires and lines. The trailer doors were still locked, the cargo was secure, and everything seemed fine. He stood by the road for a minute, sweeping the empty pasture beside him with the flashlight.

He'd never admit it, but he needed the time outside, on his feet. The cold, sharp, biting air helped. Wayne shivered and mumbled to himself, "Why is it so damned cold all of a sudden? It's August!"

The adrenaline would take a while to flush, and he was shaking. He hadn't felt this way since, well, since Afghanistan. His convoy had come under heavy fire. Later, after everything calmed down, he'd thrown up. Now, standing next to the truck, he bent down, resting his hands on his knees, and brought his breathing under control.

He forced a chuckle and groaned to himself, "Must've been the tuna at the last truck stop."

Eventually, Wayne returned to the truck's cabin. Sybil was still transfixed. He climbed up to her and ever so gently cupped her cheek with his beefy, calloused hand. He was a large man, and she was like a precious china doll to him.

Her expression softened, and her trance seemed to fade with his touch. She blinked and turned her head to look at him. She smiled wanly. "I'm okay, Wayne. I'll be okay. Let's just get moving."

"I've never deserved you, baby." He kissed her forehead and carefully climbed back down to his seat, scooping up Pinky. With his other hand, he mopped his face and took a deep breath.

Just as he reached to put the truck in gear, a terrible sound unlike any he'd ever heard before penetrated the cabin and quickly grew. Terrified, horrific shrieks chilled his soul. It sounded like hundreds of children screaming. Pinky whimpered loudly.

Sybil cried out in alarm, "Wayne!"

Wayne slammed down on the button that turned on the truck's lights. All of them. Headlight brights glared, and a blazing array of powerful LED running lights lit up the entire rig, trailer, and surrounding area in exuberant trucker glory. He yanked the truck's 200-decibel air horn.

Just then, outside, something smashed into the cabin door, rocking the cabin.

Wayne gasped, and Sybil screamed as a second and third giant fist slammed hard.

The exterior lights revealed a herd of hundreds of screaming, wild-eyed, white-tailed deer thundering out of the darkness. At least a half dozen more impacted parts of the semi-truck, collapsing dead to the ground on impact. The herd banked away, bounding down the highway, away from the bright lights and into the dark fog.

The pale white light raced across the dark landscape beyond the highway, towards the city of Fort Brazos, Texas. It washed over trees, buildings, and homes like a silken tide. It continued onward into the countryside before splashing over the nearby sprawling Joint Military Reserve Base before disappearing into the distance beyond.

The second wave, leaping and spitting electric green St. Elmo's Fire, followed closely behind, moving differently, like some berserk serpent. Every so often, it paused and diverted around or passed over certain homes, vehicles, buildings, or individuals. When it reached the Base, it hesitated as if in thought before surging forward.

The waves did not diminish. They kept going through the darkness, far beyond Fort Brazos.

911

Police Department Headquarters
Day 0. 0 Hour

The City of Fort Brazos' Police building was not a typical dull municipal building. It was an attractive two-story stucco building with arched doorways and bay windows upstairs. Deeper than it was wide, the jailhouse had been moved to a new construction steel building in the rear. Street-side, the Police building was intended to convey a sense of friendly community service for the mostly rural Fort Brazos area.

The frozen, static fog hung outside the now dark and silent office. Inside, the main squad room was dark and vague with amorphous shapes. Dust hung motionless in the air over tables, desks, chairs, computers, and two uniformed police officers sitting motionless as though in a diorama.

The cold light swept through the room, followed by the velvety, shimmering St. Elmo's fire.

As if struck by cattle prods, Sargent Derek Castillo and Officer Nara Young violently spasmed and screamed in pain as they were jolted out of their ancient Steelcase desk chairs onto the worn linoleum.

Derek's head broke his fall, banging loudly against the side of a desk. Nara convulsed on the floor before she raggedly clawed herself up, knocking a blotter and stack of papers off a desk as both expulsed their dinners onto the cold floor.

The power and lights flickered on. The air conditioning rumbled to life with its metallic shriek from old, worn-out parts, and already cold air began to circulate. The dust settled. Computers and equipment began booting up.

Rubbing his head, Derek stumbled to his feet, then collapsed sideways. "My God, what happened? Did we have an earthquake?"

Nara stood briefly, then her knees buckled, and she fell, grabbing the side of a desk to recover. She clutched her chest with one hand as she lurched to the front door and threw it open, stumbled to her knees, and threw up on the sidewalk. She staggered to her feet and, looking out into the dark fog, wiping her mouth with the back of her hand. The light shining through the door reflected off of the dense, opaque mist. "I don't. I don't see anything.... It's all just a heavy fog out there."

Derek clutched his stomach but managed not to throw up. He looked around the office. "Not a quake. Stuff's not on the floor. I used to live in California. Whatever happened, it wasn't a quake....."

Swallowing, Nara added, "I don't hear anything outside... But I remember stars."

A telephone rang. Then another. Still-booting 911-computer screens filled with a call queue. A trickle at first, it quickly flooded with the incoming calls.

Derek and Nara looked at each other and simultaneously said, "Call the Chief."

Nara reached for a phone and dialed. "I'll do it."

Derek righted his chair to sit and picked up the phone headset. "911, how can I... Sir? Sir? No, sir, I don't know what happened, is anyone there hurt or in danger? I see... Thank you for the call, Sir. Please be safe."

He punched a keyboard key and listened to the next caller, "Ma'am, Ma'am, please calm down, ma'am, who is dead? Ma'am, please say that again. How many are dead?"

Nara dialed and looked at Derek. "No answer, I'll try his cell...."

Furiously writing notes, Derek paused and looked up at Nara, raising a hand. He stopped writing, "Hey, stop. This is bad. Whatever is happening is very bad. Call the base. Right now, call the base. Something huge is going on. Maybe they know what the hell is happening."

The Hoffman's

Hoffman Family Dairy Farm
Day 0. 0 Hour

F og and darkness. Absolute stillness and quiet. No wind or crickets or any movement or sound of any kind. Like some lifeless photo negative, a ghostly farmhouse loomed out of the fog, lit by the same everywhere but nowhere dark light. It is old and well-cared-for, with rooms added on over the years. Whitewashed boards and a long porch with empty rocking chairs and a nearby garden and hothouse. An upside-down metal pail rested on the porch, with one edge slightly propped up on a stick.

As the soft waves of cold light and crackling green St. Elmo's Fire passed through, they were followed by a chorus of screams that shattered the night.

Inside, four blonde-haired, blue-eyed sisters lay in their tiny beds. 17-year-old Sandra "Sandy" Hoffman sat bolt upright in bed, gasping for air, struggling in the suddenly tangled sheets, dry-heaving her empty stomach. From their beds across the tiny farmhouse bedroom, her sisters, 15-year-old Jordan, 11-year-old Hannah, and 8-year-old Elizabeth, threw up what little they had in them, screamed, and dashed across the room to Sandra.

"Sandy, Sandy!!! What's happening?!" Tear-streaked, they clutched Sandy and each other for safety while looking nervously in all directions.

Chest heaving, Sandra held her sisters close, tears streaking down her face from the passing pain. "I don't know!"

"I'm scared!"

"What's happening?"

"Where's daddy?"

The sisters shrieked in unison as the bedroom door burst open. Their grey-haired father, Barrett Hoffman, pale-faced, sweat-soaked and shaken, Browning A5 shotgun in hand, strode inside, scanning the room desperately. His breath fogging in the wrongly cold air.

"Daddy!!!!"

One moment, the younger girls were huddled together on Sandra's bed. The next, with no passage of time that any would later recollect, they were hugging and clutching their dad. Sandra stood, pulling the sheet around her.

Their mom, Margaret, greying blonde hair all a tussle, and older brother, Nolan, with short mousey blonde hair, wild-eyed and gripping his baseball bat, arrived seconds later.

Just then, the power came back on, and lights flickered to life, and sounds from outside the farmhouse drew everyone from that moment. The sounds were of pain and fear and terror. The dogs were going crazy, and the cattle berserk.

Barrett's lips grew tight, "Stay here!"

Sandra's blue eyes flashed darkly. "Like Hell!"

The younger sisters and Margaret retreated down the hall. Margaret gathered them around her, saying, "Let's get your robes on and go check on Grandmother, girls, you know she can sleep through thunder."

Barrett opened his mouth to say something, then shook his head and took Nolan in tow towards the front door. Sandra darted to her closet and grabbed her robe, fluffy slippers, and her Winchester '94 before trotting after them.

Legs still rubbery from the awakening, Barrett, Nolan, and Sandra exited the front door to the porch. Barrett and Nolan were barefoot in T-shirts and overalls.

It was dark, with a heavy, sluggishly swirling fog. Cows out in the pasture were moaning loudly. The dogs were barking and running around this way and that, searching for whatever had tormented them. As the Barrett's arrived, the dogs skidded to a halt and then ran to them, panting. They pivoted and turned to face outward, forming a perimeter.

Lights from inside the house made the fog glow.

Nolan's voice cracked, "Dad?" Usually, Nolan would wince at the betrayal of his voice, but neither he nor anyone else noticed.

Keeping the shotgun pointed more or less at an upward angle, Barrett shivered and squinted into the darkness and rubbed one eye with the back of his hand. He grunted, "Yeah, son?"

A gust of wind lifted the fog enough to barely reveal the pasture. "Dad, I think the Johnsons' fence must've broke. There's lots more cows than there should be. Lots. Is, is that what woke us all up?"

Sandra flipped a switch by the door, and pole-mounted bright halogen floodlights around the farmhouse perimeter snapped on and stabbed into the fog sharply outlining the nearest distressed cattle. There were dark lumps on the ground among them.

Barrett sighed and frowned, and his shoulders slumped a little. "It's going to take all day to get this sorted out."

Sandra swallowed hard, "What the Hell happened, dad? All I remember are nightmares, and then we all woke up screaming."

Nolan wiped his face. "Did you dream about meteors?"

Barrett ground his teeth and didn't answer.

Sandra shuddered and looked down at the large galvanized steel pail on the porch and cautiously tipped it over with the business-end of her rifle. The chicken kept there for tomorrow's meal lay still and lifeless. "Dad, the chicken's dead."

Everyone whirled around as Margaret screamed from inside the house, "Nooo! No, God, No! Mom! Wake up! Mom! Nooo!"

General Marcus

Residence of the Commanding Officer:
FORT BRAZOS JOINT RESERVE BASE
Major General Alexander Marcus and family
Day 0. 0 Hour

In 1822, a group of Stephen F. Austin's colonists, headed by Jason Wilde, built a fort at the present site of Fort Brazos on a bend of the Brazos River. The city of Fort Brazos was incorporated under the Republic of Texas along with twenty other towns in 1837.

Today, the Fort Brazos Joint Military Reserve Base was vast, covering 178,203 acres. The main cantonment had a total population of 34,712 service and support personnel. The base was a city unto itself, with its own housing, hospital, airport, administrative buildings, support and maintenance buildings, warehouses, bunkers, and silos.

Base housing included the Commanding Officers Quarters, a colonial-style house on a mature suburban street. The simple yard was tidy and well maintained. Unopened moving boxes were stacked inside the house in every corner, with fresh signs of move-in everywhere. An African American man, woman, and twin girls lay in their bedrooms arranged like figures in a dollhouse.

The wave of cold, pale white light passed through, followed by the crackling wave of green St. Elmo's Fire, leaving screams in its wake.

Inside the Commanding Officer's Quarters, 59-year-old Major General Alexander Marcus leaped from his bed and rocked unsteadily on the balls of his feet. Broad-shouldered and trim, his T-Shirt did not conceal his still well-muscled chest. Dark-skinned, with close-cropped hair turning silver, he blinked rapidly and shook himself, looking around for danger, clutching his non-regulation blued Colt 5" 1911 .45. His stomach heaved, and he barely grabbed the trashcan next to the bed in time.

Alisha was not as lucky. Ten years his younger, Alisha was a model-perfect General's wife. With luxurious, long, dark hair, chocolate skin, high cheekbones, and large, intelligent eyes, they were quite a team. At the moment, however, her hair was a tangled mess, and she had just thrown up on the bed in front of her.

Gasping for breath, she cried out, "Marcus! What's happening?!"

Regaining his balance, Marcus desperately ran to the bedroom door, calling his daughters' names, "Faith! Hope!"

Just then, his six-year-old twins careened off the hallway wall and into his arms. He fell to his knees, hugging them close, and swept them up with one arm. He carried them to his side of the bed while Alisha folded the covers over to hide the mess. All the while, Marcus kept watching the doorway, Colt at the ready.

A wailing siren punctured the silence outside. Marcus pursed his lips, set the gun down, and reached for the phone. It rang just as he picked up the handset.

Loudly, he barked, "This is Marcus. What the…," he lowered his voice a few octaves, looking at his girls. "What's going on? Report!"

Hunting Buddies

Outskirts of Fort Brazos
Day 0, 0 Hour

Off the interstate highway, a mature crown of trees framed the well maintained but now darkened Farm-to-Market road #21 that snaked off into the distance with periodic ranch gates studying the way. Some were simple cattle gates, but some were elaborate or even stately, with cut stone and ranch brands proudly emblazoned in ornate wrought iron, swinging double electronic gates. Beyond the gates were both old and new homesteads. Many had been rebuilt with recent shale oil money. Other ranchers had invested in updating worn equipment and improved herds. Some tucked it under mattresses, saying, "This too shall pass."

Along the middle of the meandering "Farm to Market" road, in the quiet darkness, sat a dealer-tagged King Ranch Ford F-250 with two motionless men inside. The driver was handsome and greying, and the other had a full head of bold white hair and the bearing of a teacher. Both men wore comfortable but expensive hunting clothes, and behind them lay rifle bags, accouterments, and a large cooler.

The waves swept over the road and truck.

"…Shit!" Tom Parker, mayor of Fort Brazos, shook like a leaf but grabbed and held on to the steering wheel with a death-grip. An eruption of expletives he didn't know he knew spewed forth. Then he gulped a breath and suddenly remembered he was not alone, and shakily turned to his friend, "Pastor Joe" Rev. Joseph Gilmore, Pastor of First Baptist Church, Fort Brazos. Pastor Joe was trembling and on the verge of hyperventilating. The truck's windows were rolled down, and both men managed to throw up their coffee out of their windows.

Gathering himself up, Tom shuddered, "Uh, sorry about that, Joe." He reached over to steady his old friend, "Joe, are you okay?"

Pastor Joe blinked, swallowed hard, and got his breathing under control. Then he turned and looked at Tom. "Tom? What? What happened? Why are we stopped in the road?"

Both men jerked in surprise as the truck's big v8 engine rumbled to life by itself. Hands shaking, Tom reached over and turned on the radio, muttering, "I don't know, I don't know…. Let me try the radio…."

He pushed the radio station-preset buttons, but there were no signals — only static. He punched the auto-scan button, and the radio cycled through the frequencies twice before stopping on a 'new' signal. 92.5. At first, there was just a carrier with no sound. Then, a husky but familiar voice coughed to life.

"Um…hello Fort Brazos, this is Danielle Richardson, 92.5. I don't know what the hell just happened, but I haven't had a hangover like this since my last. Uh, well, that doesn't matter. Something has happened here in Fort Brazos. Alarms and sirens are going off all over the place, and the scanner is going nuts with people talking about loved ones being dead and folks running out into the street screaming. Right now, I'm trying to find out something, but the phone lines seem to be down. I'm going to stay on the air and …."

Tom and Pastor Joe exchanged glances. Pastor Joe ran his hand over his white hair and nodded, "Let's go back to town. I think our hunting trip can wait, Tom."

Tom took a deep breath and put the truck into gear, taking the next few minutes to work his way back towards and onto the interstate through the rolling fog banks. He'd turned on all the truck's extra lights and fog lights. "Joe, I don't ever remember fog like this before. What is this, England?"

Pastor Joe began to relax, and his face took on its familiar "teacher" persona. He smiled softly, "Well, you see, Tom…."

It was a moment that Tom would never forget and would relive over and over in his dreams. First, he heard the blood-curdling sound of screaming children. Then the universe shrank at the horrific sound of frenzied deer smashing into the truck. Bones and flesh shattered as they desperately tried to escape, climbing and leaping on top of each other with gnashing teeth and wide, terrified eyes.

Tom could see it coming, but there was nothing he could do. It was a living nightmare. He watched, trying to warn Joe, as a huge trophy buck with magnificent antlers smashed through the windshield, antlers, and headfirst.

Time slowed to a crawl. Helpless, Tom saw bits of glass and fur and antler and blood flying through the cabin. As he turned his head, he was able to see his friend, his best friend, and mentor, just as the antlers pierced Joe's chest. And then the dying buck kicked Tom in the head.

Seconds after the deer had thundered away down the highway, Wayne leaped out of the semi-truck, stumbling over the still quivering, dying deer, flashlight in hand, to investigate. Sybil leaned out the door, open-mouthed in horror at the carnage.

Out of the darkness down the highway, in the direction the deer had headed, the sickening sound of the impacts and crunch of bone and tortured steel approached. Wayne stood warily, waving his flashlight in that direction. Headlights careened out of the fog, and a large pickup truck emerged, flinging deer carcasses ahead of it like bowling pins

The truck was out of control, deer smashed into its grill and windshield, and swerved back and forth and then directly at Wayne.

Wayne suddenly realized his danger and crouched slightly, trying to figure out which way to run or jump. Then the oncoming truck's diver must have yanked the steering wheel all the way over because the truck turned and flipped, flying through the air, just missing Wayne as he leaped for the culvert, flashlight flying off into the pasture. The truck flew past Wayne and the 18-wheeler. It bounced and rolled over and over in a roar of shattered metal and glass into the inky darkness.

Sybil screamed, "Wayne! Oh my God, are you okay!?"

Wayne crawled out of the ditch and looked up at her, suddenly dead calm. "Call it in."

She blinked at him.

Wayne ran up to the cab and grabbed another flashlight and the emergency kit. He reached up and touched Sybil's face. "Sybil! Call it in."

"Err... Right. Okay. Yes, I'll call it in... Right."

Wayne ran into the darkness toward the wreck. Sybil scooped up Pinky and hugged him to her as she reached for the radio.

Wayne quickly tossed out road flares, then followed the broken trail of glass, rubber, and steel. The pickup truck had rolled to the bottom of the highway embankment. He played his flashlight beam over the wreck. The roll cage had done its job, and the cab wasn't crushed.

He worked his way down the embankment through the debris and climbed up the side of the truck, shining his flashlight inside. "Hello? Anybody alive in there?"

On seeing the carnage inside, he gasped. "Oh, God... Okay man, Okay, you're gonna be okay." He looked back over his shoulder and shouted, "Sybil, get help here fast!"

John & Matti

In a blur of long blonde hair and pink pajamas, Matilda "Matti" Austin's 8-year-old feet barely touched the floor as she dashed into her dad's bedroom and launched herself into his arms.

Dad was Sheriff John Austin. He'd already been at the edge of his bed, about to go and check on her and maybe do something about the mess that was mostly in the small trashcan beside the nightstand. "Matti!"

John half stood and caught his 52lb daughter like a running back, catching a football, pulling her close against his T-Shirt, and wrapping her in his powerful, former roughneck arms. "Matti, it's okay, it's going to be okay. Daddy's here."

Tears plastered blond hairs to her face. Matti looked up at her dad, and he smiled down at her. "Daddy, I had a bad dream about stars, and the dream hurt me."

"I know, pumpkin. I know. It's okay now. I've got you." He pulled a tissue from the nightstand and gently wiped the dribble of throw-up from her face.

John slowly became aware of sounds outside the window. Dogs were yelping in terror, distant shouts, and an alarm coming from somewhere. Then another. And another.

His cell phone rang as he reached for it. He answered with one hand while still holding onto Matti. "Yeah, Hector, what's going on?"

"Boss, there's some weird shit going on. Did you get knocked out of bed by something?"

John blinked, "What? You too? There are others?"

"Yeah, I already heard from Tommy and Gwyn, and I'm hearin' stuff all over the neighborhood, lots of hollerin' and people scared and shit."

"That's…. I don't know, maybe some kind of sonic boom or earthquake woke everyone up?... I don't know."

"Anyway, Boss, what do you think? Should I call everyone in? We're already long on overtime."

A couple of car alarms went off somewhere nearby. John sighed, "Yeah, though, from the sound of it, everyone's probably awake already anyway. Thanks, Hector."

"No hay bronca."

He hugged Matti closer. "Sweetie, Daddy has to go help people, but don't worry, you're coming with me. I'll come and help you get dressed."

Matti sniffed, "I can dress myself, daddy." But she didn't let go of him for a long, long moment.

John's phone rang again. "This is Sheriff Austin…."

"Sheriff, this is Officer Young. I'm sorry to disturb you, but I'm calling to ask if you know where the Chief is? We can't reach him on his phone, and we seem to have some kind of emergency going on. We're having trouble reaching some of the other officers as well."

John frowned. "I'm sorry, Officer Young, I don't know where he is. Do you know anything about what's happening?"

"Sheriff, the phones are ringing off the hook here with frightened people, but we really don't know anything yet."

"Okay, tell you what, George lives down the street, and his house is on the way. I'll stop by and see if he's there on my way into town."

"Thank you, Sheriff. I need to go help with these calls."

"Good luck. I'll let you know if I find George." John hung up and bent down and kissed Matti's golden hair. "Daddy's gotta go to work, baby."

After quickly washing her face and brushing her teeth, Matti walked calmly to her room. When she'd gone to bed, she'd left the window cracked. Now, the cold had left a layer of frost on her dresser, and she shivered and shut the window. *Why is it so cold?*

She opened her closet and considered her choices, pulling on her jeans and Lucchese boots. She shivered. She went to the back of her closet and picked out a jacket. *I've grown since last winter. It will be tight.*

She reached for her backpack and hesitated before looking inside it with a frown. She pursed her lips and muttered, "little girl stuff." She upended the bag, dumping colorful treasures on the bed without another glance. Then she opened her dresser drawer and pulled out a flashlight, checked that it was charged, and added it to the backpack along with her phone charger. She left her room and quickly walked downstairs to the kitchen and added two bottled waters, an apple, and her sack lunch her dad had made for her the night before.

Ten minutes and three more phone calls later, John had his Sheriff gear on and opened the front door, calling over his shoulder, "Matti, are you ready? We need to go."

The house was enormous. John had built it for Carolyn and the many children they'd planned to have. They'd thought they had all the time in the world, and she'd been pregnant with a boy when she died. They had already redecorated the nursery in blue, but now it was empty, the new bassinet and furniture donated to the church.

For a long time, the house had felt vast and empty. Nowadays, Matti's exuberance and love had changed it. When he'd moved back to town and built the place, there had been some snide and jealous comments he'd pretended not to hear about his 'fancy place like a mansion.' He hadn't cared then, and he didn't care now. He just couldn't bear the thought of taking Matti out of the only home she'd ever known, just so they could be in someplace smaller. Besides, he had 5 acres in the back, fenced and ready for the horse he planned to buy Matti for her birthday. He'd buy her the world if he could.

Matti already stood silently, dressed, wearing her backpack, and waiting outside the tall, heavy door. "I'm ready, daddy."

John turned and blinked in surprise. He and Carolyn had been friends since childhood. Everyone else had always known they would marry, except for John and Carolyn, of course. Now, Matti stood there with the same look in her eyes he'd grown up seeing in Carolyn's, and his eyes misted for a moment. *She looks so much like her.* "Wow, that's my girl. So beautiful and strong."

Matti saw the expression on her dad's face and knew. For a long time after mom had died, she'd seen him have that look. Only then it had been full of pain. It had always made her want to cry. This time was different. The pain was still there, but it was muted and only a shadow to his love. She smiled at him and softly said, "Come on, Dad, let's go."

Outside, it was dark and foggy, and there were unhappy sounds from every direction. "People don't like getting knocked out of bed, do they, Matti?"

Matti took up her position in the back seat of his Sheriff SUV, and John put it in gear and drove down the street, taking note that the lights were now on in most houses.

The Police Chief and John were friends and lived barely a mile apart. The lights were not on at the Chief's house. When John pulled into the Police Chief's driveway, he turned to Matti, "Stay here, Matti."

"I know, daddy."

John opened the SUV door, the sounds of sirens and distress growing. It was still dark and foggy. He looked warily about, snapping on his flashlight, then went to the door and knocked. No answer.

John walked the house's perimeter, shining his light around prominently so as not to sneak up on anyone. All was quiet. The Chief had a small deck and swimming pool behind his house that the master bedroom opened out onto. The door was closed and locked.

He knocked. "George? Hey George, you in there? Anne?" John shone his light through the window and saw two still figures lying in bed.

John tapped the glass loudly. "George, hey! Wake up, buddy!" Dogs started barking nearby.

John looked in and squinted. "Don't shoot, George. It's John Austin. Wake up in there!" He played the bright flashlight beam through the window onto the bed. No reaction. He frowned. "Oh, God no."

✪ ✪ ✪

John slowly walked back to the SUV, dialing his phone, "Officer Young? Yeah, this is Sheriff Austin. I've got bad news. Both George and Anne are dead. Stone cold. No sign of foul play - they're just dead in bed. Send someone over to secure the place and wake up the coroner, will you? I had to break into the back door. I'll wait for them to arrive."

Nara's alto voice was shaky and thin. "S-Sir, you should know, we're now getting hundreds of 911 calls… we're getting reports of, of h-hundreds of people dying in their sleep."

John stumbled and barely caught himself from falling. "What? Please repeat that!"

"Sir, there are reports of hundreds of people dead. Everyone in town seems to have woken up at the same time, or, well, they didn't wake up at all. There's no news or communications with anybody outside of Fort Brazos. It looks like we are cut off from the outside world." She hesitated, and her voice faltered, "Are we being attacked, sir?"

John visibly paled and took a deep breath. *Attacked? Hundreds of people dead?* He tripped on a loose paving stone and caught himself on a post, then hurried back around the corner of the house until he could see Matti in the back seat of the SUV and that she was okay.

"Did you call the base? Is there any word from the base?"

"Yes, Sheriff, we tried, but they don't answer. We keep calling, but it just keeps going to voicemail, and the website says they are on lockdown."

He swallowed. "Okay, listen, it's Nara, isn't it? Nara Young?"

Her voice was tight, "Yes, Sheriff."

"Yes, I remember you, Nara. You joined the force a few months ago. Okay. Nara, I don't know what's going on. Right now, whatever it is, people need us. They need us to be there for them, and we need to be there for each other. George would kick my ass if I sat around babysitting his body in an emergency like this, whatever this is. I'm going to secure his door and head-on into town. George is just going to have to wait until someone can come and collect him and Anne."

"Yes, Sheriff. Thank you. Sir, we can't find the Lieutenant or anyone higher. We... Ahhh, we could use some advice on what to do. You're the most senior law enforcement officer we've found."

"Tell me, Nara, are there any reports of fighting or violence or anything that might indicate an active threat? Any reports of panic or looting?"

There was a pause, and John could hear Nara talking to someone in the background.

"Sheriff, no, right now, there are no reports of any violence or fighting or anything like that. Just lots of scared people."

"Right. I'll take that as good news. I'm glad you are on the job there. Who's there with you now?"

"Ahh, just Derek and me. I mean, Sargent Castillo and myself, sir. The patrol officers have reported in, and we've called in everyone that is answering, but the phone service has been going in and out."

John nodded, "Okay, good job. Please call my office and tell Hector or Gwynn or whoever answers about your situation. We need to coordinate our efforts and keep each other informed. We'll figure this thing out, Nara. You and Sargent Castillo hang in there."

Bent Compass

General Marcus bounded up the control tower staircase two steps at a time while two escorting MP's tried to keep up. The last few hours had been a mind-boggling blur – one crisis after another. He had decided he needed a higher perspective on things, so he'd found his way through the chaos to the control tower. A lieutenant coming down the stairs met and followed him up the stairs to a landing halfway up. Marcus grunted an acknowledgment and tersely demanded, "Status report!"

Lt. Darryl Guevara carried a sheaf of reports but didn't look at them, "Sir, no change. Per your orders, the base is locked down. Air CAP is scrambled. It was two F-18's that had stopped over last night and were already prepped, though their original Navy pilots couldn't be quickly found. Fortunately, we had two qualified Air Force pilots available, and they are in the air. We also have gunships orbiting the base. We're still sorting out the, um, new arrivals, and, on that, ah, we have no, um, clue, sir."

"What's this about no coms?"

"Sir, there are still no coms, but local and local civilian and the civilian traffic is more confused than ours. What's worse, Sir, is that there is no satellite reception at all."

"Wait, no satellite? What do you mean? A satellite isn't responding?"

"No sir, there is no satellite connection of any kind, sir. There are no military or civilian satellites, no COMM or GPS or anything, not even civilian birds like

Direct TV. Nothing, not just ours - not anybody's, not even GNSS, or the Russians, or anyone's birds, secured or otherwise. There is no traffic of any kind, from anywhere, encrypted or in the clear. Sir, there is not even any background noise, and that's just not possible."

"EMP?"

"Sir, there is no indication of EMP effects on the ground, sir. And it is not interference — our equipment is working, even the unshielded equipment is working. Sir, no matter what we've tried, there's just no signal to receive."

"Continue."

"Sir, there is no terrestrial RF of any kind other than local traffic. Not even HAM radio - from anywhere outside of the local Fort Brazos area, and we're getting weird bounces and echoes on our own RF traffic. Also, both the secure and the public Internet is weird. It acts like it is up, but there is no inbound traffic. It's like everything is frozen."

Marcus turned and stared at him. Lt. Guevara swallowed and added, "And about the friendly fire incident, sir, nobody was seriously hurt. We're sorting it out."

Marcus blinked, grunted again, and continued his ascent up the staircase.

Lt. Guevara followed the General into the control room. It was the best vantage point on the base with its wraparound windows, given the relatively flat Texas prairie the old base was spread across.

Organized chaos ruled the room. The worry, tension, and fear were thick. Everywhere, servicemen and women were frantically talking into headsets, on phones, or otherwise engaged. All were sweating, despite the chill air in the room.

Lt. Guevara opened his mouth to order the room to attention, but Marcus waved him off, looking around, taking in the room. He walked to an observation area at the windows. Outside, vehicles raced in every direction, helicopters circled, and things more or less looked like a kicked-over ant mound. The fog still hung heavy but seemed to be clearing a little.

Meanwhile, the flight controller was talking to someone. Marcus nodded to Guevara, and the Lt. quietly said something to the flight controller, who looked up, nodded acknowledgment, and flipped a switch, putting the audio on speakers.

The radar screen showed two ascending blips with associated transponder labels. Marcus stood behind the controller and gripped the back of his chair.

(Flight Controller): Banshee, Confirmed. You have no traffic at all, any range. No radar, no IFF signals. Nada.

(Banshee): Copy Tower, no traffic. Nothing. Anywhere. Climbing at Angels 15, zero visibility.

(Flight Controller): Roger Banshee. Confirm signals check.

(Banshee): Copy Tower. Signals check. I got No GPS, No SatCom, No TACAN, No VOR. Tower, I got nothing but thee and me.

(Flight Controller): Roger Banshee. Acknowledge no signals.

(Banshee): Chuckles, confirm your compass status?

(Chuckles): Copy Banshee. Compass is bent.

(Banshee): Tower, both our compasses are bent.

(Flight Controller): Roger Banshee. Confirm compass malfunction.

(Banshee): Tower, passing Angels 30. Clouds clearing <static> There is <static> I don't <static> Wait one. What the hell?

Suddenly, there was a brilliant pulse of light through the control tower windows, from above the fog outside, and everyone flinched.

Over the radio, a loud bang and shrieking alarms blared, immediately followed by a shrill audio spike. The two blips seemed to lurch in a different direction on the radar screen, merge, and then fall.

(Flight Controller): Banshee! Chuckles! Acknowledge! What the hell happened up there?

(Banshee): ...smash <long static> clouds <static> sheer <static> sun is not <long static> losing <static> punching <static>

General Marcus's fingers whitened in their grip on the chair as he ground his teeth. "Launch SAR and another CAP but keep them at Angels 25. We must find out what the hell is happening. I want those pilots picked up and delivered to me right god-damned now! Bring the base to full combat readiness. Set REDCON 1. Full alert, full battle packs, non-essentials confined to designated shelters."

The Spire

John Austin drove carefully, weaving his way through the other first responder vehicles, wandering people, and the seemingly random strange debris that emergency situations always seemed to create out of thin air. He kept the static amber police lights and his low beams on so that they wouldn't reflect into his eyes. The fog and darkness seemed to swallow sounds and life, but dampened sound of distant sirens leaked through. Matti was curled up in the back seat. She had a faraway look in her eye. They'd made several emergency-response stops already. Each was the same.

"Daddy?" Matti's voice was quiet but unafraid. She was staring out the window into the mist.

"Yeah, hon?" John glanced into the rearview mirror. He could see the wheels turning in his daughter's head.

"Daddy, how many people didn't wake up?"

He swallowed and pulled over, and parked, flipping the emergency lights on as insurance against being rear-ended. He turned to face her. "Matti, you're safe. Nothing's going to happen to you." He reached back and put his hand on her knee. "I won't let anything happen to you."

Matti blinked and turned to face him; her head slightly cocked. "I know, daddy. I just don't understand the pattern."

John did his best to control his expression. At each stop they'd made along the way, each case was the same—one or more lifeless bodies, often with grieving family members in total melt-down. Most had the same questions: Why? What is happening? Are we at war? Some went further, asking why it was still dark and why couldn't they call their out-of-town relatives on the phone? Why is there no national TV or cable or satellite? The list went on and on, and all John had was more questions and no answers.

Some of the dead were children, and there wasn't a damned thing he could do to help any of them. There weren't even enough ambulances to remove the dead. He'd been forced to ask those who could to bring the bodies to the old Burnham refrigerated warehouse. It had gone out of business last year. The refrigeration units weren't all working, though, and a call had gone out for anyone with dry ice. John had Deputy Dalton track down any HVAC repairmen he could find to shanghai over to the warehouse.

And those had only been the calls directly on his route to downtown. He'd been careful not to say anything in Matti's presence. "Pattern? Um, what do you mean? What pattern?"

She looked earnestly into his eyes. "Yeah, it's just… well… I don't understand why there's no pattern to who lived and who didn't. They've been young and old and everything in-between."

"What? How can you know that?"

Matti gestured towards the glowing police monitors in the front seat. "Well, duh, Dad, it's on your computer screen there. It shows the list of all the calls and the age and sex of each person who died and where. They're all different ages, and I just don't see any pattern. I overheard someone say on the radio the people hadn't been sick. That they all just woke up dead. Err… I mean, they didn't wake up, and they were dead. Whatever. Anyway, everyone is just alive… or they're not. There's no in-between. There is nobody listed as sick. It just doesn't make sense."

John blanched and reached back to turn off the monitor, then stopped with his hand on the controls. He looked back at Matti. She was a bright and precocious girl, full of life. With mom gone and buried, she doted on her dad may be more than he did on her. A beautiful little girl that he knew would grow up to break hearts. Looking at her now, she was different. Maybe in shock, he thought. "This is a lot to take in, Matti. I shouldn't have left the monitors on to upset you. I'm sorry. I'm not going to leave you alone, either. You're stuck with me."

Matti smiled a won smile. "Daddy, I'm not scared. Really, I'm not. I know you're worried. You would never have taken me with you before like this, what, in an emergency, I mean, if you thought I might be hurt. You could have just dropped me at a sitter or at the Sheriff's office. I know you'll keep me safe."

John looked at her, struggling to find words. The sitter was one of the people who had not woken up, but he'd managed to keep that information from Matti, for now. He had planned to drop her at the Sheriff's office. He should have done that, he knew, but as things progressed, he couldn't bear to leave her behind anywhere... not until he understood what was going on. It was irrational, selfish, and irresponsible, and not father-of-the-year material, and most definitely against the rules. He didn't care. There wasn't a hint of any violence going on. After losing Carolyn last year, there was no way he was going to leave Matti behind somewhere.

She sucked in a breath, her eyes wide, and pulled her phone out of her pocket. "Oh my god, I need to text Isabella and make sure she's okay!" And with that, his daughter was back.

John simply stared at her for a moment as she furiously thumbed the smartphone screen. For a fleeting moment, he wondered if the sudden return to normalcy was just for his benefit. Something in her eyes. Then he sighed, checked the status monitor, and pulled the SUV back out onto the dark, mist-filled road.

Later, after more stops, another call came in from dispatch about a disturbance at Town Square. They were not far, so he worked his way through the maze of vehicles toward the center of town. He got as close as he could and parked.

Behind him, Matti asked, "Oh, by the way, dad, did you know the GPS isn't working?"

"What?"

"Yeah, I know you don't use it because, like, you already know where everything is, but I like to look at the map when you leave me in the car. Anyway, I just thought I'd mention that it isn't working. It just sits there blinking and says, "no signal."

He turned back to the console and brought up the GPS map tool. She was right. It was something that he never used. Sure enough, it said "no signal."

"Right. What else is going to go wrong?"

He got out and pulled his jacket close against the unnatural chill. It was August, after all, and he'd been lucky he'd left it in the back of the SUV, along with a duffle change of clothes. He donned his 'official' cowboy-style hat and turned to help Matti out. She was already standing there, waiting. She reached up to him, and he wasn't entirely sure if the look in her eyes was asking for comfort or giving it. He took her up in his arms and hugged her close before setting her down and holding her hand.

They worked their way through the growing crowd of people and excited voices. Not angry or dangerous-sounding, or else he wouldn't have taken Matti with him.

John paused, answering a deputy on a hand-held UHF radio, "…Yeah, Austin here. What's the…" A massive burst of static erupted from the radio, and he yanked it away from his ear. "Damn!"

Matti pulled his shirtsleeve, pointing excitedly towards the square. "Daddy, what is that?"

"I'm sorry, hon, the radio noise hurt my ear. Now, remember, stay close to me, and don't wander off." John cautiously put the radio to his ear again, "Say again? What was that? I can't hear you?"

Matti raised her voice with urgency, "Daddy, what's THAT!?" -- just as other people around them began shouting the same question, in fear and no small amount of panic. Matti pointed again towards the square.

John looked around and saw others around them also looking and pointing towards the square. "What?"

He turned. What he saw made no sense. His eyes saw it, but his brain warred with what he "knew" he should see there and what the… thing standing there now was or how it was remotely possible. The radio fell from his fingers to dangle on its lanyard. John's hand dropped to his Wilson Combat .45. Without looking, he pulled Matti behind him. His voice dropped octaves. "Stay behind me and stay close."

The dense fog began to dissipate around the downtown square, where visibility had been no more than a few feet. A crowd was noisily converging towards an enormous dark object that the retreating mist revealed. It towered above them all, in the center of the square where the City Founders / Pioneer statue had formerly stood. There were gasps and yells as people looked up, and up, and up. The tallest building in Fort Brazos was twelve stories tall, yet, looming over them was a three-hundred or more-foot-tall, impossibly slender, glassy black, crystalline spire. The fog vanished around it, and soft green electric St. Elmo's Fire roiled around the top.

"What the...."

Some people ran away, some screamed, but many drew closer to the spire, excitedly pointing, talking, and snapping pictures on cell phones. A few brave ones walked towards it as though to touch it.

Seeing this, John rushed forward and used his "Sheriff Voice" to project over the crowd. "Everybody get back from that thing! Get back! Don't touch...."

Too late. A young man, probably a college student judging by his clothes, reached out and touched it. For long moments, it seemed like all the sound in the universe was sucked away. The crowd, the emergency vehicle sirens – everything.

John bent down, pulling Matti to him. Then, the current reversed, and a crackling shockwave blew people down like bowling pins. A peal of thunder followed as the St. Elmo's Fire boiled out of the massive spire and shot vertically into the sky, parting the higher clouds of fog in an expanding gust front that swept over the City of Fort Brazos and beyond. The darkness faded as the strange night turned into day.

Amid the shouts and yells, John scooped up Matti and backed away, shouting to the crowd, "Get back! Get back, dammit!"

Matti pulled his arm and pointed up into the sky. "Daddy?"

John reached down with his free arm and pulled a sobbing woman up from the grass, dragging her upright.

"Daddy!"

"What, baby?" John pulled another person up.

"Daddy," Matti grabbed his chin, pushed it up, and pointed. "Daddy, LOOK!"

John looked up. The fog had cleared in an expanding ring around the town. He stumbled backward in shock, reflexively grabbing Matti close to him. In the sky above them was not the morning sun. There was no sun. A fireball was spreading from horizon to horizon, stretching into a long yellow-white line. And above *that* was not the big blue sky of Texas.

John's mouth hung open, and around him, the collective shouts, screams, gasps, and cries of wonder and terror swelled.

Above that ribbon-sun, what faded into the haze behind it didn't make any sense at all. It looked like... it looked like satellite pictures from space of the earth with oceans and continents -- spread across the entire visible sky. On the other side of... the world... what looked like a small hurricane seemed to be taking shape.

The fog cleared away like a curtain drawn. Dark clouds scudded along in the distance. The yellow-white sun thing, which now looked more like a thin tube, extended from horizon to horizon. Beyond the town, to the north, light shone down on... mountains.

Matti whispered, "Daddy, why do we have mountains now?"

The closest mountains to Fort Brazos were the Davis Mountains in far west Texas, hundreds of miles away.

Only, these were not the low, brown, dusty rambling Davis Mountains. No, these looked more like the Himalayas, complete with ice caps and glaciers. The massive wall seemed to stretch across half the world. And in the distance, between Fort Brazos and those impossible mountains, was a vast, violet-blue lake.

Speaking of the Horizon – there was no horizon. In the distance, the edges, the sides of the mountains, the very land itself curved upwards.

The crowd was getting loud and confused and frightened. John stood and held Matti in the crook of his arm. He looked around, saw his shell-shocked deputies arriving, and silently nodded them into action.

Matti wrapped her arms around her daddy's neck, "Daddy, if we are here, what happened to the rest of the world?"

Then John remembered something Matti had said about Stars, and he suddenly remembered a dream. He'd been standing exactly where he was now, holding Matti, looking up at the night sky as the stars fell.

"I don't know, baby." He set her down but kept her close.

John gradually recovered his senses and began moving around, Matti in-tow, reassuring people, helping people up off the ground. All the while, he kept half an eye on the impossible sky.

Somehow, some way, he, Matti, all the people, and the city of Fort Brazos had been… moved. Scooped up whole and moved inside a titanically vast hollow cylinder. A hollow cylindrical world with a sun-tube running down the center of its length. Looking up, you could see the other side of the world.

"I don't know what's happened, Matti. Someone has, someone has moved us here like a city in a bottle. I don't know who, or how, or why. But I am going to find out."

He thought to himself, *'My God, just the effort alone to do this thing is unthinkable. Why?* Darker permutations tumbled through his mind, and he wondered, *are we victims or are we survivors? Is whoever the hell did this a friend -- or an enemy?'*

Then what Matti had said finally hit him. 'Obviously, the answer to the age-old question of whether humanity was alone in the universe was self-evident and suddenly much less important to him than he would have ever imagined. More importantly, he thought, standing there looking at the other side of the world, was, *'If we are here, wherever here is, then where is Earth? And what has happened there and to everyone else?'*

Banshee Down

Fort Brazos
Day 0: 7:03 AM

Hundreds of angry and frightened people converged on downtown Fort Brazos Square, pressing against the thin cordon of Sheriff's Department deputies and police. The alien spire loomed above them, black as space. The cacophony of sirens, car horns, shouts, and pleas for help swelled rapidly.

The death toll continued to climb, and the rumor mill, the only form of faster than light communication known to man, had quickly spread the news that thousands of people were dead. People were becoming more than just angry and frightened. They wanted answers.

"What's happening?"

"I woke up screaming, and my husband was dead!"

"What is that thing?"

"What happened to the sky?"

"Are we being attacked?"

Suddenly, there was a different kind of thunder, and it wasn't coming from the direction of the spire. The crowd paused and looked up, searching the sky.

"There!" someone shouted. People started pointing at a pair of military jets high up. One was trailing smoke in an ugly, spiraling descent. The other seemed to be chasing it.

Someone nearby muttered, "This is it. We're being attacked!"

As host to a military base, Fort Brazos was home to many veterans. A squared-away older man, with close-cropped grey hair and disciplined bearing, shook his head and answered, "No, they're both ours. Those are F-18's, but that one's goin' down. No chute."

Sheriff John Austin watched as the jet fluttered down, somehow slowing and shifting direction. He pulled Matti close as the crowd watched the unfolding horror. The plane appeared to be under some measure of control. It shuddered and belched sparks, flames, and smoke as it fluttered, jinked, and stalled, nosing up for a moment, before finally nosing down, changing course even in its last moments. A fraction of a second before auguring in, the ejection seat erupted sideways on a jet of flame. The nearly vertical aircraft disappeared amid the angry volcanic fireball that followed.

The second F-18 roared low overhead in a whoosh that set off car alarms all along its path.

The veteran exclaimed, "My God, that brave son-of-a-bitch…."

John had become embroiled in crowd control, but the plane crash changed everything. Chief Deputy Hector Alonzo ran to his aid and took over, saying, "Is Okay. I got this, boss. Go!"

John nodded thanks, turned around, grabbed Matti, heaving her up in the crook of his arm, and ran back to the SUV, talking on his UHF radio along the way to the other officers and deputies. "Okay, everybody, I'm goin' to the crash site. Get Fire and Rescue over there, right damned now!" he huffed. "Get the square cleared out. Hell, clear out all of downtown. Make sure some fool doesn't shoot at that tower thing, whatever the hell it is, and start a damned interstellar war. I'll call you when I get there…."

Matti wiggled loose, hit the ground running, long blonde hair flying, and dove into the SUV ahead of her dad. The vehicle was blocked in, so John popped the curb and bounced across an empty side-lot, sirens blasting. The streets were clogged, and John cringed as he plowed across several lawns.

He nearly collided with an ancient Ford F-100 pickup truck that rocketed around a corner out of nowhere. The panicked expression on the driver's face spoke volumes. A limp woman was slumped against the driver's shoulder, and he was having trouble keeping her upright. John only had a fraction of a moment to take it in, but he knew the woman was already dead. There was nothing he could do, and he had bigger problems.

It took ten minutes to get there, but he was the first to arrive at the scene of the crash. The roar and the crackling blistering heat from the fire were incredible.

He made another radio call. "Austin here. I'm at the crash site. Roads are a complete mess. It's going to be tough for emergency services to get here. It looks like the crash is confined to the old Pontiac dealership car lot.

"The fire is raging hot but thank god the dealership went out of business years ago. I don't see any obvious ground casualties."

Matti cried out from the back-seat passenger side as she tugged on his shoulder, "Over on this side, daddy! The pilot is over there!"

John craned his neck, looking out the other window. The ejection seat had collided with a giant steel billboard — the same one that used to advertise Pontiacs but had for years simply said, "Space Rent" beneath the faded car ad. The ejection seat had almost blasted completely through the billboard but was tangled on the large steel support structure. The pilot hung loose in the chair. John jumped another curb and parked far enough away that nothing could fall on the SUV.

John continued on the radio, "It looks like the pilot ejected, but he's tangled up in that big billboard. I'm checking it out." He turned to Matti. "Stay here."

John bounded out and ran up to the billboard, shouting over the nearby inferno. "Pilot! Are you Okay? Are you injured?"

The ejection seat had done its job, separating the pilot from the plane, but it had driven the pilot halfway through the billboard steel crossbeams, and the pilot wasn't moving.

John muttered, "God," as he leaped up, caught the rusty access ladder, and climbed up and out onto the large boom.

He worked his way over to the stricken pilot whose right leg had caught on some of the steel piping. The pilot's tibia protruded from broken flesh and wept dark red blood with alarming haste. His nametag read "Capt. Finley", and his helmet was emblazoned with "Banshee."

39

The billboard chose that moment to creak, groan, shudder, and precipitously shift.

John slipped but caught himself. "Can't stay here!" He fumbled with the ejection seat harness, half wondering how he was going to get the pilot down by himself before the massive billboard collapsed and killed them both.

The pilot coughed, spasmed, and then reached up and yanked off his helmet. He gasped, revealing jade green eyes, sweaty, pale skin, bloody split lips, a shock of short auburn hair, and an angry, most definitely not-male face.

Captain Finley sputtered, "Get the fuck off me, you ape!"

One of the billboard beams supports chose that moment to snap with a vicious crack, and the entire structure sickeningly cantered three or four feet. John lost his footing and fell backward, losing his hat, but Captain Finley grabbed his arm and pulled him back with surprising strength.

Taking in the situation, Captain Finley commanded him, "Oh hell, get back here and help me off this thing, cowboy."

"Yes, ma'am," John grunted.

Captain Finley popped her harness, locked an arm around John's neck, and then screamed as she moved her shattered leg. She slumped in his arms. Her voice ragged and weak, she urged him, "Get... going."

The billboard creaked and groaned loudly as John moved quicker than he thought possible back and down the ladder and ran away from it, carrying Finley, just as the structure finally shrieked, shattered, and collapsed into a tangled mass of jagged steel and pipe.

Chest heaving, he carried her to the grass next to the SUV and gently set her down. The other jet screamed overhead again, and Finley waved weakly at it.

Matti was waiting for him with a first aid kit almost half her size, struggling to hold it up. John looked up and started to complain that she was supposed to stay in the SUV, but instead took the kit and opened it up, reminded of the times he'd done so on the oil rig years before. He cut away the ragged flight suit pants with the kit scissors, then ripped open the clotting agent and spread it over the heavily bleeding compound fracture.

Matti shouted, but he barely heard her. "Daddy, a helicopter is coming."

He hadn't heard it for some reason, but it was already hovering to land. John didn't stop working and pressed bandages to slow the bleeding. Sweat drenched her face as Captain Finley gasped, her already pale face turning even whiter.

The Black Hawk helicopter landed nearby, and a team jumped out and dashed over, carrying medical bags and a stretcher. John backed away as they arrived.

"Glad you guys are here. She's got a nasty compound fracture here, and I'm worried about the artery. I've applied clotting agent, but that's about all. You got here fast."

"Thank you, Sir. We'll take it from here." The medivac crew worked quickly, and in minutes, the Black Hawk was lifting away with the Captain. The other F-18 zoomed by again.

A fire truck and ambulance arrived as John looked down at his blood-covered hands and clothes. As he stood there, catching his breath, a paramedic ran up to him, checking him over.

"I'm ok. I'm ok. It's not my blood."

For a long moment, he stood there, transfixed. Why? Snap out of it, John! Then he realized. While he had worked on Captain Finley, she had been looking up at the sky. Through all of her obvious pain and anger, there was something else. She'd been "up there" and seen something in those green eyes. There was something about her expression. He looked up at the sun-line-thing and the other side of the world.

The firemen started spraying around the area around the fire, trying to keep flames from spreading but otherwise letting it burn itself out.

John shook himself and turned to Matti, then he smiled and looked himself over. "It's going to be a long day, baby."

He used his radio again. "This is Austin. Pilot's injured with a compound fracture and has been medivacked out by helicopter. Fire-Rescue is here on site dealing with the crash. No casualties here. What's the situation back in town?"

There was a short burst of static before Hector responded, "Boss, you'd better get back downtown. Things are under control, but they may not stay that way for long."

"I'm headed back your way."

Don't Shoot!

Fort Brazos Town Square
Day 0: 9:22 AM

When John and Matti arrived back downtown, the scene was more orderly. Police and his deputies lugged caution-striped road barricades, forming a ring around the square. The noisy, increasingly angry crowd was now, at least, held back to the edges of the central part of downtown and the square and the alien spire.

Chief Deputy Hector Alonzo met him at the scene. "Glad you're here, boss. This whole situation is un desmadre, is a disaster. Where are the feds?"

John looked sideways at Hector, then nodded upwards. No one was coming to their aid.

"Yeah, I know, boss. I'm just… I guess we are the feds, for now." Paramedics were attending to scattered injuries and helping people away. "There were a few broken bones after that," he gestured towards the spire, "Thing went boom and knocked us all on our ass." He pointed at the injured. "These are what's left, minor injuries and people shook the hell up, like that doesn't include all of us."

John nodded, "What do we need?"

Just then, all sound was sucked back into the spire again. John grabbed Matti close to him again and bent over to protect her, shouting for people to get down. No one could hear him, but people ducked and ran away quickly anyway.

This time, there was no explosion of green St. Elmo's Fire and no shockwave. This time, sound "popped" back on, as though by a switch, and at the base of the spire, a huge glowing symbol appeared. The symbol seemed graceful, delicate,

42

and bold, all at the same time, with parts that seemed to be different colors or combinations of fluorescents and colors that hurt his eyes.

Hector mumbled, "Dios, Mios… My God, I hope that isn't a countdown."

John glanced up and around. "Hector, I think we're way past countdowns. Whoever or whatever did this to us has already demonstrated their power over us. We might as well be some primitive Amazonian tribe dropped in the middle of downtown Houston. We don't have a clue what's happening, and all we can do is spit in God's eye."

Behind John, behind the barricade, someone was yelling for his attention. John turned and looked. It was a young man, probably a college student, maybe the idiot who'd touched the damned spire in the first place. One of the police officers was holding the kid back. "Sheriff! Sheriff! We need to record these symbols!"

At least a dozen people were already recording it on their cell phones.

John nodded to release the kid, who jogged over, panting. "Sheriff, we need to be recording these symbols!" His voice broke, "They could be super important!"

"Symbols? Plural?"

"You can't see it changing?"

John looked back at the spire. The symbol seemed the same. Mostly. "Color shifts."

"Yeah, I think some are outside the spectrum we can see."

John looked at Hector, then back at the college kid. "What's your name?"

"Kelly."

"Okay, Kelly, how do we record this better than all the people already doing it on their phones?"

"We have big, high-speed cameras at the University. Somebody needs to go over there, sign them out, and then set it up here with lots of data storage."

"Uh-huh. Can you do that?"

"Oh no, Sir, I don't have permission. I'm just a lab assistant."

"You do now." John turned to Hector, "Hector, get Tom Morgan to take this kid over to the University and do whatever it takes to get what is needed. Kick down doors if you have to. I don't care. Just get it done."

"Right, boss." Hector took Kelly by the shoulder and hurried him away.

John walked back over to the SUV and reached inside for the hand mic, keying the loudspeaker. He keyed the mic a few times until the noise got everyone's attention. He waited for the crowd to quiet.

"Right. Okay, everyone, right now, we are all wondering what the heck is going on." He pointed up to the sky, and gazes followed. "Myself included. I wish I had real answers to tell you, and as soon as I know more, I will. In the meantime, this tower thing, that spire there, is something we cannot ignore." He paused, looking at the faces of his friends and neighbors.

"Whoever or whatever has done this to us went to a lot of trouble. I can't comprehend how it was done or why, but whoever did it is insanely smart and very powerful. They apparently wanted us, at least most of us, alive."

Some nodded and relaxed a little.

"But like I said - very, very powerful." He pointed at the Spire. "Now, please pay attention, everyone. The last time somebody simply touched that thing, it got… angry." He waited for that to sink in.

He continued, "So, let's not make it angry again, okay? We need to know what's going on and why. So… Don't! Touch! The! Alien! Tower! Got it!!?"

There was stunned silence at his words. Especially the word "Alien." A few people managed a nervous chuckle.

"Also, if I see any of you point so much as a rubber band or BB gun at that thing, I'm hauling you off to jail and throwing away the key. Don't start a war and, Don't! Shoot! The! Alien! Tower!!!"

A few more chuckles.

John added. "Okay, last thing, for now. Everyone go home and look after your loved ones. I don't know what is next. I need you all, every one of you, to be careful. I don't know about you, but when I look up there"—he pointed up—"I'm not seeing anything that looks like other cities, roads, or any civilization. It seems safe to say that we're not in Texas anymore, but it may also mean that WE

ARE IT. There may not be anyone else—no one to rescue us. I hope I'm wrong. God, I hope I'm wrong, but every one of your lives was precious yesterday. Now…" He looked around at the silent crowd. "Now, your lives may well be priceless. Be careful. If you see something strange, call it in. The phones are working. Get help. Don't be a hero."

"The emergency plan calls for people to gather at the stadium. We'll do that as soon as we know more and can organize it. Until then, go home and take care of your families. If you can, have an adult stay with your kids at home and send another to the stadium when we get the meeting set up. We'll broadcast a live feed from the stadium on all the channels we can, so everyone can know what we know when we know it."

Hector returned from dispatching Deputy Morgan and leaned in to talk to John. "Boss, nice speech. You 'woulda made a good governor someday. Got some more bad news, though. The Mayor and Pastor Joe were in an accident out on the interstate. They're at the hospital. Mayor's okay, but Pastor Joe…."

Do No Harm

METHODIST HOSPITAL
Fort Brazos Texas
Day 0: 10:47 AM

Dr. David Duncan was haunted. A former Army Thoracic Surgeon, David had left the service after three traumatic front line tours and "retired" to the quiet community of Fort Brazos. He'd had enough, done enough, and seen enough, and was just… done. All he wanted was a quiet life. Somewhere with a decent golf course and where he could set up a nice, low-key surgical practice. With the influence of the nearby military base, the golf course was pretty good, and he had found other distractions that were starting to make his life here quite nice.

Today, however, he was not getting what he wanted. All of the top senior staff at the main hospital had woken up dead. David was now the most experienced, most senior surgeon in town. He'd found himself drafted into taking over as the de facto Chief of Surgery in the middle of a calamity of apparently Biblical proportions. So much for the quiet life.

At the moment, he had his hands deep inside the chest of a man supposedly suffering from acute myocardial infarction. But the man's heart was healthy. He stepped back. "Sew this man back up! There's nothing wrong with his heart. The chart must have been mixed up. That's the third one so far, Goddammit!"

David peeled off his gloves and surgical gown and dumped them in the bin as he stormed out of the operating room and burst out the doors into the hallway, nearly colliding with a man being pushed on a gurney. He slumped against the opposite wall, ran his hands through his carefully groomed, prematurely greying hair, and cradled a face that was normally a magnet for female attention. In years past, he'd traded shamelessly on that. Now he found it mostly tiresome.

He shivered. The air was still cold, and he was wearing scrubs. It shouldn't be this cold, for it was only August, typically one of the hottest months of the year. No one had gotten around to turning on the furnace. The hospital was bustling with movement, urgent worried voices, and shrill medical equipment alarms.

Nearby, barely discernable above the ambient hospital noise, a timid female voice said, "They're not sick."

David scrubbed his face with his hands and looked up. A pale, petite woman with somewhat wild dark hair sat primly in a nearby chair. She sat facing the opposite wall, but she seemed to be straining to see something in the distance.

David looked around to see who she was talking to, but nobody else was nearby. He sighed and looked away, assuming she was speaking to someone on her phone with Bluetooth.

"They're not sick, David." She looked right at him.

He blinked back, fatigue and confusion, "Pardon?"

He opened his mouth to ask how she knew his name, then realized it was on his nametag. "I'm sorry, miss, were you talking to me? Who isn't sick?"

She swallowed and implored him with her large brown eyes. "None of them are, but they will be soon if you don't do something."

He looked her over. She was tiny, and he thought she couldn't weigh a hundred pounds soaking wet. Her clothes were clean except for the blood on them. She's in shock, he thought. "Right, um, miss? What's your name? Let me find someone who can help you." He turned to look for a nurse or security.

"My name is Sybil. And you are Dr. David Duncan, formerly Captain David Duncan. And those men don't blame you."

David stopped cold and snapped back to stare at her. Her eyes were glassy with tears. "What... men?"

Sybil's lips trembled, and she swallowed again, and she sniffed. "The ones you keep with you that you won't let go. They all love you for what you did, and they don't blame you. You..." A tear fell. "Carl and Jose and Eduardo, and Mike and the others. You need to let them go."

He lost his balance for a moment and stumbled back, away from her. His face burned hot, and his heart raced. It was not possible. None of this was possible. "Who the hell are you? Get out of here!"

Sybil stood shakily and started to walk away. She turned back, tears streaming fast. "You have a chance to save these people, David. They are not sick." Then, she turned away and walked toward the exit.

He raised a hand to reach and stop her, but a half dozen doctors and nurses rounded the corner and pummeled him with questions.

He didn't hear any of them. It simply did not make any sense! He stood there thinking about the morning's cases. Time slowed, and suddenly it hit him like a thunderclap.

David stood up straight and blinked fast as it all came together, "My God, we're treating them for conditions they don't have. They're not sick! None of them are sick!"

Bigger Problems

Fort Brazos Town Square
Day 0: 11:12 AM

Mayor Parker, Sheriff Austin, and the surviving city leaders stood just inside the barricade, looking up at the 300-plus-foot-tall alien spire. Several university students and professor-types aimed cameras and instruments at it and talked excitedly a few feet away.

Tom asked, "Have we contacted the base?"

John nodded. "They are not answering. There is a notice on the website that the base is on lockdown. I sent Gwynn Daltry over there to knock on the door. She radioed me a few minutes ago. She said she tried to drive up to the base security gate but didn't make it that far."

Tom looked sideways at him.

"She says they waved her off, but when she tried to talk to them, they fired shots."

Tom bristled, "They what!?"

"She says they didn't shoot right at her, but the message was clear: Go away, don't bother us. Whatever's going on, Tom, they're not in a talking mood yet."

Tom shook his head. "They're going to come marching in here to take over, you know…. Situation like this."

Councilwoman Gloria Vargas nodded. Her long, jet black hair was streaked with silver and held back in a ponytail with a turquoise and sterling silver hair clip. "Tom, this is going to be trouble. I've heard a little about this new General Marcus over there. He's been there less than a week, and I also hear that he has enough medals to snap an oak tree, and he wears them to bed. One of those types. Do you really think he's going to be willing to take orders from us? Congressman Taylor was in D.C., and everyone else was in Austin for the special session. We're the highest-level governmental officials around, and we're all city or county! There's not a single surviving federal-level official we've found alive."

Tom chuckled. "Gloria, you've always had a way of cutting through the bull. I think you're probably right. They won't comprehend reporting to us. That's a horse pill they won't want to swallow."

John cleared his throat. "Prevailing Constitutional Authority. Let's all just hope that they remember what that is."

Tom looked at him, nodding. "My God, I'd always thought about that stuff as an exercise in pointless bureaucracy."

John added, "Yeah, but there is State continuity and Federal. The military will want to proceed under Federal continuity protocols and will say that trumps our State protocols. We're going to have to work fast on this and figure something out. We may have to appoint a Governor so that he can appoint a congressman or senator... I don't know."

Gloria pursed her lips. "We will need to schedule elections, which will have to include the base personnel, too...."

Tom nodded, "I expect that the Military probably has their own continuity protocols as well. This whole situation is going to be messy, but we have to do it. They're not going to like the idea of reporting to a small-town city government instead of the President and Joint Chiefs."

Gloria turned to John. "Sheriff, you know that I opposed your election."

John smiled, "Yes, ma'am. I noticed that, at the time."

She put her hand on his shoulder. "Now that we're faced with the end of the world, or the beginning, or whatever the hell is happening, I want you to know that I think I underestimated you. When you came back, I just saw you as that guy that left town, made it big, then came back to lord it over all of us so you could position yourself to run for higher office."

"I've been accused of worse, ma'am." He wanted to get angry but held himself in check.

She glanced up at the sky and then over at the spire. "I still don't know if I like you or not, and I'm still not convinced of your motives... But, I think it is time for truth between us. Why did you come back? I know that now may not seem like the time...."

John smiled thinly. "Okay, time for truth. Why not? You want to know why I came back?" He pulled Matti forward into the group and got down on one knee. "Matti, this is Councilwoman Vargas and the Mayor and other City Council, people. You know some of them, right?"

Matti stood tall and nodded solemnly.

"Matti, please tell the Councilwoman why we moved back to Fort Brazos."

Matti smiled sadly, "Miss Vargas, we moved here because this is Daddy's home and where he fell in love with my mom. Daddy and Mom wanted lots of kids, and they didn't want to raise them in Houston or some other big city. They moved here because of..." For a moment, her lips trembled, and she continued defiantly, "Because of me."

John stood up and looked at Gloria and the others. "I moved back here," he paused, "I moved back home because Fort Brazos is my home, and I love it here. I never expected that when I did, that people would treat us differently, like we were outsiders, just because I moved back and had money."

He pulled Matti close to him. "Carolyn and I tried to ignore the way we were treated, but it hurt the way that some people sucked up to us and others treated us with suspicion and... jealousy. I worked my ass off to accomplish what I did. I never expected a parade, but now that we're speaking honestly, I guess I never knew how few friends I really had."

Tom's expression was pained, and the others were all mixed.

Gloria narrowed her eyes. "You want us to feel sorry for you? You didn't answer the question about running for higher office."

Matti looked like she was going to kick the councilwoman, but John tightened his grip on her shoulder. "Councilwoman Vargas, I believe that rumor started with you, did it not?"

She blinked and stammered, trying to form words.

51

John smiled. "I thought so. That's okay. I understand. Those were different times, and now…"—he nodded towards the spire— "…and now, it all seems pointless and childish, doesn't it?"

Gloria composed herself quickly. "Okay, Sheriff. Fair enough. We have bigger problems now, and we need each other. I am sorry I underestimated you. I doubt we'll be friends, but, all things considered, I think we are all family now. Family members may not get along, but we stick together." She bent down and extended her hand to Matti, "Matilda… Matti, will you accept my apology to you and your dad?"

Matti considered the offer, "Miss Vargas, I know you're scared. I'm scared. I think we all are. Right now, I think you mean what you are saying." She took Gloria's hand and then held onto it when Gloria tried to stand. "But remember this. When you're not scared anymore, remember what you've said. Remember that we're all now family like you said. Don't forget it, because I won't forget, and I'll be watching you." She released Gloria's hand.

Gloria's eyes widened, and she looked up at John as she stood. "My goodness, it seems like this is my day for underestimating people."

John lowered his gaze. "Councilwoman, councilmen, Mayor, I'm going to ask us all to apply our collective and formidable talents, intelligence," he smiled at Gloria, "and guile, to whatever it is that we will be facing in the coming days and beyond. I have a feeling we're going to need every ounce of it."

Tom cleared his throat. "All right, then, people, we've got a lot of work to do on many fronts. I figure we've got a day at most before the military decides to roll into town, possibly with guns blazing. We need to be ready."

A pair of F-15's roared overhead before racing off into the distance.

Sensibilities

Sanches Veterinary & Equine Center
Day 0: 12:11 AM

Years before, Dr. Eva Sanchez had not simply inherited her father's Veterinary practice. She had redefined it and grown it to become the most trusted and respected practice for a hundred miles. Where her father had been kind and respected, she had become revered and beloved. Sought after. People flew their animals in to see her. None were more important than any other. She treated all with the same energy and almost mystic insight and empathic diagnostic skills.

Her secret? To her, it was all just hard work and a personal stubbornness that bordered on the pathological. She refused to give up on what she believed in.

At the moment, she had her arm deep inside a mare whose foal was presented wrong, and she was all alone at the center. None of her help had yet shown up for work. *End of the world or some such excuse. Tell that to this poor mare.*

"It's going to be okay. It's okay. Your baby is going to be just fine. You just let me help you, sweetie…."

Behind her, a low, familiar voice called out, "Need some help?"

Eva bit back a dozen inappropriate words her momma would have spanked her for. She gritted her teeth and glared over her shoulder at Dr. Jacob Becker, who was already pulling off his jacket and rolling up his sleeves. She snapped, "I'm not talking to you! You… you…! Get your skinny butt over here!"

He hadn't waited for the invitation. He stepped into the stall and went to work, helping her. He had done the same many times before. They were philosophical

53

enemies. He was an Agriculture scientist specializing in genetically modified crops. Eva hated everything genmod stood for. It was dangerous and spoke to the hubris of man. Everything about him grated against her, both personally and politically.

Their arguments were legendary on campus. Everyone knew they loathed and despised each other. They were oil and water. Fire and Ice. And frequent, hopelessly passionate, lovers.

Later, with the foal standing on wobbly legs and the mare doing well, Eva and Jacob washed off. After a few moments of silence, she swore, "Oh hell," and rushed into his arms.

He held her close, stroking her hair. She often called him a string-pole for the way he towered over her. He, in turn, often called her a pixie. They stood, silently holding each other, for a long time.

"Jacob, what is happening? What does all this mean? Where are we? What happened to the sky?"

He pulled her closer. "I don't know. Someone has gone to a great deal of trouble to create an entire world out there and deposit us into it. That implies there must be plans for us and that we must have a high value of some kind to whoever has done this. I just hope that when we find out just exactly what that value is, that it speaks to a destiny, we can live with."

Eva sniffed. "Listen to you, Mr. Deterministic, talking about words like destiny. If you keep it up, before long, you'll talk about God's will and such."

Jacob smiled, "I always felt that if there was a God, that snapping his fingers to create a universe just isn't very impressive. Creating the conditions for the universe and allowing it to evolve into his... *design*... would be a lot more impressive. A lot, lot harder. So, whether or not God actually created the universe, it works out pretty much the same way to me."

"You are such a strange man."

Before today, before this terrible day, Eva had never wanted to be seen being publicly affectionate with Dr. Becker. It just wouldn't do. Everyone knew they hated each other. Her friends hated his friends. Now? Today? She realized that she didn't give a damn anymore. Maybe she never really had.

She took his hand, and they walked outside together, lost in their own thoughts. Neither noticed the behavior of the other horses. None were jittery or noisy. They simply and calmly watched Eva and Jacob as they walked by.

They walked out into the pasture. Eva's four German shepherds followed in watchful formation. Jacob stopped and turned to face her with a serious expression.

She looked into his eyes and suddenly pulled back, her eyes widening as she took in his expression. She grimaced and shook her finger at him, "Oh God no, no, no, you don't!"

He smiled gently, reaching out to stroke her hair. "Give me a chance."

She tried to step backward, but the dogs were right behind her, blocking her, actually pushing her forward. She didn't notice. "Don't you dare! Not now!" Tears formed as she pointed to the sky. "Not because of this!"

"Eva...." He swallowed and continued. "No, not because of this. I had already planned to do this before.... Before all this happened. It's what I was trying to tell you yesterday when we... when we fought."

She bit her lip, "I... I know. I knew I think. Damn you!" Her tears began to stream unabated. "Nobody has worse timing than you!" She hit him in the chest once, then again and again, but her heart wasn't in it. "Nobody makes me crazy like you!"

"Eva?"

"No!"

He sank to his knees in front of her, reached into his pocket, and pulled out a ring box.

"No!"

Jacob smiled gently. His expression was loving, patient, and kind. He was confident in her answer. "Will you marry me?"

She slapped him, but he didn't flinch.

She immediately regretted it, "I'm sorry... I'm sorry! I didn't mean that. I just... I can't! This is crazy. This is all insane!"

He waited.

She looked up at the crazy sky but couldn't focus on anything through her tears. The breeze was gentle and soft. There was an unnatural chill in the air, but it was warming slowly. Her anger and fear drained away as she looked back down at him and stared into his ruddy, gentle face. The universe shrunk to just the two of them.

Eva decided to accept it. She would share her life and her fears with him, no matter what was to come or how short it might be. It no longer mattered to her what anyone else would think or say. She would take the leap. She had never dreamed of being able to do that with anyone, least of all with the insufferable Jacob Becker.

Somehow she knew, though, in that moment, that he was the only man that she had ever truly loved. Her chest heaved, and she nodded quickly, and he put the ring on her finger. She fell into his arms.

Softly panting but watchful and alert, the dogs silently took up cardinal positions around them.

Flying Blind
Fort Brazos Joint Military Reserve Base
Day 0: 1:04 PM

Chief Master Sargent Harrold Anders was on a mission from God. Whatever the hell was going on, HIS boys were going to be ready. The emergency or whatever it was that was happening had immediate repercussions for everyone at the base. The CO had given orders, effectively converting a peacetime reserve stateside training base into an active-duty firebase with a fully patrolled and guarded perimeter. Fully mustered and equipped units stood up in preparation for action with unknown, possibly even *Alien*, hostiles.

On the plus side, most of these men had been deployed at least once to active theatres in the Middle East or elsewhere. They at least had some idea of operational security. The bad news was that this was still an unmitigated clusterfuck, and they would be lucky if friendly fire were the only bad thing that happened today. He forced himself not to keep looking up at the sky, just like he was continually berating everyone around him that did the same.

"All right, you worthless losers. I don't care if we have to fight aliens shooting ray guns at us or bug-eyed monsters. You - will - be - ready! You can bet your asses that whatever does come won't be green mars women with big tits looking for husband material! Whoever has done this to us has no fucking sense of humor at all!"

Behind him, two Humvees collided in a metal rending crash. Harrold's face twisted in a rictus of fury and his chest swelled in rage as he whirled about.

CONTROL TOWER

General Alexander Marcus surveyed the sprawling Joint Reserve Base from the wide control tower window. His dark brown eyes were worried, but decades of discipline kept it bottled up and tucked away. He stood ramrod straight in his crisp Air Force BDUs and, notably, a belted sidearm. After the initial hours of chaos, he had taken time to make sure he was parade-ground sharp. His close-cropped grey hair covered his shade-of-night skin. He had shaved and made sure the other officers took at least some time to do the same, including the issue of sidearms, along with fresh marine guards in full battle rattle.

On the tarmac below, the Humvee collision caught his eye as he looked out over the sprawling base. He could not hear what was being said, but he watched CCM Anders gesticulate wildly, shouting something most certainly unpleasant, as the drivers involved wilted under the verbal fusillade. Just as quickly, Anders had the situation resolved and traffic flowing again.

Marcus chuckled darkly. In his deep baritone voice, he quipped to the Lt. Darryl Guevara, "I'm glad Anders is on our side."

Darryl Guevara smiled, "Yes, Sir, roger that." Guevara had not needed extra time to clean up. He had been on duty and was always fastidious, a picture-perfect example of the whip-smart Cuban immigrant-son working his way up the ladder.

Marcus turned away from the window. "Sitrep? How's our pilot?"

"Sir, Captain Finley is out of surgery. The injury is serious, but they saved her leg. She'll be out of action for some time. She asked to see you."

"Good, take me to her."

Guevara opened his mouth to speak as the elevator chimed, which was odd because it wasn't to be used during the crisis — it wouldn't do to have officers stuck in an elevator in a time of need. The doors opened, and Captain Gail Finley grimly rolled her wheelchair out into the control room, with an orderly fussing over her, carrying an IV bag.

Marcus tossed a surprised glance at Guevara, then strode over. "Captain Finley, shouldn't you be in the base hospital?"

Gail was pale, with a dew of sweat on her forehead and her hair plastered back. Her eyes were fiery, though. Marcus could see how her reputation had been earned. After the crash, he had asked for her and her wingman's packets. She was known for getting what she wanted and working harder than anyone else to get it.

Gail cleared her throat, "Yes, Sir, but this is not a normal day, Sir."

"No, Captain, it sure as hell isn't. I've spoken to your wingman about what happened, but I want you to tell me what you saw, in your own words. However, first, Lt. Guevara?"

"Yes, General?"

"Record this interview. Any detail may be important later."

"Yes, Sir." Guevara raised his eyebrows but quickly fished his smartphone out of a pocket and started recording.

General Marcus nodded. "Go ahead, Captain."

Gail took a deep breath, winced, and began to speak. "Sir, we were flying in the blind up there. It was dark, and there were no air currents at all." She paused.

A pilot himself, Marcus thought about it. "Wait, what did you say?"

"The air was completely still. There were no currents, of any kind, at any altitude. There was nothing. All just dead air, the whole way up."

"Okay, are you sure it wasn't just your instruments?"

"Yes, Sir, 100%. I flew an EA-18G Growler for a while last year doing EW testing. I knew what I was doing, Sir."

Marcus took a breath, thinking. "I'm sure you did. All right, Captain, then what happened?"

Gail squirmed in the wheelchair as the orderly tried to adjust her IV. "Sir, just as we passed Angels 30, something happened. We passed through those static clouds and fog into clear air. There was indirect light from somewhere, but no stars or moon. Just clear black sky."

General Marcus nodded.

She closed her eyes and concentrated, "There was this thing… a pale line across the sky and all of a sudden it…." She opened her eyes, "General, any other day, I would be afraid to report this for fear of being put on psychiatric leave.

You see, a bolt of green lightning shot up from the deck, raced past us and up and out into space… and… it *splashed* against the line-thing. Then the line lit up like it was an old-fashioned fuse. As it caught fire, the whole sky lit up in a flash. I know it couldn't have been, but in my mind, I was thinking *nuke*."

Marcus sighed, "I think we all know why you didn't see any stars or the moon. You were up high; did you see any other aircraft or structures of any kind on the ground?"

"No, Sir. Nothing."

"Okay, continue."

Gail stared right through him, remembering. "Sir, after that tube thing lit up, everything went crazy. We were slammed by a jet stream that just… just wasn't there a second before. It tossed us around like toys, and Chuckles clipped me good. Not his fault, Sir."

"I don't think he was at fault, no. However, tell me something. You think the sudden change in air movement wasn't just coincidentally simultaneous to the… err… ignition event, you think they were connected?"

Gail nodded sharply, "Sir, I've been going over it and over it in my head. I saw… I saw the world up there. As you know, we're inside a hollow cylinder, Sir. I think the air moved because until the ignition event. It wasn't. The world wasn't spinning…."

Marcus blinked at her. "So…."

She could sense how he was struggling with it all. Just like she was. The events had given her a certain clarity. She knew it was vital for the General, and everyone else, to get a grip on what was happening. He needed, hell, she needed to hold onto at least the illusion they comprehended what was going on.

She continued, "So the Coriolis isn't generating the gravity, or it wasn't, before. I think the Coriolis was engineered to keep air and oceans moving. You see, Sir, whoever put us here may be godlike engineers, but it isn't magic. It's physics, and at least some of it makes some sense. It implies they have some form of artificial gravity holding everything in place vertically, orthogonal to the surface, but until the spin, the world wasn't, well, it wasn't really turned on. Once the spin started, I imagine the artificial gravity phased out, or else there might, maybe, interference patterns?"

Marcus paused for a moment. He asked, "Captain, what is your academic background?"

Gail blinked. "Sir, I have a Masters in Aeronautical Engineering from Cal Poly, but I'm…."

He waved her to stop and let the silence draw on as he rocked back on his feet. "Captain…."

He shook his head. "No, Not anymore. Major Finley, you are ordered to get yourself looked after, and after that, you are going to be my go-to problem solver until your leg heals. You are medically grounded anyway. Take some pills, get some sleep and report back to me at 0800 tomorrow… Assuming we have an 0800 tomorrow, that is."

He continued, "Major, you should know that the entire senior staff was off base when all of this… when our change of venue occurred. We were changing command, and the old and new staff members were in a big huddle at a conference at the Pentagon, following Operation Pearl Chalice. Normally, I'd be up to my neck in senior staff officers. I'm going to have to field promote if we're going to get anything done around here, and you're my first victim."

Looking stunned by the turn of events, she started to say something until he waved her off.

"Orderly, take the Major back to the hospital and make sure someone sits on her if that is what it takes to get her to sleep. Then you, personally, are responsible for getting her here and looking after her medical needs while she is away from the hospital. The confused orderly opened his mouth to speak as well, but Marcus cut him off.

"It's okay. I'll make it official and go through your CO. Now, go."

Gail stayed upright at sitting attention until after the orderly wheeled her back into the elevator.

Marcus nodded approvingly. He noticed that this time, she had let the orderly wheel her out instead of insisting on doing it herself. He returned to the window, followed by Guevara.

"Lt. Guevara take notes. Get with mission planning. I want to see what is out there. I want to send out drones to do mapping immediately around the base and spreading out from there. I want to compare our records with what is out there right now. What is different? I don't trust whoever did this to us."

Guevara snagged a nearby clipboard, flipped the forms to their blank side, and started writing.

"Yes, Sir, we don't really have a mapping group to do this… and we really don't have a working mission planning group."

"You're right. I know we don't, but we need them now. Put together a list of candidates with the best available skills, and I'll approve the formations."

"Yes, Sir."

"Schedule a senior staff meeting for four hours from now. Agenda items to follow, and I damned-well want answers at the meeting."

"Yes, Sir."

"We need a SIGINT group to go looking for anything they can find. If someone's lost on the prairie with a walkie-talkie, I want to know about it. I want ears-on 24x7, and I want everything recorded."

"Yes, Sir."

"Organize patrols away from the base. There's got to be a reason we are here. Find it. Coordinate recon patrols with mapping, keep in constant contact and vector recon to anything at all unusual, and have close air support on hot standby."

"Yes, Sir."

"I want to set up long-range recon mapping, with tanker and fighter escort. We need to know if anyone… else… is in this place with us. I want to know how long it will take to map this place. I don't care if we have to start with somebody's kid's Celestron telescope and point it UP – I want maps, and I want to know what is out there," he pointed out the window and upwards. We need to know our ground."

"Yes, Sir. I think the mapping group may need to be bigger…."

"I want a plan on my desk by this time tomorrow."

Guevara swallowed, fighting the urge to roll his eyes.

"I know what you're thinking Lieutenant, planning here is not used to working at this pace. Well, tough. I didn't change the planet. Someone else did. Kick 'em in the ass and get it done. Oh, and you'll need your own Captain's bars to get the right kind of boot imprint, so go update your uniform, Captain and report back in 30."

✪ ✪ ✪

Twenty minutes later, Captain Guevara returned with fresh insignia, carrying a sheaf of photos.

Marcus nodded in approval then looked questioningly at the photos.

"Sir, these are photos from Major Finley's wingman. There's something you need to see." Guevara spread the photos across the table and aimed an overhead light down on them for emphasis.

Marcus's jaw dropped. There was an enormous, tall, thin black spire rising from the center of the City of Fort Brazos. "Why didn't we know about this? Has anyone talked to them?"

"Sir, the base was in lockdown when some Sheriff's deputies approached. They were warned off, and we are not taking civilian calls."

"Warned off, how?"

"Warning shots were fired, Sir."

Marcus winced. It took all his self-control not to swear out loud. He shook his head, "This is my fault. Dammit. We're looking for goddamned space aliens when there is that… that thing rising above the city we should be protecting! And… And we SHOT AT the deputies, coming to us for help?!"

Captain Guevara didn't hesitate, "Sir, warning shots were fired for their safety after they continued to attempt to approach the base perimeter."

One of the servicemen in the communications area half stood and urgently motioned for the Captain, who stepped over to investigate. After a quick exchange, he called to the General, "Sir! You're going to want to hear this."

As Marcus walked over, the speaker crackled then steadied, "…repeating: This is Danielle Richardson on KFBR, with an update on today's disaster. There are conflicting reports, but some say the number of dead is in the tens of thousands. Killed… murdered in their sleep… and if you heard that big explosion, some people say they shot down one of our airplanes over the city. I've heard the Police Chief is dead, many of the City Council and even Pastor Joe. There are reports of explosions and gunfire, and from my window, I can see emergency vehicles and people wandering around everywhere in shock. There is chaos, and I cannot get through to 911. Several people are talking about seeing stars falling…. My God, this is a nightmare…."

Several people in the tower gasped in shock. The airman added, "That's the gist of it, Sir, it is rambling and contradictory, but it is the only news we have from outside the base."

"Thousands of people dead? Sweet Jesus! Captain, I don't recall any reports of dead on the base. Are there any?"

He hesitated, "No, Sir. None reported. It was touch and go after the friendly fire incident, and the other… situation, but there were no serious casualties."

Activity in the room had stopped, and all eyes were on the General. He ground his teeth. "Okay, people, we may have a nuclear, biological, or chemical attack on our hands! We know that Major Finley wasn't shot down, but that just adds to the confusion. We don't know what is happening. For all, we know there may be active hostiles or even terrorists."

"What is our readiness status? What do we have available for immediate action?"

Guevara hesitated for a moment, "Sir, it's a mess right now. We finished the Pearl Chalice exercise just two weeks ago, and most of the equipment is in the maintenance cycle. Most of the remaining officers we actually have onsite are out organizing the… new arrivals. The best company-level group available now is Captain Moss's 3rd Company. As of an hour ago, they reported 80% readiness. Everything else is well below 50%."

General Marcus nodded. "Okay, cannibalize what we have to but get the rest sorted out. Meanwhile, I want 3rd Company in full MOPPS gear and full combat load-out, and I want them at the gate in 30, and I want close air support and get me some eyes over that town right fucking now in a rotating CAP."

Marcus addressed the rest of the service people in the control tower. "People, we are going to protect the civilians. Period. I want to know the exact operational status of our armored command – how many of what units are deployable right this minute." He paused and pointed at the photos. "We will expand the security cordon around this base, and we will secure the town, and we will secure that thing standing there! We may need to evacuate the civilian population to the base reservation."

"Have the base hospital prepare for incoming casualties and establish triage. Tell them there are reports of thousands of civilian casualties."

"People, we are operating in the dark. We need actionable intelligence. Rules of Engagement are to avoid action if possible and report back. Protect the civilians. Do not shoot civilians unless hostile action is shown. If possible, avoid action, report back, and call for reinforcements."

He paused and looked around the room. "Something has apparently killed our people. We don't know who or what, but it's obvious we ain't in Texas anymore. If damned bug-eyed monsters attack, then call for help, and we'll hit back with everything we've got."

Detente

City of Fort Brazos
Day 0: 2:49 PM

The column of light armored vehicles and Humvees thundered into town, flanked by Apache attack helicopters and a squadron of F-15's for emphasis. The closer they got to downtown, the more the Humvees had to slow down due to all the other vehicles already on the road. People stopped and stared, and a few waved. As they arrived at the square, weapons drawn, they called out on loudspeakers, ordering people to stand down. People watched and gradually went back to what they had been doing before, generally ignoring the soldiers.

A platoon rushed towards the spire, and a lone figure walked calmly out into the space in-between, hands raised.

The platoon leader, Lt. David Garreth, shouted, "Sir! SIR! MOVE ASIDE!"

Chief Deputy Hector Alonzo very carefully forced a smile and raised his hands higher, "Lieutenant, I know you have your orders, but, please, please! Don't shoot, the alien, tower. Please do not make it angry, and, whatever you do, don't touch it!"

FORT BRAZOS CITY HALL

Garreth and his platoon circled the room, still in full MOPPS, but with weapons pointed in discrete directions.

Gloria Vargas wrinkled her nose at the smell.

Several seats were empty. Their former occupants were among the dead. The hasty meeting was called as an expedient location for the conference call with the base. Tom and John, with John's shirt still blood-stained, as well as several City Councilpersons, gathered around the speakerphone.

Tom summarized, "… so you see General, the alien tower, people are calling it the "Spire," by the way, is under continual observation. We are recording these symbols as they appear, and we've pushed the cordon back even further. With everything that has happened, we don't think the object is actively dangerous. Whoever put us here could obviously hurt us or kill us anytime they want, especially considering all the casualties."

There was a pause from the other end of the phone line. Marcus's voice was strained. "How bad is it, Mr. Mayor? How many dead? How many injured? Do you need to evacuate the civilians to the secure base area?"

Tom looked at John.

"Ah, General, this is Sheriff Austin. We're still counting, but the number of dead is already over three thousand, approaching four thousand. We set up an unused warehouse as a morgue, and we're digging up all the dry ice and refrigeration units we can find."

After a long, long pause, Marcus's voice dropped to a subterranean rumble, "My God! Mr. Mayor, we had no idea, and we've failed you completely. Please tell me what you need. What is the ongoing threat? How many wounded?"

The councilpersons and Mayor and John all shifted uncomfortably and shook their heads at each other.

"Ah, General, this is Sheriff Austin again. We have a few injuries to deal with, but almost all are minor. Lots of them, but minor. We have a triage set up, but there are no serious or critical patients, and there is no current military threat that, uh, that we are aware of."

General Marcus's tone darkened. "I don't understand. How is that possible?"

John continued, "General, you need to understand. We were not… attacked. Everyone either woke up today – or they didn't. We're all either alive or we're not. Do you mean to say that this didn't happen at the base also? We'd assumed that was contributing to your… preoccupation there."

A long and uncomfortable silence followed.

"Mr. Mayor, I don't know what to say. We have had… um, difficulties here, but there were no deaths here. None."

There were gasps from around the conference table.

General Marcus continued, his voice dropping octaves and volume, "What has happened in your city is… is worse than 911. My God. It only happened in the City. This must be a biological or chemical attack! I can understand not attacking the base itself. The city is a softer target. It must be some kind of attack!"

There were worried and puzzled looks around the table, but John and others adamantly shook their heads.

"General, this is Sheriff Austin again. We've had NBC training, and this just does not fit that pattern. People were side by side, and some woke up, and some didn't, and nobody is sick or symptomatic." He paused for a moment, thinking. "It is random across all age groups, races, and sex, and it also includes livestock and other animals. None of our post-911 sensors have detected a thing, and we've looked. Hard. We only have a handful of hazmat suits anyway. I've been on at least a dozen death calls myself. Oh, and again, nobody is sick. There is no sign of anyone being sick or anything like you would expect from an outbreak of some kind."

A staffer brought in a manila envelope of reports and handed it to the Mayor, who looked it over, frowned, and handed copies to everyone.

In the pause, Marcus inquired, "Lt. Garreth, are you nearby? What have your tests shown?"

Garreth shuffled closer to the speakerphone, his MOPPS gear noisy and clearly uncomfortable. In a muffled voice, he answered, "Yes Sir, General, I'm here. All the preliminary tests are negative. There is no indication of an NBC event. Everyone here seems very healthy and alive. I haven't seen anyone with so much as a cold, Sir."

Marcus answered, "Thank you, Lieutenant. Maintain status until the medical team gives final clearance."

"Yes, Sir, General." Garreth shuffled back to a neutral corner.

John and the others read over the latest report. He looked around at them. These were practical men and women and leaders of a thriving agricultural community. He reread the numbers and saw it in their eyes. John reached for a piece of paper and did some arithmetic. As the realization sunk in, people shook their heads in anger and horror.

Marcus began, "Mr. Mayor, Sheriff? I'd like to…"

John cut him off, "General, excuse me, but there is new information." He ran his hand through his hair and continued, "The, ah, the hospital is reporting that all of their previously sick patients, that is, those who woke up at all, are now symptom-free from their diseases and illnesses. Several almost died from treatments they didn't need anymore. In short, General, there don't seem to be any sick people in Fort Brazos. None, zero, nada."

John paused, then continued, "General, I think things are pretty clear now. We've all been kidnapped, abducted by forces unknown. The entire military population is untouched, but the civilian population has been, well, we've been selectively culled, like some herd or someone's garden, while our sick have been healed. The forces that did this to us are saying, 'Look what we did. Not only do we have the engineering knowledge to create an inside-out planet, but we know your biology better than you do yourselves. We put you in this world, and we can take you out.'"

General Marcus responded with a carefully neutral but still dismissive tone, "Ah, look, Sheriff, things are happening fast. It is too soon to draw too many conclusions yet."

Gloria surprised everyone by speaking up. "General, this is Councilwoman Vargas. I don't particularly like Sheriff Austin, nor do I agree with him on many things. Right now, however, you need to listen to him. He is not some bumpkin backwater Sheriff. He's got a Masters in Petroleum Engineering, and an MBA from Wharton, and several patents. Look, you don't know any of us, but we're all smart people. General, how many people did you say died on the base?"

"Again, none, Councilwoman."

John jumped in. "General, we are, of course, glad to hear that. We've had enough loss of life as it is. Look, whoever put us here in this place is sending a message. They selectively woke some of us up and some they just didn't. Think about it. They let all of the military personnel live and only culled the civilian population. They did it to show us they can. We live or die at their whim."

The silence that followed was palpable. Finally, Marcus spoke, "Mr. Mayor, Councilwoman, Sheriff, I need to confer with my staff here and bring them up to speed. With your permission, I will send people to help with your casualties. Is there anything else you need right now that I can help with?"

Tom nodded to the others. "General, no disrespect to you or your fine men here, we don't want to turn the city into a militarized camp, and I think putting a ring of tanks around this Spire would be considered… impolite to our alien… hosts. We've seen what happens when someone simply touched the damned thing. I think that if you could supplement our police and sheriff office personnel with some MP's to keep the curious and foolish away from the damned thing, it would be appreciated."

"Mr. Mayor, I'll pull the heavier forces further back if you will agree to direct participation by my people with yours in the study of and any… interactions with the alien tower. We are now all in this together."

Tom looked around the table. Some seemed happy with the idea, and some not, but no one raised an objection. "General, I think we can live with that."

Gloria spoke before anyone could stop her. "General, this is Councilwoman Vargas. You should also know that we have officially invoked the Continuity of Government protocols."

Marcus snapped back a reply, "Councilwoman, Mr. Mayor, I suppose that is your right, of course, but are we getting ahead of ourselves? Isn't it too soon for that?"

Tom turned to John, "Sheriff Austin, please tell the General what you told me earlier."

John took a deep breath. "General, we have thousands of our people dead. Thousands. All of us, including you, have been kidnapped and deposited in an… well… an alien world of some kind. Our people need something to hold on to. Are we going to continue our way of life? We cannot let this descend into panic, chaos, dictatorship, or every man for himself. Our people need reassurance that this is still a Republic. Maybe it isn't the United States anymore, but dammit, if we are here, then this is still Texas! Texas began as a Republic, and it looks like maybe it will have to be one again. We owe it to our people to show them they do have a voice and that we are still a civil society of laws."

Marcus replied in an even tone, "Okay, Mr. Mayor, Sheriff, Councilpersons, please rest assured that you have my, our, unwavering support. Whatever you need. I suggest we set up a face-to-face meeting as soon as possible."

Tom added, "Thank you, General. We'll look forward to it. I know you've only just taken this post and that we have not had the opportunity to meet as yet. I regret that we must do so under these circumstances, but we are glad you are here."

"Thank you, Mr. Mayor. My wife and I have not even unpacked all the boxes yet from the move. I had been looking forward to meeting you and getting to know your community. To be honest, I had expected this to be my last command before retirement. I think all of our futures have been reset for us."

Tom pursed his lips, "Of course, General." Dottie seemed to emerge from nowhere and handed Tom a sheet of paper. He read it with his glasses on the tip of his nose, nodding, "We're all looking forward to meeting you and your family. I understand you have twin girls?"

"Ah, yes, Mr. Mayor. Faith and Hope."

"I'm glad they are here with you, then... So many have family that, well, that are not with us in Fort Brazos and may never see them again. Oh, also, ah, General, we meant to ask about your brave pilot, um, Captain Finley. She almost died, making sure her plane did not hit the high school. I hope she is Okay?"

Marcus answered, "Yes, Mr. Mayor, Major Finley is doing well. I intend to bring her with me when we meet. If there is nothing else, I will sign off now."

"Thank you, General. We'll coordinate on the meeting and look forward to meeting you soon."

Garreth and his men quickly left the room.

Tom reached over and semi-dramatically thumbed off the speakerphone. "Whew! Thoughts, anyone?"

Gloria blew her nose, "Leave the doors open...."

Councilman Bragas drawled, "I think he thinks we're power-mad and trying to take over the world."

Gloria added, "He's going to be trouble. You wait and see. He will march in here, thumping his chest full of medals and take over."

Tom looked at John questioningly, "I thought you said the pilot was a Captain?"

John raised his eyebrows. "So did I."

Tom continued, "Well, maybe you can get her to talk some sense into him. You did save her life after all."

Dr. Talib

The wild-haired young lab assistant tugged at Dr. Leo Talib's perfectly tailored Saville Row shirt. Again. "Dr. Talib?"

Dr. Talib was Assistant Dean of Language Studies at Bonham State University. He was a gifted polyglot, fluent in fourteen languages and passible in a dozen more. A frequent and heavy globetrotter, he was urbane, cultured, and darkly handsome at 35.

Leo's parents had both been diplomats. His mom American, and his father, French Algerian. Never in one place long, he'd grown up in Algiers, Paris, Brussels, Bogota, Beijing, London, and, after the death of his father, Washington D.C. His mother had then gotten sick, and her care had bankrupted them. He was stuck in America.

Despite everything, he could tell you which square meter any given French wine derived from, which dynasty a particular Chinese vase came from, or which dialect of Mayan was inscribed on an ancient artifact. Many people wondered what he was doing at Bonham State University. He often asked himself the same question.

Now, today, he had barely recovered from the morning's wake-up electrocution when he'd been rousted by an unsympathetic Sheriff's deputy from the cot in his tiny office, where he'd been huddling, contemplating his bleak future.

He could still feel the rough hands of the hulking deputy who had practically dragged him from his office. Later, on the way from campus to what passed for a downtown in this godforsaken place, he'd learned that he was the new acting departmental Dean. Apparently, that old fossil Dr. Gloria Rubenheim had blessed the world by not waking up this morning. Or ever again.

Oh, and there was a black, apparently, 'alien' tower-thing looming over the city.

Leo had hated everything about Dr. Rubenheim and, worse -- having to work for her. When he had been recruited to this remote community on what seemed like the far side of the moon, he was led to believe that, after a brief transition, he would take over the department when Dr. Rubenheim retired. He had just turned 30 and had his whole life in front of him. The plan was to stay for a few years, write several books and publish frequently, and then upgrade to a nice civilized institution, preferably on the continent. By then, with his department head credentials and experience, he could safely regail his enlightened colleagues with tales of life in the wild wild west.

Once he'd arrived, however, their relationship had soured. The old bitch had refused to step down, just to spite him. She'd even told him so and seemed to take great pleasure in tormenting him.

Since then, he'd suffered for five years under Rubenheim's tyrannical rule, and even if he did transfer elsewhere, it would be as an "Assistant" Dean at a nowhere school. He'd been trapped.

The bitch had tried to sabotage him several times, hoping he'd trip up so that she could ruin him for good. When Machiavellian academic maneuvers failed, she'd had the gall to, somehow, arrange for a willing coed to try and, imagine it, seduce and discredit him. He wasn't gay, though rumors persisted; he was just bored with such childish games and vacuous mental pygmies.

His parents had found him to be a difficult child to raise and eventually had him tested. They never treated him the same afterward and became distant, as if they couldn't relate to him anymore, or that perhaps something in the testing results had frightened them. He knew his IQ was somewhere well over 190, but he'd kept that to himself. He knew he was far more intelligent than most anyone around him. Often, however, the decisions and behavior of other people completely dumbfounded him. He'd found he had a talent for languages, which became his life and obsession, that, and his penchant for style.

Style was something that seemed utterly foreign to the inhabitants of Fort Brazos. Not that there weren't more than a few people who simply equated money with style, but none seemed to comprehend the Zen of true style and its intersection with Fung Shui. He was a castaway, trapped on the vast primitive Texas prairie.

Now, though, he truly was trapped, kidnapped along with the rest of these provincial Neanderthals by, he shook his head, by damned space aliens. The universe hates me.

"Dr. Talib!"

For what seemed the 500th time, he bit back a retort and forced a smile, "Yes, Kelley, what is it?" Just shoot me and get it over with.

Kelley practically jumped up and down, the mop of his sandy hair flopping about, pointing excitedly at a nearby collection of laptop computers scattered precariously on a jumble of boxes, "Please, Doctor, look at this!"

For just an instant, Leo allowed himself to imagine that the young man had a shaggy wagging tail and a long, drooling dog-tongue hanging out of his mouth. He sighed and followed Kelley over to the laptop screen.

"Okay, what am I looking at? You know technology is not my forte." This wasn't true at all, but it was an affectation he chose to cultivate.

They were standing under a collection of portable fabric-roofed pavilions. A dozen people darted back and forth from the barricade line, bringing more equipment, dragging more power cords and lights, and bringing – his stomach fluttered – American coffee and donuts. Nearby, police officers stood idly, drinking that same vile coffee, watching what he and the others were doing as though he might suddenly decide to steal something.

Kelley hovered over one of the notebook computers, like some spastic bird, tapping keys and pointing excitedly at the screen, "See that?? Look at that, would you?" Kelley picked up a disposable coffee cup and drained it. Leo realized he'd lost count of how many the young man had consumed.

Leo was looking, but it seemed no different than before. "Kelley," he reached out and put his hand (lightly) on the young man's obviously unwashed shirt shoulder, "please slow down. What are you showing me?"

"Oh, right. Yeah… uh…," Kelley typed furiously with one hand while he angled the screen with the other. "It went by so fast I didn't see it at first. Watch…. *this*…!"

Leo leaned in closer. On display was a recording of one of the symbol-change transitions. Only now, there was something different. Something very, very familiar. He did not wait for Kelley. He bodily moved Kelley out of the way and took over the keyboard, typing fast. Kelley's attention was quickly distracted by a slender grad student with long curly brown hair and a shy smile. She brought him coffee and cupped his hands as she gave it to him. They wandered off together to the next tent.

My God… There's audio embedded in this… Leo's fingers flew as he downloaded the software he needed, and the outside world faded from significance. He was in the Zone. Minutes later, he looked around and found a pair of headphones. He wiped off the damp ear muffs. Universe knew where they had been.

He hit <Play> and watched and listened. Then he played it again. And again. And again. The universe shrank around him as he listened.

For perhaps the first time in his life, he was no longer bored. He slowly took the headset off, not even noticing that it had rumpled his hair.

"Kelley!"

Kelly dashed back in, "Yes, yes, Doctor?"

"Has anyone else seen this?"

"No, Doctor, I was just about to…."

"Don't. This is important. Nobody must see this yet. It could be vital; do you understand? I need to listen to this in a quiet place -- it is too noisy here. This ahh… this signal has much more information than we thought. I need to work on it…"

"Sure, Dr. Talib. I'll send copies out to everyone."

Leo shook his head. "Kelley, please don't. Not yet. If others get involved right now, we'll have a hundred different opinions." He looked Kelley in the eyes,

"Kelley, this is my gift. Language is my gift. I'll work on it, and I will take it to the College and the City Council, and I'll tell them what a great job you are doing. Can you put this on a memory stick for me? Then, keep looking for these and send anything new directly to me and no one else."

"Sure! Sure, Dr. Talib, I'll do that right now and keep working on it."

"Thank you, Kelley."

Magnifying Glass

On Approach to Fort Brazos
Day 1: 09:32 AM

General Marcus glanced over at Captain Guevara in the seat next to him, who was taking photos out the window, and then smiled inwardly as he returned his gaze to Major Finley in the helicopter seat across from him, her shattered leg in an awkward-looking cast. She was forced to keep her cast jutting out to the side, twisting her in her seat. Her face was pale, and her jaw was set. The vibration must be excruciating, but she hasn't complained once. She's tough. He'd read the report on the severity of her injury and subsequent surgery and privately wondered how well he himself would be holding up after less than a day. *You'd still be on your back, old man, asking for more pain meds, provided you were even still conscious, and you know it.*

After her visit to the control tower, Marcus had sent word ahead – she was to sleep, even if they had to tie her down. The doctors had been horrified that she'd evidently snuck out of ICU in the first place. Reportedly, after returning to the hospital, the Major had listened dutifully to the doctors excoriating her for risking her health and possibly her life. Thirty seconds into the lecture, she'd closed her eyes and passed out on her own before the sedative could even be added to her IV.

He shook his head. *At least someone got some sleep.* At around 7 pm, the sun-tube had started to dim gradually. By 8 pm, its fiery yellow had softened to a remarkably moon-like silver glow. Through the night, breaths were held, and everyone had wondered if and when the sun-tube would re-ignite. He'd eventually returned home and held his wife and the twins close to him for a couple of hours, comforting them and answering what questions he could.

He'd returned to duty just before 4 am, and paced back and forth in the control tower, waiting. At around 6 am, the suntube began to brighten again, and everyone breathed a collective sigh of relief. By the top of the hour, it returned to full brightness. He was new to the base and to Texas, so he'd asked when sunrise normally happened here. Apparently in August, sunrise occurred at around 7 am and sunset at around 8 pm, so their abductors seemed to be keeping the same schedule.

Before yesterday, though it now seemed like an eternity ago, he and his wife Alisha had been unpacking boxes. This was a new command, a safe command far from physical danger. His biggest genuine concern had been how his six-year-old girls would adapt to their new home and whether they would encounter racial bigotry as a family of African American descent in a remote Texas city.

The base was mainly a training center, home to units between combat deployments. It was an administrative posting, but he knew it was probably his last. What came next would be retirement or commanding a desk at the Pentagon. Now, he was the commanding general of, apparently, the sole outpost of humanity in a new, probably hostile alien world.

The Boeing Chinook CH-47 helicopter was a singleton flight. Captain Guevara had wanted gunships to accompany them, but Marcus had overruled. Arriving in an unarmed transport was calculated to convey both power and restraint -- to the townspeople as well as to the alien spire, assuming it, or perhaps 'they' were watching.

They had flown a winding course around the outside perimeter of the region - the demarcation zone between the new world and the abducted one. The roads were simply chopped off, and the virgin landscape began. They had also flown around the edge of the enormous lake, or perhaps it was an inland sea, that now sat between the base, the town, and the mountains.

Those mountains were like a barrier wall, complete with glaciers. Glaciers! He now knew that beyond those mountains was an ocean. They were at the tip of a vast continent that, so far, appeared devoid of visible structures or cities. A large river drained either end of the massive lake, and other pilots reported prominent "natural" harbor inlets that begged further investigation.

After following the edge of the lake, they had circled the town, and it was clear that these were self-reliant people. Everyone seemed busy doing something, and the radio reports of people wandering aimlessly about and of violence seemed entirely untrue. At least from the air, there were no signs of civil unrest, and no one seemed to be waiting around for someone else to show up and save them or tell them what to do. He'd flown over disaster areas before, many times. This was very different.

They overflew a caravan of hundreds of vehicles headed towards a warehouse district. Most were vans or pickup trucks carrying what were obviously bodies covered in sheets. Far, far too many bodies. There had to be thousands of them.

Marcus keyed his mic over the helicopter noise, "Captain Guevara?"

"Yes, Sir, General."

Marcus swallowed, looking down at the procession. "Captain, I do not want those vehicles interfered with at all, but I want an honor guard there. At the warehouse and all along the way. Chopper them in if you have to. I want these people to know. Strike that. I want *our* people to know we are all in this together."

"Yes, Sir, I'll get right on it."

"Thank you, Captain.... Pilot, let's move on, now."

In the distance, the spire glinted darkly.

They continued their spiral path into town. As they drew closer, the spire looked like it might have been some giant javelin piercing the heart of the city.

"Major, you've been reticent. Give me your thoughts."

Major Finley's face was slightly damp with sweat. She tried to hide her grimace, and she willed herself to ignore the pain, just as she had ignored the doctor's order to stay behind.

"Sir, somebody went to one hell of a lot of trouble to shanghai an entire city, the base, and all the area around it, and plant us here like this, like my mom might have grafted a fruit tree branch. Lakes, oceans, mountains, continents, hell, a whole world inside a giant bottle? Sir, I am trying to comprehend it all, and my brain is fighting it. Beyond the city, beyond the base, the landscape is... Well, it is both sculpted and beautiful, and parts of it seem almost cookie-cutter duplicated like portions were copied and pasted to fill space. But it's not all the same. On those mountains back there, I could see what looked like alpine forests, and from what we can see, um, above us, on the other continents, they are not the same climate zones as here. Some are clearly very tropical, and some desert."

"Cookie cutter, huh? I think you may be right. Look into the mind of our abductors, Major, and tell me what you deduce from this?"

"Sir, I think whoever did this realizes that we, humans, need a diverse set of climate zones to create an overall sustainable ecosystem. Whoever built this place thinks very long term. What scares me is whether this is an Ark or an Ant Farm. Sir."

Marcus looked sideways at her. "Worried some alien kid has a giant magnifying glass, and he's going to start frying us?"

Finley stared at him, her eyes hard and cold, "Sir, I think they already did that, and thousands of civilians are dead."

"Jesus, Major, I hope you and that Sheriff are wrong."

"Sheriff, Sir?"

"Yes, Major, it seems that the Sheriff who pulled your ass out of that billboard, cute trick ending up there, by the way, had much the same thought as you did. He called it 'a culling' and that whoever put us all here did it as an object lesson."

Finley's lips tightened, "Sir, I did everything I could to avoid crashing into anything that looked…."

"Relax, Major, I'm quite proud of how you handled yourself. It's just that now, your handle may change to Billboard Banshee or just Billboard.

Finley's face tightened, and she fought furiously to bite back a retort. Her pale cheeks heated beet red. Looking him in the eyes, she realized he was not baiting or berating her. He seemed sympathetic. She swallowed hard and forced a smile. "Could be worse, Sir. I suppose I could end up as Pontiac."

Marcus grinned, "I think I like you, Major. Don't let it go to your head."

"No, Sir."

As planned, they kept a discrete distance from the spire and landed at the agreed-upon location, a football practice field near the High School. A jumbled collection of civilian and law enforcement vehicles waited. A small crowd stood at the edge of the field, holding onto their hats and loose clothing as the wash from the large twin turboshaft helicopter's massive blades washed heavily over the area.

Marcus stepped out of the helicopter with care, straightening his dress Air Force uniform, which he'd ordered for all present, instead of combat BDU's. Another message he hoped would inspire a positive reception.

In the bright light of the suntube in the sky above, his dark black skin contrasted vividly with Major Finley, who seemed bone-white in comparison. She was frustrated by a wisp of auburn hair that kept escaping her uniform cover and falling into her eyes as she struggled with her cast. He kept an eye on her as she levered herself out with crutches, her jaw set firmly against the pain. Her body language made it very clear she did not want help. On the other hand, it wouldn't do for her to fall on her face. He waited nearby, just in case. She soldiered through it and lurched into position by his side, flanked by Captain Guevara, with his darker, Cuban complexion. Their uniforms were crisp and professional, with their service ribbons adding color.

The group wandered towards the civilians. It wasn't quite a march, but there was discipline in their movement, even with Finley on crutches.

The Mayor, the surviving City Council members, and Sheriff Austin advanced in a bunch to meet them at a point halfway between the ground vehicles and the bone-shaking, ridiculously loud helicopter.

Gloria nodded towards the General and nudged Tom in the ribs, his bruised ribs. She didn't notice him wince as she said into his ear over the ebbing helicopter noise, "See? Like I said, he's got enough medals to snap an oak tree!"

Tom grimaced, "Yep, Gloria, when you're right, you're right." The General was the oldest in the approaching group,

The noise and rotor wash subsided. The city officials significantly outnumbered the General's party. The General extended his hand as he approached. "Mr. Mayor, members of the City Council, Sheriff, I am General Marcus, and I am truly sorry that we must meet under these terrible, extraordinary and, frankly, mind-boggling circumstances. It is my sincere hope that going forward, whatever happens, we can all work together in solidarity."

Tom took the General's hand firmly. "General, I wish," he nodded towards the others with him, "we all desperately wish these circumstances had never happened. I think we're still in shock."

He released the General's hand and turned to his party. "Allow me to introduce the members of the City Council we've been able to locate so far: Councilwoman Gloria Vargas, and Councilmen Dale Hubbard, Jack Burdger, and Wylie Hickum. Also, Sheriff Austin, whom you spoke with on our call."

General Marcus nodded. "It is our honor to meet you. With me today are Major Finley and Captain Guevara. With murmured greetings, everyone shook hands."

Tom gestured towards the vehicles. "General, if you and your party will accompany us, we'll proceed back to the council chambers."

The group merged and slowly walked towards the waiting vehicles. A gentle wind blew across the football field, but the pervading chill was out of the air, and the temperature had settled at a cool, for Texas, 78 degrees Fahrenheit. The mood was somber, and the conversation muted and scarce all the way into town.

Balance of Power

Fort Brazos City Hall
Day 1: 10:06 AM

I n the council chambers, the council members settled in at the back around a raised curving desk. The room was not large, but the building they were in was new, modern, and well-appointed, benefiting from a recent resurgence in taxes on natural gas royalties. The members seated themselves behind their nameplates and individual microphones. Several spots were empty. The council was elevated several stair-steps above the rest of the room.

The stenographer took her place to the side, and Tom jotted some notes on a yellow legal pad. Sheriff Austin stood to the side. Marcus, Finley, and Guevara were directed to front-and-center seats facing the council.

Tom leaned into his microphone, "This meeting is called to order. Today we will dispense with the usual formalities. However, this meeting is being recorded in keeping with the seriousness of our situation and the shocking and extraordinary events of the last day. Several of our members are absent. We all hope they are Okay, but we have no real choice to push ahead and declare an emergency quorum."

"For the record, in attendance are myself, Mayor Tom Parker, along with City Councilwoman Vargas, and Councilmen Hubbard, Burdger, and Hickum. Also, under the circumstances, we have asked Sheriff John Austin to be here. He is the senior surviving member of law enforcement in Fort Brazos and can address emergency services questions."

He glanced down at another sheet of paper, "Also in attendance, from the Joint Military Reserve Base, are Major General Alexander Marcus, the base commander, Major Gail Finley, and Captain Darryl Guevara."

"Let me begin by restating what we recently learned from the General. Specifically, there are no reported deaths among the military personnel, contractors, or dependents located on the base's grounds. This is in stark contrast to the absolutely crushing number of civilian dead."

He paused and looked around at the other faces in the room. The soft hiss of the air conditioning was the only sound.

"I will tell you that our citizens are going to be more than shocked and suspicious when they find this out. I can't begin to imagine what conspiracy theories will flare-up. Things could get very ugly, very fast. For this and other reasons, the council has decided that nothing will be held back from the people. We will begin daily public briefings today. We ask that you join us at those briefings to share what the military has learned."

Tom paused. Marcus had noticeably stiffened, and his face had gone firm but blank. The Captain and Major both struggled to be still and rigid.

Tom shook his head, "General, I gather you are not 100% in agreement?"

Marcus controlled his expression, barely. "Mr. Mayor, I... Sir, my natural inclination is to gather information, not rush to judgment, and share information only as needed. There is just so much we don't know yet, and so much that we think we know that is obviously just supposition and may well be wrong. I am worried that rushing to inform the population before we are confident in the facts might be destructive. That by saying one thing one day and something different the next will sap confidence and trust. But then, my mission and requirements are different from yours."

Tom nodded, "Yes, General, in many ways, you are right. We don't know much at all, do we?" Gloria and the others started to object, but Tom raised his hand and shook his head. "But that cuts both ways. If we wait until we know things for a fact, the citizens will think we are holding back. And we would be. No, General, the Council has decided that we will inform the people of what we know and what we think we know. We will tell them we may be wrong and that we probably are wrong on many things. But there will be no secrets here. We have to mourn and bury our dead. We have to figure out what we are going to need to do to survive. Hell, General, we need to start counting food! We can't manage this crisis by holding back and creating doubt among the people. They need to trust us."

Marcus started to speak, but Tom raised his hands to stop him, adding, "General, you should also know that we received a call from Dr. Nakamura on the way over here. He's the Dean of Science and Technology at the University."

Marcus blinked at the mention of Bonham State University. In all the confusion, and with his newness on-station, he'd completely forgotten there *was* a University in Fort Brazos. The awareness of it sent a wave of hope through him that perhaps their chances of survival might not be quite so bleak as he'd privately feared.

Tom continued, "Dr. Nakamura is also the Astronomy department head and took the initiative to use the observatory to look at," he nodded upwards, "well, at the other side of the world, to see what is there."

Several of the council members chuckled softly to each other. There was no mirth in their expressions. Tom saw the puzzled looks on Marcus's group's faces.

"General, we ah, we all know Dr. Nakamura. He's been a fixture here for ages. We were all just a bit surprised that he took the time actually to step away from that telescope to bother to call…."

Marcus nodded, "Yes, I know the type. I've had my people begin the process of mapping the area around the base and around Fort Brazos, but we've only just begun. While we suffered no casualties at the base, I should also add that we have been dealing with our own problems, including being short-handed. As part of my assignment here, we were in the middle of a reorganization, and almost all of the senior officers were off base at a conference when these series of events occurred. This led to the initial confusion, including the incident at the gate, when our sentries turned away your deputies. I sincerely apologize for that."

Tom and the rest of the council turned and looked to Sheriff Austin. John stiffened, then replied, "General, I'm just glad that nothing more serious happened. My people were shocked to be shot at, and word has·spread. I suggest that your guards and my people meet in public and make nice. People are talking about what happened, and rumors are spreading, including some blaming the military for this whole situation. We don't need the incident to fester into something that we will all regret. Our people need to trust each other."

Marcus nodded, "I agree, and, again, I deeply regret what happened. Events on the base were confusing, and there were initial fears of an active enemy threat, and we are still sorting things out. I will personally and publicly apologize to your deputies, as will the guards."

John and the Council momentarily wondered if the General would elaborate on precisely what events had been so confusing on the base.

Instead, Marcus asked the Mayor, "What did Dr. Nakamura find?"

Tom shook his head and frowned. "I'm afraid I have bad news. Or at least, I think it is bad news. Dr. Nakamura reports that as far as he can tell, and he cautions that there are areas covered with weather patterns he can't yet see, and he can only see the *other* side of the world, but he reports no cities, structures, roads, or anything that looks artificial. Also, Dr. Nakamura and others have measured the interior dimensions of this… place that we are in. I don't understand all the details, but they bounced a radar beam around, and apparently, this world is almost 4,000 miles long, and it is nearly 2,000 miles from the surface on this side, to the surface on the other side." He glanced at handwritten notes in front of him, "That would make the interior surface area be about 27 million square miles. That's more than the surface area of," he looked at the notes again, "The United States, Russia, Canada, China, Brazil, Australia, India, and Argentina, combined, and, so far, it looks like we are all alone in it."

The room fell silent as the numbers sunk in.

Marcus nodded gravely, "Our pilots report seeing no other cities or structures as well. As far as we've seen, this is a virgin world. That includes radio traffic or other signals. There is nothing but our own signals and from the city here. I'm glad, by the way, that things do not seem as bad as what your radio station person – I think her name was Danielle – was reporting on the air." He paused, "Still, we've only seen a fraction of things from the air so far. I am worried that it is premature to tell the citizens we are all alone. This could cause panic."

Tom grimaced at the mention of the reporting from the radio 'personality.' "Rest assured, I will have words with Miss Richardson about her ravings on the air. Her words may have caused more panic than anything else that's happened since. Certainly, it was gasoline on the fire."

John interjected, "General, I think we all know we're on our own, here, that is, at least, that nobody's coming to help us. This is no time to hide things from the people or, worse, leave the false hope of outside aid, and, by extension, leaving open the hope that any of us will be able to talk to or see our loved ones from outside Fort Brazos, possibly, ever again."

Marcus took a deep breath. "Mr. Mayor," nodding to the others, "Council People, Sheriff, we're not going to always agree with each other. This is one of those times. We don't know what has happened to us. We don't know how we got here or who did it or what their motives are, or how or if we can get back home. Are the actors that did this good or evil? Are their motivations something we can even understand? We don't know whether they think our lives and our future are significant or not." He nodded towards John, "And if, Sheriff, you are right about this being a 'culling' - it seems clear to me that if they are willing to sacrifice thousands of us like that, our abductors may be enemies and not our friends. They may be doing this to experiment on us and test us and find out our weaknesses."

Marcus smiled grimly, "On our way here, we flew around the area. We have a video to share with you. During the flight, Major Finley, here, said something that stuck with me. She said that she wondered whether we were in an Ark or an Ant farm. I asked her if she thought that meant some alien hooligan kid might be out there with a magnifying glass ready to incinerate us one at a time." He paused, then continued as all eyes turned to Major Finley, who held up well under the stares and scrutiny.

"You see, the Major here said that she thought maybe whoever did this to us had already used that magnifying glass, so to speak, to murder our civilians. I tell you, we must all work together if we are to survive. What worries me more is the very fact that none of the military died. That tells me that our abductors wanted to save us, so they could see how we fight. On the other hand, I'm not stupid."

He waved a hand upwards, "Whoever could do all this and put us here, really may just think of us as ants. The technology to create an artificial inside-out world? It makes us look like primitives, Neanderthals, or worse, in comparison."

The council members worriedly talked amongst themselves. Gloria had the look of someone who had been holding something back. She sneered at the General, "So, you think the military is more important and we civilians are expendable?"

Marcus had decades of practice at keeping his expressions and body language under tight control. He did not quite keep the wince from showing.

Tom turned to Gloria, "Gloria! I hardly think the General is some heartless monster."

Marcus cut off her retort, "It's Okay, Mr. Mayor. The Councilwoman has a right to ask. Let's cut to the chase. What she really wants to know where we stand, and whether the military is going to take control."

Gloria raised an eyebrow.

Major Finley and Captain Guevara didn't quite shrink back, but they did their best to imitate silent statues.

The council erupted into shouts and accusations. Everyone had been thinking the same question, either consciously or not.

The sharp crack of Tom's rarely used gavel silenced the tumult. "Order!" he demanded. Gloria and the others slumped back in their leather upholstered chairs. "Okay, General, just where *do* you stand? I remind you, we have voted to invoke State Continuity of Government protocols. We are forming a committee to draft a plan, including elections for a President and possibly a constitutional convention, to craft a representative republic government. We believe the people would reject anything else, and we believe it works."

Marcus leaned back in his seat and considered, letting the silence grow. Finally, he tapped one of his service ribbons and looked at Gloria, "Councilwoman, the United States military, today, is a rare thing. We don't fight for conquest; we set people free. This ribbon, here? This is my Global War on Terrorism service medal. I commanded a group that commanded a group that did the heavy lifting. This other ribbon," pointing to another, "is because I was good at shooting at paper targets, and this one over here is my Air Force Longevity Service Ribbon – because I've been stubborn and hung in there all these years and learned how to play the game of politics. All these bits of fabric are thank-you's for being a good boy and doing my job well."

"I have served my country for over three decades. I command thousands of men and women, and I live in a house the taxpayers paid for. My service has not made me wealthy, but I've been respected and trusted with the responsibility for the lives and honor of my people."

"Before we were all abducted, I had looked forward to a quiet and safe command, and to eventual retirement, and to watching my girls grow up. I wanted to serve my country. I'm not a megalomaniac. I have no interest in trying to 'take over,' and I doubt my good men and women would even let me if I tried."

He paused a moment, then leaned forward and lowered his voice, "I will not, however, stand idly by and let tyranny take root here, and I will not obey unlawful orders from an illegitimate junta. My daughters will grow up free."

Tom and half the council bristled and angrily stood, shouting "How Dare You!" and various expletives at being called a junta.

John set his jaw and walked into the space between the council and the seated Air Force officers. He looked at the council and raised his arms, palms outstretched. "Stop this!" He turned back to the General, "You too, General. All of you, settle down! We're all angry and scared of whoever has done this to us, but" he pointed at Marcus, "*He* didn't do it, and neither did we and, I am pretty sure that none of us, not one of us, are the kind of person who would stand for tyranny.

Gloria narrowed her eyes. "Nice speech, gentlemen, but General, who the hell are you to decide what is lawful? Why should we trust you?"

Tom swallowed and looked at Gloria, "Look, Gloria, I know your first husband was an Air Force officer, and I know he was an ass, but don't let that color your judgment here. The General is new here, and we don't yet know him, so trust will not be easy, but we've got to work through this."

Gloria glared at Tom with a look that might just be able to melt the alien spire.

John turned to Marcus, "General, you and the personnel at the base are all citizens here. Any vote will include them, and you and they represent a third of our overall population."

Tom leaned into his microphone, "General, will you obey the civilian government?"

"Mr. Mayor, Council, I give you my word. The military is sworn to protect you. It is we who are expendable. Word has spread about what happened to

the civilian population, and I must tell you, every man and woman in uniform is filled with righteous fury. God help whoever has done this if we ever get our hands on them."

Tom nodded. "I'm sure I believe you. However, you didn't answer the question."

Marcus took a deep breath, "Councilwoman, Mayor, we have a long road in front of us all. We're clearly going to have to organize a new government. I pledge that I and the military will obey that new government, assuming, that is, that said government is indeed legitimate and doesn't descend into chaos, or worse. We will all have a say in what it looks like."

Gloria chided, "That's very Politic of you, and you have the big guns."

Marcus bristled, "I will not march my legions into Rome and take over, madam."

Gloria retorted, "Oh, so you do have a Caesar complex?"

John stepped between them, arms outstretched to break up the confrontation, and Tom used his come-to-order voice, "That's enough, Gloria! The General is not our enemy. We need each other!"

John added, "Remember everyone, there are no more factories making spare parts and supplies for those guns, tanks, and planes on the base, or for that matter, for anything in the city, either. We're going to have to be smart, and we're going to have to work with and trust each other."

Tom glanced at Austin, then back at the General, suddenly worried. "How about it, General, how long can you keep the planes flying?

Marcus thought for a moment, then looked at Guevara and Finley's grave expressions. "We're not sure yet. We need to do a new inventory, we… we received new supplies just before… before this happened. We need time to sort things out. Regardless, it is finite. We intend to use our resources as much as needed to secure and map as much of the area as we can, while we still can."

Gloria, still fuming, glowered at the General and started to speak, but Tom waved her down. Marcus's dark black cheeks heated with a tinge of crimson, but he held his tongue.

John considered aloud, "We need to do more. We need to inventory all of our resources, civilian and military alike, and we must restore trust between the civilians and the military before the conspiracy theories explode into violence."

A tense silence filled the room.

Marcus took a deep breath and nodded to himself, "Does anyone have a Bible?"

Everyone stared at him in surprise, then most started reaching into their desks or bags. Tom's eyes widened, and he nodded. "Yes, just a moment." He likewise reached into the desk in front of him and retrieved a well-worn Bible. He handed it across the desk to Austin, who gave it to Marcus.

Marcus stood up, pursed his lips, and held the bible to his heart. "I, and all my officers and men, swore an oath to support and defend the Constitution of the United States and to obey the orders of the President. Well, I don't know where exactly we are now, but this isn't the United States anymore. I will, however, make a pledge here today. On the life of my wife and children, on the lives of the men and women who serve under me, I swear that we will serve and protect the civilian population, and we will obey the lawful orders of the civilian government. So help me, God."

Two hours later, the meeting broke up. The council filed out. Some were still angry, especially Gloria, but most were just tired and worried. There was much to do.

Outside the chambers in the foyer, Marcus, Gail Finley, and Darryl Guevara waited, with Finley stubbornly refusing to sit, leaning on her crutches. As John exited, he was joined by a tired-looking Chief Deputy Hector Alonzo. Marcus caught John's attention and called to him, "Sheriff?"

John and Hector walked over. John answered, "Yes, General?"

Marcus nodded thanks, "Sheriff, it looks like we'll be working together quite a bit for the foreseeable future. I want you to know that you can count on me for anything you need. In the meantime, I believe you have met Major Finley?"

John turned to her and extended his hand, "I hope that your injury heals quickly, Major, and, I have to ask, I thought it was Captain?"

Gail grimaced and narrowed her eyes, then released a crutch long enough to shake his hand, "Thank you, Sheriff, for pulling me off that billboard. I hope nobody was hurt on the ground?"

Marcus interjected, "You are correct, Sheriff, it was Captain. The Major has been promoted."

John hesitated for a moment, sensing some hostility from the Major. He shook his head and smiled. "Call me John, and, no, nobody was hurt on the ground. You saw to that, and you should know that everyone in town knows that you almost gave your life to make sure that was the case. The building you avoided at the last second was the High School."

Gail's eyes widened, and she blanched. Her lips parted to say something, but John stopped her. "Thankfully, the school was empty at the time, but that doesn't matter to the town. You're a hero, and we all thank you for your selfless actions."

Gail closed her mouth with a click and blinked.

Marcus smiled, "Congratulations, Sheriff, you may be one of the few people ever to leave the Major speechless – whom she didn't have to salute."

Gail's face had become a mask again.

John nodded, "Happy to oblige, General. Now, what can I do for you?"

"Sheriff, I understand there are still many civilians unaccounted for. I'd like to offer what manpower or any other assistance I can to help."

John considered the offer, then looked at Hector, "General, this is Chief Deputy Hector Alonzo. Hector, what do you think?"

Hector thought about it, unimpressed by the Air Force brass in front of him, "Sure boss, we've got a lot of ground to cover. There are a ton of ranches, houses, businesses, and shacks we need to visit. It's gonna take a lot of time to get out to them all. A lot more time than I like. People could still be hurt and need help. We also need to take, well, take a census to find out who all is here, who was out of town, who's visitin', and who's dead. Seems like every place we visit gives us a lead on someplace else we should check out. It's makin' the process take forever."

Marcus nodded and offered, "How about this, Sheriff, Chief Deputy, how about I detail as many vehicles and squads of men and medics I can scrape up to accompany your deputies. Then, as you have to split up and check out more and more places, my people can help fill in the gaps, help with communications, evacuations if needed, and so forth."

John exchanged glances with Hector, "I'm grateful for the help, General, but a bunch of armed soldiers spreading out across town may play into those conspiracy theories and the fears our lovely radio DJ was helping create."

Marcus didn't hesitate, "Very well, Sheriff, nobody seems to be shooting at us, so my people will leave their weapons in their vehicles and will keep a discrete distance. Nobody wants a scared or injured citizen to think they are being invaded. Your deputies will be in charge. My people will only assist and carry food, medical, and emergency supplies for any who may need them. Will that work?"

John nodded, "Sounds like a plan, General." He extended his hand to Marcus, and they shook.

Marcus smiled, "Good. Also, I have drafted Major Finley here to be my top advisor. With her leg being broken, she's grounded from flying for a while, and she seems to have a unique grasp of events. I've also tasked her with being my direct liaison to you and your City Council."

John looked at Gail and hoped that her almost-hidden sour expression was not aimed personally at him. "I'm looking forward to working with you, Major."

Gail smiled thinly but managed not to say something caustic about the 6'2" cowboy towering in front of her. God, how she hated working with dumb hicks. "The pleasure's mine, Sheriff. Anything your people need, you just let me know."

Copy & Paste

Warehouse District
Day 1: 11:13 AM

S am Nellis was worried. Like most people, he had not gone to work but had instead huddled with his family, waiting for news. Eventually, after his boss had not called to check on him, he'd called himself. His boss was among the dead. Sam was now the senior manager of the CoMart regional warehouse/distribution center. Eventually, stores were going to be expecting shipments of food and other goods, and they'd be knocking on the warehouse doors. He'd called the police department and asked for help protecting the warehouse in case things got out of hand.

Fort Brazos was the largest city for quite a distance. As a result, it was the regional distribution hub for many businesses. Modern warehouses (distribution centers) were designed to minimize the amount of time any given piece of merchandise was there. Efficiency was measured in terms of reducing the number of days or hours before a carton turned around and shipped to its final destination. As a regional hub, that meant a lot of total inventory passed through them. The logistics meant that while the intent was to keep things moving, there was still a lot of inventory sitting around at any given time.

Sam parked his new Chevy Tahoe in the empty parking lot, nodded at the two policemen sitting outside in their car, and entered the building through the administrative offices in the front. He made his way back to the cavernous warehouse area and closed the door behind him, the sound echoing into the distance. He hit the controls to turn on the lights high in the rafters, and it took a few moments for them to flicker and warm up to full brightness. The lights came on in sequence, starting at his end of the building and then coming to life further and further away.

The building was not enormous as warehouses go, but a half-million square feet was nothing to sneeze at. He started walking down the central aisle; his gently scuffing footfalls were the only sound. After a few moments, he began to realize that something was wrong. It was not a feeling of danger, just that something wasn't right.

Then, he stopped in his tracks and looked ahead at what was there, instead of what was supposed to be there, what he remembered to be there. He knew exactly how many of the towering shelves were there, how many forklifts, and every aspect of the facility. He could sketch everything out from memory, blindfolded.

His jaw dropped as he looked ahead and realized what was different. The building didn't end where it was supposed to. It kept going and going, and going. Somehow, it was now vastly larger than it had been before.

What happened to the Hoffman's?

Hoffman Dairy Farm
Day 1: 2:27 PM

S heriff Austin had spent the day filling in the gaps of the census, and well-being checks his deputies and the assisting military personnel had been performing. It was a chaotic process. There were so many small farms, ranch houses, gas stations, stores, and businesses. It was inevitable that some would be missed. All the groups were periodically reporting back their findings, and John was making the rounds, trying to make up the difference.

His eight-year-old daughter Matti was with him, as much to keep him company as for him to keep an eye on her. At the moment, he was following up on a call from Tom. Apparently, one of the City Councilmen, Barrett Hoffman, had not been heard from or accounted for, and John had been asked to personally check to make sure that Barrett and his large family were OK.

John drove down the picturesque "FM" Farm-to-Market road, alongside the well-maintained white-painted fence line of the Barrett family dairy farm. It was a big place, and the house or other buildings were not visible from the road. He turned into the gate and followed the uphill winding road to the farmhouse. As he topped the hill, he slowed as he saw a Humvee and another Sheriff's Office SUV parked in the circle driveway in front of the house. The number on the Sheriff's vehicle was Grayson Miles'.

There were no people in sight.

John picked up his UHF radio handset. "Grayson come in?"

97

"Grayson?"

He waited, then keyed the mic again, "Ah, this is Sheriff Austin. I'm here at the Barrett place, and it looks like Grayson beat me here, but he's not answering the radio. Have you heard from him?"

There was a moment of static before the reply, "No, Sheriff, we haven't heard from him in a while."

"Acknowledged. I'll check it out."

He turned in his seat to face Matti, "Matti, I want you to stay here in the car. Okay?"

Matti was busy doing something on her tablet computer. She looked up and flashed a brilliant smile. "Sure, Daddy."

John got out of the SUV and stood and listened. It was quiet except for gentle farm animal noises in the distance. He called out, "Grayson?"

No answer, but there was a lot of ground and many buildings to cover.

He walked up to the front door, which was ajar. He pushed the door open and called inside, "Sheriff's department. Is anyone home?"

The hairs on his neck stood up. He wasn't sure what it was, but something was wrong, and he could feel it.

He heard the car door open behind him, and he whirled around to Matti's voice, "Daddy? My computer's all messed up!"

Something was very wrong. He blinked. Then he stopped breathing, and his world slowed. Matti was wearing his leather jacket, which was huge on her and holding up her tablet computer. Just then, there was a flash, a streak of light, and her tablet exploded in a cloud of sparks and glass.

Matti shrieked and threw the sizzling tablet away from her. She ducked down, looking in every direction.

There was something – a thin thread of some sort extending from Matti's tablet towards *something* next to the fence. A large, weird plant looked like a man-sized aloe-vera plant that he hadn't noticed before. Someone must be hiding behind it.

"Matti!"

John never consciously remembered what happened next. As he ran towards his daughter, there was movement at the plant thing, and then something thunked hard into his chest – into his top-shelf body armor that he'd paid for himself and that he'd bought for his other deputies with his own money. Gossamer strands led back to the plant. The next thing John remembered was finding his Wilson Combat .45 in his hand and firing at whoever was hiding behind the plant.

Then, two more objects struck his chest and knocked him backward a half-step. John reloaded and emptied a second magazine into the plant. It began to wilt, but not before a fourth, softer impact into his body armor. Then, the plant slumped over. There was nothing behind it. John reached for another magazine but found he'd already loaded and fired his two spare magazines.

Just then, he'd reached Matti. He swept her under one arm and ran around to the back of his SUV. Matti needed no encouragement to hide. He set her down, opened the back door-gate, grabbed the rack-mounted Remington 870 shotgun, and peeked around the curve of the vehicle.

The plant was sluggishly trying to move away. John advanced toward it and emptied the shotgun into it. It stopped moving. He looked down at the dark, slender barbs protruding from his chest and body armor. Careful not to touch them, he tried to brush them away with the slide of his .45, but they resisted. He slapped them harder, and they fell away.

He ran back around the SUV to Matti. He fell to his knees, checking her over as she trembled. Finding no injuries, he pulled her close and embraced her. "Matti! Matti!"

As he drew her close, the tears started, and she cried, "Oh daddy!"

He stood and held her to him and looked back at the unmoving creature. He kept the SUV between them and the beast and opened the passenger side front door. He picked up the UHF radio handset. Only now did he realize how much his chest was heaving. He took a moment to catch his breath.

"This is Sheriff Austin. We've got trouble out at the Barrett place. Call the General and tell him there is some kind of… an alien creature here. There may be more. Tell him to bring his guns and get the hell out here right now."

✪ ✪ ✪

John had bundled Matti back in the SUV and backed it out and away from the farm, down to the road. He reloaded the shotgun. He kept the engine running and reloaded his empty .45 magazines.

In the distance, he heard them coming. The distinctive thud-thud-thud of the helicopters swelled until there was no other sound. "Stay in the car this time, Matti. The helicopter may kick up a lot of debris, and you could get hurt."

Matti nodded obediently.

He stepped out and waved at the three approaching helicopters. One was a Sikorsky HH-60 Pave Hawk troop carrier, and the other two were AH-64 Apache gunships. The troop carrier slowed to land in the adjacent field while the gunships zoomed ahead towards the dairy farm, banking this way and that. A trio of F-15's shrieked overhead.

General Marcus was in his camo BDU's, with a sidearm. A heavily armed group surrounded the General, ran to John's SUV, and took up tactical positions around it. John bent low next to the side of the SUV, facing away from the farm, and shook hands with Marcus.

John shouted over the helicopter noise, "General, I'm glad to see you and your men, but should you be here yourself?"

Marcus grinned crookedly, "I'm staying here with you and the chopper, Sheriff. If the aircraft give clearance, the platoon, here, will go investigate. Tell me what happened. What is waiting for us?"

John shook his head, "General, all I know is that I arrived to find one of your vehicles and one of mine parked at the house, but nobody was around. Then, a creature of some kind attacked us, and I shot it. It took three clips of .45 and eight twelve-gauge rounds to kill it. It looks like a man-size plant – a cross between a porcupine and an Aloe Vera. It shot barbs at us, but my vest stopped them."

Marcus looked around, "Us?"

John swallowed and rapped on the SUV window. Matti bobbed her blonde head up, smiled at him, then ducked back down again. "We were just checking on Councilman Hoffman. Nobody has reported any danger or violence, so I kept her close to me. My daughter, Matti."

Marcus grimaced, "My God, man, I'd be terrified for my daughters if that had happened to me!" He knocked on the window, and Matti poked her head up again. She looked at her dad, and he nodded. Matti looked at Marcus and smiled weakly. "Young lady, you are very brave."

This time, she smiled brilliantly, flashing her perfect eight-year-old teeth and liquid blue eyes, and looked back at her dad. He nodded again, and she ducked back down again, out of sight.

One of the soldiers, a radio operator, stepped close to Marcus and spoke into his ear before stepping away again.

Marcus nodded, looked at the platoon leader, and raised his thumb. "Check it out, Lieutenant!"

Two more helicopters had delivered more men. Marcus detailed a platoon to guard Matti and the helicopters and then proceeded at a trot up the road to the house along with John and a cordon of flanking soldiers. They stopped at the body of the creature. It had gone flaccid and bled out a viscous coppery fluid. Regardless, Marcus had three men keep it under guard, their rifles aimed at it, while others stood guard, looking for others.

Marcus started to poke it with his boot, then thought better of it. The creature was large and heavy, and its… fronds… were thick and muscular. Lying flat, it was over seven feet long. Wicked-looking barbs protruded from the edges of some of the fronds. Now that the creature had fallen over, its base could be seen. It looked like a mouth of some kind surrounded by large lumpy hand-like structures. The center of the creature was grey and somewhat iridescent. All around the center part were small round bulbous, almost glass-like protrusions.

"All right, nobody touches this damned thing. I want it isolated and quarantined. Sheriff, let's keep going. I want to talk to the survivors."

They rounded the house and stopped briefly at the scene of a struggle. There were rifle cartridges, blood, and drag marks. On the side of the barn was the body of a dog.

101

It had been impaled with a long dart-like barb. A long strand of silken material, resembling a fiber optic strand, extended from the barb into the dirt and dust. Nearby, drag marks led to the open doors of the large and well-maintained barn.

Soldiers stood guard outside. Inside, hazmat-suited medics attended to the survivors who had not already been medevacked. The bodies of the others lay where they'd been found, sunken and emaciated. Drained. Clear plastic sheeting separated them all.

A serviceman helped the General, and then John don a hazmat suit. John winced from the bruises he'd received from the impacts on his vest.

They entered the barn. John ground his teeth at the sight of the body of his friend, Deputy Grayson Miles. Miles was recognizable only by his uniform. Barbs protruded from the vest protecting his chest, but his throat had been ripped out by other barbs that had almost completely severed his spine below the chin.

More of the strands were everywhere, along with the ragged remains of the cocoons everyone had been wrapped in. In a corner near the entrance, yellow tape encircled the completely dissembled parts of the patrol's equipment and weapons and what had to be the remains of a lever-action rifle of some kind.

Barrett Hoffman, his wife Margaret, and their son Nolan were dead. The grandmother's body had been found upstairs in the house, though the assessment was that she had been one of the unlucky civilians who had not awakened at all. Sisters Sandra, Jordan, Hannah, and Elizabeth had survived and were being treated. Their two-year-old brother, Vicktor, had later been found hiding in a cupboard in the house dehydrated and had been whisked off on one of the helicopters along with Sargent Washington and Specialist Simmons. Corpsman Mendez was among the dead. Lieutenant David Garreth had survived and now lay next to Sandra Hoffman. Both were hooked up to IVs and had bandages covered the barb wound areas.

Marcus knelt down next to David while John looked on. David blinked several times and tried to sit up.

Marcus put his hand on David's chest and gently pushed him back down. He spoke softly, "Lieutenant, can you tell me what happened?"

David wheezed a cough and nodded, "Yes, Sir. We arrived here with Deputy Miles. Sargent Washington found signs of a struggle around the house, and when we investigated, we were attacked by something. It came out of nowhere and shot us all with those barb-things. The last thing I remember is feeling like I did in stun-gun training, but worse. The next thing was the corpsman working on me, waking me up, cutting me out of that damned cocoon." He shivered.

Marcus stood and turned to the nearest corpsman. He pulled him aside, away from the survivors. He ordered, quietly, "Report, Corpsman."

The corpsman came to attention, "Yes, Sir. All the victims were… cocooned. We cut away the material; it apparently has a numbing effect of some kind on the victim's skin. We were careful not to touch it without protection, although it now seems to be dissolving and breaking down. The surviving victims seem strong, Sir. They weren't, uh, well, whatever was done to those who didn't survive was not done to the survivors. They were all lined up in a row, and the ones that died were first in line. It looks like the survivors had simply not been gotten to, yet, Sir. We think the survivors will all be Okay. The paralysis seems to be wearing off."

"Thank you, Corpsman. Although, I'm not sure how any sane person could be simply "Okay" after going through this." He looked over at the remains of Corpsman Mendez and stiffened, "Sweet mother of God, what could do this?"

John took a deep breath, "General, I can show you what did this and how."

"What do you mean?"

John smiled grimly, "Four ways. I believe what happened was in the field of view of the dash-cam in my vehicle and at least partially in view of Deputy Miles' vehicle."

Marcus stood straighter and brightened, "That could be vital, Sheriff. What are the other ways?"

John tapped what looked like a button on his uniform shirt. "I'm wearing a body cam." He gestured towards the body of Deputy Miles. "And so was Grayson Miles."

Fallout

Council Chambers
Day 1: 9:15 PM

The last of the video clips finished playing on the large projection screen. The grizzliest was the video captured by Deputy Miles' body cam, including a point-of-view sequence showing what the creature had done to him after death. John reversed the video to pause on the image of the attacking alien creature. The council, Sheriff Austin, General Marcus, Major Finley, and Captain Guevara sat in stunned silence, most of them green in the face. Two of the council members were visibly shaken and had thrown up.

Tom broke the silence, "Aliens. My God. Is that thing what kidnapped us?"

Gail quietly spoke, "There is no technology. It is all biological."

John wondered aloud, "She's right. It sure doesn't seem like some all-powerful being capable of building this world and putting us here."

Marcus added, "It's a test. They're testing us."

Gloria swallowed and asked, "What are those threads attached to the barbs for?"

Marcus observed, "In the video, the barbs didn't change course, they were ballistic, so the strands are not for guidance."

Gail shook her head. "Unless they have some biological purpose of some kind, I think they may be for telemetry. Perhaps barbs send information back down the strand, about the target, to the creature. We should have the wound areas examined to determine if anything more happened than impact damage. There could be some kind of poison or something else in the wounds."

Tom rested his face in his hands, "First the awakening, then the culling, then the alien spire, and now we have homicidal walking plants killing our people, and we still have a lot of our people unaccounted for."

Several people shifted uncomfortably, and Councilman Hickum broke his green-faced silence, "Should we... should we say anything yet? Maybe the General is right. This will cause panic!"

Councilmen Hubbard and Burdger exchanged disagreeing glances. Burdger spoke up, "We must say something. We must warn the people!"

Tom grimaced, "General, what do you think?"

Marcus looked at Hickum and then quickly at each councilperson before answering, "Mr. Mayor, Councilman Hickum, I had objected to immediately telling the citizens about our guesswork and suppositions." He pointed at the creature freeze-framed on the screen. "That... that thing is not a supposition. It is real. It killed my people and yours. We must assume it was not alone, that there are others out there like it. Also, I would be surprised if there were no other dangers, more tests, as it were, that we have not yet seen. Your people, no, *our* people, need to know the real dangers they face. Our children need to be protected. Every person still alive is precious. We cannot allow more to be lost because we were afraid to tell them."

John sighed, "At least we know we can kill them. Our weapons can kill them."

Gloria cocked her head and smiled wanly, "Yes, you certainly proved that, didn't you?"

John looked at her. There was something in her voice. For a moment, he was apprehensive about the wheels turning behind her eyes.

Tom and the rest of the council nodded enthusiastically. "Yes, Sheriff, thank you from all of us, from all of Fort Brazos. Congratulations."

John shook his head. "Don't thank me. I was a fool. I should not have had Matti with me. Still, we need to warn people what to look for. When word gets out, people could start shooting any bush or cactus that the wind catches."

Gloria jumped in, using his first name, "John, there is no way you could have anticipated this happening. Even the General here, in all his military zeal, didn't see this coming. He ordered his men to go out without carrying their weapons or wearing body armor. No, Sheriff, your quick thinking and bravery probably saved the lives of the General's men as well as the poor Hoffman children. God rest Barrett and the other's souls."

John backed away, "No, no…."

At that moment, Matti appeared in the doorway, beaming and smiling hugely. She launched herself at her dad, blonde hair flying and her boots clicking on the tiled floor. "Daddy!"

John caught her with one arm and pulled her tight, and lowered his gaze at Gloria, not even wondering at the coincidence of Matti's appearance at that moment and in a closed session meeting. *She's up to something.*

Marcus stared at Gloria and slowly shook his head. He pursed his lips and inhaled deeply. "Mr. Mayor, Councilpersons, I will coordinate with the Sheriff, here, to deploy as many men, vehicles, and resources as I can find to protect the city. We'll establish roving patrols, checkpoints, and whatever makes sense. I'll have hot teams on standby to respond to reports of any new encounters or other suspicious activity."

John pointed Matti towards the empty seats customarily reserved for the audience. She kissed him on the cheek and quietly sat. He nodded to the General, "We can organize additional neighborhood patrols inside the city with trustworthy people. There are many ex-servicemen and other auxiliaries we can organize, and of course, we have lots of good men and women who are licensed to carry. We can set up training classes and refresher classes. We also need to figure out how to coordinate the communications between us and the military. The 911 system can gather reports from the population, and we can filter out the non, Uhm, non-alien-related problems."

Marcus nodded to Guevara and Finley, "Excellent. If you can find some room for my people, we can set up a communications node at your location, with some of my people, face-to-face with yours. That should improve both the speed and quality of our interactions. We'll create redundant telecommunications paths between here and the base, so we won't be out of touch if a phone line is cut – whether on purpose or not."

"And one more thing that I'm sure some of you will not like since you have reminded me that the civilian government is, frankly, you people. You are, for now at least, the equivalent of our House of Representatives and Senate, combined, into just you council people and a mayor. I have a special responsibility to make sure that you are all individually protected. So, I am assigning marine guards to what is now our capital building, here, and, until a Secret Service or equivalent is formed, protective details for each of you."

Gloria cast a smoldering glare, "You will do nothing of the sort! I will not be a prisoner! I will not be put under guard by you or anyone! I will not..."

Tom cut her off, "Gloria! Stop. Just stop. The General has a point. I don't like it any more than you do, but we are not just a small town anymore. We are *it*, and we are, well we are at war. We can't very well protect our people if we let our vanity prevent us from using our common sense. There are only five of us. Six, if you include the Sheriff here. If I were a bad guy, I'd want to take out the city leaders, wouldn't you?"

Gloria winced at the word 'War.' So did the other council members.

Gail turned to Marcus, "Sir, may I add something?"

"Of course, Major."

Gail stood up on her crutches. "Mr. Mayor, Council people, Sheriff. The United States people have lived with the direct threat of war, either originating beyond the oceans, or some remote nuclear threat or, more recently, from dangerous but isolated terrorists. In living memory, we have not had wars fought in our cities like Europe or other parts of the world have had. Americans don't have living memories of hostile armies marching and fighting in our streets. We see it on TV taking place in other countries, but it's still something abstract remote to civilians. Now, today, in this place, for the first time since, what, the Civil War, an American city is under direct threat. Possibly even under siege. We've been mass-kidnapped and suffered mass casualties. Fort Brazos is now a wartime city, a city at war, and we have no allies to call upon. We've encountered a single enemy, who might well be the equivalent of the Japanese midget-submarine discovered outside of Pearl Harbor before the main attack. Perhaps this is all being staged to see how we react and how well we fight back.

Perhaps it was an isolated incident, though I don't think we can afford the illusion that we were all brought here for purely innocent and benign reasons."

She inhaled, and her expression darkened, "Can we afford to assume that worse is not coming? Can we afford not to take steps to protect our leadership? This is *History* we are making, assuming there is anyone left to remember it in the future. How will history remember us? That we were too scared to act? Or that we stood up to face the evil that comes and make them pay a price they will forever remember?"

The weight of her words hung over the chamber, and a long silence followed. Marcus put his hand on her shoulder and motioned for her to sit. He nodded to himself, "The Major, I have found, has a way of cutting through to the heart of things."

John smiled, "Perhaps we are seeing a bit of how she got the call-sign I saw on her helmet? Banshee, I think it was?"

Gail's eyes flashed, and a hint of red colored her cheeks.

Marcus leaned back, "I expect you're right, Sheriff. And, Major, I believe you are right as well. This is not a civil disaster. This is not even a military one. It is, honestly, a disaster of biblical proportions. We must all be careful as we rewrite the rules."

Tom sat up straighter in his chair. "Okay, then. General, please let us know what you need from us. We have a lot of work to do. I believe it is time for us to address the town. We will use the football stadium for a public gathering. We can fit, what, fifteen to sixteen thousand in it? We will broadcast the feed on every channel and radio station.

"We'll bring in food and coffee and whatever we need to get things done. Also, I imagine that you and your staff will be spending a great deal of time in the city, away from the base. We'll find permanent places for you to stay, but in the meantime, I invite you to stay at my house, General. I'm sure others here have spare bedrooms as well?" All nodded, except for Gloria, who hesitated, then grudgingly nodded.

John added, "I have several extra rooms at my house, as well."

Marcus frowned, "That is very generous of you all. In the spirit of getting to know each other, I accept the invitation. However, I will not impose on your generosity any longer than it takes to make other arrangements or for my people to set up tents for us. We may be at war, but the spirit of the 3rd Amendment about quartering troops in people's homes is essential. We do not need to create new sources of friction and resentment unnecessarily.

Tom ceremoniously cracked the gavel. "Let's get started, people."

Harold and Danielle

The Manticore Pub
Day 1: 11:23 PM

Air Force Chief Master Sargent Harrold Anders was tired. Bone tired. Despite being in peak physical condition, the events of the past non-stop seventy-two hours had taken a heavy toll on his 49-year-old body. The base was no longer on lockdown. The patrols he had organized were in full swing, and the sound of helicopters crisscrossing the area was constant. He wasn't 18 anymore. Sitting in Fort Brazos's only Irish pub, he waited for his stout. The impossibly young, perky coed girl who eventually served it didn't help.

He sat alone, near the back, and silently nursed his beer, still numb with the shock of events that he'd been too busy to let catch up with him. His grey eyes stared into the distance, and he let himself relax and think of… nothing. It was his personal form of meditation, away from all the responsibilities and the crushing weight of the new reality, and of the need to stand as a granite anchor to all the men that looked up to him and needed to see that someone was not afraid. He wasn't afraid; however, he wasn't sure what he was.

In the corner of the pub, an Irishman strummed a guitar and sang a ballad with tears streaming down his face singing the English folk song 'The Unquiet Grave':

The wind doth blow today, my love,
And a few small drops of rain;

ACCIPITER WAR

I never had but one true-love,
In cold grave she was lain.

"I'll do as much for my true-love
As any young man may;
I'll sit and mourn all at her grave
For a twelvemonth and a day."

The twelvemonth and a day being up,
The dead began to speak:
"Oh who sits weeping on my grave,
And will not let me sleep?"

"'T is I, my love, sits on your grave,
And will not let you sleep:
For I crave one kiss of your clay-cold lips,
And that is all I seek."

"You crave one kiss of my clay-cold lips,
But my breath smells earthy strong;
If you have one kiss of my clay-cold lips,
Your time will not be long.

"'T is down in yonder garden green,
Love, where we used to walk,
The finest flower that e're was seen
Is withered to a stalk.

"The stalk is withered dry, my love,
So will our hearts decay;

So make yourself content, my love,
Till God calls you away."

Anders wondered who the singer had lost. For that matter, he wondered how many in the room hadn't lost *someone* on Awakening Day. He sipped his beer and stared into the distance, trying to find some logic, some sanity. Some hope.

Ten feet away, Danielle Richardson sat at another table, also alone. She was mortified. She had gone on the airwaves and simply panicked. Freaked out. Gone nuts. Over the edge. Lost it. Now, nobody was yelling at her or even laughing. Not that anyone was laughing about much of anything right now, it was just that no one would talk to her or look at her at all. Everyone was avoiding her. She wasn't stupid, and part of her knew that one reason why nobody wanted to talk to her was because, to one degree or another, everyone else had been just as scared as she was. Confronting her would force them to think about how they themselves had been terrified. At least, she hoped that was it.

So now, here she sat, sighing to herself for the thousandth time, wondering what disaster would befall her next. She looked up out of her fifth, at least, Jameson whiskey and noticed the barrel-chested soldier staring at her from across the room. His hair was brown with a tinge of grey. A red beret was tucked into his camouflage uniform epaulet, and his expression was... scary.

She blushed hotly, and her temper flared. God, he must hate me, but the asshole doesn't even know me! She downed the rest of her Jameson, inhaled deeply, stood up, and marched to his table, her vintage heels clacking on the tired linoleum.

In her most resounding, trademark radio announcer voice, she commanded him, "Okay, Damn it! I'm sorry, Okay? Just... Just leave me alone!"

Harrold snapped out of his reverie and blinked at her. He had no idea who she was or what she was talking about, but he was taken aback. Her eyes and face were ablaze, and he could not stop himself from sucking in his breath at her. She was like some raven-haired Valkyrie.

Danielle teetered for a moment, and from the now blank expression on the man's face, she realized what she had done. "Oh, God. I'm…. I'm really, really sorry. I'm so stupid!" She turned to flee as the failure and frustration of her world came crashing down on her.

Harrold stood and said one word. "Stop." He did not raise his voice, but his nearly thirty years of military experience carried more than enough iron. Everyone in the pub stopped what they were doing and stared.

Danielle's heart skittered and thudded hard, and for reasons she didn't quite understand, she stopped and turned back to face him.

Harrold spoke softly this time, willing her to be calm. "Who are you, woman?"

Reactions

Outside of town, at the Hoffman dairy farm, a gentle breeze flapped the edges of the freshly erected military tents. The plant-like alien corpse had begun to decay rapidly, and debate had raged over what to do with it. The temporary compromise had been to fly in a refrigerated isolation tent from the Joint Reserve Base, along with portable generators.

Tents were erected over the area where the creature had attacked Sheriff Austin and the other side of the farmhouse, where it had attacked the Barrett's and, later, Lieutenant David Garreth's men and Deputy Miles. At the barn, where the victims and survivors had been cocooned, plastic covered the entire structure.

Everywhere, hazmat-suited people took measurements, photos, video and tagged and collected samples.

A nearby pasture had turned into a military landing field, with fully a dozen helicopters and several V-22 Osprey's coming and going at any moment. Dozens of mobile infantry trucks, a dozen Bradley Fighting Vehicles and other light armored vehicles, and even a half dozen M1A2 Abrams tanks had converged on the farm and established a perimeter. AH64 Apache attack helicopters orbited overhead, and an air cap of F-15's circled high above.

Throughout the surrounding countryside, an entire company of soldiers searched on foot for signs of other alien creatures or anything out of the ordinary. Should they find anything, or should anything find them, their orders were to back off, if possible, and radio in anything suspicious.

❂ ❂ ❂

Next to the landing field, numerous large tents were the center of a frantic beehive of activity and were surrounded by a cordon of troops and light armored vehicles. Three marine guards stood ready outside the large command tent, wearing tactical vests, body armor, helmets, and eye protection. Two carried H&K UMP 45's, and the third wielded an FN M240b medium machine gun.

Inside the tent, General Marcus sat flanked by Major Finley and Captain Guevara on folding chairs at the back of the tent, behind narrow folding tables. Small microphones were positioned so they could be heard over the outside vehicle and aircraft noise. All three wore Airman Battle System-Ground (ABS-G) digital-pattern camouflage uniforms and sidearms.

Gail's naturally pale face was chalky and drawn, and her auburn hair was in mild disarray as she struggled to find a comfortable position for her cast-covered leg. Her crutches were in arms reach behind her. Captain Guevara's much darker Cuban-heritage complexion did nothing to conceal his grave, tight-lipped expression.

Marcus's jaw was set, and his dark black skin shaded the sphinxlike expression he labored to project. The current situation both apocalyptic and of biblical proportions. He knew he had to exude confidence, whether he really felt it or not.

A harried young female corporal operated a notebook computer connected to a projector. The projection screen was currently blank, except for the emblem of the Joint Reserve Base. A stack of papers and computer gear grew several inches as another corporal dashed into the tent with another armload, deposited it on the table, saluted, and nervously retreated.

As he began to exit the tent, he stepped back and aside as a Lieutenant entered, followed by the surviving Fort Brazos City Council, Tom Parker, and Sheriff Austin. Marcus, Gail, and Captain Guevara stood as the group entered. An assortment of scientists from Bonham State University followed on the heels of the council, including Dr. Nakamura, Dean of Science and Technology, and Dr.

Leo Talib, (newly) Dean of Language Studies. Several rows of folding chairs had been placed behind more narrow tables. Wireless mics were scattered on the tables.

The mood was somber, and the group fell silent as Marcus stood and tapped the microphone. He took a deep breath, "Thank you all for coming. Please be seated." He waited while the council took the front rows, and the scientists meandered around the other seats, gradually choosing their seats. As he often did, John decided not to sit but instead stood to the side of the row of council members.

"First of all, based on our previous meetings, I'm sure that some of you are concerned about the military presence outside."

Gloria leaned into a microphone and quipped, "One little alien that Sheriff Austin already killed, and you launch an invasion!"

Tom grimaced, "Gloria, please, we talked about this!"

Gail bristled and started to speak, but Marcus cut her off, "Mr. Mayor, it's Okay. Before all this happened, yes, this would be an extraordinary action that would have probably required the President's authorization on U.S. soil." He paused and passed his gaze across the other council members. "Councilwoman, yes, I ordered all the commotion you see outside, and I'm not going to apologize."

Her eyes widened, and she half-stood in indignation.

Marcus held his hands in front of him, raising a finger for each issue: "First, we all woke up in an alien world, Second, thousands of citizens are dead, Third, we find an alien tower in the middle of your town, Fourth, we lose an EA-18, and, Fifth, an * ALIEN * shows up, and murders five people, cocoons the rest and nearly kills Sheriff Austin, here, and his daughter, and, Six, we have no way of knowing whether others if its kind might be able to track it or may come to investigate. So, Yes, madam councilwoman, I'm not taking chances. We don't know if there are more of those things out there or what other dangers there may be. If I didn't send this show of force and even more people died because I didn't take it seriously, then we'd be having a different conversation. You all would, rightfully, crucify me for incompetence."

Gloria's expression softened from hostile to mulish, and she sat back down.

116

John spoke in a low baritone, "Gloria, he has a point. The rules have changed. This is as close to a biblical apocalypse as I think you can get, and we are, all of us, literally, in a brand-new world."

Marcus raised an eyebrow at John's choice of words, then continued, "Thank you, Sheriff. Now, the good news is that we have not found anything else so far. After all that has happened, I would rather respond with overkill than to put any more lives in jeopardy."

Tom spoke up, "Thank you, General. We are glad that you are here and available if we need you." He smiled, "Of course, the farm-to-market road outside was pretty well demolished by all your vehicles, but that's a small price to pay."

Several people chuckled nervously.

Tom continued, "Changing the subject, General, the council is asking that, after today, we hold a daily joint military/civilian briefing, to be televised. We'll bring selected government, law enforcement, and university leaders to speak on what we've learned. We'd like for you to provide a daily military briefing, as well."

Marcus nodded and smiled thinly at Gail, "I'll be there as much as I can, but I'm assigning Major Finley to take the lead as my direct liaison officer. She can't fly for a while, so she needs to earn her keep somehow."

Gail swallowed and shifted uncomfortably in her chair.

Tom smiled softly at the Major and exchanged looks with the other council members, then nodded to Marcus, "Thank you, General. We look forward to working with Major Finley."

Marcus took a deep breath, "Okay, then. You all came here to find out the latest we know about the alien that attacked us. Let's get this show on the road. First slide, please."

An image of the bullet-ridden plant-like alien creature snapped onto the screen, and everyone shifted positions and strained to see the picture better, and the scientists exchanged hushed, excited whispers.

Councilman Dale Hubbard quipped, "Damn, Sheriff, do you think you put enough holes in the thing?"

John sighed and shifted on his feet, his heart not really in it, "You can buy me a new vest, Dale."

Dale grunted darkly, and Councilman Jack Burdger murmured, "It looks like a cross between a plant and a porcupine."

Dale squinted, "…and a spider."

Marcus nodded to the Corporal, who advanced to the following image. This time, the creature's body had been spread out to its full seven-foot-long length, with measurement markers next to it. The Corporal cycled through a dozen more images taken from different angles.

Marcus pursed his lips and continued, "We will provide copies of all the images to any of you who want them via email or thumb-drive. The next image shows how the body of the creature started to decompose."

Several images were displayed showing a time-lapse, showing the creature begin to flatten and turn a sickly oily brown.

"As I am sure you all remember, there was considerable debate about how to move the body safely and where to take it. While we were arguing, the thing started to basically melt into the ground. We were afraid if we tried to move it, it would fall apart, and we would lose too much, ahh… evidence."

John leaned forward, "Has the refrigeration worked?"

Marcus nodded again to the Corporal. The next photo was obviously taken inside the tent, and the creature was still intact, if somewhat more flattened. "Yes, it seems to have at least slowed things down. We need to have your scientists figure out what to do next."

Everyone in the room turned to look at the short Asian man of slight build in the center, second row. Dr. Takumi Nakamura was the Dean of Science and Technology. His hair was black with streaks of grey, and his surprisingly light grey eyes were bright with distant concentration as he gazed at the projected image. He did not notice the sudden attention being focused on him.

Tom reached over and gently nudged him.

Nakamura, whose classroom reputation was to stand a foot away from the whiteboard and mumble into it as he wrote with one hand and erased with the other, turned and blinked and very softly spoke, "Ahh, yes, Mayor?"

Tom leaned over and pushed a microphone closer to Nakamura, "Dr. Nakamura, can you share your thoughts on how we should proceed with the investigation, the examination, and study of the creature? How should we proceed?"

Nakamura smiled shyly and picked up the microphone. He drew it close and then held it there, lost in thought. The moment stretched out uncomfortably, and several people cleared their throats. Those who knew the professor knew it was impossible to rush him.

Marcus put on his best 'I will be patient… I will be patient….' Expression.

Finally, Nakamura nodded to himself. "We must establish a new department, a Xenobiology department, with experts in biological disciplines, chemistry, physics, materials sciences, genetics, pathology, expertise in all the known phyla morphologies, and, I think, animal husbandry and veterinary medicine. In addition, we need to begin studies to project behavioral characteristics, intelligence, and any evidence of language or technology. We don't know if this was an intelligent creature, of just some predator endemic to this new world."

Everyone in the room exchanged looks. No one had before suggested that the creature might not have been intelligent – that it could simply be a… beast.

Dr. Nakamura continued, "The old life sciences building on campus is currently unoccupied. Its renovation was nearly complete before recent events. It was scheduled to be the new microbiology studies center. It has suitable isolation equipment we can adapt to this situation. It is relatively remote and is at the edge of the campus. If we were to set up a lab at the military base, we'd have to start from scratch and move a lot of delicate equipment that we don't have replacements for, and all the researchers would have to continually go back and forth from campus to your military base. We should, therefore, repurpose the building as the new Xenobiology lab. Lastly, we need military expertise to assess the creature's offensive capabilities, its defensive capabilities and begin projections and analysis of potential weaknesses in the context of how we defend ourselves against it."

Marcus leaned back in his chair, "Thank you, Dr. Nakamura. That's a lot to think about, and it sounds like it will take time to organize that. In the short term, how do we gather the most information from the creature before its condition degrades too completely?"

Nakamura thought for a moment, "Unless someone has a better idea, we will need to go ahead and freeze it solid as soon as possible. In the meantime, I suggest we find a way to extricate it from the ground so that we can x-ray it, do a sonogram and a CT scan. In addition to that, we should take soil samples where fluids have bled through. Assuming it has cellular structures like earth organisms, the freezing process may rupture cell walls and physically alter its physical structure and even change its chemical composition. However, we appear to have few choices, that is until you can secure more subjects for study, preferably still alive and without so much tissue damage."

Marcus stood and looked around the roomful of anxious faces. "I think it is important for us to all understand just exactly what this creature is capable of. The next images are, frankly, gruesome. However, as your Sheriff pointed out, we're in a new world now, with new rules." He nodded at the corporal. She held his gaze for a moment and did her best to hide a hard swallow before tapping the key.

The first image showed a medium-sized brown Australian Shepherd dog that a clutch of wicked thorn-like projectiles had impaled. Gossamer strands trailed from the end of each barb. The dog had been almost ripped in half. Several in the audience sucked in their breath.

The next image showed a row of bodies, some living, some, clearly, not. The dead were shriveled and cocooned. The living were surrounded by the tattered remains of their cocoons but were stiff and rigid, their faces paralyzed in a rictus of terror.

The next image was of Sheriff's deputy Grayson Miles, or what was left of him. It was evident that the creature had shown particular interest in the deputy. One of the professors bolted from their chair, knocking it backward, and fled the tent, retching loudly outside.

"Oh my God."

"Sweet Jesus."

The council members turned shades of green, and many in the room were either teary-eyed or turning crimson shades of fury. Or both.

In the back of the tent, Dr. Leo Talib stood. He waited patiently for the room to settle down and to be recognized. The side discussions continued unabated, especially among the academics.

Marcus looked at Talib and used his microphone to speak over the noise, "Yes, and you are, sir?"

The son of American and French-Algerian diplomats, his accent and innate sense of authority had literally been imbibed in his mother's milk. He'd selected his most serious Saville Row suit but studiously ignored the mud on his now priceless leather shoes from Piccadilly. As a child, Talib had secretly watched his parents practice their speeches when they thought no one was watching. Their voices had been so different — more focused, confident, and authoritative. He had learned from them and developed his "teaching voice" as well as what he used now – his "wise and authoritative" voice.

He picked up a microphone and very briefly paused, "Thank you, General. I am Dr. Leonard Talib. I am, apparently, now this world's leading expert on languages. I have been studying the glyphs which have been appearing on the alien spire, and I have made a discovery."

Several people stopped their conversations, saying "What?" and "What did he say? A hush fell over the room.

Marcus's eyes brightened, not only at the prospect of new information but just as much because of the diversion from the grizzly object lesson on the projection screen. "Yes, Doctor, please tell us what you have discovered."

Talib paused, looking around the room, making sure he had everyone's undivided attention. "Many of you do not know me. First, allow me to explain that I am fluent in fourteen languages and quite passable in a dozen more. I have been working with a small team to study the alien glyphs. So far, you should note that none have actually repeated. I say actually because my first discovery is that the symbols appear in multiple versions that are overlaid with portions that vary in spectra beyond normal human visual acuity. Simply put, only rare humans can see the majority of colors represented, and some of the colors are beyond that which any human can perceive. I believe we are being given a primer on the alien language, and that language has color permutations many orders of magnitude more complex than any human language."

Gail leaned forward to her microphone, "Excuse me, Doctor, but how do we know that these color variations actually mean anything? Couldn't they be... artistic?"

Talib smiled gently, controlling his breathing and keeping his irritation in check. "Thank you, Major, that is an excellent question, and that was naturally my first thought as well. However, digging deeper, I have discovered what I believe is definitive proof that these color variations, including multiple hues in a single representation, have, in fact, separate meanings. You see, within the visual change of each glyph, I, with my team's help, have discovered additional embedded data. That data is formatted in a way the aliens knew we *would* recognize." He paused and spoke with conviction, "That data is, in fact, compressed audio waveforms that are unique to each color variation. They have given us an audible representation of their symbology, and it is stored, rather conveniently, for us, that is, in a standard MPEG audio format. They wanted us to find this information."

Someone gasped, and urgent murmurs broke out among the academics.

Marcus urged, "That is great news, Dr. At least I think it is. Can you show us an example?"

Talib held up a thumb drive. Marcus nodded to the corporal, who worked her way around to the back of the tent to retrieve it, then returned, plugged it into her laptop, and played its video file.

On the projection screen, Dr. Talib's handsome dark face filled the screen, and his recorded self-briefly repeated his findings in careful, patient, knowing tones. Then a video of the alien spire appeared and zoomed to the constantly changing alien symbols. The image then transitioned to a split-screen, with a still image of a glyph symbol on one side and a complex audio waveform on the other. Then, Talib's voiceover explained that the audio about to be played was only that which was in the human hearing range, but that the total data was much more complex.

Then the audio played, and all the murmurs and side conversations abruptly ceased. The audio was not harsh or bizarre. It was not alien, but it was. There were two voices at different pitches and octaves. They were ethereal and achingly majestic, stretching and crying and reaching into your soul like some silken goddess. No, not a goddess. This was the sound of angels singing, making mere humans seem coarse and thin and vain and dirty and small.

Then the video stopped, and the room was utterly silent, save the sounds from the military vehicles and aircraft outside.

The moment stretched on, and Marcus cleared his throat. "Well, um, Dr. That was…."

Talib interrupted, "Please excuse me, General, but that was not all."

"There's more?"

"Yes, General. Please play the second file."

The corporal found the file and played it. The calm image of Dr. Talib filled the screen again, with an expression this time that was patient and perhaps sad. "Ladies and Gentlemen, I discovered another audio waveform that appears to be appended to every glyph I've examined so far. As you will hear, it is quite different from the first one I played for you. However, this waveform is identical for each glyph, and it is in spoken English." His image paused on the screen, knowing the reaction that would come.

Half the people in the room leaped to their feet, and everyone began talking excitedly to each other. The corporal paused the video.

Marcus tapped the microphone, "Please! Please be quiet. Let's hear this."

Everyone sat back down, some faster than others. A strong wind gust shook the tent.

The playback resumed, and the recorded Talib continued, "The following audio is concise, less than twelve seconds long, and was very compressed and, in contrast to the glyph audio, is entirely within human range. The following is the entirety of the audio message."

The screen split again with Dr. Talib's face on one side and a short audio waveform depicted on the other. It played. In English, the voice sounded male but with nothing other than a generic, vaguely computer-generated-sounding accent.

> *"The sound you have just heard is the voice of your enemy. The destroyer of your world and countless others.*
> *Learn it well.*
> *Vengeance shall be yours."*

Two hours later, the meeting broke up. Dr. Talib, Dr. Nakamura, and the rest of the University delegation clustered in the center of the tent, engaged in a raucous debate, or what amounted to one for their collegial dispositions, over peer review and the academic evils of jumping to conclusions. Dr. Talib tried to leave the discussion and kept looking in the council's direction, but Dr. Nakamura and three others blocked his exit and pummeled him with questions.

John and Gail were deeply engrossed in discussions over maps of the area and resource planning and allocation of soldiers, deputies, and police. John stood over the maps, explaining local geography issues, while she leaned back against a table, propped up by her crutches, keeping her leg and cast at an angle.

Across the tent, Marcus, Tom, and Gloria had pulled up folding chairs and sat in an isolated huddle. Captain Guevara and the other council members met together in another corner.

Gloria nodded towards John and Gail and looked at Marcus with a telling expression, "General, I had begun to wonder if we were going to have a problem with those two working together? Her body language and everything about her fairly screamed that she detested him."

Marcus considered his answer, then shrugged, "I wasn't sure either, at first. Now, though, I've gotten to know Major Finley a little better. She blames herself for the crash, you know. I think that having your Sheriff pull her out of that billboard, combined with her injuries, was an affront to her... pride. She's a very driven young officer, and I think she needed her current duties to get her mind off it and let her focus on doing something useful – and, vanity allowing, important."

Tom smiled, "And it also showed her that you trust her and don't blame her for the crash."

Gloria looked at Tom and then Marcus, "You know, we are going to need their youth and strength if we are going to survive, aren't we?"

Tom cocked his head, "What are you getting at, Gloria?"

She chortled, "I mean, Tom, that we are going to need leaders like those two. They're young and strong and, well, they're popular."

Marcus pursed his lips, "Councilwoman, Mayor, why are we sitting here? What did you really want to talk about?"

Gloria and Tom exchanged worried looks.

Tom took a breath, "We're here, General, to talk about new civilian leadership. You, and, we, need to decide how to proceed with forming a new government that can have a chance at being popularly accepted, and is seen as being legitimate to all parties, and has a chance in hell of working in this new world we find ourselves in."

Gloria grimaced, "What Tom isn't saying, General, is that we need to be the adults in the room and stop bickering and agree on what to do next."

Marcus leaned back and sighed. He took a drink from his bottled water and considered. Tom and Gloria waited.

After a time, he leaned forward, "Okay. Historically, the United States population was made up of, what, seven or eight percent veterans and active service? They've always been an important if minority voting bloc. Here, though, the percentage is much higher, over thirty percent, and our security situation is literally life and death. Representation in this new society will need to be different, and I don't just mean there are more votes."

Tom shook his head, "We still need a civilian head of state...."

Gloria started to speak, but Marcus smiled and raised his hands, "Yes, I agree, but we need to think of how to give confidence to both our military and the civilians."

Gloria narrowed her eyes, "What, you want to turn in your medals for a suit, General?"

Marcus gazed at her and frowned, "Councilwoman, unlike some, I am not a politician, and I have no desire to be one or to be anything other than an Air Force officer. The people, *all* the people, need to feel like their vote is real and that it counts. I do not want to be President, and that is not what the people, our people, need for me to do. I am military through and through, and that's all I ever want to be."

Gloria seemed doubtful.

Tom nodded, "Taking you at your word, General, do you have any suggestions on how to proceed?"

Marcus shook his head and groaned, "I should have paid better attention in civics class."

Behind them, the University delegation continued their debate, arms waving.

Nearby, Gail stood up on her crutches and leaned over next to John at a large map. John nodded as they quietly talked. Gail focused intensely on the map. Their heads were almost touching as she traced her finger along the line of a road.

Gloria glanced over at them and considered, pursing her lips, and then smiled. "Gentlemen, I think I have an idea."

Ghosts

Before the crisis, there had not been an isolation ward at Methodist Hospital. There was an emergency plan, somewhere, for dealing with some unthinkable disease outbreak, and there were undoubtedly procedures for dealing with contagion. The Hoffman attack survivors, however, were beyond scary. They'd literally been captured and cocooned by an *alien* creature. Were they contaminated with some dread pathogen or worse? Countless Hollywood horror movies had inspired rampant fears and whispers.

With so many previously ill patients somehow cured, much of the hospital was now empty, so clearing out and isolating a section of it was far easier than anyone would have otherwise believed possible. An extensive military security detail, both inside and out, stood guard while both military and civilian doctors and medical personnel had sealed off the impromptu isolation ward, complete with layers of plastic seals and hazmat suits.

The Hoffman family survivors, Sisters Sandra, Jordan, Hannah, and Elizabeth and their two-year-old brother, Vicktor, along with the Lieutenant David Garreth, Sargent Washington, and Specialist Simmons, had all been whisked to the isolation ward, stripped, scrubbed, examined, x-rayed, CT-scanned, whole-body-imaged, and sonogramed. Despite shrieks of protest, their every orifice had been exhaustively and deeply analyzed. Their fluids and excrements were microscopically studied and preserved. Blood samples were taken on the hour, and their every word and movement was remotely monitored and recorded from multiple angles. In the end, they had all been thoroughly examined in every way the doctors could think of. Each was interviewed repeatedly until tempers flared.

The military doctors were led by Commander (Dr.) Gwyneth Elliot and her staff. The senior surviving civilian doctor was Dr. David Duncan. Commander Elliot was called a force of nature by her supporters and other names by the rest. At 5'4", she was not of imposing height. However, as a former Olympic biathlon athlete and Silver Medal winner, her physicality was intense, and her very red hair and hazel eyes only added to her vitality and presence.

At the moment, she and Dr. Duncan sat alone in the video monitoring room, watching the survivors. The room was not large, and their rolling office chairs were close.

On the video monitors, the survivors could be seen as all being up and active. The younger children were running around, playing a game of some kind. Seventeen-year-old Sandra was sitting cross-legged on a bed in animated conversation with Lt. Garreth. Nearby, Sargent Washington and Specialist Simons lounged at a small table, playing cards and laughing about something.

Dr. Duncan seemed rapt by what he was seeing. Commander Elliot studied his profile.

She smiled softly, "David?"

It took a moment for him to react. He blinked and took a breath. "I'm sorry, Gwyn, I just cannot believe how quickly they have all… bounced back."

She reached out and touched his face. They'd been lovers for a time, but it had cooled. His darkness was something she had never been able to overcome. He could not let go of his nightmares and his ghosts. She had not seen him since before…. Before the awakening. He seemed different now.

"David, what else is going on?"

He chuckled, "You mean, aside from the end of the world and the beginning of this one, thousands of people dead, aliens, and, oh, people being completely cured of incurable diseases?"

She thumped him on the back of his head and retorted, "Yes, jackass, besides that!"

He didn't flinch from the thump, which surprised her.

He smiled and answered quietly, "I think... I think that I'm re-evaluating my life... and my ghosts."

She'd been with him often enough when he would awaken from his nightmares, and she knew about the men who (then) Captain Duncan had somehow managed to save from their wounds, only to see them all subsequently die from a mortar round as he'd finally left the surgery tent to get some rest. It had been the event that drove him from military service to seek a quiet life in Fort Brazos.

She rested her hand on his. "Good."

He continued, "Do you remember when I called you about the patients not being sick?"

She inhaled sharply, "Of course! We nearly lost several patients of our own! You saved their lives, David, not to mention the broadcast message that went out to everyone asking them to, what was it, 'have their medicines tested before they took anymore?' That was inspired. None of us figured out what was happening as fast as you did."

He sighed, staring into the monitor, "Well, I can't take credit for that. It honestly had not occurred to me either. How could it, really? We are doctors. We're trained to look for problems, not the lack of them. Anyway, it wasn't my idea. You see, there was this strange woman in the hallway. I don't think I've ever seen her before, by the way. I had just come out of surgery where I nearly killed a heart patient who no longer had a heart condition, and I was... I was in a bad way. Then, in the hallway, there she was. She called me by name. She told me the patients were not sick – and that I needed to let go of my ghosts."

He turned to Gweneth, and his eyes were misty. "Gwynn, she knew their names."

Her eyes widened, "Well... I suppose that's not the strangest thing that has happened lately, is it? It sounds like she was right on both issues, doesn't it?"

On the video monitor, the children were jumping up and down on beds, and young Sandra and the Lieutenant were laughing about something. Sandra's smile was brilliant, and she brushed her long blonde hair back behind one ear.

Lieutenant Garrett seemed to enjoy the attention. Elliot smiled, "I think they are all going to be just fine, except for that young man -- he is going to be in serious trouble."

Duncan put his other hand on hers and squeezed, "I think there is going to be a lot of that going around." He turned fully towards her and took her hands in his own. "Let's go to my office."

She straightened in her chair and sat up straight, pulling slightly back and away from him. Her expression stiffened, betrayed by only a glimmer of a smile. "Why? Why go to your office? What can we do there that we cannot do here?"

He returned her deadpan, "Well, you see, Gwynn, my office has shades and a lock on the door."

She thought about it, considering whether now was the right time for such things or if she even really wanted to reignite their romance. She stared deeply into his eyes for a long moment and suddenly realized just how fast her heart was beating. It was the apocalypse, after all. Who knew what might happen tomorrow? "Well, if you put it that way...."

Beast

Highway
Day 4: 9:19 AM

The highway that passed through Fort Brazos and along the border of the Joint Reserve Base reservation extended for another forty-five miles in either direction, in what people were already calling north and south. East was spinward, towards the massive lake and barrier mountains and the approaching hurricane that was creeping down the upward curve of the horizon. North and South were down the axis of the cylindrical world. After forty-five miles, the road simply ended, its edge sharply sliced off. Beyond it lay the vast interior of the new continent.

General Marcus had decided to establish a small forward operating base at each end of the interstate. Men and materials could be easily trucked down the highway to the checkpoints. Those checkpoints would serve multiple functions, not the least of which would be as the jumping-off point for ground scouting parties tasked with investigating anomalies observed from the air and as hubs for the planned 'Lewis and Clark' ground exploration teams.

The road itself was strange. All the little towns and side-roads that used to be there were gone, replaced by a field of tall grass, and the road no longer curved towards or around non-existing towns or landmarks. It was now straight as an arrow, with the same discolorations eventually repeating over and over. Like the landscape around it, it had been "copied and pasted" into its new shape and direction.

It wasn't just for military use. A small trickle of prospective 'mountain men' had begun to head out into the wilderness, to see what they could see, to test themselves, or to simply escape the organized and structured world. To make their own destinies or die trying. No-one stopped them. However, an announcement had been made requesting that they let someone know their intentions, so no one would think that perhaps something had happened to them as it had to the Hoffman's. The checkpoints were a jumping-off point into the new wilderness.

Construction equipment was already on-site at the checkpoints. People, building supplies, and supplies-in-general were being hauled by both military and civilian trucks and vehicles. Wayne and Sybil Blanchard owned one of those. Although they had been on the highway carrying a load on Awakening-Day, the Blanchard's were not Fort Brazos residents. Now, without a home and stranded, they had happily accepted the work.

Their 18-wheel truck and trailer hummed along the long grey ribbon of concrete. Sybil sat in the passenger seat, holding Wayne's Chihuahua Pinky, watching the approaching storm out her window. Her long dark curly hair was tied back in a ponytail.

"Wayne?"

"Yeah, hon?"

"Are you sure we're getting paid for this?"

Wayne thought for a while before answering, "Well, in the long run, I don't think anyone really knows what form of currency or exchange we're going to end up with. But the military has been good to me so far. I feel good about doing this and helping, and the company sure is a lot better than it was in Afghanistan!"

"God, I sure hope so!"

He chuckled, "Maybe the new money will be bottle caps, like in that game."

Sybil closed her eyes and groaned, "Well, at least they're paying for the gas, maintenance, and food. That's something!"

Wayne squinted out the windshield into the distance ahead.

"What's going on?" he mumbled.

Far ahead of them, a desert-colored Humvee had suddenly swerved and collided with something. As they drew closer, smoke began rising from the Humvee.

Sybil stiffened, "Did they hit someone?"

Wayne hit the brakes. Big trucks don't stop on a dime, but he managed to safely stop within a hundred feet of the stricken Humvee. No one had gotten out of it yet, but there did not seem to be another vehicle. Wayne frowned and looked at Sybil, "Call it in, and stay in the truck."

She didn't question his decision to leave the truck and investigate. Smoke was still rising from the Humvee, and she had no idea whether it might catch fire and burn or kill any survivors. She reached out and grabbed his beefy arm before he left, though, her eyes level and firm, "Be careful."

He managed a smile and reached for his shoulder-holstered Beretta M9 he'd started carrying after news of the Alien attack had spread like wildfire. He checked the magazine, nodded at Sybil, and exited, climbing down the side of the truck cabin and trotting forward to the Humvee as the smoke and crackling sound of fire grew.

He yelled, "Hello? Is anyone alive in there?"

The Humvee was at an angle, its undamaged driver-side facing him, but oily black smoke poured out of the open window.

He called out again, dashing around the vehicle, "Hello? Is anyone hurt?" As he reached the other side, he skidded to a halt.

In front of him was a thing… It was black, thickly armored in front, a gaping mouth with shark-like teeth, an array of tiny eyes, and had a massive horn that Wayne had no doubt was responsible for shredding the Humvee. It had six legs, and at the moment, was… eating what was left of the occupants of the Humvee…. Wayne could not tell how many that might have been. It looked like a cross between some kind of dinosaur, a small rhinoceros, and, well, a mythical hellhound.

Over the crackling of the blazing fire, it had not yet noticed Wayne, who did not even reach for his Beretta. The paltry 9mm round would only make the thing mad. He gently started backing away, willing the beast not to notice him.

He almost made it.

As he backed away the way he had come, the thing flung half a camouflage-covered leg away and snorted, shaking its head back and forth before locking its attention directly on Wayne. It growled a sound like rocks being crushed. Wayne was a big man. Civilian life had softened the edges, but he was still thickly muscled underneath. He'd never been a sprinter. However, he suddenly discovered he could run a lot faster than he'd ever imagined possible.

The beast clawed the ground and took off after Wayne in an undulating, sinewy, six-legged gallop. It was slow to start, inertia being what it is, but it quickly picked up speed. It thundered after him, quickly gaining ground.

Wayne could feel it closing the gap behind him, and he knew he wasn't going to make it back to the truck in time. He started to reach for his Beretta, thinking that perhaps by some miracle he might at least slow it down, when a sharp, angry crack erupted from the truck, and the beast stumbled to a stop, shaking its head madly.

Sybil hung out the window of the truck cabin and fired her Rock River AR .308 again, and the bullet spalled across the thing's armored head.

Wayne reached the side of the truck and never remembered how he had gotten from the ground to the side of the cabin, "Hit it again!"

Sybil fired, again and again, emptying the 20-round magazine while Wayne climbed inside, gunned the idling truck engine and pulled on the powerful 200-decibel air horn, then shoved the truck into gear to run the thing over.

The truck lurched forward and slammed into the beast, which went flying into the air, bounced, and rolled to its feet. It shuddered, raised its head, roared, and shakily galloped off the road, disappearing into the tall grass.

Facing the People

Fort Brazos HS Stadium
Day 4: 9:00 AM

T he Fort Brazos High School football stadium was one of the largest in Texas, with a capacity of 16,000. Its cost had been controversial, and the vote regarding its construction had been quietly added to a low-turnout and otherwise dull and unremarked-upon routine ballot. Some citizens had been outraged, especially at the nearly $50 million cost, but the die was cast, and it was, really, a very nice stadium, even if the price tag could have sent all of Fort Brazos's students to state college for years to come.

Today, the stadium would be filled to capacity, with 1,500 more seats placed on the playing field. There were no players, no cheerleaders, and no marching band. There were no banners or mascots. The concession stands were empty, and there was no levity at all.

An elevated stage had been erected – one that was usually used for graduation ceremonies, concerts, and special events. This event would be unique in many ways and would be broadcast live to everyone in Fort Brazos, the Joint Reserve Base, and streamed to the smartphones of anyone, not near a TV.

Organizing it had been a whirlwind, and not just because of the physical logistics. This was the first major public meeting since Awakening Day. People were scared and still mourning for their dead. No one knew what was coming next.

In the distance, the approaching hurricane had slid down the horizon until it was almost hidden from view behind the barrier mountains. The sun-tube was dimming overhead, and the brilliant stadium lights could be seen for miles. On stage were General Marcus, Major Finley, Captain Guevara, Mayor Parker, Councilwoman Vargas, and Councilmen Burdger, Hickum, and Hubbard. Sheriff Austin stood to the side. Also on stage were Dr. Nakamura, Dr. Talib, and Dr. Duncan. The stage itself was mirrored on the giant video screens at either end of the stadium.

Security was tight, with police and marine guards in very visible evidence. The crowd, however, was probably the quietest the stadium had ever held. Tom, Gloria, and Marcus stood together, to the side of the stage, in animated but hushed conversation. Each, in turn, shook their heads and gesticulated their points of view before gradually nodding agreement and shaking hands. They walked to their places on the stage.

A hush fell over the stadium as Tom stepped to the podium. A gentle wind tussled his light grey hair, and his soft green eyes were a little watery as he took a deep breath.

"Citizens of Fort Brazos, this town meeting is being held to inform you of what we have learned so far and to discuss certain other issues. However, before we begin, I would like to say a few words." He paused, looking down, then looked back up again, "My friend, our friend, Pastor Joe Gilmore should have been here today. Like so many other loved ones, he isn't. But if he had been, I know he would have filled our hearts with hope and peace and told us not to be afraid, for God has not given us the spirit of fear, but of power and of love and of a sound mind. We remember how we all felt after 911 and the terrible feelings of pain and righteous rage.

Today, we are here, and we know not what happened to our world. All we know is that so many of our loved ones are dead and that we have been ripped from our own world, abducted and deposited here, in this place. Why? How? Who did this? Our hearts cry out in pain and grief, and we are all here, separated from the rest of our world and loved ones, and I wonder, is this how Noah felt after the flood?

All I can say is that we must not panic. God has given us many brave and brilliant people amongst us. We must have faith and not be fearful. I believe we are here for a purpose beyond that intended by our abductors. I believe we have a destiny, that we will rise, and we will survive and overcome, and that we will find out who did this to us, and we will make them pay a terrible price.

So, have faith and pray for our loved ones, pray for what we have lost, and pray for those who lead us to be wise and strong.

Thank you."

He looked left to right, across the sea of faces, sucked in a breath, and stood tall. "We're now going to play a video slideshow on the monitors and on your TVs at home. This video will show you what we've seen and learned about this world and the threats we face. You'll see the alien creature that murdered the Hoffman family members and our brave soldiers. You'll see the first daily military briefing, and you'll see a report from the hospital about the healthcare concerns with our medicines. You'll see video taken from long-range aircraft from the Joint Reserve Base as well as from the University telescope. You'll also see the alien spire in the Town Square, the symbols on it, and you'll hear from Dr. Talib, who will describe what he's discovered hidden in those symbols."

"In short, you will be shown everything we know so far. I will caution that some information may be wrong. To be honest, there was a heated debate about whether we should wait until we were more certain of the facts or not, but the decision we made was to provide full disclosure of whatever we learn when we learn it. I'm sure that, over time, many things we tell you will turn out to be incomplete, mistaken, or simply wrong. That can't be helped. This is a dangerous new world we are in, and you deserve to make your own decisions based on the best information available."

He paused and looked briefly at General Marcus, "That being said, General Marcus has… impressed upon me that there may come a time when military and defense-related information may be withheld. We simply don't know who is listening. However, such decisions will be made based on the need to protect our survival. Not of our 'way of life' or to protect a 'national interest' or sovereignty. Those things don't appear to mean much anymore. We now must be concerned with our very survival, possibly of the human race."

He pursed his lips and gazed across the crowd. "After the video, each presenter will be available to answer questions. Before we start, however, I'd like

Sheriff Austin to address certain concerns that many have been worried about. John?"

John walked across the stage to the podium, boots clicking on the springy boards, as Tom stepped aside. Following Tom's example, he waited a moment, looking across the stadium.

"First of all, I'd like to thank everyone's kindness and support for our deputies, police officers and for the courage and dedication of our military. We have shed blood together, and your outpouring of love and the help that everyday people are giving, pitching in in so many ways, is humbling. Thank you."

"Second, I want to address one of the top concerns that you all have made known – the issue of food and supplies and how long they will last. I have good news on this, as well as some frankly bizarre news. The good news, in short, is that we do not appear to have a short-term problem with food or supplies. In fact, if you look up the horizon, you can see vast fields of grain. There is more than we can possibly eat, and there are plans in motion to harvest and store as much grain as possible. It appears our abductors do not want us to starve."

Low, uncomfortable laughter drifted across the stadium.

"Also, more good, and some strange news. As many of you know, Fort Brazos is home to many regional distribution centers for all sorts of things, so we already have an oversupply of most things we might need anytime soon. However, the strange part is next. He looked up at the giant video screens and pointed. An aerial photo was displayed, showing the Fort Brazos warehouse district's huge distribution centers.

"This photo was taken a couple of years ago, and some of you will recognize it from the Chamber of Commerce brochures." He nodded offstage, and the photo slide to the side of a split-screen. On the other side of the screen was another photo. Parts of it looked the same, but the size and scale of several of the warehouses were vastly larger.

"As many of you now know, our abductors apparently thought our warehouses weren't big enough. Not only are they now much, much larger, but their contents were also duplicated."

John returned his gaze to the crowd. "So, nobody needs to panic over food or supplies. There will be no price gouging and no hoarding. Most stores have already voluntarily, and of their own accord, kept prices where they were. Thank you for that. Meanwhile, I'm sure it will come as no surprise that the council will be announcing price freezes."

"When I say no hoarding, I mean it. Don't make this an issue that will force us to act on. If your neighbor is in need of something, help them, just as you would want them to help you. Just like you would have done without thinking after a tornado or flood. At the same time, if you have supplies you don't need, make a list. We'll work out some kind of way for people to trade, buy, sell or simply give things they don't need to those who do."

"Third is power." He paused as a photo of a power transfer station was displayed. "I'm sure everyone remembers the high-tension power lines that ran from the lignite coal power plant into the city. Well, they're not there anymore." The image was replaced with a photo of power lines converging onto a black box. A man in a hardhat was standing next to the box, which appeared to be about as long and wide as the man was tall. John gestured up to the photo, "Instead, power to the city is now apparently coming out of this black box. When the utility engineer, Gerry Evans, touched it with an insulated pole, a shockwave blew him back twenty feet."

The audience gasped.

"I'm told Gerry is recovering nicely at Methodist Hospital. Meanwhile, the military has placed a permanent guard around the power station. Curiosity nearly killed Gerry. Don't follow suit, people."

"Speaking of safety, the Fourth point is about safety. You've all heard what happened at the Hoffman ranch and that there are dangers in this world. With the help of the military, we are increasing our patrols day and night. We're also going to organize additional neighborhood watch patrols, and we are going to conduct weekly firearms safety and marksmanship classes. No one is going to tell you not to be armed. However, all of us could agree that we need to do it in a safe and responsible way. Just because the alien looks like a damned plant doesn't mean we need to start shooting any bush that waves in the wind. I don't want any hurt from stray bullets and friendly fire. Also, we need to coordinate our efforts so that if we find more of these creatures, we can maybe even capture one alive, so our scientists can learn more about them and their weaknesses. Hear me on this, everyone. I want no heroes out there. If you see something, back off and call it in, if at all possible."

"Lastly, we encourage you to report suspicious things but please only use 911 for true emergencies. Our system is already overloaded. We're working on a new set of numbers for you to call for different kinds of emergencies. Until we have that ready, please help us keep things under control."

John stepped back from the podium, and Tom nodded his thanks. John retreated to the side of the stage again.

Tom retook the podium, "Thank you, Sheriff. And with that, let's start the video."

If anything, the crowd was even more subdued after the hour-and-a-half-long video. Volunteers spread out, handing out bottled water.

Tom stood and returned to the podium again. However, Gloria also stood. She approached the podium and exchanged words with Tom off-mic for a solid minute.

Finally, Tom turned and spoke to the crowd. "Ladies and Gentlemen, I have asked Councilwoman Vargas to make an announcement."

He stepped to the side, and Gloria took the podium, adjusting it for her lower height. "People of Fort Brazos, there is another concern which I know many have talked about. That is, to be blunt, who will be 'in charge' now that we find ourselves not one city among many, in a state among many, and in a country of many -- but as the only city in a whole world. Some have argued that the military should make all the big decisions. Others have argued that we need a constitutional convention to decide upon an entirely new form of government. Perhaps, in time, when we better understand this new world and our place in it, it will be time for esoteric debate over forms of government. For now, however, we already have a representative form of government, and we need a clear understanding of who is in charge so that decisions can be made in a crisis." She paused and raised her voice, repeating and emphasizing the word, "Crisis?" She snorted, and not a few people chuckled. "I think we can all agree that we are in a crisis-filled world right now. Our military is used to reporting to a President and Joint Chiefs. Well, right now, all they have is me," she waved her hand at the other council members and Mayor, "and these!"

"The Mayor, City Council, and General Marcus propose that we hold an election for a President and Vice President, who will be concerned with issues broader than just our city." She nodded at Tom, "Mayor Parker is a very fine man, and Fort Brazos is lucky to have him. We propose that this new office of the Presidency be separate from the Fort Brazos city government. The City Council would act in the role we're all used to being filled by a congress and Senate. The President would be commander-in-chief of the military and of the other towns and cities. I'm sure we will get around to creating in this new world. As new communities are established, they will be represented. Someday, when there are enough of us, we'll grow to have a full Congress and Senate, as our forefathers established."

She looked across the stadium at the expectant faces. Many were nodding agreement. She raised her voice, "Do I have a second?"

The crowd growled approval.

Councilman Burdger stood, "I second the motion!"

Councilman Hubbard followed, "Here here. I third."

The rest of the council stood in solidarity, along with General Marcus, Major Finley, and Captain Guevara. Tom smiled at her for the camera. He started towards the podium, but she raised her hand and did not yield it.

She then gripped the edges of the podium and leaned into the microphone. "Fort Brazos is facing an uncertain future in a new world. I cannot comprehend how we got here, and I don't know about you, but it all scares the hell out of me."

A ripple of nervous laughter drifted across the stadium.

"Look, I'm just a small-town City Councilwoman and businesswoman. We need someone to lead not just this town - but be the leader of this world. This new… Texas." She gestured to the vast panorama overhead.

Then, she nodded offstage, and another video began to play, to the apparent surprise of no one except for Sheriff Austin. It was the uncut video of Sheriff John Austin's encounter with the alien creature at the Hoffman farm. John had objected to the full video being shown. While everyone knew in general what had happened, now was the first time the entire scene was shared, not only from the bodycam perspective but also from the dashboard cam of his Sheriff's vehicle. The whole stadium was rapt as they witnessed the events, and of their Sheriff's quick and decisive action, including his breathless dash to scoop his stunned daughter Matti out of the way, and his battle with the creature itself was shown in slow motion, his .45 blazing in precision aim, even as he ran. The creature's thorn-like projectiles arced across and sank into his bulletproof vest, and his bullets punched through the creature's leathery plant-like skin, raising a greenish coppery spray.

The video ended, and Gloria leaned into the microphone again, "We need someone who is smart and who has been successful in the real world. Not an intellectual, but a self-made man and leader who can lead us to a better future."

John stood stunned with a deer-in-headlights expression, shaking his head no. Gloria walked across the stage and reached up to put her hand on his shoulder. She looked out across the stadium, and someone started clapping. Then another, and another until everyone in the stadium stood and joined the thunderous applause. She pulled on his sleeve and almost dragged him towards the podium.

She leaned into the microphone again, "I nominate Sheriff John Austin, who we all know is brave, isn't afraid to get his hands dirty, who is a native son and was a damn fine ballplayer. But most of all, he believes in Fort Brazos. He could have gone and lived anywhere in the world after his success, but he came back home to serve our community."

She looked down, swallowed, and spoke again, "I have to confess that I misjudged John Austin. When he returned, maybe I was jealous. I admit that. I thought he was only here to further his own political ambitions. I also admit that I am responsible for some of the rumors to that effect, and I apologize for that. I have, however, come to know John and his lovely daughter. I've listened to his wise words in council meetings. I've seen his intelligence and generosity to the community, not the least of which include the donation of a brand new elementary school in memory of his beloved late wife, Carolyn. He is an engineer and earned his MBA from a difficult and prestigious university. He has many patents to his name, and we've all now seen his bravery. I give you, Sheriff John Austin! The first President of New Texas!"

John leaned down to speak into Gloria's ear, "Gloria, I promise, somehow, someday, you'll pay for this!"

She replied with a knowing smile, "And now, for the office of Vice President, we have another nomination. After much debate, it was decided that the Vice President should be nominated from the ranks of the active-duty military. Our candidate is a decorated pilot. She started working on her pilot's license before graduating high school." She glanced over her shoulder at Major Finley, who suddenly realized what was happening. The dread terror on her face was all the confirmation Gloria needed that their choice had been the right one.

"She earned her Bachelor's and Master's Degrees in Aeronautical Engineering and was first in her class. She is a veteran of 89 combat missions. When she was called upon to investigate the skies above Fort Brazos after The Awakening, her airplane was severely damaged. Somehow, she wrestled control enough to direct it away from buildings or homes into a vacant parking lot, missing the High School and undoubtedly saving the lives of many innocent civilians. She bravely stayed in her plane until the last possible moment, before ejecting, and was severely injured."

"Thank God she is Okay. This remarkable young woman is here today sitting behind me, and she had no more idea this was about to happen than our dear Sheriff had. I am told her Air Force call-sign is Banshee. I talked to General Marcus and to other officers and pilots who know her, and evidently that moniker suits her. She simply refuses to give up. Ladies and Gentlemen, people of Fort Brazos, we need people like Major Gail Finley and Sheriff John Austin to lead us into this unknown future!"

"The Mayor, the council, and General Marcus have all endorsed these candidates. Others are, of course, free to submit their names for candidacy, and we will set the election date shortly."

The rest of the council stood around him and ushered John and Gail to the podium. Thunderous applause swelled like a living thing, with shouts and yells of approval. A few people were more restrained, assuming John and Gail's reluctance was feigned, but John had built a solid reputation even before Awakening Day and was very popular. As a young man, he'd left town to work in the oil fields and later worked hard to earn an engineering degree and filed several patents on improvements and inventions for oilfield equipment based on his first-hand experience. He'd gone on to earn an MBA at Wharton, and built a successful business, which he'd sold for a substantial profit, then moved home to marry his high school sweetheart. They had Matti and been very happy. An accident had taken her from him and Matti, and together, they'd won the hearts of the people of Fort Brazos as a loving father and daughter and much-liked Sheriff.

At 6'2", he was tall and lean, with high upper body strength from his oilfield days. He dressed well, with tailored shirts, Lucchese boots, and a robust and rugged appearance.

While unknown before Awakening Day, Gail had become a hero for quite nearly sacrificing herself to prevent civilian deaths from her plummeting aircraft. It didn't hurt that she was young, at only 32, a slim 5'9" and rakishly attractive with short auburn hair and forest green eyes, although, at the moment, all color had drained from her face. Despite that, even on crutches, she moved with a lithe unconscious swagger.

In short, they were both very attractive, intelligent, and already popular. They were also horrified at not only being so suddenly and publicly ambushed but at the very prospect of having the weight of the entire world placed on their shoulders.

John and Gail stood before the podium. John sighed, looking out at the crowd. He shook his head again and looked over at Gloria again before speaking.

"Will someone, please, help me figure out a way to get even with Gloria for drafting us like this."

Gloria's face flushed crimson, but the crowd reacted with understanding laughter. She was famous for being a pain, but she was 'theirs.'

He continued, "New Texas, huh? I think I like the sound of that. What do you think?" The crowd roared approval.

Then, Matti bounded onto the stage and into his arms, and the stadium shook to its foundations.

He looked at Gail, trying to fathom what she was thinking. She swallowed and held his gaze with grim, steely determination. He could see that she was going to spread some of the blame onto him for this. He could also see in her eyes that she would do her duty.

The applause diminished enough for him to speak, "Some of you know my daughter Matti, and some of you knew her mom, Carolyn. When I was young, I couldn't wait to leave town and see the world. I saw it, but I came back for Carolyn and to start a family. I've been all over the world.... The old world.... There are, or there were, a lot of nice places and people out there. I learned that what I really wanted in life was the girl I'd loved since we were kids and to grow old with her, here, in Fort Brazos." He swallowed, "I never got the chance to grow old with Carolyn, but we loved each other, and she gave us the joy of both our lives, our daughter."

He hugged Matti to him. "Before Awakening Day, all I wanted to do was to raise Matti and help my hometown. Now, the world has quite literally changed, and it's changed us with it. On Awakening Day, we lost far too many of our friends and loved ones. At first, we weren't sure how many we lost. We had no way to know who was in town, who was visiting, or just passing through. As of today, though, more numbers have come in, and those numbers tell us something. Some of us called the deaths a culling. That whoever abducted us and put us here was making a point, telling us how truly powerless we are – that they put us here, and they can take us back out again. As of today, the numbers tell us that the dead... our dead... number not approximately, not close to, but * exactly * five percent."

145

The only sound in the stadium was that of the wind and a few birds. Beyond the barrier mountains were flashes of lightning and a dark, ominous rising storm.

"I only learned this information as I was on my way here. Honestly, it has left me rather stunned and numb. I believe our abductors wanted to make it crystal clear. They picked a number and simply exterminated a clean five percent of the civilian population. To. Make. A. Point. Whoever they are and whatever their reasons were for doing this, it is clear to me that we were both important enough to go to all this trouble for and important enough for them to think it was necessary to do the culling. They want our attention."

He paused and looked across the sea of faces, "Well, they've got it. And now, Dr. Talib tells us that our abductors tell us that they aren't the real enemy. Maybe that's true. Maybe they really saved us, and we'd all be dead, otherwise. Maybe they think we're too stubborn to work with and that the culling was necessary for us to take them seriously. I don't know. What I do know is that they wiped out so many of our friends, or fathers, mothers, brothers, and sisters, like they were so many garden pests. They went to a lot of trouble to put us here, so they spanked us to keep us from screwing things up. They want us here for a reason. They want us to do something. I think they want to use us against this 'other' enemy they talk about."

He turned to Gail, and she nodded agreement. He continued, "I'm making a vow, here and now. We *will* protect and raise our children. We *will* find out what really happened. We *will* make them pay. And our abductors? One day, somehow, someway, there *will* be a reckoning!"

The audience stood in ovation, and the roar of approval and thirst for vengeance could be heard by every surviving living human being.

Break, Break...

Highway
Day 4: 9:22 AM

Ahead of them, on the highway, the burning wreckage of the Humvee billowed black smoke. The dark, six-legged creature disappeared into the high grass of the vast prairie that curved upwards in the New Texas sky. After slamming into the beast, the 18-wheeler was rolling slowly forward down the two-lane road.

Wayne and Sybil exchanged worried glances at each other, then back out the window while Sybil reloaded the rifle. She swallowed, looking at the Humvee, gauging their likelihood of driving around it, "I think we can make it around the wreckage. We're closer to the checkpoint than we are to Fort Brazos."

Wayne stared at the road ahead and squinted, "I can make it around it, and I'm more worried about getting stuck if we try to turn around, anyway." He looked at her again and reached over and clenched her shoulder.

She looked into his eyes and nodded sharply. "Do it!"

Wayne pulled the air horn again for a long blast, then gunned the engine and threw the truck into gear, closing the gap between them and the Humvee quickly. There was just enough room to swerve around the now roaring flames without losing control. The deep-throated crackle and heat of the fire flashed through the truck cabin as they raced past.

They both worriedly watched the rear-view monitor, but the creature had vanished.

Wayne smiled crookedly, "You did great, sweetie. You saved my life. If you hadn't shot at that thing, I'd have been a goner."

Sybil smiled shyly, "Good thing it was you out there. I'm a better shot."

Wayne choked back a retort, then thought better of it, "Yes, yes babe, you are."

The tension dragged out for two full minutes as they both tried to cope with what had happened. Wayne took a deep breath, "Did you get through to the checkpoint? What did they say?"

She shook her head, "No, I think we're out of range, and there was some weird shrieking static on the CB... hurt my ears. I had to turn the squelch way up."

"Okay, keep trying. Someone might hear you, even if we can't hear them."

Sybil safed the rifle and set it aside before reaching for her water bottle and taking a long swallow. She picked up the CB handset, took a deep breath, and started, "Break, break…."

Ambushed

Fort Brazos HS Stadium
Day 4: 9:36 AM

Thunderous applause still shook the stadium as John and Gail did their best to come to grips with being suddenly 'volunteered' to run for President and Vice President. Behind them, General Marcus, the City Council, and Mayor stood in solidarity. Captain Guevara and Hector Alonzo stood at the wings of the stage.

The expressions on Gail and John's faces were admirably composed. However, Marcus thought to himself, there was still quite a bit of a 'deer in the headlights' look in their eyes.

John had spoken for a while and then yielded the podium to Gail. She had lurched forward on her crutches, and John had adjusted the microphone for her. The people were still staggering under the crushing weight of their dead loved ones. Waking up inside an artificial alien world didn't help. Her near-immolation and bravery in avoiding crashing into the high school had made her more than just popular. Her selfless example shone a bright and shining hope on an unknown future. The ovation was already standing before she said a word.

Gail had thought she could handle or deal with anything that came her way in life. She was young, strong, and driven. She hadn't even told anyone about the letter in her breast pocket, the one confirming her acceptance into the elite Air Force Thunderbirds. She'd received it the day before Awakening Day.

Now, standing there in front of thousands, she barely felt the throbbing pain in her shattered leg, but a new emotion gnawed a hole in her stomach. It startled her. It was not fear of physical danger, rather, a more generalized fear of… fate. She knew other emotions very well – anger, pride, the joy of flying that she truly lived for, rage, wonder, and, oh how she knew ambition.

But this…. She'd planned out her whole life and knew what she'd wanted since she was a young girl. Everything she had done in her life had been done to execute that plan, and she'd been right on track. She'd known, *known* she'd be a Thunderbird since the first airshow her dad had taken her to. Dad had filmed her leaps of joy as the ironbound formation had ripped through the sky overhead. She'd made it! She'd earned it. She'd always known she would and that she'd go on to become the youngest or one of the youngest woman Air Force generals on record.

She'd had a plan.

Now, she found herself leaning against a podium in a high school football stadium, with glaring bright lights nearly blinding her, in some sort of alien apocalypse, with thousands of people applauding her, wanting her to be, what? Vice President of perhaps all of what remained of humanity?

She looked back at General Marcus and read the many levels of his expression. He seemed confident in her and perhaps even proud. She also saw in his eyes that he was… amused and something else that caused her to flash in anger. She knew he'd never admit it, but he was glad it was her at the podium and not himself.

She mouthed, 'I'll get you for this… Sir.'

He nodded knowingly back at her.

She turned back to face the crowd, and the applause subsided. She took a breath and forced herself to smile.

"This is not what I had planned for…," She shook her head, "It's not… It's not what I…."

Many laughed softly, allowing her time to compose herself.

She took a deep breath, "Look. I know that none of us had planned for any of these recent events to happen. As I was standing here just now, I was thinking about how I'd had my life all planned out." She unconsciously patted the letter in her pocket. "All I've ever wanted to do was fly." She swallowed, "… and I'm sure that many of you had your own plans for your lives and for your loved ones."

Silence sighed over the crowd. "Until now, I admit that I have been burying myself in my work and not truly facing all that has happened to us. Our destiny has been unalterably changed. We must either come to accept this or reject the mantle of our new burden."

She paused and looked across the sea of faces. She took another deep breath, and her eyes misted, "We can't. We simply cannot turn back. We are in the new world, and our ships have burned and sunk behind us. We have our fate, our future, and I thank God you all, all of you, are here. We are not alone. We will face this together."

The enthusiastic applause was swift and strong. A few scattered people stood, then more quickly followed until all joined the ovation.

She waited for it to wane, "I have but one request of you." She paused, gathering their attention, "As I said, this is not what I planned. I just wanted to fly. I'm sure your Sheriff would say something similar." She glanced at him, and he nodded gravely. "So, if you are all willing to draft Sheriff Austin and me to do this, to drag us out of our lives and throw us into new ones, then you must promise us something in return." A few soft chuckles sighed into the pregnant silence that followed.

"If you can ask us to do this, then you must also ask each other to be open to what is to come for all of us. All our lives have changed and will be changing in ways we cannot yet imagine. If you can ask us to do this, then we can ask you to be brave and accept and perhaps even embrace the changes that will come for each of you. I suspect that a great many of us shall soon be called upon to reach beyond ourselves and seize our collective new destiny."

It took a moment for the thought to sink in. Then, this time, the crowd rose almost as one, nodding, applauding, some with tears streaming down their faces.

A slender young dark-skinned Corporal walked briskly up onto the stage behind the council and stopped beside Captain Guevara. The young man's face was a mask as he saluted. He spoke into Captain Guevara's ear. Guevara grimaced, nodded, and reached for his cellphone. He studied the screen, swallowed, and returned the salute, and nodded to the Corporal to leave, who disappeared as quickly as he could without actually running.

151

Guevara stepped over to Marcus, tapped his shoulder, and spoke into his ear, trying to be heard over the crowd.

Marcus managed to keep a stoic face, turned to look Guevara in the eye, and reached for his own phone. Just then, the crowd noise spiked in response to something Gail said. Marcus read the Flash Priority Message on his screen:

FROM: FOB ONE - CHECKPOINT WEST
TO: COMMAND FORT BRAZOS
CLASSIFICATION: OPSEC ALPHA
PRIORITY: TOP
LOCATION: APPROX. 20 MILES EAST OF FOB ONE
WEST
ENEMY STRENGTH: ONE (1) CREATURE REPORTED, SIX-LEGGED. NO APPARENT TECHNOLOGY
SUBJECT: NEW SIGHTING, QRF DEPLOYED
NEW SIGHTING REPORTED BY CIVILIAN TRANSPORT. ATTACK ON SINGLE HUMVEE ON HIGHWAY. OCCUPANTS ALL KIA. NO CIVILIAN CASUALTIES. ENEMY WITNESSED BY CIVILIANS AND REPORTED AS NEW UNKNOWN TYPE. QUICK REACTION FORCE DEPLOYED PER COMMAND FORT BRAZOS STANDING ORDER. QRF REPORT TO FOLLOW AS AVAILABLE. END MESSAGE

Marcus took a deep breath and put his phone away. He reached over and tapped Tom on the shoulder, then pulled him aside, cupping his hand over Tom's ear and gave him the news. Tom looked up at him, swallowed, and motioned for the rest of the council to join them in a huddle.

Their expressions grave, they stepped back to the middle of the stage behind John and Gail. Tom stepped forward and put his hand on Gail's shoulder, gesturing to use the podium.

Many in the crowd had noticed the drama unfolding on the stage, and their murmuring had quickly spread. When their Mayor stepped to the podium, a hush fell over the stadium.

Tom smiled sadly and took a deep breath. "Citizens of Fort Brazos. My friends. It is my duty to report to you that there has been another attack."

The crowd erupted in shouts and cries and an equal number of people calling for silence, so they could hear what came next. Tom waited patiently for calm. It did not take long.

"What we have been told is that a military vehicle was attacked by a single alien creature, about thirty miles west of town and that there are reports of military casualties. There are no reports of civilian casualties at this time. Moments ago, a military force was dispatched to the scene. However, it is too soon for us to know anything more. There are no reports of attacks or sightings anywhere else, and we do not believe there is any immediate danger here in the city. That said, out of an abundance of caution, we are going to ask that you all calmly and carefully go home. Look after your families and your neighbors. We'll notify you as soon as we know more."

It Heard Me

The Marine V-22 had been the fastest available ride from the stadium out to Forward Operating Base One, at the northern end of the highway, which was a beehive of activity. Marcus and Guevara exited the ramp. Gail had been left to deal with the Council and begin to face her fate in the impending election.

On the trip over, they had circled the scene of the attack a few times. Air and ground units had scoured the area but found no sign of the creature that had attacked the Humvee, but it was clear from the empty brass scattered around the smoldering remains of the vehicle that the men had at least tried to fight back. The search continued, but there was nothing Marcus could add, and, truth be told, he really should not, personally, be in the hot zone. Four men he'd never met had died there – Lieutenant Marshall Sherrard, Sargent Nelson Black, and specialists Delon Smith and Keanu Campbell.

They had landed near what was being affectionately called the 'Truck Stop.' A growing tangle of civilian and military vehicles was being processed, primarily for unloading. The FOB was surrounded by an outer ring of double-stacked K-rails and a quickly growing set of walls and guard towers. The highway had been turned into a makeshift runway. It was temporarily surrounded by cyclone fencing until more permanent walls could be built. Light armored vehicles patrolled inside and outside the camp, and a platoon of M1A2 Abrams tanks was emplaced at strategic locations around the perimeter.

Nearby, a collection of double-wide trailer homes had been set up for housing and office space. A prefabricated steel building was half-constructed and appeared to be intended as warehouse space to house the growing pile of building materials, equipment, and general stores.

Standing next to one of the 18-wheel civilian trucks was a large, beefy man and a short busty woman with somewhat wild curly hair. A corporal took pictures of the truck, especially the front grill, which had taken some damage.

Marcus and Guevara trotted over to Wayne and Sybil. The corporal's eyes widened at the sight of such lofty rank, quickly stiffened and saluted. Marcus wasn't 'just' a general anymore. He was now the highest-ranking military officer in the entire world. The moment the salute was returned, the young man escaped as quickly as decorum would allow. Sybil seemed pensive and worried, and Wayne stiffened, but Marcus could see how he had repressed a salute. Wayne was a large man with flowing long hair, but he would always have 'military' stamped on his bearing.

Marcus sized him up and liked what he saw. He extended his hand, and Wayne shook it firmly in his large, calloused hand. Marcus nodded in greeting, "Hello, I'm General Marcus, and you are?"

Wayne was tired, but he had never been intimidated by rank, even when he'd been in uniform. He respected it, but life was too… busy to worry about who had more flashes on their shoulder… or stars. "I'm Wayne Blanchard, and this is my wife and protector, Sybil."

Marcus raised his eyebrows, smiled, and took Sybil's hand. "Glad to meet you, Mrs. Blanchard. May I call you Sybil?"

Sybil had been listening but seemed to be elsewhere at the same time. She blinked Marcus into full focus. "Yes, of course, General, please do." She paused for a moment, making an inner decision. She smiled, "Oh, and General, I believe you have two darling girls, Faith and Hope? How are they, and your wife, Alisha, coping with their dad suddenly becoming so important?"

Marcus's eyebrows twitched ever so slightly, then he grinned widely, "Well, Sybil, for some reason, they don't seem to react with the same fear and dread and requisite reverence that I've come to expect from others, but I suppose I'll manage."

Sybil flashed a brilliant smile, "Someone has to remind you of those feet of clay, oh august General."

Marcus laughed aloud, "Well, I suppose I'll have to temper my Nebuchadnezzar-like aspirations."

Guevara looked at Wayne questioningly, but Wayne shrugged and waited.

Marcus smiled again and then stepped closer to the truck to examine the grill. The damage was significant. A large, dented area looked as though they had collided with a rock or boulder. "I'm glad that you two made it out unharmed, and I'll see to it that your truck is repaired. In fact, I think I'll have them pull the whole grill off and see if the scientists over at the university can learn anything from it. That said, as I'm sure you can guess, I need to hear from you, firsthand, everything you can tell me about what happened."

Sybil reached over and touched Marcus on the arm, "General, I'm… I'm so sorry about your men. Maybe if we'd gotten there sooner…."

Marcus took a deep breath, "Sybil, you stop right there. My men were not your responsibility. They were mine. This was my mistake. I should have ensured that all traffic out to this FOB was protected by armed convoys, including you and your truck. Their deaths are on me. I will not make the same mistake again. All future transports will be in armed convoys."

Sybil nodded slowly. Wayne looked at Marcus and upgraded his opinion of him.

Captain Guevara kept his face a mask but stood straighter, willing his solidarity to a man he'd only known a short while, but who seemed to be evolving before his eyes into a larger figure.

Wayne swallowed, "Well, General, there's not really a lot to tell. We were making our way down the highway when we saw the Humvee turned sideways on the road, with smoke coming out of it. All we could see was the good side. We stopped a ways back, in case there was something volatile in the vehicle, and I got out to see if there was anyone I could help."

He paused, looking down at his feet for a moment, "There was nothing, I mean, nothing I could do. Those men had been torn to pieces by that thing. It had ripped apart the Humvee like it was tissue paper. I think it had not heard us pull up because of the fire, but all of a sudden, it looked up from what it was... doing, and it saw me."

Marcus nodded, letting Wayne tell the story without interruption.

Wayne stared into the distance, "It was big. It was black and had red spots, and it was armored. It was like a cross between a dinosaur of some kind, a rhinoceros, and... a hellhound. I think it was, like, really, really heavy. When it started chasing me, I could hear how hard it crunched the pavement as it ran. Oh, and it has six legs and a mouth full of triangular teeth, kind of like shark's teeth."

He paused, reliving the moment. "I ran back to the truck, but I wasn't going to make it. It was about to catch me when my savior, here," he pulled Sybil close and hugged her to his side, "shot it with her .308."

Marcus cocked his head and looked at Sybil, "You wounded it?"

Wayne and Sybil chorused, "Oh no, not at all!" Wayne continued, "The bullets bounced off it, but they startled it. It gave me enough time to get back to the truck."

Marcus smiled approvingly at Sybil.

She shrugged, "I was shooting 150-grain boat tail hunting rounds. They just left a smear on that thing's armor. Maybe if we had, like, tungsten sabot penetrator rounds, they'd do some real damage."

Marcus looked at Guevara, who nodded thoughtfully, "I'll add that to the list, Sir."

Marcus smiled, "Thank you, Sybil, and not just for the information. Thank you for keeping your head out there. Both of you." He stepped closer to the front of the truck and examined the damaged grill, "I take it, that's when this happened?"

Wayne swallowed. "I got back in the truck, and Sybil emptied a 20-round magazine into the thing. Just made it mad. I gunned the truck and rammed it. It, like, it just bounced off us, got up, and left. It didn't run away, not like it had chased me – I think it just got tired of playing with us and left."

Marcus nodded again, "Any other thoughts?"

Wayne looked at Sybil and back to Marcus again, "Yes, Sir, Sybil and I were talking about this earlier. We couldn't reach anyone on the radio. We were too far from the city and too far from the FOB. There's no cellular coverage out there either. Vehicles should have long-range communications gear, in case of emergency."

Marcus thought for a moment, "Thank you. Someone had mentioned putting up expeditionary relay towers along the road. We'll make sure that gets done ASAP. Also, thank you for your patience and for filling me in. Now, I have a couple of questions."

Wayne and Sybil nodded.

"First, you said the Humvee was on fire, and yet the creature was still... attacking the occupants. How did it react to the fire?"

Wayne blinked in surprise, "You're right. I hadn't thought of that. That thing was right up there, with its head inside the vehicle. There was flame and smoke there, and it didn't seem to care. Any animal I know of would have avoided the fire."

Marcus pursed his lips, "Well, it sounds like it is not from our neck of the woods, for sure. Let me ask another question. You said it looked up, suddenly. Any idea what made it sense you were there?"

Sybil smiled shyly, reached into her jeans, and handed a memory stick to Marcus, "No, but maybe you can tell something from the dashcam video."

Marcus's eyes widened, "You have video?"

Minutes later, they were all looking at the dashcam video on a flat-screen inside one of the double-wide trailers. At first, all you could see was the burning vehicle on the road ahead. You could hear Wayne and Sybil discussing it and the sound of Wayne leaving the truck cabin. Moments later, Wayne entered the frame of the video and worked his way around the side of the wrecked Humvee. Off-screen, Sybil could then be heard calling 'Break Break' on the CB. There was movement on the far side of the Humvee, and moments later, Wayne could be seen running back towards the truck. Sybil could be heard cursing, and there was the sound of scrapes and other noises from the truck cabin as the massive black creature slid around the corner, chasing after Wayne. The crack of Sybil's rifle was sharp and loud, and actual sparks seemed to fly when the .308 rounds struck the creature's frontal armor. The video played out, showing the truck ram the alien creature, followed by the sight of it trotting off into the tall grass.

Marcus rubbed his chin. "Rewind it to when Wayne went around the corner of the Humvee."

A Corporal dragged the progress bar backward and then clicked play. The video played again until the point at which movement could be seen on the far side of the Humvee.

Marcus held up his hand, "Stop. Rewind to when Sybil starts talking on the radio."

The Corporal complied, and the scene repeated.

"Stop – right there. Zoom in on that movement."

The picture enlarged, and the backside of the creature could now be seen. Its hide was dark and roughly textured, so at a distance, it had not been immediately apparent what it was. Then, just as Sybil's voice could be heard speaking on the radio, in the enlarged image, the head of the creature popped into view, staring directly at the cab of the truck. At Sybil. Then its head swiveled to the side, where Wayne had been approaching.

It was very quiet in the trailer for a long moment. Then, Sybil swallowed hard. "It * heard * me." Wayne put his arm around her.

Marcus frowned. "It's just possible it did. However, you were a distance away inside the cab of your truck. It did not initially react to Wayne approaching it. Instead, it reacted when you started broadcasting on your radio. The thing is alien... maybe it can hear radio waves?"

New Arrivals

Ninety minutes later, at the Reserve Base's main conference room, Marcus had settled into another string of meetings. He'd been briefed on the latest long-range reconnaissance flights and their inherent logistical challenges since there were no other bases or landing strips anywhere in the world to land at. They'd stripped a KC-135 refueling tanker down to the bone to maximize its range. However, they were taking it in stages. The grand total of three KC-135's at the base were the *only* KC-135's. Period. They simply could not afford to lose one now.

The conference call with Dr. Nakamura and the City Council had taken another hour and a half to convey the changes in the sun-tube. Marcus could see that there was going to be a problem with the man. Dr. Nakamura was clearly brilliant, but the man simply could not be hurried.

After another half dozen briefings, Marcus had ordered a short break. He'd retreated to his office, eschewing visitors and using the time to organize his thoughts.

The next meeting would be about the elephant in the room that he had ordered the entire base to keep quiet about. In the chaotic hours after Awakening Day, it was soon apparent that there were no casualties among the military and dependents. Of course, they had not been aware of the shattering death toll among the civilians at the time.

Unbeknownst to anyone outside of the Joint Reserve base, there had very nearly been a high death count amongst the military, but for very different reasons. The Fort Brazos Joint Reserve base had an area of 178,203 acres. The main cantonment at the base had a total population of 34,712 active, reserve, civilian contractors and support staff, and dependents.

On Awakening Day, an additional 12,825 military personnel had awakened to find that they had been abducted from their home military bases, from around the Earth, and deposited inside the confines of the Fort Brazos Joint Reserve Base.

These "New Arrivals" had been taken from the militaries of around twenty other countries. In the confusion that followed, shots had been fired, but, miraculously, there were no serious casualties. The New Arrivals had been deposited in remote areas of the base, which reduced their immediate interactions with the indigenous Joint Reserve Base personnel, or each other, as many were mortal enemies of the other.

The situation had been confusing and chaotic, and it was some time before he had begun to accept that the New Arrivals hadn't actually been invaders. Marcus admitted to himself that this had contributed to his initial lack of focus on events taking place outside the base. He'd ordered a complete lockdown, which had also resulted in warning shots being fired at approaching Sheriff's deputies, who'd been dispatched to check on the base and request assistance.

Now, he'd returned for an update on the status of the New Arrivals. He had already met with their individual commanders to get a feel for them and whether he thought any were going to be problems. Some of them were definitely in the 'Problem' category.

A census had been taken by now, and his staff had a reasonably high confidence level regarding each person's identity. That was because they had discovered that fully translated personnel files for each and every New Arrival had been conveniently placed in a flagged electronic folder in the base's computer system. In fact, there was a vast database of records from each of the New Arrival's home military. It would take years to comb through it all.

They'd managed to repurpose existing buildings and set up temporary quarters for everyone using expeditionary supplies. Everyone was now fed and sheltered, and all but the most trusted were disarmed. Still, some of the more suspect forces had been organized in more isolated areas, with firm but polite MP's looking out for their… security.

He was still the most senior NATO and allied country officer, but it was unclear if officers and men from non-American forces would accept his authority. He was confident that many, especially from countries that had conscripted their soldiers, would want to leave military service entirely. For that matter, given all that had happened, he knew that many of his own men and women wanted to leave.

No one knew why they'd been brought here or what dangers they would face, so could he afford even to consider letting anyone go?

Would it be possible to integrate some of them into a new "Fort Brazos Military?" Who would they swear allegiance to since all of their home countries were gone? Should he disband them and only accept the crème of the willing crop? How would their ranks be integrated, and who was senior to whom?

As he sat back down in the conference room, he eyed the senior officers from most of the New Arrival contingents. Not all had arrived with their dress uniforms, but each had done their best to be presentable in what they had or could borrow. Aside from Americans, the assembled officers represented, in alphabetical order, Australia, Brazil, China, Columbia, Egypt, France, Germany, India, Iran, Israel, Japan, North Korea, Pakistan, Russia, Saudi Arabia, South Korea, Turkey, UK, and Ukraine.

The numbers of troops from each military service varied but were very nearly all frontline or even elite forces, with no support or administrative personnel.

A few, like the North Koreans, were outright belligerent and, despite the evidence of the 'sky' above them, were utterly unconvinced that this was not all some Machiavellian plot by the evil Americans dogs.

Marcus's face was impassive, but he sighed inwardly and thought to himself, "There's going to be hell to pay for this from the City Council when they find out I've been keeping this secret."

Not What We Seem

Temporary Morgue
Day 5: 10:00 AM

A fter the stadium rally and the hour and a half long teleconference with Dr. Nakamura and General Marcus, and the City Council members, Gail and John had met for several more hours into the night. Gail ended up sleeping on the oversized leather couch in Mayor Parker's office. She pretended not to notice the three Marine guards that now followed her everywhere she went.

John had scooped up a sleeping Matti and taken her home. Like Gail, he'd tried to ignore the marines he himself had acquired, but his deputies had not. Sheriff's Captain Robert Morales and Chief Deputy Hector Alonzo had organized their own security detail for John, including Deputies Thomas Morgan and Caesar Willis. Hector and Robert alternated shifts, as did the deputies. They'd made it clear to the Marines who they thought was in charge of 'their person.' The Marines were polite but unmoved.

The first meeting of the day had not taken place at City Hall, but instead, at one of the central distribution center warehouses that had been "enlarged" by their abductors. Gloria had seen to it that Gail had a fresh uniform and had her personal beautician stop by to make sure that Gail "was presentable." Today, there were camera crews from the three local news stations following them around. Gloria had been more than a little jealous that Gail had needed very little help from the beautician.

They had toured the vast warehouse and posed and asked questions in a live broadcast. After that, they'd stopped at Ray's Diner for a late breakfast/lunch.

The camera crews stayed outside but filmed them through the windows. The proprietor, Ray, was excited to have them there. The fact that half of them were years-long customers who already ate there several times a week was almost forgotten. Now, these people were leaders of the *World*. Ray's wife, Josephine, fawned over Gail, in particular. Their son Ray Jr. "would have been" at the high school (had it not been closed due to the emergency of Awakening Day), and did Gail know that Ray Jr. had been Texas All-State? She was convinced that Gail had saved his life and that Gail would never, ever, pay for her meals at Ray's Diner!

The seating was cramped, the linoleum was worn, but everything was (as always) spotless. The small tables in the diner had been pushed together, and the council sat facing each other across the picked-over debris of their meals. For most of the meal, they'd talked in small groups to the people closest to them across the table. All of them were pensive.

Tom tapped his water glass with a spoon. The side conversations died away. Everyone knew what was next. "Ladies and gentlemen, I'm afraid it is time."

✪ ✪ ✪

Other than Gail, all had been to the temporary morgue before, some of them, many times. The facility had been an empty warehouse with a refrigeration section. They'd called up all the HVAC people in town, fixed the refrigeration units, and added portable chillers when there was no more room in the refrigerated section. Now, the 50,000 square foot building teamed with workers wearing coats, carrying clipboards and tablet computers.

The camera crews had followed them to the warehouse, but the security details blocked the doors and herded them to a staging area where the Council and Presidential candidates would later hold a press conference.

The sheer number of Awakening Day dead had overwhelmed everyone. There were not remotely enough body bags or ambulances, or hearses. The bodies had been organized, then re-organized and re-organized again as the continuous stream of personal cars, trucks, and vans had arrived, with grieving family members, neighbors, or friends carrying the bodies. The "receiving" area had been set up so that all the other bodies were not in sight.

Commander (Dr.) Gwyneth Elliot had been 'drafted' to manage the morgue and the post-mortem examinations and investigations being conducted. She'd been dividing her time between duties at the Joint Reserve Base hospital, the quarantine at Methodist Hospital, and the morgue. She looked younger than her 39 years. Decades of biathlons helped, but today her shoulder-length red hair was pulled back, and her face was lined with worry.

After the brief tour, the group met in a small office area conference room attached to the central warehouse.

After everyone had sat down, Tom began, "Doctor, please tell us what you have learned."

Gwyneth hesitated, picking up one of the water bottles clumped in the middle of the table. "First is what I hope is good news. As you know, there were only a small number of children among the Awakening Day dead. What you don't know is that there were no children left without a parent – there were no orphans. Furthermore, all of the children who did… die… had something in common. All of them had serious life-shortening genetic disorders or defects. Some of them, we found, had not been aware of the problem."

Tom leaned forward, "So, our abductors were kind enough not to make any children orphans, but they didn't mind culling five percent of us or eliminating genetically… inferior children?"

Gloria sat back in her chair. "We're like… flowers to them. They're like, gardeners, weeding out what they don't like."

Gwyneth took a drink of water. "That's not all. There is a commonality with all the bodies we've examined so far. After we had noticed that decomposition was slower than expected, we took a harder look. What we've found is that all of the bodies have no living biome of any kind within them. The only conclusion I can draw is that…" she looked down at the table, twirling the water in the bottle. "This is going to sound crazy. These people, all of them, did not die on Awakening Day."

"What?!"

"What do you mean, they didn't die?"

"Of course they did! Thousands died that day!"

"Who does she think she is?!"

Tom slapped his palm down on the table, "Enough! That's enough, everyone. Let her finish." It took several seconds, but eventually, everyone quieted down.

Gwyneth took another drink of water. She sighed, "After I tell you, we're going to want something stronger than water."

The anger and hostility vanished as everyone saw the seriousness on her face.

Tom interjected, "Everyone – we're all in pain over the friends and loved ones we lost. Don't take that out on the doctor. She has what may be the worst job imaginable right now, and she deserves our support and respect."

Councilman Hickum nodded, "Here here."

Gail reached out and put her hand on Gwyneth's. "Tell us."

Gwyneth looked up, and there were tears in her eyes. "What I'm trying to tell you is that all those people did not die on Awakening Day. Those bodies have never, ever, been alive."

Blank stares answered her.

She added, "Look, inside our bodies are lots and lots of bacteria. There are over 500 species of them. Bacteria are much smaller than our cells. In fact, there are ten times as many bacteria inside our bodies as we have cells. What I'm telling you is that none, as in zero, of those bacteria, are alive inside the Awakening Day dead. They were not killed, and there is no cell damage. They are all intact. They're just not… alive. It is as though they were created to exactly copy what was there, but there was never a… spark of life."

John cocked his head, "You mean the bodies are, like, copies?"

Gwyneth turned and stared at him. "No, Sheriff. I mean that those bodies? All those bodies? They're like us. We are all… copies. The ones out there were just never… turned on."

Pandemonium and despair broke out around the table.

Gail and John blinked almost as one and turned to each other, "Of course."

They looked at Gwyneth and saw that she'd already reached the same conclusion.

Gloria spoke out over the noise, "Doctor, tell us, how do you know? How can you know this?"

Gwyneth nodded, "Every organism constantly consumes and burns chemical energy and creates waste products. It is a continuous cycle. There are no waste products in their bodies. They were never alive. Also, we looked at their DNA and their chromosomes. The telomeres were... new. Over time, as we age, our telomeres, well, the short version is that each time a cell divides, the telomeres get shorter. All of the samples we have tested are the same. They've never been alive.

Gail swallowed, "You tested survivors, didn't you?"

"Yes. Starting with myself."

"And you found the same thing."

Tears fell down Gwyneth's cheeks, "Yes, in every person and animal we've tested. ALL OF US... all of us are copies. We were all awakened that day, brought to life, but those out there," she nodded towards the morgue area, "Those bodies were never alive."

John and Gail looked at each other. She stood, bumping the table with her cast, "Don't you all see it? It all fits. The duplicated land we see outside, copied and pasted. The warehouse we saw this morning altered and expanded as if it had always been that way. This whole world was *manufactured*. Our abductors.... Somehow, they scanned and Xeroxed us and put us all here."

Gloria broke the dead silence that had followed, "After all that we've been through, I just don't know how people will react to this. It could tear us apart. Doctor, who knows about this?"

Gwyneth looked around the table, "I did the tests back at the base, and it was compartmentalized, so only a handful of people have any part of the picture. However, sooner or later, someone else will figure this out. It will come out."

Three and a half hours later, the Council, Mayor, John, and Gail stood outside at the news conference site. Dr. Elliot had not joined them. The security details positioned themselves a discrete distance from them. While they'd been inside, rain from the hurricane, which, to everyone's relief, had broken up on the other side of the barrier mountains, had soaked the area. They stood under a large gazebo in a popular park. The rain had slowed to a drizzle, and the outside light was fading. Lights had been erected inside the gazebo.

Tom stepped up to the portable podium. His wife Dotty had picked out his dark grey 'funeral' suit and matching tie for him to wear that day. The edges of his grey hair fluttered in the wind.

He looked into the cameras, "As most of you know, we have more dead than there is cemetery space for. Some have suggested a mass grave. However, the Council has decided that a new National Cemetery will be constructed to honor and commemorate the friends and loved ones we lost on that terrible day. We will ask for proposals for the design of a monument, and we will hold a public vote to choose the most appropriate one. "

"If you already have a family plot and wish to bury your loved one there or to have them cremated, you may do so. Every person who died that day will have a plot permanently assigned, with some form of remembrance marking. If a family decides to inter their loved one somewhere else, and later decides to have them moved to the National Cemetery, their place will be permanently reserved."

"We understand the frustration that some of you have expressed about the decision to hold all the remains here at the temporary morgue. Because of all that happened, we needed to make sure that everything possible would be done to understand what happened to us and how."

"As of tomorrow, any family that wishes to retrieve the remains of their loved one for burial or cremation elsewhere may begin to do so. Until the new National Cemetery is ready, each of you may make arrangements for what ceremonies or visitations you wish to make. We will do whatever we can to help and be respectful to you and to your friends, and loved ones remains."

"General Marcus has already assigned security to the facility, and I'm told an honor guard will be formed, much like that at Arlington National Cemetery, back... back home on Earth."

"In the meantime, the doctors here will be conferring with our scientists at the University to try to make sense of all the information they have gathered. Thank you."

So Shall It Be

Council Chambers
Day 5: 6:00 PM

I
t was still raining by the time they arrived at the Council Chambers. The Council and Mayor did not take their places on the elevated platform. They randomly slumped into the seats in the audience area. Councilman Dale Hubbard and Councilwoman Esmerelda Collins lay down, sprawled across several seats.

For almost twenty minutes, no one spoke. All were emotionally drained and exhausted. Then, the silence was broken with a knock at the big double doors, and Chief Deputy Hector Alonzo and Deputies Willis and Thomas arrived with a large assortment of Chinese food, pizza, hamburgers, and drinks. They stayed long enough to help sort out who got what and then retreated out the doors.

The mood was somber and appetites mechanical.

Tom took a single bite of his burger, chewed for a moment, then asked aloud, "So, are we real people or just lab rats? Are the real versions of ourselves still alive back home?"

Gail held chopsticks and a to-go carton of Pad Thai in her hands but didn't eat. "Whoever has done this to us is so much more advanced than us that I cannot believe that they would go to all this trouble just to test us like lab rats. They already know more about us and our biology and everything else than we do ourselves. I believe they intend to use us to fight the enemy that they referred to in that audio that professor played to us."

170

Councilman Hickum leaned forward, "If they're so damned powerful, what do they need us for?"

John shook his head, "That message said that it was the sound of the enemy who destroyed our world. If, and I mean if, that is true, and assuming that our real enemies aren't manipulating us, then we have no home to return to, and they think we will be motivated to fight this other group. Remember, they didn't kill any of the military on Awakening Day."

Gloria snorted, "Right. They want us to fight some other alien race that has supposedly destroyed our world. They want us to fight them, how? With what? The sheriff's pistol? The General's tanks? Even back on earth, we could barely get to the moon!"

Tom sighed, "But... are we real? Do we have souls?"

Gail lifted a bit of food with the chopsticks and sniffed it but put it back down. "We have no way of knowing how our abductors actually did it. However, some theories I've read about the possibility of teleportation required that the original... object being teleported must be destroyed in the process, and all the quantum information about the original is transmitted to the other location. That information is used to re-create that object at the other end. As for whether we are real... I know that I feel real to myself. I can remember all my life back to when I was three. I have my memories, and I feel like myself. As far as our souls go, if we have them, I would prefer to think that we would somehow know if they were gone."

Esmerelda Collins hadn't touched any of the food. Her family had been among the original settlers in Fort Brazos, and they had a substantial dairy and cattle business. She sat up and joined in, "There's been quite a bit of talk in the cattle genetics industry about cloning. If I remember, one of the problems with that first cloned sheep was that its telomeres had remained the same length as the adult, so the clone's cells thought they were old, and it died at an abnormally young age. Its offspring, however, were normal. Telomeres are bits of DNA that protect the ends of your chromosomes. Normally they shorten as cells divide — so the older you get, the shorter the telomeres."

"So, if we are clones, whoever did this managed to recreate us at our current ages and with all our memories intact. I should point out that giving us lengthened telomeres might mean they want us to live longer."

Gloria's eyes widened at a thought, "If we've been copied, or even if we haven't been, how much time has gone by back home on Earth?"

Tom slumped back in his chair. "I promised, I insisted that we would not hold anything back from the people."

John shook his head, "No, Tom, it was the right call. We really don't know what this means. Dr. Elliot seems like a very competent woman, but she could be wrong. There could be different explanations for the things she discovered. This knowledge isn't something that impacts public safety. It doesn't really tell us anything about why this has happened to us. Going public now, so soon after our friends and loved ones died, could be crippling. We owe it to the people not to go off half-cocked about this. We need to have Dr. Nakamura's scientists study this very carefully. By the time he does come to any conclusions, we'll have had a lot more time to think about what it means and how to tell the public."

Tom's eyes were haunted, but he gave a thin smile. "I think we should invite the spiritual leaders from the different faiths together for meetings to quietly discuss the deeper meanings behind all that has happened to us. We should get their input, first, on how to talk about all this. I wish Pastor Joe were here."

Gloria surprised everyone by reaching over and putting her hand on Tom's shoulder. "He was a good man, Tom. It's not your fault, and you know he'd tell you that if he was here. I imagine his choice of words would have been… colorful."

Tom nodded and patted her hand back. "Okay, everyone, let's change the subject. We need to talk about the election, and we need to propose a new governmental structure. There'll be no Mayflower Compact here. We all know how much of a total disaster that was and how badly that worked for them. I believe we need a system that will be similar to what our people are used to."

Councilman Hubbard chimed in, "We already have voting districts for the Council members."

Gail adjusted her position and her cast, "I know this is self-serving, but what about the base? We're still organizing and counting, but there may be more… ah, more people and dependents there than we'd thought. Those people now represent a large percentage of our overall total population. They need to feel that their votes count."

Tom nibbled his now-cold hamburger, "Oh, I completely agree, and that was my intention. I'm worried about what would happen if we create a parliamentary division between the city and the base. I think it would ultimately nurture an 'us versus them' attitude. I think we'd be better off in the long run by establishing separate voting zones or districts on the base."

Esmerelda stood and stretched, "You mean, you want a balance, like two houses – a Senate and a House, with one being districts and one being global?"

Gail had been staring at the newly created world maps on the wall. Her eyes narrowed, "Oh."

John turned to her, "What?"

"Global. Meaning, what about people outside of Fort Brazos and the base? Homesteaders and colonists, who move out into the world?"

Gloria's eyes widened, "Move out into the wilderness? Now? With those creatures out there killing people? Who would be crazy enough to do that?"

John pursed his lips, "Gloria, people have already started slipping away out into that wilderness. Some people are just not made to live in cities or anywhere near them. Back home, that could be hard to do. There was always someone else around the corner, someone else who owned the land. Here, though, it's wide open. Nobody knows what is really out there, and there is nobody but yourself to answer to if you take the leap."

Tom scratched his head, and everyone paused to think. He sipped his drink, "Okay then, for now, we have an at-large representative who is responsible for matters outside the city and base."

Councilman Hickum rubbed the stubble of his five o'clock shadow, "Yeah, like, who owns all that land? And who owns those crops?"

John raised his eyebrows, "Hmmm, you mean like the land grants the Republic of Texas gave out to settlers to encourage immigration?"

"Yeah, maybe."

Gloria shook her head, "Oh Lord, are we going to have old west range wars again?"

Tom sighed with a half-smile, "Oh, I think we can manage to keep the land and assay office records on an inflammable medium of some kind and make them digitally public record for all. I'm sure that Esmerelda's family's cattle baron ambitions can be moderated."

There were soft chuckles from around the room, and Esmerelda's face reddened a little.

Tom continued, "I think that, for now, we can announce that there are more crops out there than we have the ability to harvest. If people want to go and do that, we'll pay them for the amount they harvest, we can give them a percent ownership in what they harvest, and we can establish central grain repositories. Anyone that wants to work hard should profit from that work, accordingly."

Gail had been looking something up on her smartphone during the conversation. She put it down and looked up, "I'd like to make a suggestion on a model for representation."

Tom and the others smiled.

"I was looking at the way some countries organized their representation. In the Philippines, they have, or, maybe had 24 Senators who were elected at large. Half were elected every six years, and they had a two-term limit. Whoever got the top-12-most votes became a senator for the whole country. So, if we did something similar, the Senators would represent everyone by popular vote, and our 'house' members could be elected by district."

Tom nodded slowly, "Okay, I suggest we come up with three or four models, and then we have a quick public referendum. We can put a time limit on it and even schedule a constitutional convention for some time in the future, like maybe a year from now."

Gloria nodded, "Second the motion."

Dale added, "Third."

Tom looked around the room, and everyone was in agreement. "So shall it be, then."

Analysis

Bonham State University
Day 5: 6:35 PM

Thornhill Hall had the largest projection screen of any of the lecture halls at Bonham State University. It was a large room, with lots of tables and comfortable swing chairs. The projection screen displayed an endless progression of PowerPoint slides, videos, and still-images concerning everything learned so far about the new world around them and the creature that had attacked the Hoffman farm.

Students and faculty streamed in and out of the room, uniformly disheveled from little to no sleep. Prohibitions on food and drink in the room had been forgotten. Coffee and drink service, as well as food and snack trays, lined the walls, and the tables were littered with laptop computers, tablets, reams of printouts, and not a few people who had succumbed to exhaustion and passed out. A half-dozen undergrad students quietly worked their way through the tables, picking up crushed soda cans, coffee cups, water bottles, and food wrappers.

Presentations had included (preliminary) studies on atmospheric composition, gravity studies, soil and plant analysis, post-mortem statistics and analysis of the dead, photographic studies of the landmasses and oceans visible in the 'sky' above them, spectrographic studies on the 'sun tube' or 'sun line' or whatever the thing was, as well as radar map analysis, and much, much more.

Dr. Takumi Nakamura presided over it all, with the rest of the surviving senior faculty and administrators arrayed behind him on the dais as a review panel. Each presenter had, in turn, been grilled by Dr. Nakamura and the panel. Their methods and conclusions were all challenged, and each was sternly reminded of the virtues of academic circumspection.

A Xenobiology 'departmental review committee' had been established, with department heads from many disciplines participating. Dr. Jacob Becker was on the committee, and Dr. Eva Sanchez was empaneled as an adjunct subject-matter-expert member (and the only veterinarian).

Seated away from the established and respected department heads was Dr. Leo Talib. After his dramatic announcement regarding the discovery of the hidden messages in the glyphs appearing on the alien spire, Dr. Talib had expected to be the celebrated focal point of future investigations. Instead, ever since that tumultuous meeting, he had been sidelined and marginalized. What little assistance he received was a complete waste of time. Every step he'd taken had been dissected. Every conclusion he'd reached had been scorned as being both premature and done without consulting relevant experts in related and relevant fields.

Leo sat rigid in his chair, forcing himself to project confidence and dignity. He would not give Nakamura the satisfaction of seeing him stew.

The current presenter was the Computer Science department head, Dr. Bill Franks. He had just demonstrated the first computer mapping model of the new world, based on the imagery so far available.

After he finished speaking, Dr. Nakamura sat silently, thinking for a long moment before asking, "Dr. Franks, I have a side question. Please tell us how all of our data is being backed up, now that, well, the rest of the world appears to be gone?"

Bill's eyes were bloodshot, and his shirt was uncharacteristically half-untucked. He nodded to himself before answering, "Yes, that's a fascinating question, and I asked myself the same thing. As you know, somehow, the rest of the public and the academic Internet II are still active, but in a more or less frozen state. We think that whoever abducted us and put us here also must have somehow spidered the entire Internet and copied it and its functionality. Everything still mostly works, but no new information is being added on Internet sites outside of Fort Brazos.

He looked down at his laptop and clicked something. A new image was displayed on the projection screen. It was a small black box with an almost organic look to it. It was connected to an equipment rack in a data center.

Bill continued, "You've seen this before – this is the... Alien... black box that all of Fort Brazos's wired telecommunications terminate into, kind of like a tiny version of the black box the power lines now come out of. We don't know what it is or how it works. There does not appear to be any power being connected to it or any connection of any kind. It's just a... brick that all of our telecommunications have been wired into."

"We thought it was a completely static copy of the Internet. However, we soon realized that we are able to make changes to the Internet resources we have access to. For example, our students quickly discovered that they could update their social media pages with new information. Then we noticed that our backup jobs were still running without error. Our remote cloud storage is still backing up data. If we disconnect the black box, we lose connection to it and everything else, but the data was there when we plugged it back in. (he carefully omitted the political firestorm that happened when others found out that he had disconnected the black box. What if the data had all disappeared!) When we look at how much storage space is available, the best answer we can discern is that we are only limited by the mathematical limitations of our own software to store, track and retrieve the data. I caution, however, that that is, of course, a very preliminary finding."

"We are, of course, also rounding up every resource we can find to back up the data locally, but who can say where it is all really going?"

Dr. Nakamura nodded thoughtfully, "Thank you, Dr. Franks. I'm sure all of us have considered that whoever was responsible for building this artificial world and putting us here is more than capable of reading our mail, presuming, of course, that they would even care what is in it."

Half the panel around Dr. Nakamura nodded grimly, as did Franks himself.

Dr. Nakamura thumbed through a schedule, never once looking at Leo Talib, "I believe that next up is Biochemistry?"

Before anyone could respond, a handful of breathless students burst into the hall and dashed towards the stage. Dr. Nakamura and the others stood up warily.

The student in the lead, an olive-skinned, dark-haired young woman, one of Dr. Nakamura's astronomy post-grads, pleaded, "Professor! You've got to come outside right now!"

Dr. Nakamura didn't move, "What's this all about? Why are you here, Nenet?"

Nenet ran to a stop at the foot of the dais, and the other students clumped up behind her, nearly knocking her down. She gulped a breath, "Please, Dr. Nakamura, you've got to see this! It's the suntube. It's changing!"

✪ ✪ ✪

The crush through the lecture hall doors had very nearly resulted in injuries. However, stern shouts and warnings from the faculty and staff had restrained everyone just barely enough to prevent catastrophe. In the quad outside, everyone quickly spread out, hands reflexively shielding eyes from the brightness and many hands pointing in the same direction.

It was well known, at this point, that looking directly at the sun-tube did not cause injury, any more than staring at a bright fluorescent light fixture would hurt you, but generations of "don't look directly at the sun" didn't change habits overnight.

It was early evening, but still, a couple of hours until "sundown." In the distance, the approaching hurricane had slid down the horizon and bunched up behind the barrier mountains. Strobing lightning flashes could be seen beyond the peaks, and the storm seemed to be breaking up and splitting in two, wrapping the edges of the mountains.

Perpendicular to the mountains was the thin "sun-tube" or "sun-line" that stretched from pole to pole down the length of the cylindrical world. Ever since Awakening Day, the thin line of light had burned brightly down its entire length and slowly faded to a moon-like level of brightness until it brightened again in the "morning."

Until now, the sun-tube had been uniformly bright down its length. Now though, all that changed. Instead of a solid line of light, a bright spot had formed, concentrating the aggregate light output into a bulging pulse that ever-so-slowly propagated down the length of the tube. In its wake, the suntube quickly dimed.

Familiarity

T he Manticore Pub's dark wood paneling and worn, golden-brass fixtures were warm and welcoming, and it was now open around the clock. It was a popular spot for many in the military. For CCM Harrold Anders, it had become more than his favorite haunt. It was where he often, somehow, accidentally, bumped into Fort Brazos's most infamous radio DJ, Danielle Richardson.

Tonight, like everyone else there, they had gathered to avoid talking about whether the sun-tube would light again in the morning or whether there would be a morning. Tonight, they would sit and drink and think about anything else.

To Anders, Danielle was an impossible woman. They had known each other for mere days, but it seemed a lifetime. She drove him completely mad. Harrold had loved all three of his ex-wives, he was sure. None of them, though, had so profoundly and irretrievably captured his heart. For the first time in his life, he knew the battle was lost. He didn't care. Harrold was a fearless and physically powerful man. He was the senior enlisted man… in the world. He inspired dread and devotion in the hearts of men. Now, though, and from the very first moment that he met this woman, here, at this very table, he knew that she had effortlessly conquered his heart.

Danielle sat next to him with a lover's familiarity. Indeed, they had become lovers that first night they had met. Not simply lovers, but the kind of earth-shaking, angels weeping kind of lovers she'd only read about in her trashy novels. He was impossible and infuriating, and… and… she knew that she was his forever. She had not believed it was possible in the real world. *Maybe we're not in the real world anymore.*

It was not just the way her heart had raced the first time they had met before she really understood what was happening. This was the kind of love that she suspected most people only ever dreamed about. It absolutely terrified her, and it was happening so fast. And she didn't care.

At the moment, their doubts and fears lay beneath the surface. A Bonham State University coed waitress had just served them two perfect pints of Guinness.

They sat back and listened to the Irishman singing. He'd become a fixture at the pub. More and more people had started coming to the pub. No doubt for all sorts of reasons. They came and listened and, quite often, sang along. There was something cathartic about it as they listened to him sing Eric Bogle's 'The Green Fields of France.'

Well, how do you do, young Willie McBride?
Do you mind if I sit here down by your graveside?
And rest for a while in the warm summer sun,
I've been walking all day, and I'm nearly done.
I see by your gravestone you were only 19
When you joined the great fallen in 1916,
I hope you died well and I hope you died clean
Or, Willie McBride, was it slow and obscene?

Did they beat the drum slowly, did they play the fife lowly?
Did they sound the death march as they lowered you down?
Did the band play The Last Post in chorus?
And did the pipes play the Flowers of the Forest?

Did you leave a wife or a sweetheart behind
In some faithful heart is your memory enshrined?

ACCIPITER WAR

Although, you died back in 1916,
In that faithful heart are you forever 19?
Or are you a stranger without even a name,
Enclosed in forever behind the glass frame,
In an old photograph, torn, battered and stained,
And faded to yellow in a brown leather frame?

Did they beat the drum slowly, did they play the fife lowly?
Did they sound the death march as they lowered you down?
Did the band play The Last Post in chorus?
And did the pipes play the Flowers of the Forest?

The sun now it shines on the green fields of France;
There's a warm summer breeze that makes the red poppies
        dance.
And look how the sun shines from under the clouds
There's no gas, no barbed wire, there's no guns firing now.
But here in this graveyard it's still No Man's Land
The countless white crosses stand mute in the sand
To man's blind indifference to his fellow man.
To a whole generation that were butchered and damned.

Did they beat the drum slowly, did they play the fife lowly?
Did they sound the death march as they lowered you down?
Did the band play The Last Post in chorus?
And did the pipes play the Flowers of the Forest?

Ah young Willie McBride, I can't help wonder why,
Do those that lie here know why did they die?
And did they believe when they answered the cause,

Did they really believe that this war would end wars?
Well the sorrow, the suffering, the glory, the pain.
The killing and dying, were all done in vain.
For Willie McBride, it all happened again,
And again, and again, and again, and again.

Did they beat the drum slowly, did they play the fife lowly?
Did they sound the death march as they lowered you down?
Did the band play The Last Post in chorus?
And did the pipes play the Flowers of the Forest?

Danielle glanced over at Anders and could see the dampness in his eyes. Almost, anyway, since it was hard to see through her own tears.

Across the room, in a darkened booth in the back, sat two young people. One of them was an Army Lieutenant with Ranger flashes. The other was a young fair-skinned woman with long flowing blonde hair. They were leaning across their table, holding hands, looking into each other's eyes, and speaking softly.

Harrold chuckled at the sight of them, "My, my, my."

Danielle leaned into him, stroking his arm, "What?"

Harrold nodded towards the booth in the back, "Those two lovebirds, the Ranger and the blonde girl. Do you know who they are?"

Danielle sniffed and squinted a little, "Isn't that…."

Harrold smiled, "Yep. That's the Hoffman girl and young Lieutenant Garrett."

"I thought they were in quarantine?"

"Doc let 'em out today. The whole bunch was driving the hospital staff up the wall."

Danielle giggled, "Look at them! That poor boy doesn't stand a chance!"

Harrold looked into Danielle's eyes, "No, he sure doesn't."

Shattered

Town Square
Day 6: 7:41 AM

T he next morning, every living soul stood outside and watched as the sun-tube burned across the sky, not the long thin line of yellow fire. Instead, it was now a much brighter "patch" of brilliant light that mimicked a sun moving around a terrestrial world. The daylight grew in intensity as the bright spot inched along, giving a moving shadow to where you stood instead of the fixed shadow from the day before.

Presumably, as it moved across to the other end of the world, it would gradually grow dimmer, into night. Everyone hoped and prayed the process would begin again anew in the 'morning.'

The crowds gradually melted away, abuzz with talk and speculation. Gail and her detail had gone back inside Town Hall, and she had kicked her shoe off and curled up on the couch with one leg tucked under and the other jutting out with the cast to read her email. Sun-tube light now streamed through the office where Gail had made a vain attempt to sleep the night before. She just had not been able to shut her mind down.

Vice President? She had gone over and over recent events in her mind, looking for the mistake in her actions, the flaw in her strategy, the wrong words said, anything that would help explain how she had ended up in this predicament.

What had she done wrong?

She was effectively being kicked out of the Air Force, out of the life she loved. Worse, it felt like every time she turned around, she kept running into… him. She knew it was irrational to blame him. He had never been anything but polite and understanding and insufferably, maddeningly proper with her. He'd also seemed as genuinely surprised and unhappy with the present situation as she was. Worse still, as she had started to work with and get to know him better, he'd turned out to not be remotely as dumb as she'd first thought. *No*, she corrected herself, *as you first assumed*. Far from it.

She was even beginning to, well, maybe, tolerate him a little. His daughter, though…. The corner of her mouth twitched. Matti was a force of nature and impossible not to adore.

It was a goddamned shotgun wedding. She knew there were even rumors that the two of them were an item….

She lowered her head, chin resting on her chest, and she closed her eyes for a moment. There were too many things, too many changes, too many….

Just then, she winced as a sharp pain stabbed her ears and the window glass shattered. A sonic boom filled the world and rolled on and on. Bits of glass cut her face and arms in a few places, but she didn't notice. Before she consciously thought about it, with one foot bare and the other still in the cast, she had dashed out the door, running to the exit, towards the sound. She was faster than her security detail, but only by a single stride. She stopped dead in her tracks, yards beyond the front doors, stepping barefoot across the broken glass.

Across from City Hall was the Town Square. In the middle of the square, where the memorial statue used to stand, was the massive, towering black alien spire. Until now, it had been displaying a seemingly endless series of glyphs. Hidden in those glyphs was the now-famous soundtrack – the 'sound of our enemies.'

The glyphs were gone. Now, the spire had been swallowed by an enormous… Earth, or, presumably, some sort of hologram, of earth. The image was achingly beautiful, with all the familiar colors and shapes of delicate clouds and cyclonic storms. She gasped. It quite literally took her breath away.

A crowd of people stood around the square, shouting, pointing, filming with their smartphones. Then, the scene changed, and the Earth receded from perspective and a vast cloud of spacecraft, surrounding a giant, moon-sized 'mother ship' hove to, slowing to a stop relative to the Earth. There was a unanimous sharp intake of breath around the square as people cried out in fear and anger.

Then, a flurry of tiny flashes of light erupted from the ships. Moments later, brilliant pinpricks blossomed on the earth. Gail fell to her knees.

The hologram of the Earth and attacking spacecraft faded away and were replaced with the image of a creature no one had ever seen before. It was shown next to the darkened silhouette of a human male. The creature was almost twice as large. It had two clawed legs and two sets of arms with smaller claws, one large and one small. The large set appeared to have some sort of sharp weapon attached. The smaller had more mobile-looking 'hands' and carried technological devices of some kind. The creature had a large beak with iridescent glyphs painted on it and feathers or some feather analogue, like some nightmare bird from Hell.

A low, unaccented voice boomed over the entire town,

"People of Fort Brazos, behold! See now, the slayer of mankind, destroyer of your world."

It was a brisk cool but pretty morning, and Danielle Richardson had been up early, watched the new sun-tube thing, and had stopped at Greta's Café on the Town Square. She had been eating a breakfast Crêpe Romanoff when the towering alien spire had gone berserk, shattering windows and knocking everyone to the ground. Around her, many people immediately started taking pictures and recording video on their phones. Nearby, the young man and woman operating the bank of cameras permanently recording the alien glyphs on the Spire got back to their feet and frantically adjusted the cameras, some of which had been knocked over.

Everyone was staring at the enormous holographic images. Danielle grabbed the edge of the table and pulled herself up. As she did, she noticed the nominee for Vice President, Gail Finley, stumble out the shattered City Hall doors, blood trickling from cuts on her face and arms, barefoot on one side and stopping unevenly with the large plastic cast on her other leg. Her uniform blouse was untucked and rumpled.

Danielle didn't think about it. Maybe it was the remnants of Journalism school, she never knew why she did it, but before she was consciously aware, she had her own phone out and started recording Gail. Close on Gail's heels, several Marines dashed out the door and surrounded her, but Danielle still had a good angle. As the alien voice spoke, Danielle saw the emotions raging on Gail's normally impassive face. The face of the cocky fighter pilot turned prospective leader of their world.

Gail's eyes widened as the voice announced the fate of Earth, showing the flash pinpricks of light across the surface of the birthplace of mankind, apparently from some kind of weapons that the massive cloud of alien spacecraft had launched.

It flashed through Danielle's mind that she and, well, just about everyone was still in a state of denial about what had happened to them. The crushing agony of the thousands of dead was so intense as to seem unreal. Their homes and familiar surroundings were all still there, and yet you could go have breakfast on the square and almost feel like nothing had happened. There was still some kind of normalcy and irrational hope that, somehow, someway, it was all a bad dream. That they would wake up and everything would be the way it was before... before the horrors of Awakening Day, and the terrors which had followed.

Now, that thin, tattered blanket of denial was blasted away by the shockingly loud, flat, almost robotic, alien voice.

Gail's eyes welled with tears, and her jaw quivered for a moment. Then she set it. Hard. She drew her lips thin and stood back up, awkwardly at first, with the cast, but forced herself to stand ramrod straight. Her hands and knees were bleeding, her hair was astray, her chest was heaving, and her fists were clenched. Gail's eyes blazed with incandescent fury, and her milky pale skin flushed darkly. To Danielle, it seemed as if Gail actually grew taller in those moments, swelling in size. When she'd first emerged from the building, Gail's eyes had widened in shock and horror. Now, they were hard as diamonds.

The expression was mirrored on the Marines, and she could hear their collective growl of righteous anger. Then, Danielle thought her phone's camera had gone out of focus until she realized that her own tears had blurred her vision. She kept recording even though she could no longer really see anything clearly.

✪ ✪ ✪

Sheriff, and Presidential candidate, John Austin, had been up that morning, already dressed in his tan uniform, checking his overnight messages and email. He sat, drinking coffee at the kitchen table. Chief Deputy Hector Alonzo sat across from him, checking messages on his phone. The rest of his newly imposed security detail were split up, half outside the house, the other inside. It was early, and Matti had a few more minutes before her alarm would go off. There was precious little new information about the attack on the highway. The offending creature had not yet been found.

In the five hours since he had collapsed into bed, there were 68 new overnight emails from Dr. Nakamura, Dr. Talib, and others at the university. There were 22 email reports from the Police department and another 47 from his own Sheriff's department. The Mayor and City Council were responsible for another 31, and General Marcus's staff had contributed 56 reports and updates. There was another twenty-some-odd from other sources, and while he had been drinking his coffee, 27 more had flowed into his email inbox.

At least the apocalypse had the silver lining of having killed junk email.

He'd finished skimming subject lines and a handful of more urgent messages when the entire house shook from an explosion. "What the Hell?"

Everyone dashed outside. His house faced in the Town Square's direction, and a good portion of the enormous alien spire was always visible. Even from this distance, he could see the Earth hologram and hear the distant alien voice.

His detail had surrounded him before he realized it.

He called out, keeping his eyes on the massive apparition, "Matti!"

"Yes, Daddy." She was already standing next to him, barefoot in her pajamas, her long golden hair tousled and fluttering in the breeze. "I'll be ready in two minutes, Daddy."

Two minutes later, with his phone ringing nonstop, he stepped up to his Sheriff's department SUV, but Hector had already taken the driver's seat. John's eyes flashed, but Hector did not yield.

Hector simply said, "Let's go, Boss."

Matti was already in the back seat, dressed and wearing a baseball cap, her long blonde hair tied back, holding her backpack in her lap.

High above the Town Square, the alien voice editorialized. The image of the alien with avian features rotated.

"This is your enemy. The closest analogue to their species, in human experience, is Avian. Their race is aggressive. You might call them Accipiters, from your root word for Hawk. They have a complex social and reproductive structure and are users of advanced spacefaring technology. Culturally, their use of genetic bioengineering is innate. They routinely alter conquered species to fill roles in their empire."

General Alexander Marcus had also been up early, eating breakfast in the spartan officer's mess. The shock wave felt like a small earthquake. He leaped from his plastic and metal chair, which flew backward behind him and dashed for the exit. Moments later, he, Captain Guevara, and several others pounded up the control tower stairs. The control tower main room windows were the highest observation point on the base. He arrived, and the crowd around the windows parted.

Although the Joint Reserve Base was many miles away from the actual City of Fort Brazos, the new reverse curvature of their world meant the city was more visible. In the distance, the holographic Earth was clearly visible over the city.

"Where's the live feed?!"

A corporal on the other side of the room shouted, "Over here, Sir!" He didn't wait for orders to turn up the volume. The large monitor showed a live feed from Town Square.

"... "The Accipiters arrived in your star system in a migration swarm of approximately sixty thousand spacecraft. They launched kinetic projectiles from far beyond your orbital reaches and were timed for more or less simultaneous impact on all of your military bases, strategic assets, and the population centers near them. Those areas of your world that appeared to be in protracted conflict across entire regions were simply sterilized."

"Nothing remains of the world you knew."

At Bonham State University, the shockwave had rattled the buildings. Students and faculty rushed outside to see what was happening. The University was only a couple of miles from the Town Square, and the alien hologram was clearly visible and audible. The mood was a jumble of awe, fear, excitement, and, to a lesser degree, panic. People pointed upwards, and most, it seemed, recorded the scene with their smartphones.

Dr. Leo Talib had been asleep on the couch in his new office, late of the unlamented Dr. Gloria Rubenheim, who had been among the 5% culled by the aliens on Awakening Day. He'd been up all night, again, struggling with deciphering the alien glyphs and had only fallen asleep two hours earlier.

The boom of the shockwave and the godlike alien voice had shredded his gossamer dreams and shaken him from the couch. He wiped his face and shakily started towards the door to see what was happening. An array of large-screen video monitors littered the office, each with live feeds from different viewing angles of the alien 'spire.' The thought of that term made him bristle with irritation. *It should be called an obelisk, in honor of ancient obelisks with their symbols and markings, but no, the Luddites here had called it a 'Spire.'*

As he passed the monitors, he stopped and stared. Some of the views showed a massive hologram of some kind. The kids operating the permanent cameras had tilted the lenses to capture the sight. Some of the cameras, however, were still aimed at the base of the Spire. Alien glyphs were still appearing but were now changing rapidly, keeping pace with the voice of the robotic-voiced narrator.

Next to the alien glyphs were more symbols. These were radically different from the glyphs he had grown used to. The style, shape, color, and structure were totally new.

"My God, it's a new language, and it is keeping pace with whoever is talking." His eyes widened, and he moved quickly to his chair, grabbed a notepad, and began making notes without looking down. "This is a live Rosetta Stone of English spoken word in time with two alien written languages!"

Tom, Gloria, and the rest of the City Council had been having a working breakfast at Ray's Diner when windows shattered, and the entire building felt like it was going to flip over.

Dazed, stunned, and bleeding from minor cuts from flying glass, they had stumbled outside, looking up at the hologram.

ACCIPITER WAR

On the pronouncement *"Nothing remains of the world you knew,"* Gloria's face fell as all the emotional armor and detachment she had built up since Awakening Day suddenly collapsed. Her knees buckled, and she gasped, "No....." Tom caught her before she hit the ground.

The other council members reacted in similar ways, crying out in shock and anger, and fear. Some prayed, and others just kept shaking their heads in denial.

For a moment, Tom looked into Gloria's tear-filled eyes. They had battled each other politically for years. Now, for the first time, they were just two people in pain. He gently helped her to her feet. She nodded thanks, and he let her go.

A small crowd gathered around the council members and Mayor. Many held hands or held close the person next to them as they stared up into the sky and the impossible alien hologram.

"...We were only able to save some of you. Of all your world, we selected you. In the moments before your annihilation, we scanned your city, your military base, and some other military resources from around your planet."

"We scanned and preserved your global digital network. All the servers, and nodes, including all the digital facsimiles of your literature and art, as well as history and popular entertainment, are preserved for you so that you have at least some record of what you have lost."

"Here, in this world that we have created for you, we have reconstructed your city and surroundings. Those that survived were restored. The essence of yourselves was preserved, what you would call your soul. You are still who you were. You are yourselves."

192

✪ ✪ ✪

John had no idea how fast Hector and the other vehicles had driven, sirens blaring. However, there were several moments when he had desperately gripped the hand rests and glanced worriedly back at Matti, who seemed nonplussed about it all, with all the supreme confidence of the very young.

John's SUV and those of his other men and the Marines screeched to a halt near the Town Square, and they burst out of their doors to see what was happening. Matti was right beside him, clutching his hand.

John looked down into her eyes, and while there was some fear in them, she mostly just channeled all her love and trust in him. He hoped that he would live up to her absolute faith in him.

"In the time that has passed since the attack, your enemy, whose name you could not physically pronounce, has modified your planet to suit its needs and beliefs. The surviving population of your planet was subsequently collected, evaluated, and cataloged. The genetic structure of humanity and your world's major life forms were recorded and assessed. Afterward, most were discarded and recycled. Those few humans who were allowed to survive were re-educated to perform suitable tasks, and many were genetically altered to fill niche roles."

An image was displayed of an enormous structure, viewed from high above. It looked more as though it had been grown rather than built. It bordered a large lake or inland sea that looked disturbingly like where

Chicago had once been. Long antlike columns of humans could be seen entering one side. The view zoomed in and a much, much smaller number of humans, and what perhaps had once been humans, shambled out the other side.

One woman near the square fainted at this sight, several people fell to their knees and vomited, and horrified parents pulled their children close and covered their eyes.

The voice paused for long moments.

"The Accipiters reseeded your planet with plants and animals suiting their needs. Using your term, your planet was Terraformed. Your cities were torn down and recycled into building and manufacturing materials for your enemy's new colony world."

"This is how your world appeared before the arrival of the Accipiters."

The holographic projection changed, and the image of the Earth returned.

"Many of your years have passed since these events began. This is how your world appears today."

The holographic projection changed again. The image of 'old' Earth faded. Next to it, a new globe appeared. The familiar swirls of weather systems now covered a very different world. Many of the colors were wrong, with deep violets and very unearthly greens and even some smears of orange.

"Your enemy has done the same thing to thousands of other planets and civilizations across the galaxy. You are not unique. The Accipiters destroy any diversity of life, flora, or fauna that does not meet their standards. They incorporate and modify what sentient and non-sentient life forms they believe are useful. The Accipiters employ a vast array of such creatures to do their work. Without exception, all are conditioned, sometimes genetically, to worship them."

The voice paused again.

"We did not save you, humans, in order to preserve your species.... You were saved and put in this place to form the nucleus of a force that will grow and go forth into the galaxy, fight your enemy, and defend others against them."

"We have already begun to teach you about some of their subject races. We will teach you more. You will learn. While you are in this world we created for you; you are hidden and protected from the Accipiters. You will grow, learn and avenge your planet. We will give you tools and knowledge, but you must learn *how to absorb the new knowledge we share and adapt it to your needs."*

"We will provide tools and knowledge, but you must do the work yourselves. You must rise to this challenge. We will not fight. You must learn the science and make the technology your own. We have done as much for you as we can. Who we are does not matter. We will not reveal this to you."

Green fire crackled around the base of the spire in a deep basso roar. The hologram disappeared, revealing the dark towering spire again. Lightning flashed from its top and ripped across the sky in actinic fury and thunder that shook the world.

"Heed this warning: You must accept this destiny, or we will sterilize this place, start over, and find another race to take your place."

Shangri-La

Joint Reserve Base
Day 6: 8:12 AM

The alien voice had stopped and then looped to the beginning of its message. Inside the control room, there was fear, stunned silence, anger, and rage. A lot of rage. A circle formed around General Marcus. For long moments, he gathered his thoughts and emotions. He surveyed the faces around him. No one spoke. The only sound was from the equipment and air circulators.

Around him was the control room staff as well as most of the original senior officers. Of the New Arrivals, only the allied commanders were present. Marcus took the time to look into each of their eyes as they waited.

He spoke softly, but there was no hesitation or timidity in his voice. It was a Command voice he'd had many years to polish, supremely focused and direct.

"It would seem that we have a choice to make. If all of this is true, then we must, all of us must decide whether we will accept the fate they described for us as a race. Each of us in this room gave an oath to protect our country. Now, our country…," he paused and nodded to the allied officers, "Now, our *countries*, our world may be gone forever. All that is left is us and a single small city. Had these Accipiters landed and fought us on the ground, I know that we, all of us, would have fought them with all our might."

He looked around at their faces again, "But, they didn't want a fair fight. They killed us from orbit and then, and then they raped, butchered, and damned our world."

Loud murmurs of anger filled the room.

197

"Whoever it is that put us here is obviously powerful, but they want us to do their dirty work. They think that if we have nothing left to fight for, that we'll somehow go 'out there' and fight these things. Also, if it is true that these Accipiters are all over the galaxy, then we're going to need a lot more than just *us* to fight them. All our rifles and tanks and planes won't do squat against spaceships. Obviously, our abductors are not stupid, and they have to know that we will need more of us as well as better weapons and especially spacecraft of our own."

"And they did pretty much say that they would give us the tools we would need."

"Of course, that's all nice and theoretical. On the other hand, they also threatened that if we didn't cooperate that they'd find someone else to do the job."

The room turned quiet again.

He scanned the faces in the room. "What they are describing is not something that we could accomplish in a year or ten or even a hundred. The galaxy is big. Enormous. It takes thousands of years for even *light* to go from one end to the other. They're talking about a generational war – that we would need to become a warrior race that leaves our children and loved ones back in this Shangri-La hidey-hole and goes out to fight the baddies."

He let that sink in.

"Right now, though, we're all going to have to decide is whether we accept this fate, this destiny. This… ultimatum."

"None of us signed up for this. I can only tell you that as for me, I will stand. I will stand against these Aliens, and maybe, just maybe, I can make them regret what they've done. My life's mission will be to make them come to fear us. To fear the words Human, and Texas and Fort Brazos!"

The growl of agreement was almost subsonic, and the room vibrated with it.

"You, and all the men and women who serve under you, must decide whether you want to simply give up. Lay down, die, and let humanity perish without even a whimper."

He took a deep breath and implored them, "Or, whether you will join me and take the fight to these Accipiters. Who knows, maybe, someday, we can save someone else's world."

Do or Die

Council Chambers
Day 6: 10:00 AM

T he council chambers were deathly quiet. The recordings of the alien message had been replayed several times, each from different angles, showing varying details. None of the replaying's had lessened the blow. Each seemed like another nail being hammered into mankind's coffin.

General Marcus and Captain Guevara had choppered in, John Austin and Gail Finley were seated next to each other in the middle of the seating area across from the raised council seating. Gail's cuts and bruises had been treated and bandaged, as had those of the injured council members.

This meeting was closed-door. No notes were being taken, and the cameras were all turned off.

Tom sighed, "Well, our abductors don't mince words, do they? What was it you called them, Gloria?"

She stared into the distance and replied in a small voice, "Gardeners."

Tom leaned back in his leather chair, "Gardeners, huh? So, I guess these Gardeners see these Accipiters as an invasive species messing up the neighborhood, and it is beneath them to get their hands dirty?"

John snorted, "And we're not worth the effort to save or defend except to serve their purposes?"

Gloria's eyes were bleak and bloodshot, "They said many years have passed. What does that mean? How long have we been gone?"

Deep silence filled the room.

Marcus grunted, "Well, they left that detail, and a lot of other details out, didn't they?"

Gail slammed her fist on the chair-arm. The noise shook a few of them out of their collective trance. "So, they scoop a handful of us people off a murdered planet and expect us to become, what, their Mercenaries?"

John shook his head, "Or, slave army."

"Oh, thank you so much, John, for that lovely mental image."

Marcus slumped back into his seat, "If the Gardeners could do all these things – My God, they built an entire world! Then they kidnapped us, Xeroxed us, and set us up here, and all under the Accipiters' noses, 'in the seconds before our Annihilation,' then I cannot believe that they could not have had the technology to stop the attack in the first place."

Tom grimaced, "I suppose we only know what they've told us, and we still know nothing about the … Gardeners. They certainly haven't shown themselves to us!"

Gail looked sideways at John, "So, slaves, huh? Fight or die, like, what, gladiators?"

John stared at her grimly.

Councilman Hickum jumped into the fray, "It's the dying thing that has all of us going, right? They said we must accept our fate, or they would find someone else to do it for them?"

Councilwoman Esmerelda Collins rubbed her temples, "So, they want to turn all of us into cannon fodder to fight their war?"

Marcus shook his head, "No Councilwoman, the more I think about it, the more convinced I am that they chose Fort Brazos for very specific reasons, and not just random population to turn into an army."

John nodded, "I think I see where you are going with this, General. The Gardener announcement said that they had specifically chosen Fort Brazos. Fort Brazos has always been a more isolated, independent city. We're not part of a big Metroplex like Dallas or Houston. We're an independent community."

Marcus grimaced, "Yes, well, an army does not exist in a vacuum. It must have support. For every single frontline combatant, there are many more people needed to keep them supplied. Then there are all the people who provide medical care, and more, still, who build all the weapons, vehicles, uniforms, electronics and equipment, food, and on and on. There is a military ratio, called 'Tooth-to-Tail' of the number of people to support a soldier or soldiers versus the number of actual front-line combatants. That, however, ignores all the civilians who are needed to provide support for the people providing support. Not just the Military Industrial Complex, but the civilian society that provides the ultimate economic and societal foundation."

"The Tooth-to-Tail ratio today is much lower than it was, say, in World War II, but it is also true that the way we fight has changed a lot. At the same time, the percentage of deployed forces responsible for logistics functions, and base and everyday support functions have both increased, including the use of civilian contractors."

Esmerelda sighed, "So, you are saying that the civilians of Fort Brazos are supposed to become what America was in World War II? The 'engine of democracy,' with all the sacrifice and rationing and sitting around waiting for the staff car to arrive with the gold star and folded flag?"

Gail's eyes narrowed, "Councilwoman, I think you may be right, and worse, they want the civilians to become the baby machines to supply the future soldiers as well as to be the civilian workforce providing for the military's needs. They did say that 'we would grow.'

Esmerelda winced, "Major, as a cattlewoman, I know something about managing a herd. You have to protect them from predators and provide them with food and room to grow." She pointed to the maps on the wall showing the vast fields of grain and the open world beyond. "That's what they've done here. They picked a strong bloodline and built a nice ranch away from the wolves, where the *herd* can grow."

Gloria raised her head up, "But we've had predators. People have died!"

John shook his head, "They said they are teaching us. I suspect that they've introduced us to only isolated examples of the creatures, the enemies they expect us to fight in the future so that we would learn about them."

Esmerelda spat her response, "Yeah, like an immunization – give us a weak version of the virus so we can build up an immunity. So, what if a few cells die?"

Councilman Hubbard sighed, "Oh god, that's so…. This can't be happening!"

Gloria slumped her head onto her crossed arms, "I'm still hung up on the bit about us being copies, Xerox's of ourselves."

Tom nodded slowly, "I know what you mean, Gloria. I feel like I'm reliving my college philosophy classes – 'What makes a man a man,' or, in our case, what makes a human, human? What about our souls? What are we now? Are we all like the Jewish Golem, animated creatures in the image of man? God, I wish Pastor Joe was here. I know he would have the existential part of this all figured out."

Subdued silence fell over the group.

John took a deep breath and stood. He looked around the room and the drawn expressions on everyone's faces. "Existential questions aside, we must face the fact that they've given us an ultimatum."

Gloria looked up, her eyes bloodshot, "We cannot just declare one way or the other. We cannot just impose a decision on the people."

John nodded, "We were going to hold an election anyway. I think it needs to become a plebiscite. The people must declare what they want. Item one is whether to accept the alien's demands."

Gloria sat up straighter, "Well if Item One doesn't pass, I suppose none of the others will matter. Assuming we are not all suicidal, then Item Two is to accept or not accept the newly proposed form and structure of government, and how representation will work or vote on a Constitutional Convention."

Gail asked quietly, "They only said we must accept their demand, but they didn't say what that means. Is it something that can be declared, or is it a majority vote? How much of a majority will the aliens accept? If the measure passes, does anything happen to the people who vote no?"

John replied quietly, "You sure do cut to the heart of things sometimes, don't you? As to whether these Gardeners are so bloody-minded that they'll kill anyone who votes no, we all know that they killed 5% of us civilians just to make a point."

Tom shook his head, "I find it hard to believe that they could do everything they've done, including copying us, without knowing something about our psychology. They must know that it's just about impossible for humans to agree 100% on something. I think they must expect that some will say no, and knowing that, they wouldn't go to all this trouble just to wipe us all out because some of us say no. To your point, though, they might just be bloody-minded enough to cull those who say no. Can we justify telling people that, though? Isn't telling them that if they vote no, they might be killed, setting us all up to fail? What trust would people have?"

Councilman Hubbard answered, "Most of the people will read between the lines, and the rumor mill will run wild on this. Everybody will be asking the same question, but can the Gardeners read our minds? Will a Yes vote under duress satisfy them?"

Gloria leaned forward and opened her mouth to say something, then she shut it and slumped back in her seat.

John shook his head, "I just don't know. Perhaps all we can do is to tell people to vote their conscience."

The pause was longer this time.

John looked at the General, "What about the military? Will your people go along with this?"

General Marcus stood, "I think the majority will support it, and we need to ensure my people have a voice. However, I'm afraid that's a more complicated question than you realize."

Tom said evenly, "Is there something you have not told us, General?"

Marcus took a deep breath, gravely looking at their faces. "I suspect that you may already know. You see, there are more people at the Joint Reserve Base now than there were before Awakening Day."

Tom nodded, "General, we're honestly not very surprised to hear that. There have been rumors about strange things happening at the base."

Marcus kept a straight face, "Yes, Mayor. Things were, are, very... chaotic at the base. On Awakening Day, the situation very nearly ended in bloodshed. We're, honestly, still working on sorting things out."

Gail was still seated. John turned to her, looking down at her, "You knew?"

Gail leveraged herself up on her cast and stood to face him. "Yes."

Strong murmurs of disapproval washed over the room.

He shook his head, "And you were *ordered* not to tell us?"

Gail drew her lips tight, "Yes."

Tom lowered his voice, "General, how many?"

"12,825, from the militaries of 19 other countries, including some hostile to the United States."

The room erupted in shouts of anger and confusion.

"What?"

"My God!"

"How could you keep this from us?"

"Where did you put them all?"

"From what countries?"

"Are they armed? Are they a danger?"

"What were you thinking?"

Marcus had expected the response, and perhaps worse. "Major Finley and all personnel were under strict orders to keep this a secret. On Awakening Day, we barely avoided a small war. Like you, we did not know what was going on. Was it an invasion or attack? At first, we thought it was perhaps some kind of Terrorist attack, but when we encountered the foreign troops, everything nearly, literally, blew up."

"We also quickly discovered that parts of the base had… changed. Then, when the suntube lights came on, and we all found out that we were not on Earth anymore, everything came into question. Were there spies or imposters among us, or even among the civilian population?"

"Then there was the Stalker attack – an attack by an actual goddamned *alien* that killed my people and yours. The longer I waited to tell you, the worse I knew it would be."

"It has only been in the last day or two that I have really started to get a feel for the New Arrivals and their officers. Now, however, a decision must be made about what to do with them, and it is not just a military decision."

John said, "You mean, do we conscript them into this army of the Gardeners?"

Marcus shook his head, "No, Sheriff. The issue is not as complicated for those from Allied Powers. We have precedent and regulations for dealing with those, but quite a few are not."

"Many were originally conscripted into their home country's military, some under the force of threat to their families. Many may not wish to voluntarily continue in any military service. What do we do with them? Would the civilian population of Fort Brazos accept them? Do we exile them to the wilderness?"

"The non-allied forces who do want to… enlist all came from different militaries and traditions. What do I do with them? What is the right rank for each person, and do they deserve it? Will our own men and women agree to serve underneath any of them? For some, like the North Koreans, can we, ever, trust them?"

John's jaw dropped, "North Koreans?"

Marcus nodded to Gail.

Gail leaned back against the chair, "There were some Americans among the New Arrivals, as well as units of various sizes from Australia, Brazil, China, Colombia, Egypt, France, Germany, India, Iran, Israel, Japan, North Korea, Pakistan, Russia, Saudi Arabia, South Korea, Turkey, the UK, and Ukraine."

Esmerelda looked thoughtful, "More genetic diversity? You realize that, right? I mean, Fort Brazos is mostly white, with a fair amount of Hispanic and not a lot of black. All these people will have a different ethnicity, and many won't speak English. Assimilation won't be easy."

Marcus nodded, "Yes, Councilwoman, that thought had crossed my mind."

Gloria cocked her head, "So, you didn't know if you could trust us, and you've been worrying about all this on your own?"

Marcus smiled, "At first, no, none of us really trusted each other, did we? I suppose I wanted to be able to tell you the whole story as well as to tell you how I recommend we deal with it. I was taught, whenever possible, to solve the problem myself before bringing it to others."

Tom scratched his chin, "So, you're saying that Item Three on the Plebiscite needs to address the question of these… New Arrivals?"

"Partly, yes. I think that Item Three should ask whether the people of Fort Brazos are willing to accept the New Arrivals into your community. Those among them who wish to remain in military service will need to swear allegiance to the new government. In addition, we need to be very clear that the military will have strong representation in the government. I think that the basic outline of that is Councilwoman Vargas's Item Two, but we need to make sure that the military personnel feel that they are not marginalized and are directly referenced."

Esmerelda stood, "And what of those who choose to do neither? Will their leaders drag them to follow them into some kind of exile? To set the stage for a conflict with us at some point in the future as they go out and set up tin-pot dictatorships?"

Gloria stayed seated but took stock of Marcus's eyes. "That's what really worries you, isn't it?"

Marcus let his façade slip a little and sighed, "Would you have me just shoot the ones I don't trust? Imprison them? If I send them off into the wilderness, they'll blame us for exiling them, even though that's what they asked for. Also, it's not just the North Koreans, there are religious hardliners in some of the other groups, and I'm sure that many of them still think this is all some kind of evil American plot."

Councilman Hubbard added, "It's not just your new arrivals. Some of the civilian population won't want to be part of this new society. Some of them will want to leave and strike out on their own."

John looked at him, "I think that can actually work to our advantage, Councilman. We can offer to outfit and supply any civilian who wants to leave and provide them with a radio to communicate with us if they choose. They could end up providing a lot of useful information in the long run."

Tom smiled, "And they can trade information for supplies."

Gloria pondered, "Even if we ask everyone to submit to the government here and not go off and create oppressive colonies elsewhere, once they leave, they'll largely be on their own. Part of the Plebiscite needs to be that they will all have representation in the government. That they and their descendants will always be able to call on us for help and that they will always have a say in their future."

Esmerelda frowned, "There's something else that's going to be a problem with all these soldiers from other countries." She paused and waited for everyone's attention, "I expect that they are mostly men?"

For a moment, the room fell silent as the thought sunk in. Then, in near unison, everyone sank back in their chairs.

"Oh hell."

"That's just great."

Gail blinked, then her eyes widened, "Oh."

Gloria shook her head, "Well, they're not going to go off and build very productive new colonies without women, are they? Have you added up the numbers?"

Marcus nodded, "The population of Fort Brazos, including the University, is 86,837. The population of the base and its territory is or was 34,712. Now, it is 47,537. So, instead of the already unbalanced total male to female population of 55% to 45%, now, with the addition of the international forces, the balance is at about 60% men, 40% women."

Councilman Hubbard sighed, "There will be trouble. Eventually."

John looked at Marcus, "How do we… how do we protect our women?"

Gail answered harshly, "A bullet in the head for rape."

Gloria grimaced, "Cut their balls off."

Tom shook his head, "At the rate people are arming themselves, I pity the fool rapist."

"No!" John frowned at Tom, "I will not have vigilante justice in our town. We will have justice and due process. If they're found guilty, then either shoot them or exile them to another continent." He turned and looked at Gail.

Gail nodded and smiled thinly, "I can live with that."

There was a long silence as people shifted uncomfortably in their seats.

Tom wondered aloud, "Speaking of exiles and colonies, will the Gardeners allow the creation of colonies that don't directly contribute to this war of theirs?"

John shook his head, "They've demonstrated they can hurt us or kill us. I think if we just ignore them and try to quietly try to farm and ranch this world that they'll not only know it, but they'll punish us, or worse. Like you said earlier, they must know that humans don't 100% agree on, really, anything. Whatever the answer we give, I think they'll want to see that most of us comply with their demands. I think the Plebiscite, with its direct vote by the people, is the clearest signal we can give."

Many hours later, John sat at his desk at the Sheriff's office, going through reports with Hector. John was, after all, still the Sheriff. Hector would become the new Sheriff after the election. It had taken little effort on John's part to make sure that happened. Hector was liked and respected in the community. They were alone in John's office. The security detail was camped outside the door.

John yawned, leaned back, and rubbed his eyes.

Hector studied him for a moment, "You've looked better, boss."

John chuckled, "Tell me something I don't know."

"You've been spending a lot of time with the Bonsai lady."

John bit off a retort, "You know perfectly well it was 'Banshee.' Don't be an ass."

Hector leaned back and frowned, "People are startin' to talk, you bein' Fort Brazos's most eligible bachelor and all."

John groaned, "Et tu, Brute?"

Hector grinned broadly, "Still, she's not too bad to look at, but she's too skinny, and she's a cold one. You could do better. You remember my cousin Belynda? She's been dying to meet you. She's got long black hair down to her butt, and she's built like a…."

John closed his eyes and tuned him out. Hector had previously tried to set him up with one of his sisters. "Hector…."

Hector laughed, "Look, boss, I know there ain't nothin' goin on, and I know you haven't had a moment's privacy, especially with your little gang of marines out there makin' sure you can't have no fun. I just thought you should know that tongues are waggin." He leaned forward, this time serious and concerned. "I'm just tellin' ya', be careful. One mistake and the political coyotes will be pickin' your bones."

John shook his head, "I know Hector, I know. I'm just trying to do everything I can to keep the Gardeners from picking *all* of our bones."

Demons

Methodist Hospital
Day 6: 11:21 AM

L ike Dr. Talib, Dr. David Duncan also had a new office as the result of Awakening Day. Now, as acting Chief Surgeon, he'd been up all night as well. He'd been reviewing an endless stream of reports and findings, but what had left him unable to sleep were the phone calls and emails back and forth with Commander Dr. Gwyneth Elliot and the world-shaking findings about being "copied" and more. He had been sworn to secrecy, but Gwyneth had needed a sounding board.

The truth was that he had spent the last two hours numbly 'staring into space,' as his mom would have said.

The hospital was not very close to Town Square, but the shockwave had been noisy enough. Fortunately, the hospital windows had not been broken.

After his army service, he had moved here for the quiet. To get away from his demons and ghosts.

Now, this. One revelation and shock after another.

He closed his eyes and sat there. The aliens had decreed that all of their futures were tied to what would no doubt be a never-ending forever-war of, quite literally, astronomical proportions.

As for his ghosts, despite what that crazy woman had said in the hospital corridor, he still talked to them. They had been with him so long it was hard to imagine not having them around.

His desk still had the belongings of his predecessor in it. He hadn't gotten around to clearing it out. He reached down and opened the bottom drawer. In it was a dusky bottle of Bunnahabhain single malt scotch whiskey and a pair of glasses. He picked up the scotch and set the bottle on his desk. He stared at it for a full two minutes before picking up one of the glasses as well.

Reporting

92.5 FM and Live Video Stream
Day 7: 8:06 AM

"Good morning Fort Brazos. I'm Danielle Richardson, and welcome to the "The Danielle Richardson Show. Yesterday was truly a historic day for Fort Brazos and humanity itself. Today we're going to recap yesterday's events, but that's later. First, and only on the Danielle Richardson Show, I have an exclusive video. And no, I don't mean yet another angle of the hologram thing in Town Square. That's being covered to death everywhere else."

"No, what I'm going to show you on my live stream is something you haven't seen. The raw, uncut, unedited exclusive video of the personal reactions, as they happened in real-time, as our candidate for Vice President witnessed the alien broadcast."

"Now, you all know that I was not a fan of Ms. Finley from the start, and I've talked about the dangers of the Military Industrial Complex gaining too much power over our lives. I had nothing against her personally. I'm sure she's a fine officer and all that, but the idea of her being a heartbeat away from the Presidency is something that concerned me greatly."

"And so, let me set this up for you. Yesterday morning, moments before I was about to pay for my morning coffee and crêpe at Greta's and head to the station, the aliens did their thing. I'm not sure what they're compensating for, breaking glass and eardrums like they seem to enjoy doing, but there I was in the middle of it."

"So what, you say? So were lots of other people too? And you'd be right. What was different is that I was only a few feet away from City Hall, and that's where Major Finley burst out the shattered glass doors. She had one foot still in the cast like we're all used to seeing her in, and the other foot bare, running right across all that broken glass to see what was happening. A bunch of soldiers followed like they could protect her from the hologram or something."

"Anyway, I'm not sure why, but instead of filming the hologram, like everyone else, I turned my phone towards her. There was just something about her. I confess that she was so… vivid, so larger than life even. I just couldn't take my eyes off her. As you watch the video, I think you will see what I mean, even though she never says a word."

Pinky

In the day of the attack on the highway, Wayne and Sybil's supply run to the Forward Observation Post had been scheduled as a quick day trip, so they'd left Pinky at the Vet's office for a checkup and grooming, assured they'd be back the same day to pick him up. In the aftermath of the attack, they had been politely but firmly invited to stay put while the investigation played out. There was also the not so minor issue of replacing their truck's front grill.

Three days later, they were finally back at the Vet's office to pick up Pinky. They sat in the waiting area, along with a half dozen other people, several of whom had unhappy pets on leashes. The 1970's-era Spanish architecture was well worn but also well cared for. It had been tastefully redecorated to soften some of the harsher characteristics of that period. Its bold lines and accents had clearly been updated with a woman's touch.

Wayne fidgeted as they waited. It was taking much longer than they had expected.

Sybil extended a slender arm behind him and pulled herself close to him. "It'll be Okay, Wayne. I'm sure they're just super busy right now. I'm sure Pinky is Okay."

"I should never have left her here alone."

"She'll forgive you. Just be glad she wasn't with us on the highway."

He grunted and slowly nodded.

The inside door opened, and a petite Hispanic woman with long dark hair and large black eyes stepped through. "Blanchard?"

Wayne and Sybil stood and met her at the door.

"Hi, I'm Dr. Eva Sanches. Can you come with me, please?"

Wayne nodded but glanced a worried look at Sybil. There was something in Sanches's tone that didn't sound right.

They followed her to a small examining room, where an assistant sat with Pinky, who lay on an examining table. Pinky looked up, and at the sight of Wayne, she leaped into the air with a joyous Yip! She danced around the examining table, yipping and letting everyone know that her person had arrived.

Wayne sighed with relief and extended his arms to pick her up. His brilliant ear-to-ear smile filled the room. Pinky gleefully jumped into his arms. He held her to his face, and she licked his nose and cheeks in delight.

Sybil turned to Eva, "Doctor, we had the sense from you that maybe not everything was right with Pinky?"

Doubt shadowed Wayne's face, but he focused on cuddling Pinky.

Eva picked up a clipboard and scratched her head. "Ah, yes. I have a question first. You indicated on the form that Pinky had been neutered at some point in the past?"

Sybil nodded, and Wayne answered, "Oh yes, when we adopted her two years ago. Why?"

Eva nodded but did not seem surprised. "Well, it is quite obvious that Pinky is your dog, so there was not a switch up. I expect this will be a surprise then. You see, Pinky is no longer fixed. She is no longer neutered."

Wayne and Sybil answered in unison, "What?"

Eva looked down and sighed. She was tired and had not slept in two days, and she'd had trouble keeping food down. There was just too much to do that could not wait. "This is not the first I've seen. In fact, every formerly neutered animal I have examined is no longer neutered. It has all been undone."

Sybil paled, "What? How? ... what?"

Eva nodded and grimaced, "It seems that the aliens who put us here wanted us to be fruitful..." she paused as a frown came over her face, "...and multiply."

216

The color drained from Eva's face as a dawning realization came over her. "Oh... my."

Wayne blinked in confusion, but Sybil looked into Eva's eyes, and both of their jaws dropped. Sybil sucked in her breath and covered her mouth, her own eyes growing wide. "You don't think?"

"Oh, God."

Wayne held Pinky to his cheek, "What is it, dear?"

Silent Storm

First United Methodist Church
Day 7: 12:00 PM

Tom Parker, Mayor of Fort Brazos and Senior Deacon at First United Methodist Church of Fort Brazos, stood at the pulpit. It was early, and the suntube light shone through the stained glass. A photo of Pastor Joe hung on the pulpit, and there were flowers everywhere. The pews were packed, and it was standing room only. John Austin, Gail Finley, and Marcus Alexander were also present. The Fire Marshall didn't object to the overcrowding. He was on the third row.

The choir had sung with aching sorrow and passion. The projection screen slowly scrolled the names of the dead. There were thousands. Photos of loved ones were taped and pinned to every free surface in the room.

Tom looked out across the congregation. He saw fear. Lots of it. He also saw bone-crushing sadness, anger, denial, confusion, and, on many faces, the blank stares of the lost. He recognized all those feelings and more from his own heart.

He began, "It should not be me, standing here. It should be Pastor Joe. He died, and I lived." He gazed across the room, "I know that many of you have had the same feelings about your lost loved ones. Joe died in my arms, killed by a deer through the windshield of all the crazy things. An alien monster didn't kill him. He was taken from us in an accident only minutes after the aliens spared him the fate of so many other of our loved ones. They wanted him to live, but he died in a stupid accident, and I do so dearly wish he was here to encourage and inspire us." Several people burst into tears. "I would trade places with him in an instant."

"We've all lost people we loved, and they were taken from us in the most callous way, by powerful aliens who simply wanted to make a point, to emphasize their power over us."

There was a rough stir of anger throughout the room.

"Since then, we've had one revelation after another. We all woke up in an alien world, apparently the sole survivors of Planet Earth. Aliens have attacked us, and families have been destroyed." He looked directly at Sandra Hoffman, who sat in the second row with her surviving siblings.

A lean young Army Lieutenant, David Garreth, sat very close, next to Sandra. Her lips trembled at Tom's words, but she nodded to him. People in the pews around her gently reached out their hands, touching her shoulders and whispering love and support. She fought to remain strong for her remaining family. Her sisters buried their faces in her, and she pulled them all close. David's face was tight with protective defiance.

Tom smiled softly, "I'm going to play for you something that Pastor Joe recorded after the 911 attacks." He looked up at the projection screen, and the names faded and were replaced with a video recording of Pastor Joe standing at the same pulpit. He'd been younger, and his hair thicker, but the grace and vitality that defined him were plain.

"Howard Washington Thurman was born in 1899 and died in 1981. He was an African American author, philosopher, theologian, educator, and civil rights, leader. He was the first prominent African American pacifist. His theology of radical nonviolence influenced and shaped a generation of civil rights leaders. He was a key mentor to leaders of the time, including Martin Luther King Jr. He wrote the following:

I share with you the agony of your grief;
The anguish of your heart echoes in my own.
I know I cannot enter all you feel
Nor bear with you the burden of your pain
I can but offer what my love does give:

The strength of caring,
The warmth of one who seeks to understand
The silent storm-swept barrenness of such a loss.
This I do in quiet ways,
That on your lonely path
You may not walk alone."

"We will never forget what has happened in these last few days. We will always remember where we were when it happened. It is a savage inflection point in all our lives. We will mourn and bury our dead. We will find out what has happened and why and who was responsible, and, in the fullness of time, I'm sure that our brave young men and women will venture out with terrible purpose and find those who did this evil and heinous thing."

"In the days, weeks, and years ahead, we must, however, decide who we are and what we stand for. Will we apologize for and excuse the actions of our enemies? Will we worry ourselves into inaction, fretting over what we must have done or said to make people so mad at us that they would do such a thing? Do we deny that evil is a real and dreadful thing, relegated to the dustbin of primitive thinking? Aren't we too evolved for that?"

"Or will we accept that however kind and sophisticated and educated and loving and accepting we are of other people and their beliefs, that there truly is evil in this world. That there are people who despise us for who and what we are? Do we forget all that we have learned about what happens when one people looks at another and decides that those people are not really people at all? Do we forget the lessons from the millions killed by Hitler? By Stalin? By Mao? By Pol Pot?"

"Throughout human history, century after century, Genocide has been with us. One group of people decides another is subhuman and then does its best to wipe them out. Is this really any different? There is a group of people in this world who believe that anyone who is not them, who doesn't believe as they do, doesn't dress and act as they do, is their righteous and mortal enemy."

"I'll get in trouble for saying this. I love my fellow man—all of them, from every corner of the globe. However, I also know that some of my fellow men will happily slash my throat and my children's throats while my cheek is turned. I hope and pray with all my heart that we can reach

220

these people. That we can show them love and kindness and pull them from the abyss of their hatred."

"I, for one, will not hide my head in the sand and pretend that there is no evil in this world. I will not cower in the shadows. I will stand with my family and my community. I will freely give hope and shelter to those in need, just as I will give hope, shelter, and support to all the brave men and women who are our sword and shield."

The video playback stopped, and the frame froze on Pastor Joe's face, with his full head of energetic white hair, brilliant blue eyes, and prominent nose. Joseph Gilmore had authored 28 books on spirituality and had lent his 6'2" frame to many mission trips building churches and homes. He'd lived in the same simple two-bedroom house for decades and had just celebrated his 68th birthday a week before Awakening Day. He'd truly been a pillar of the community, and his continence radiated faith, intelligence, determination, and love. The image faded and returned to the scrolling names. Tom turned back to the congregation.

Tom choked out the words, "It's not fair…." And the room swelled with "No's" and surging anguish. He swallowed and paused, gazing at all their faces.

"It's not fair. No, not any of it. What has happened to us all is no less than biblical, like Noah after the flood. Many of us are asking questions about what it all means, and has God forsaken us? Does he even exist? How could he let this happen?"

"The truth is that I'm just as overwhelmed as you are, although, somehow, I just know that if Pastor Joe were here, he'd find a way to shine a light on it and make it understandable to us and inspire us all the same."

A few people chuckled softly. "I also know in my heart that Joe is looking down on us, and if he could, he'd slap me on the head and tell me to have faith and to believe that somehow, in all this, that God still has a plan for us."

"What I can tell you is that, yes, it seems that we are all that is left of humanity. There is no one left to call. It's just us. Joe's not here, but *we* are. We need to decide what we, *as a people*, represent and what we are to become. Will we just fade away and die with the rest of our world? I admit to you that I have had moments when my faith has failed me, and in my personal fear and despair, I've had fleeting thoughts that may be just fading away would be better than living with this pain and anguish and a terrifying and unknown future. I have thought about it. I know many of you have, too."

"But here's the thing. I keep reaching the same conclusion. If we let it all go, there will be no one to tell our story. If we quit, then all of history, all of humankind's pain and suffering, all of our triumph and joy, all of our glorious triumphs and failures, everything we've learned about the universe and ourselves, everything that makes us unique in the universe, will be forever lost. If we quit, then what was the point? Don't we then betray the souls of all who came before us? Why did we bother to pull ourselves out of the mud? Why did we claw our way for thousands of years, generation after generation, out of ignorance and despair and dare to begin the process of reaching beyond our world to explore others?"

"Compared to the geologic history of Planet Earth, Mankind was a blip, a shining spark of life reaching beyond itself to strive to improve itself and find meaning in the universe."

"Do we surrender to our fears and our sorrow and anguish? What would our loved ones, who we lost, have told us?"

He paused and waited, "What would Pastor Joe have told us we should do?"

He looked around the room. At first, the congregation shifted uncomfortably in their seats. Slowly, people started to look up from their tears and anguish, and the mood began to lift. At first, there were a few angry nods, but gradually the room filled with a murmur of defiance that burned away the fog of fear.

Tom smiled thinly and nodded. "You see it, don't you? He would have told us that we must live! We are not alone. There are other peoples amongst the stars who our common enemy would also snuff out. We are being given the opportunity to transform the pyres of our lost world into a beacon of hope. There is indeed a purpose for our existence. We must have faith and bring light and love and hope to our unknown neighbors…" He swallowed, "And, I'll add one more thing that I also know my friend could not have brought himself to say, but it is in my heart, and I believe it to be true. I say… I say that we must also teach these Accipiters, these enemies of light and life, the true meaning of despair, and what it means to be the mortal enemy of mankind."

What awaits us in the dark?

Ammunition Bunker # 1: Joint Reserve Base
Day 7: 1:51 PM

G eneral Marcus, Captain Guevara, a handful of senior officers, and CCM Anders stood inside the lower level of the ammunition bunker. Like all such structures, it was designed with safety protocols to prevent damage to other facilities in the event of a catastrophic failure. Its reinforced concrete and steel structure was primarily underground and shaped so that the force would be directed upwards instead of outwards in the event of an explosion. The bunkers were not much to look at from the outside. Low to the ground and outfitted with heavy lightning rods and weatherproofing, most of the structure was underground. This particular bunker had been built in 1973 and had three levels.

The base had never been designed as a front-line facility. It was deep inside the United States, and the only really serious enemy concern had been that of a nuclear missile or terrorist attack. The military stores on the base were significant but mainly devoted to repair and training. The stockpiles were deposited in a series of bunkers, with some redundancy in case of disaster.

In light of their situation, Marcus had ordered an inventory. They wouldn't be receiving any new supply shipments. What they had was what they had. He'd also ordered that any and all spent ammunition cartridges and casings be recovered for potential reload and reuse, including a thorough sweep of all practice ranges, something that was sure to keep a lot of otherwise unoccupied soldiers very busy for a long, long, long, long, very, very long time indeed.

224

During the inventory of Bunker # 1, the specialists in charge had "hit the alarm" when they discovered that something was wrong. Each level had its own blast doors. When they reached the bottom, they discovered a new set of blast doors that had not been there before. Each freight elevator only went down one floor, and they discovered a new elevator on the bottom floor. After much discussion, a single squad of heavily armed marines followed a Tech Sergeant downstairs and took covering positions behind him while he opened the door. It was not locked.

Hours later, after a thorough search, the bunker and its new… additions were deemed safe. Marcus and the other officers now went through the new door and stairs to the 4th level.

Marcus managed to keep a straight face, but several officers sucked in their breath in shock. It was not only a 'new' level, but it was also huge, and there were yet more new doors. In total, ten new levels had been found. The construction of each level contained multiple redundant fire and blast barriers made of a suspiciously non-manmade-looking alloy.

Marcus was immediately reminded of the Warehouse space that had been "enlarged" by the aliens. Seemingly countless shelves contained what must be an astronomical amount of ammunition of all types and sizes. It was all clearly labeled.

Guevara walked over to one of the warehouse-style shelves and opened a sealed ammo can, removing a box of NATO 7.62x51mm rifle ammunition. The box looked similar to a standard one, but there was something odd about it. Guevara opened the box. Inside, the cartridges were wrapped in a very thin film that looked as fragile as a soap bubble. The film was clearly vacuum-sealed around the ammunition. He showed it to Marcus and the other officers.

CCM Anders reached for and took the box. He pressed his thumb firmly into the film, but it resisted. Next, he removed a water bottle from his gear and poured water on the film. The water beaded and rolled off. Shaking his head, he took out his service knife and slit the film with it. The film immediately shriveled up and fell away, dissolving into a tiny ball.

He nodded thoughtfully. "Smart, Sir. Like plastic, the film is waterproof or at least very water-resistant, and it is resistant to poking that would break most any kind of plastic film this thin. Also, vacuum sealing the ammo like this will probably increase its shelf-life a great deal. Also, I don't know if anyone has noticed, but the air in here is cool and dry – even more than on our own levels, and I don't see any ducts or hear any air moving. All in all, if everything is sealed like this, then I expect it will help with shipping it in the field. It is already sealed and waterproof."

Preliminary searches of the other bunkers had revealed similar but as-yet unopened 'new' doors and, presumably, more levels.

Marcus frowned. He looked around the room and then at his officers. "For any kind of engagement that our force level could carry with them and expend, this looks like years' worth of supply."

Guevara added, "Assuming we are to do lots of fighting, we'd eventually use up even this much ammo. Perhaps they are giving us enough to last until we build up the infrastructure to manufacture a sufficient supply of new-made ordinance?"

Marcus nodded, "I think so, yes. However, it also implies to me that the aliens think that our current weapons can actually be of use against these enemies, at least in some kind of limited engagements, on the ground. Any enemy smart enough to conquer the galaxy could swat us like flies from orbit and would adapt to our weapons and tactics. I think they are providing enough inventory of the things that we already know and understand that we can use until we learn to do better, perhaps from captured weapons and technology that we acquire along the way."

"Captain Guevara, please have the arms bunkers also checked. I will be surprised if we don't discover the same kind of, um, changes there as well. For that matter, I want every building on this base checked out, top-to-bottom. Let's find out what other surprises they have in store for us."

CCM Anders looked at Marcus. "Sir, if I may ask, we're locked inside a hollow world. How are we supposed to go out and fight some galactic menace? Back on Earth, the best we had were chemical rockets to get us into orbit and barely to the moon."

Marcus smiled grimly. "Chief Master Sargent, that question has been keeping me up at night. These 'Gardeners' clearly are on their own timetable. They're only telling us what they think we need to know. They're feeding us baby food in a highchair. What will happen when they let us down and we start walking on our own? Will we be the innocent toddler walking alone into the dark woods? On Earth, were we just living in a fairy tale, with only our brothers and sisters to fear?"

Guevara added, "… and what awaits us in the dark wood?"

Leaders

Joint Reserve Base
Day 7: 4:00 PM

General Marcus studied the faces of the officers seated in the conference room. He looked around the room and reflected upon how it was not an elaborate or richly appointed room or even one built in the last decade. It was just another anonymous-looking conference room in a building that looked like so many other U.S. government buildings. The normalcy of the room belied the fact that it was now located inside the last surviving outpost of humanity.

He thought to himself, *We're trapped inside this hollow world, given an ultimatum by our kidnappers that we must fight what will likely be a generational struggle against an entrenched, galaxy-spanning enemy. Quite a tall and mind-bogglingly ambitious order for a species that never put anyone beyond our own moon.*

The conference room was sealed and swept for anything that shouldn't be there. Armed Marine guards stood outside the soundproof doors. Across from Marcus sat four officers of varying rank and even more varying uniforms from different nations. Each of those nations had been allies of the United States.

To Marcus's right was Colonel Gideon Markovic, late of the Israeli Defense Force. Gideon had risen through the ranks, leading mechanized infantry and increasingly sensitive duties. Gideon was of medium height, with light hair and dark eyes. He was Israeli by way of Russian Jewish refugees who had fled to the United States and later immigrated with their young son to Israel. His confidential personnel file, provided in the database left by the Gardeners, had been interesting reading. His wife Carmit and two girls, Anat and Brach, had not been 'rescued' by the Gardeners, and the crushing weight of it all rested on the man's unyielding and determined shoulders.

Next to Gideon was Lieutenant Colonel Martin Williams of the Australian Intelligence Corps. Martin had worked up the ranks within Intelligence both in the field and in command, in the Middle East and other exotic places. He was an unassuming-looking man, bland in almost every way. He looked like an overworked, uninspired accountant. An uninteresting and very forgettable accountant. Marcus knew from his file that Martin had cultivated that look and had even had surgery to enhance it. He was both brilliant and shrewd. He'd had no family to leave behind, only his country and planet. After recent events, even his well-practiced façade was drawn and apprehensive.

Next to Martin sat Brigadier General Sabrina Chilton of the United Kingdom's Signal Brigade. Sabrina was rakishly thin, with short bobbed, slightly graying blond hair and soft blue eyes. Her face was a strong one. She had served for twenty-six years, fifteen in Signals. At the time of the attack on Earth, she had been on a multi-country trip and made a courtesy stop at a forward operating base. She and that unit had been scooped up like the other "New Arrivals."

Sabrina was the senior ranking officer among the survivors of the friendly nations. She was also fiendishly good at her job, providing Strategic and Tactical Communications for the Royal Army. What she seemed to have a natural-born talent for, though, was Electronic Warfare.

Sabrina's husband had died in an accident years before, and she was a single mom with a teenage daughter, Nicole. Thankfully, Nicole had been accompanying her when they had been abducted. Unfortunately, she'd planned to drop her daughter off at a boarding school in Switzerland on one of the return legs of her trip, and Nicole knew it. Sabrina sat stone-faced. Despite the fact that she'd 'arrived' here with an intact unit, she only knew a few of them, mostly by reputation. None of her headquarters staff or day-to-day colleagues had been with her. She knew no one in this place except for her daughter, and Nicole wasn't talking to her.

Next to Sabrina sat Colonel Cesar Salangsang, commander of the Philippine Army 54th Engineering Brigade. He was 52 years old and well-liked by his men.

At 5'4", he was the shortest person in the room, but he radiated an intense vibrancy and strength. His toothy smile was how most of his men thought of him, but then, most of his men gladly and literally moved mountains for the man. Woe be unto those who were only there to mark time. Unlike so many other officers, Cesar did not berate or curse those who fell short. His glacial stare of disappointment and pity usually sufficed. When it didn't, enthusiastic 'encouragement' from the wayward soldier's more enlightened fellows would help them find their way to the light. His men were immensely proud that their brigade always had the best performance ratings.

Now, Cesar's smile was etched on his face like a bas-relief. Darkness haunted his eyes, though. He had had an extensive family that included both his and his wife's parents, surviving grandparents, as well as his own nine children and six grandchildren, and an extended family whose annual reunions brought an ever more dizzying explosion of children, teenagers, and family of all ages. He loved his work, but his family was what he had lived for. He and units of his brigade had been building a forward operating base on one of the Southern Philippine Islands. It was for a renewed effort to project force against Islamic insurgent groups as well as Communist rebels. Construction had been taking place under regular fire from snipers and mortar fire. Amid that fire, Cesar had frequently been seen, leading by example, driving construction equipment, and directing the efforts of his men. Now he was here, with the rest of his men, and like so many others, his entire family was forever lost.

Marcus opened the meeting with a grim smile, "Thank you all for coming," *As if they could refuse!* "I've asked you to join me here today to discuss the future. You've all seen the alien's demands, and you've all been given information packets summarizing what we know so far about these supposed enemies we're being told we must fight. In addition, each of you has received a summary of each other's backgrounds."

Sabrina's eyes briefly narrowed, but she remained quiet, her hands folded on the table.

Marcus noticed it and nodded, "I see some of you are suspicious. Good! I'm suspicious as hell about all that has happened. Still, these so-called Gardeners seem to have a gun to our heads. We are as technologically inferior to them as rats in a scientist's maze. We can either choose to go along with their demands or wait and see if they really are willing to wipe us out and start over."

He looked around the table, "I'm going to ask this right now. Do any of you want to do that? Are you willing to go through door number two and see what happens?"

Except for the air conditioning, it was deathly quiet in the room. No one moved.

Marcus nodded, "Yes, well, that's one reason why I had all of you go to the warehouse morgue and see the dead. I wanted to make sure that you saw for yourselves how easy it was for these Gardeners to prune us back. Not just an arbitrary amount, either. They killed exactly 5% of the civilians, and not a single military man or woman."

Marcus knew that the morgue experience had affected all of them, himself included. Seeing thousands of dead bodies tended to make an impression. No-one turned away from Marcus's gaze.

"Good. Now, let me make myself crystal clear. I don't like this, I don't trust this, and I intend for us to do everything we can to keep a knife in our boots, a gun up our sleeves, and eyes on the back of our heads. Yes, dammit, we're being used. Manipulated. Possibly even enslaved for some sort of sick alien gladiator games pitting one race against another. I don't know. None of us knows. All we can do is try to organize ourselves and prepare as best we can. And Survive."

He paused for a moment, searching the faces around him. He took a breath, "One of the first steps is organization. That is why I've asked you here today. Until Awakening Day, this base was in the middle of the continent, far from conflict. It was a lot of things, but what it boils down to is that we were a place to train, a place to repair and reorganize after deployments, and a place for the politicians to dump any unit they could find, so that they could close other bases in the losing party's districts."

Twinges of smiles touched their faces, and Cesar's eyes widened.

Marcus chuckled, "What? What's the point of the apocalypse if you can't badmouth your now deceased lords and masters?"

Gideon broke the group's silence, "General, if I may ask, why this base? Why Fort Brazos? If they wanted us to fight a war, why not a front-line base full of front-line troops and equipment, or even, say, your Fort Hood?"

Marcus nodded slowly, "Colonel Markovic, that very question has haunted me, and the Gardeners have certainly not gone out of their way to hold our hands and explain their reasoning in terms we understand. They're testing us, a step at a time to see if we somehow measure up."

Sabrina's voice was the husky voice of a life-long smoker, "What did you decide, General?"

Marcus looked at each of them in turn. "Colonel Williams, you're the Intelligence expert. Tell us what you think."

Williams didn't flinch, and Marcus silently wondered if Williams was physically capable of flinching. He answered in a measured voice that was unremarkable in every way. "General, a military is an extension of the will of the people it serves. Your geographic location was somewhat remote, and the city itself was not part of any of the larger metropolitan areas. Its people felt themselves to be independent. Your base had a broad cross-section of specialties and skills. While the units here were not active combatants, most personnel had served tours in active war zones. When you combine its existing units with the, as you called us, the New Arrivals, you have the raw materials, the building blocks to assemble and grow a force structure that has a broad array of support organizations and, potentially, with the civilian workforce in the city, a supply train to field an effective force. These aliens, the so-called Gardeners, are playing the long game."

"Thank you, Colonel. I would add to your assessment that none of the New Arrivals were delivered here with anything larger than small arms. We have a lot of equipment here, but most of it is not combat-ready – it was here to be repaired, upgraded, and made combat-ready! We don't currently have enough men and materials to field in full strength or provide a supply chain for a traditional deployment. We're going to have to repair and train and cross-train. My plan is to completely reorganize the units here and establish new ones. You four officers are the beginning of the process. You have the backgrounds and experience we need, and we need to start integrating the New Arrivals."

Cesar smirked, "Some of the forces from other countries will not be happy."

Marcus nodded, "You're right, Colonel, and in some cases, they won't be happy no matter what I do. In the meantime, I will make it clear that this is just the start. We, of course, have existing units here that will continue under their current command structure, but I need to adapt to our new circumstances. I also fully realize that we have no clue what we'll eventually be facing. The organization we build will need to be flexible and adaptable."

He paused and looked around the table. "Also, I will tell you four first. This will be a meritocracy. Just because you will be among the first to be assigned new commands does not mean that you are somehow entitled to said commands. Time in rank does not mean what you're used to anymore. Based on your individual and very detailed records, another thing provided to us by our abductors," he paused for a moment to let that sink in. Everyone shifted uncomfortably at that revelation and the myriad implications that came with it. "I believe that you are the right people for the jobs, but I may be wrong, or someone better may come along."

Marcus let that sink in for a moment. "There's something else, as well. Before we go further, I need to know if each of you will be willing to swear allegiance to the new government being formed here. And, I'm going to ask you to do that now, even before it is formally in place. I need you. What's more, I need you to take a leap of faith. If you are unwilling to do so, I understand that volunteers are being sought to go out and explore this world first-hand."

Everyone stiffened. Reactions varied from tightened lips to widened eyes, but these were disciplined, experienced officers and leaders.

Marcus went on, "This is a new reality, people. We may be sitting in a place that *looks* like it did before Awakening Day, but it isn't earth. This is all a re-creation of our environment." He thumped the table, "This table didn't exist on Earth. It is also a re-creation. If you go outside, you can look up and see other continents that have eco-zones that resemble the places you came from. They're not original either. This is all a completely brand-new world, fresh off the alien assembly line."

Marcus looked down at the table for a moment before continuing, "I'm going to tell you all a secret. But before I do, I need you to raise your hands and swear your allegiance to the Republic of New Texas, or whatever we end up naming the place, and that you agree to join and serve under my command. This is non-negotiable. We'll write up something fancy later, and you can sign whatever parchment we come up with, but for now, on your honor, I need you to put your hands on your hearts and swear. Or leave."

All four looked at each other and slowly rose as one.

Marcus stood and put his hand on his own heart. "Repeat after me, I, your name, swear on my honor, allegiance to the Republic of New Texas."

They did.

"And I agree to join the New Texas military and serve under General Marcus's command, under the authority granted by the civilian government."

They so swore.

The reality sunk in as they pledged their fates to a people and a General they did not know, in a world they didn't understand, and to a terrifying and uncertain future.

Marcus waved them back to their seats and remained standing. "What I'm about to tell you is currently known only to the civilian leadership and a few officers. A moment ago, I told you that this place we are in is not the original." He tapped the table, "Like I said, even this table was not on Earth. This building wasn't there either. They were scanned by the Gardeners and then reconstructed here. Some things are different. For example, we discovered that the ammunition bunkers have many new and vastly larger levels with perhaps decades' worth of ordinance in them."

Martin's eyes flickered for the briefest of moments, "So, they must expect that we will be using our existing weapons for some period of time, which implies limited ground conflicts since we would likely not be able to operationally support any kind of extended engagements."

Marcus nodded and continued, "Agreed. We've found other changes. Civilian warehouses were similarly, ah, expanded. However, the secret you will now have to keep is not about the buildings or the land outside. It's about us. None of us are originals either. Our bodies were also scanned and then re-created here and brought to life. We have medical proof. All those dead bodies you saw? They were never actually alive. They were re-created just like us—but the Gardeners chose not to breathe life into them."

Cesar's jaw dropped. Gideon slumped back in his chair, blinking. Sabrina sat rigid, unmoving, staring at Marcus, and Martin shook his head and quietly said, "Of course."

Marcus looked at Martin and nodded for him to continue.

Martin spoke with his dry, measured, unremarkable voice, "Now that I think about it, it makes sense. These aliens scanned us and our environment. They didn't freeze-dry us and everything else, haul it all the way here, and then unthaw us. That would be a huge amount of… mass… to move. Also, moving mass like that might be either beyond their capabilities or at least beyond their ability to do so while the Accipiters were watching. Much easier to scan and move everything as data. No, they had to travel a presumably vast distance to wherever this place is, likely far, far away from our solar system and the invaders there. Once here, they built this world and terraformed the land to meet our needs. Then it makes sense that they would, ahh, print or by whatever technology, replicate us and everything else on location, in situ."

Cesar whispered, "Our souls…."

Marcus remarked, "The latest working theory is that the scanning process may well have been destructive. The implication was that they did the scanning moments before we would have been destroyed anyway. They only took people and places that were about to be destroyed by the alien attacker's kinetic bombardment, leaving no evidence of their tampering. The Gardener announcement did state that we are still who we were, that our essence was preserved. I, personally, choose to believe it means that we are indeed who we were and that our souls, whatever that really means if it means anything at all, are still our own. I believe I am -- who I was."

Marcus allowed the soul-searching moment to stretch, then he asked, "People, are you all still with me?"

Thoughtful and somber, they all answered, "Yes, Sir."

"Good, I expected nothing less from each of you. Let's get down to business. Colonel Salangsang, I'm promoting you from Lieutenant Colonel to full Colonel. The rest of you, I'm keeping at your current rank, at least for now. As we go forward, that could change with circumstance and our needs. However, I don't really think that will happen. Each of you is of sufficient rank for the slots I'm appointing you to."

"Colonel Markovic, I am ordering you to organize and command a new unit, what I'm calling the 1st Mechanized Infantry."

Gideon stiffened, and Marcus held his hand up, "Colonel, we only have enough people and combat-ready equipment to form, at best, an understrength Brigade, and that will be with a lot of less than perfectly operating equipment. You're going to figure out what we have here, across pre-existing personnel and New Arrivals, and cherry-pick your first string for 1st Company, 2nd Company, and so forth. You'll be competing with other commands, of course, and there will be some serious horse-trading going on. I want to see how well you handle yourself creating and leading a new Brigade and how well you whip them into shape."

"Yes Sir."

Marcus looked at each of them before continuing, "Understand, people, that whether or not you hold on to your commands depends entirely on yourselves."

Everyone nodded.

"Good. Now, Colonel Williams, I'm assigning you to establish our Intelligence group. We'll name it after we figure out what it needs to look like, but you are going to be this world's spymaster. We need military analysis of what the civilian scientists decipher from the aliens. We need to lay the groundwork for how we will organize and manage Intelligence operations as we, however, it's supposed to happen, go out and start fighting these bad-actor aliens, the ones the Gardeners called Accipiters. I need you to build a table of organization – what skills and experience you need and how many people to start with, then you can horse trade like everyone else. We'll create a review board to resolve assignment conflicts and make sure we put our men and women where they are needed the most."

Martin nodded, "General, as I understand it, there are inhabited worlds being threatened by these Accipiters that we are being charged with trying to protect,

God, help us. That said, the enemy of my enemy will not always be my friend, but I expect some of those we encounter may at least be valuable as resources for trade and strategic intelligence. Of course, the interesting challenge will be how to gather intelligence on planets where we humans will not exactly be able to blend in."

Marcus smiled, "Then I suppose you'll just have to invent a whole new kind of tradecraft, Colonel."

Martin allowed a small smile and nodded.

Marcus lowered his gaze, "One more thing, Colonel. Your immediate first priority will be to review each of the other New Arrivals, starting with those from unfriendly nations. I need your analysis of how we can best make use of them while minimizing, hopefully, the risk that they'll bite us in the ass later on. Figure out what we can salvage from this mess."

"Yes Sir."

Marcus turned to Sabrina, "Brigadier Chilton, like Colonel Williams, you are going to need to create and figure out what the size and composition of 1st Signals and Electronic Warfare will be. I'm keeping you at your current rank, for now, because you have experience running a larger organization already, and I fully expect that we will eventually need you to build a new one at least as large as what you previously commanded."

Marcus looked around the table, "People, I know that we will have holes and missing skillsets. I will need each of you to prioritize and assess how to fix those shortcomings. We have to work around them and train for critical slots we are unable to fill. We also need to think about saving irreplaceable knowledge that may reside only in the minds of our most experienced people. We can't do everything at once, so let's figure out what the worst holes are and how to plug them."

"Lastly, Colonel Salangsang, I'm ordering you to create and command the 1st Combat Engineers. There are existing units here on base that you will be able to draw from, in addition to your own men. 1st CE will be very, very busy. First, we need to assess what needs to change on the base itself. Second, we need to better plan and build new Forward Operating Bases on this continent and elsewhere in this world. Third, I have no doubt that we will need your services when we eventually start venturing out and meeting our cosmic neighbors, and, before anyone asks, no, I have no clue about how we're supposed to be able to accomplish that."

"Yes, Sir."

Marcus looked around the table and saw the weight on everyone's shoulders. "One more thing. All of us have lost. We lost our whole damned planet! We lost friends and loved ones." He looked at Cesar and Gideon, "Some of us lost children and spouses. I know. Just remember, ALL of us in this world have lost. All of the men and women who serve under you have lost. I need you to inspire your people, to lead them, and to give them hope and a purpose."

Marcus rose and stood at attention. The others followed suit. What he did next broke military tradition. He saluted first. Gideon, Martin, Sabrina, and Cesar snapped parade ground salutes in return, each according to their respective nation's traditions.

Marcus stabbed the intercom button on the conference room phone. "Captain, please bring it in."

Moments later, Captain Guevara opened the door and pulled in a rolling clothes rack. Hanging on it were four new uniforms, already adorned with name tags and rank insignia.

Hunting Party

Highway
Day 8: 10:11 AM

T he dark hulk of Lieutenant Marshall Sherrard's Humvee still lay on the burnt and blackened highway. His horrifically shredded remains and that of his men, Sargent Nelson Black, Specialist Delon Smith, and Specialist Keanu Campbell, were carefully and respectfully removed.

After the attack, desultory grassfires had burned parts of the area around the road. Fortunately, the fire did not spread far because the ground was still damp from the hurricane that no one had bothered to name.

Now, a forensics effort was underway. Photos, measurements, and samples were collected by an understandably nervous team of army specialists and civilian scientists (mostly their Teaching Assistants and Lab Assistants), with notable exceptions like Dr. Jacob Becker and Dr. Eva Sanches, who had literally rolled up their sleeves and joined in. They quietly talked amongst themselves as they scraped surfaces for samples while a dozen or more video cameras recorded everything.

They were not alone on the highway. 2nd Bradley Fighting Vehicle Platoon of the newly minted and not yet organized 1st Mechanized Infantry Brigade surrounded the burnt-out vehicle with four supporting Bradley Fighting Vehicles and four hastily up-armored Humvees, with their squads of riflemen, machine gunners, and specialists.

In the surrounding area, a pair of Stryker Platoons maneuvered in an expanding search pattern. Two entire companies of men walked in tight wedge formations, following the vehicles. Overhead, AH-64 Apache Helicopters circled and searched for the hexapedal alien creature that had attacked the Humvee, and from which Wayne and Sybil Blanchard had barely escaped with their lives.

Everyone present had been briefed on what had happened and now seen firsthand the carnage wreaked. Before Awakening Day, the civilian scientists might have cringed at the intrusion of the military and the weight of metal deployed. Now, after all, that had happened, they were more worried about what might be lurking about, concealed in the vast rolling fields of tall grass that surrounded them.

The search had continued in the area ever since the attack. However, that morning, "something big and black" had briefly been spotted only a mile away and in the general direction. It had initially been seen leaving on the Blanchard's dashcam. Nothing had been seen since, and the trail was getting cold.

Like the newly formed 1st MI, the Joint Reserve Base's "Command Center" was a work-in-progress. The base had never been intended to be either a front-line operating base or even to directly manage combat operations from afar. It had been a training center, logistical operations center, repair depot, and many other things.

Today, General Marcus paced back and forth across the now-scuffed maple floor of the indoor basketball court that had been picked to serve as the new, "temporary" Command and Control Center. Long rows of cafeteria tables were laden with computers, displays, and work areas, some bowing in the middle under the weight of equipment. What had started as a rough circle had rapidly morphed into multiple rows, each focusing on different areas of responsibility. A continuous stream of civilian contractors and tech ratings added more to the room by the hour. Someone had found some huge flat-screen monitors and set them up at the end of the central operation's row of tables.

Marcus suspected they had come from retail stores back in the city, judging by the discarded boxes and packaging and the newness of their design. He made a mental note to ensure that they had actually been paid for and not simply "appropriated." Then the thought suddenly hit him that there would be no more new-model monitors, computers, cellphones, or other high-tech gadgets. Possibly, ever. They would need to be careful with what they had and make it last.

At the moment, the screens showed aerial and ground perspectives of the ongoing search near the scene of the highway attack. He fought the urge to grind his teeth at the lack of progress. He knew he had to set an example, now more than ever. What frustrated him more was that he was comfortably on the base with a nearby steaming cup of coffee while the "real work" was being done miles away. He'd let his enthusiasm get the better of him when he'd shown up in person at the scene of the Stalker attack. He'd later chastised himself for that. Professionally, he knew where his place was and that his men needed him right where he was, safe and protected and alive to lead them not just today but tomorrow and the day after.

To his left stood Colonel Markovic. He'd only had hours to begin to organize 1st MI, but the deployed units in the search were all composed of men with multiple tours of experience. It would take time to build working cohesion and forge them into well-oiled teams, but they all knew their roles and responsibilities for now.

Brigadier Chilton, Lt. Colonel Williams, and Colonel Salangsang watched the unfolding events from the side, staying out of the way.

Marcus took a breath, then looked sideways at Gideon, "Well, Colonel, what do you recommend now?"

Gideon thoughtfully chewed his gum, which Marcus knew was a polite substitute for a cigarette – and probably one stronger than American brands. He turned away from the screen to face Marcus, "Sir, I think that while the ground is firm, it is still too wet to try burning the field, and I'm scared about what would happen if it got out of control, even with the network of creeks and streams and tree lines to provide fire breaks. Also, the civilians at the scene had reported the creature was not afraid of fire. Sir, I think we need to use dogs."

Marcus raised an eyebrow, "Won't that be rather hazardous for the dogs? I don't want to waste them. You saw what it did to our men on the highway."

"Yes, Sir, but there are ways to hunt dangerous game."

Marcus nodded thoughtfully. "I see where you're going with this. A couple of years ago, I was invited to a feral hog hunt by General Carlisle on his family ranch. They used dogs and eventually took down a 600-pound feral hog. I remember it was big, black, mean, and nasty."

Gideon blinked at him.

"They're descended from imported Wild Boars brought over from Europe by early settlers."

Gideon nodded, "Yes, I see, Sir, that's it exactly. I watched that dashcam video from that trucker family several times. The beast was big, and while it eventually moved fast, it was somewhat slow to start. I think well-trained dogs would work, and we do need to track it down before it is too late."

Marcus pursed his lips and nodded. "Make it happen. We need to get this thing, and, Colonel," he lowered his voice, "Remember, our abductors are testing us. I'm worried about what happens if we don't show them we can handle it."

Gideon's eyes widened, and his mouth parted briefly before he clamped it shut with a click. He swallowed, "Yes, Sir, I hadn't thought of that."

Marcus looked back up at the screen before continuing, "Colonel, between you and me, I sometimes wonder if I will ever sleep through the night again.

Service dogs were trained for many things. However, tracking big game or alien creatures was not exactly high on the list. A call was put out for a hunting guide/tracker and dogs. Before long, one name rose to the top of the list. Frank Yaegar, a somewhat famous local businessman, rancher, and long-time globetrotting big game hunter. He not only had a prize set of dogs but had spent decades hunting everything from grizzly bears in Alaska (with a bow), to big and dangerous game from Canada to Africa.

Twenty minutes after the call, a marine V-22 Osprey landed at the Yaegar ranch on the outskirts of Fort Brazos. Frank was stocky, with the weathered look of someone who'd spent much more of his life outdoors than in. He had explained that the dogs might become distraught and not cooperate well inside the large and noisy aircraft. He'd been outside talking to and soothing his dogs when the V-22 had roared overhead. He was taken aback when his dogs didn't become at all agitated or upset.

He had selected a half dozen of his most experienced dogs, two labs, two pointers, two foxhounds, and his prize bloodhound. They had looked him in the eye and then calmly trotted up the loading ramp as though they'd done it a thousand times.

Frank slowly shook his head and walked behind them, his engraved Hambrusch .700 Nitro Express African Safari "dangerous game" rifle in the crook of his arm, and his well-worn safari hat, vest, and gear. In the lead was his tall and slender 32-year-old daughter Mira, also an accomplished hunter, carrying her own Hambrusch, chambered in .500 Nitro Express. She'd been on every big hunt with her dad since she was 9. She wore a broad-rimmed safari hat shading her face and long sleeves, leaving little of her fair skin exposed.

The loadmaster, Sargent Dickey, stood at the foot of the loading ramp. He was a 20-year veteran of the corps, and he took everything personally. The lives of his men and the success of whatever their mission might be were his personal responsibility.

He started to say something about civilians bearing arms on *his* aircraft. For a moment, he and Frank locked gazes. Their eyes traded both the deadly seriousness and self-discipline that came from decades of hard work and facing personal danger. There was also no small amount of fear. Fear at the shocking series of events that had occurred, starting with Awakening Day. Fear of failure. Perhaps most of all, they gauged in each other a steadfast refusal to give in to that fear. The moment passed, and Sargent Dickey nodded at Frank and moved to secure his passengers.

When the Marine V-22 landed on the highway, there were four Bradley's nearby from the 1st Bradley Fighting Vehicle Platoon, along with their Humvees and individual squads. Lt. David Garreth, (newly) commanding, stepped forward to greet the Yaegars and their dogs.

Behind them, the V-22, having delivered its cargo, rolled down the highway for a Short Take-Off, its alternate way of taking off that saved fuel.

Over the noise, Lt. Garreth extended his hand and shouted, "Sir, Ma'am, thank you for agreeing to help with the search. General Marcus personally asked me to assure you that my men and I will be here to protect you."

Mira smiled wryly and answered in a quiet voice she knew Garreth wouldn't hear, "Wasn't that what Lt. Gorman said to Ripley?"

Garreth squinted, shouting, "What's that, Ma'am?"

Frank knew his daughter well and assumed she'd said something suitably sarcastic. He shouted back, "Thank you, Lieutenant. We're glad to help and will be even happier for you and your men to keep us off the menu."

Garreth led them down the road to the scene of the attack and pointed out the path the alien creature had taken when it retreated. The noise had abated, but there were still many vehicle engines running and aircraft orbiting overhead. Frank and Mira leaned their heads close to each other and conferred. Frank patted her on the shoulder, and they separated. She took the dogs over to get the scent.

Dr. Eva Sanches and a heavily armed corporal met her and the dogs at the edge of the scene. The dogs and Eva were immediately comfortable with each other, and Mira relaxed a little. A lot of people do not react well to being surrounded by that many dogs. Eva nodded to Mira and held out a bloody strip of fabric covered in alien saliva for the dogs to scent.

Behind Eva, Mira could see evidence of the carnage. She'd seen men die before. She'd seen what a lion could do to a man. This was... worse.

Mira looked over at Garreth and Frank and nodded. She spoke to the dogs, "Find!"

Garreth spoke into his UHF radio, "Armor maintain 75-meter distance rear, platoon line in front, moving direct northwest." Though his voice did not tremble, the situation's stress kept his tenor slightly uneven. Garreth was, of course, a trained veteran of life and death situations. He wanted payback for the Stalker attack, but the creature they were hunting was unlike anything he or his men had ever experienced. That Sheriff had killed the Stalker with his sidearm and a few shotgun blasts. The trucker lady had shot this six-legged beast with a .308, and the rounds had simply bounced off. He was grimly determined to prevent more casualties. He was 24 years old and hunting a bullet-proof alien monster. His adrenaline surged, and he'd never felt more alive.

The total complement of the 1st Bradley Platoon, including drivers, was 40 men. The Humvees were left on the road, including Lt. Garreth's Platoon Command Humvee, and their crews disembarked to join the Bradley's infantry. The squads formed a protective formation around and ahead of the Yaegars, with the Bradley's following close by.

Frank led with the bloodhound while Mira followed with the rest of the dogs. The dogs were excited and very alert. Not long after leaving the highway, the bloodhound stopped, sniffing and looking, then changed direction. The path zigzagged. Each time they encountered search vehicle tracks or the trails of the soldiers, there was a delay while the scent was reacquired. Overhead, Apache AH-64 attack helicopters circled, following their progress.

After an hour and a half, the progress slowed.

Garreth asked Mira, "What's happening, Ma'am?"

Mira shook her head, "Please don't call me Ma'am, Lieutenant. It makes me feel old!" Her expression turned serious, "We're slowing down because we are getting closer."

Garreth nodded and spoke into his UHF radio, "Trackers say we're getting closer. Everyone stay sharp!"

Suddenly, the bloodhound stiffened, then ran ahead on its short legs, barking. The other dogs were faster and raced forward while their humans struggled to keep up.

They all stopped at a small clearing. The dogs ran in circles. Frank and Mira stood back-to-back, rifles ready, grimly expecting death to charge from the tall grass. They glanced at each other with nervous smiles.

Garreth shouted, "Dogs have it, Danger Close!" He spoke into the radio, "Trackers say it is here, close by. Does anyone have eyes on?"

<No Movement, Sir. Air cover says they don't see anything either.>

Garreth looked questioningly back at the Yaegars.

Frank nodded, "It's here, Lieutenant. It's close."

Garreth called on his radio, "Infantry, fire when ready. Armor, fire on my command."

The dogs suddenly stopped running around in circles and instead surrounded the Yaegars, guarding them, herding them back. All except for the bloodhound, who walked over to an area of disturbed dirt and sniffed. Its hair stood up on its back, and it bared its teeth, growling low and harshly, backing away. The other dogs reacted swiftly, putting themselves between the patch of dirt and the Yaegars.

Frank and Mira swung their rifles in the direction of the warning. Mira shouted at Garreth, who had turned his back to look in the other direction, "Lieutenant!"

Garreth whirled about, rifle ready, but there was nothing there. He ran towards the Yaegars and stopped in front of them. He called into the radio, "Report! Does anyone have a visual on the target?" Garreth's head and voice were cool, but his heart blazed with fear and excitement.

Just then, the ground shook, and the dogs reacted by pushing against and biting the Yaeger's pants legs, desperately trying to move them away from danger. The bloodhound yelped and ran for its life, around and behind the Yaegars.

Garreth's heart stopped, and his pupils dilated. He shouted again into his radio, "It's here! It's under the ground! Close ambush front, out of the ground!"

A mound of dirt swelled upwards, and Garreth fell backward as the soot black-armored creature clawed its way out with its six limbs and burst from the ground, shaking the soil and roots from its head and bellowing in a rock-grinding, air-ripping, basso roar.

In an instant, the dogs were on it, dashing in to snap and bark and dance away as the creature's maw snapped at them in a loud crunch.

Scrambling to regain his footing, Garreth fired his RRA Tactical Carbine, chambered in 458 SOCOM. The 350 Grain armor-piercing rounds made divots in the creature's armor plates, enraging it, but did not penetrate. More shots rang out as the platoon had rushed back in, but none found purchase. The creature spun around, charging and snapping at the dogs and converging men.

Frank and Mira fired their big game rifles at the massive creature's flank, which left bigger divots. Franks .700 Nitro Express 1000 grain bullets dug deeper than Mira's .500. There was a small spray of the creature's blood. It screamed an ear-shattering cry and whipped back around to confront what was hurting it, its armored tail swiping in the opposite direction. One of the Labrador Retrievers didn't move fast enough and was slammed by the tail with a sickening crunch, spray of blood, and a dreadful whimper from its crushed lungs as it was flung more than forty feet away.

The creature roared again. Mira whistled, and the dogs disengaged and returned to surround herself and Frank, and as a group, they backed away. More rifle fire rained down on the creature from Garreth and his men, but it only seemed to make it angrier.

Frank and Mira looked at each other and nodded. She fired her .500 Nitro Express as Frank stood ready with the .700. The creature twisted and leaped into the air, whirling around to charge Mira, screaming its rage. Frank fired into its dripping, gaping maw, and Mira chambered another round and fired a heartbeat later. It yanked its head away and spat viscous fluid, clawing the ground. More fire concentrated on the beast, and it flinched as a 7.62 squad automatic weapon raked its side in a shower of sparks.

Garreth made his decision. Their rifles were clearly ineffective, and the civilians were too close to call fire from the Apaches. The Bradley's had moved closer. He keyed his radio again, "Sargent Washington, engage the target!" He turned and dove into the Yaegars, arms extended, "DOWN!" Frank and Mira were already dropping when Garreth flew into them, shielding them with his body.

Sargent Washington's lead Bradley was armed with a Bushmaster M242 mounted 25mm chain-driven autocannon, firing M919 Armor-Piercing, Fin-Stabilized Discarding Sabo Tracer rounds at a velocity of 3,600 feet per second. The initial five-round burst was overkill. The tracer rounds made the fire look like some kind of laser weapon as they ripped the creature open from end to end. The rounds were not explosive, but the effect was the same. The pressure wave from the 25mm shells liquefied the internal organs, and the creature effectively exploded, showering the area with noxious greasy fluids and offal.

Five more rounds followed, plowing the dirt underneath before Garreth could radio out, "CEASE FIRE! CEASEFIRE!"

Drowning Sorrows

Reinhardt Distributing
Day 8: 3:25 PM

S heriff John Austin drove his Sheriff's Department SUV up to the developing scene outside Reinhardt Distributing, the largest beer, liqueur, wine, and bar supply distributor in Fort Brazos. Like many other warehouse operations in the area, it served Fort Brazos proper and the whole multi-county geographic region surrounding it. Chief Deputy Hector Alonzo sat in the passenger seat, and two Humvees full of John's 'temporary' Marine guards stopped just ahead and behind John's SUV.

A barricade had been set up outside the distributorship, and nine police cruisers sat at various angles with their light bars flashing. Police Captain Wayne Marchant stood behind one of the cruisers, resting a bullhorn on the roof of the cruiser while he studied the enormous warehouse with binoculars. All the visible entrances and doors were closed. The handful of windows in the business office attached to the warehouse were boarded up from the inside.

Before John could exit the SUV, his marine guards were there, opening the door for him but making it clear how unhappy they would be if John tried anything so foolish as to try to move anywhere without them. Hector left the group and walked over to talk to Captain Marchant.

Hector returned after a couple of minutes, "You're gonna love this, boss. Seems the warehouse workers have barricaded themselves inside and are refusing to come out or to make deliveries. They're drinking and eating the merchandise. I figure they can hold out a long time eatin' bar pretzels, peanuts, limes, and cherries. Meanwhile, the ones that aren't passed out are stupid drunk, except for the ringleader, a Mr. Darnell Lewis. Mr. Lewis has no criminal record, boss, but shots were fired when Captain Marchant's people arrived."

John nodded, "What do you think?"

Hector grunted, "Well, boss, I don't see any bullet holes anywhere, and maybe those boys in there just shot in the air as a warning, but booze and bullets don't mix well."

"What does Marchant say?"

Hector turned his head and spat tobacco, "Cap'n wants to go in guns blazin, boss...."

John shook his head, "They're bottled up inside and drunk already. Let 'em just pass out from it, and Marchant can walk in quietly and scoop them up."

One of the police officers backed away from the police line and approached John's group. She was black, with shoulder-length straight black hair and a bright face. She was at least 5'10 and walked with the easy gait of a lifelong athlete.

Hector went to speak to her, then ushered her through the guards to John. "Boss, you remember Patrol Officer Naomi Lamar?"

John reached out to shake her hand and could sense her nervousness. Not about himself, but something else. "Yes, I remember Officer Lamar and some sort of incident with a basketball, a barbeque pit, and a Doberman last year?"

Naomi glanced over her shoulder at her Captain twice, then back at John, frowned, and then her eyes widened before she opened her mouth to explain, but John held his hand up, "It's Okay, Officer, I'm teasing you. You appear to be worried about something. How can we help you?"

She looked into his eyes and realized there was no derision. She relaxed slightly, "Ahh, Mr., I mean Sheriff, I know Darnell Lewis, we went to school together, we still live in the same neighborhood, and our families know each other. I can tell you he is not a bad man. He's smart and hard-working. I don't believe he wants to hurt anyone. I'm not sure he could if he tried. Darnell's sister and mom were both part of the Awakening Day dead."

John nodded, "And what about the other people in there?"

Naomi shook her head. Darnell's probably more intelligent than the rest of them put together. They're following his lead. I know it."

Hector put his hand on her shoulder, "A minute ago, Sheriff said we should just let them all have their fun and pass out drunk and clean up the mess after, and nobody'd get hurt. What do *you* think?"

Naomi looked from Hector to John, "I don't believe Darnell would hurt anyone, but he might hurt himself. I'm afraid that's what he's really in there to do.

John looked at Hector, and Hector nodded before asking, "What did Captain Marchant have to say about this?"

Naomi's lips tightened, and she hesitated, glancing back over at the Captain.

John sighed, "That's Okay Officer, I think we get the picture."

Just then, John's cell phone, along with Hector's and his detail leader's phones, all rang. John looked at the caller-id. It was General Marcus.

Moments later, John thumbed off the call and looked at Hector. His detail tightened the circle around him.

"Hector, I'm putting you in charge here. Go help Captain Marchant find a better way to deal with this situation. I've got to go."

Hector nodded, "You got it, boss."

Pieces

Bonham State University
Day 8: 6:37 PM

When the remains of the plant-like "Stalker" creature had been delivered to the University for study, the old Life Sciences building had been appropriated. It had been near the end of a complete renovation. The major construction was done, the walls were painted, and new drop ceilings were installed. Taped-down cardboard and plastic still lined walkways protecting the new carpet from moving equipment and construction worker's dirty boots, and much of the shiny new furniture had yet to be fully assembled.

As a school with a heavy focus on the agricultural sector in general, including animal husbandry and the veterinary sciences, certain facility areas were designed for the examination, surgery, or necroscopy of animals of all sizes. Provisions had been made so that animals could be efficiently moved in and out of both special and multi-purpose rooms through adjacent loading docks.

One of those rooms had been modified and now resembled a cross between a surgical theatre and a small lecture hall. The surgical area was now surrounded by tempered glass walls and special air conditioning and filtration units.

In the wake of the "Stalker" incident, many changes had been hastily made to the room, including "clean-room" equipment and negative pressure and air filtration equipment on loan from the Joint Reserve Base. It also sported a newly constructed "airlock" and numerous UV lights to aid in room sterilization. The seals were configured to fully close in the event of a power failure. A changing room had been added so that personnel could don bio-hazard protective suits.

Even though quite a few people had been in close proximity to the Stalker remains without apparent ill-effect, Dr. Nakamura had insisted that "proper" controls and precautions be put in place. With input from the infectious disease experts and the military on biological, chemical, and nuclear warfare, a set of procedures for handling current and future specimens were drafted.

Today, the audience area was full of both military and university representatives, self-segregated into cliques and groups. The pungent smell of ozone and fresh paint hung in the air. Equipment hummed gently while everyone waited for the delivery of the remains of the creature that attacked the soldiers on the highway. Everyone had seen the images of it from the trucker's dashcam.

For those not present, a live video conference had been set up. The Council, Sheriff Austin, and Major Finley watched the remote video from the council chambers, while General Marcus did the same from his growing new command center. Their absence had quietly fueled some speculation regarding safety. However, as people filed into the small room, its size had made it obvious why — there wasn't enough room.

Amid the growing murmurs of quiet conversation, the mood was of equal measures dread and excitement. The lights dimmed, and a hush fell over the room as biohazard-suited men carefully wheeled a large olive-drab steel crate into the room. It looked old and well used and had stenciled writing on the side, including "DO NOT DROP" and "THIS SIDE UP" and instructions on opening "Breather Valves" before opening.

Behind them, two more men carried between them another olive-drab metal container with military markings. They set it down and retreated, along with the first group. Moments later, they re-entered the room, carrying more.

Dr. Nakamura stood and walked to the glass, looking inside at the growing collection of steel boxes that looked more like an ammunition dump than specimen containers. He stabbed the intercom button, "What is all this? Where is the creature?"

One of the biohazard-suited men turned and walked to the glass, pressing the intercom button on his side. "Sir, I don't understand your question." He pointed at the pile, "It is in those."

"What do you mean? It was supposed to be big. What happened? Why are there so many of these dirty boxes? Did it melt like the other creature did?"

The man's face was visible through his headpiece. His expression was confused for a moment, then his eyebrows raised, "Oh, no, Sir, it didn't melt. The thing was big, and these are all the pieces we could find…."

Nakamura blinked in horror. "Pieces!" He took a sharp breath, "What do you mean, pieces?"

The man shrugged without answering.

"Stop! My god, what did you people do?"

"Ah, Sir, all I know is that they said it was damned hard to kill."

The Hangar

Remote area of the Joint Reserve Base
Day 10: 9:42 AM

Sargent Ramirez and Corporal Dobson were part of the search detail, combing through every building and structure on the base, looking for anything that shouldn't be there. It was an enormous base that had grown in leaps and lurches ever since it was initially founded by a group of Stephen F. Austin's colonists in 1822 on a bend of the Brazos River. Most of the base had been built up and torn down, paved over and rebuilt yet again many times. Some of the oldest surviving areas were now used for dead storage or, in some cases, training areas, including aircraft breach and tactics using the hulks of old military transport aircraft.

One of the more iconic surviving structures was a truly titanic hanger originally built to base and service dirigibles. It had been slated for demolition several times, only to receive last-minute reprieves so it could be used for one pet project or other, or, more often than not, as a handy bulk storage warehouse for disused and no longer manufactured, but possibly useful for some obscure reason in the future, aircraft parts and assemblies.

The fuselage of a Boeing 737 rested nearby, fitted with boarding ramps, and various shipping containers and other aircraft viscera lay nearby. It had been used as the training area for a training operation just two weeks prior to Awakening Day.

The surrounding tarmac was as old as the dirigible hangar, cracked and worn, but it had been kept clean, and the potholes and cracks were filled and kept in moderate repair. The grass and bushes around the hangar were slightly overgrown. Since Awakening Day, some priorities had changed, including landscaping maintenance around disused parts of the base.

Dirigibles had been enormous. So, the hangar itself was even bigger and taller, with massive vertical doors made up of narrow panels designed to open almost the entire width and height of the structure.

Ramirez and Dobson parked their door-less, unarmored Humvee in the parking area adjacent to the human-sized doors on the side of the hangar. As they exited the vehicle, Sargent Ramirez held up his hand, signaling Dobson to stop. There was a shimmer around the building.

Dobson squinted, "Sargent, do you hear that? What is that noise?"

Ramirez grunted, "You mean besides my tinnitus?"

Dobson bit back a retort and struggled to maintain a straight face. "Sargent, there's a high-pitched sound coming from the hangar. I thought I heard it driving up, but now that the engine is off, I can hear it for sure. Hurts my ears too. Oh, and Sargent, it's not hot today, so why is there a heat shimmer around the building?"

Ramirez squinted and stared at the building for a moment and then knelt down and picked up a piece of landscaping gravel. He tossed it towards the hanger. A few feet from the hanger, the small rock impacted... something and sprang back out again towards the Sargent, who barely dodged it as it sprang off the side of the Humvee. Nothing else happened for a second or two, and then a loud voice began screeching from around the corner, back towards the massive doors in front.

Ramirez nodded urgently to Dobson, and they quickly got back into the Humvee and circled around, at a distance, to the front of the hangar. Alien glyphs, like the ones that everyone had now seen on that alien spire in the middle of downtown Fort Brazos, now played across the enormous hangar doors.

Sargent Ramirez's expression tightened. "Corporal, get on the radio and call this in."

I'm....

Dr. David Duncan blinked and looked up from the papers on his desk at the sound of light knocking at his office doorway. He smiled broadly, and his face brightened as he quickly stood and moved around the desk to greet his guest properly. "Gwyneth! God, I'm so glad to see you! I've missed you so much."

Dr. Gwyneth Elliott smiled tightly and rushed into his arms, not bothering to close the door behind her or, any longer, to conceal their relationship. Had David not been fairly sturdy and athletic, the force of her embrace might have knocked him backwards a step or two. He sometimes forgot she was a former Olympic athlete.

She did not release her grip on him, and he hugged her tighter, realizing something was wrong. "What's happened? What's wrong?"

After a moment, she let go and turned away, and walked over to his floor-to-ceiling window. As the hospital's new Chief of Surgery, he'd inherited the oversized and too expensive, in his opinion, office from his predecessor, who had not survived Awakening Day. It was only a 4-story hospital, but the window gave a nice view of Fort Brazos and the distant upwards curvature of the horizon.

Gwyneth mumbled, "Why, whatever could be wrong? Alien abduction? Thousands of people dead. Aliens? We've been Xeroxed and genetically altered? Diseases cured? Oh, and *Monsters*? Then there's the end of the world apocalypse, and somehow we're the plucky survivors chosen to fight a galactic war?"

David walked over and stood behind her and put his hands on her shoulders. They stood there in silence for a while before she relaxed a little and leaned back into him. He gently answered, "Nope, that's all old news. Been there, done that." He paused and lowered his voice, "Now. Tell me, Gwyn, what's wrong?"

She stayed there for a while, quiet, leaning into him. She sniffed and wiped away tears she hadn't realized she'd cried and brushed back her shoulder-length auburn hair before turning to face him. When she did, her face was strong, and she looked deep into his eyes.

"I'm pregnant." She watched the wheels turn in his head.

His first reaction was happiness, then confusion, followed by, "That's… What? How is that possible? I can't. I had a vasectomy years ago!" His expression was more confused than accusatory. "And isn't it too soon to tell?"

Gwyneth clenched her eyes tight for a moment, relieved, frightened, and ecstatic at his reaction. Part of her had feared he might reject her. She hugged him tight and put her head on his chest. "Don't worry, you are most emphatically, and quite empirically, the father. Besides, why not? After all, I had my tubes tied years ago. Why on Earth… I mean, why shouldn't I be pregnant? We make quite the pair."

She disengaged, took him by the hand, and led him to his overstuffed couch. Their relationship had been an on-again, off-again thing for a couple of years. It had been off-again before Awakening Day, although just now, she couldn't remember the reason why. As they sat, she reflected that this couch was where they'd reignited things in the chaos that followed Awakening Day. She smiled at the realization that this was where the new life growing inside her had been conceived. She couldn't rationally know for sure that it was the place since it had not been the *only* location they had made love, but somehow she knew. It calmed her nerves.

As they sat, she touched his face. "It's on the early side to detect, but I've triple-checked it. Also, I did some calling around. Apparently, you and I are not alone. There have been other reports of pregnancies with circumstances like ours, but they were curiosities. I'm not sure, but I suspect the OB/GYN's were afraid to say anything about it, in case they were wrong. We've all seen the baby booms that happen after things like big power blackouts and such. The doctors I've talked to rationalized that that is what was going on and that in the… heat of the moment, perhaps birth control measures had not been, well, effectively used.

David swallowed, "I expect that they were actually right, at least about the trauma of recent events causing people to… seek comfort in each other."

Gwyneth nodded, "So, I made some more calls, and it turns out that there are reports that pets and livestock have been de-neutered. Un-neutered?" Her lips twisted into a wan smile as she thought about it.

David's expression tightened, and he shook his head. "Those fucking alien bastards. They un-fixed us so we would reproduce more and have lots and lots of babies that will grow up and fight in this damned war of theirs."

Gwyneth was quiet for a moment, then put her hand on her belly. "I had the same reaction when I figured it out, but now…."

He thought aloud, "You know females are socially and biologically conditioned to want and protect their babies."

Her eyes flared in anger, and she punched him in the chest. "Don't be an idiot, David. Of course, I know that, even though it is really too soon to feel it." She looked deep into his eyes. "David, if what these aliens, these 'Gardeners' are saying is true, then everything has to change. We are it. We are all that's left of the human race. Regardless of what happens next, you know as well as I do that we're in a dangerous new world, and there will be casualties. Perhaps a lot. And if we have to go to war, there will be even more."

She continued, "My God, David if we *don't* have a baby boom, we might soon have negative population growth. With everyone so depressed about what has happened, that wouldn't be surprising. And there is no immigration from anywhere else to replenish us. If we don't grow, humanity may just wither away."

David gently brushed her hair and thought about it. Then he took her hand, stood, and walked them back to the window. He pulled her close, stood behind her, rested his hands on her stomach as they both looked out onto Fort Brazos. The bright spot on the sun-tube was early in the day cycle. Light glinted from the oceans on the other side of the world.

In unison, they both said aloud, "I love you."

David chuckled and kissed her hair, pulling her even closer.

Gwyneth softly shook her head, "So, what now?"

Dr. Nakamura

The wood-paneled office of the President of Bonham State University was full of polished relics and memorabilia, some dating all the way back to the University's founding in 1892. Assistants and volunteers kept everything neat, dusted, and organized. When Dr. Takumi Nakamura had survived Awakening Day as one of the most senior professors on campus, he'd given no thought to who would take over running the place. Circumstances, however, had conspired to catapult him from being Dean of the School of Science and Technology to become, effectively, the leading scientist in the world. It did not take long for him to be drafted into the office and role of University President.

Now, he was responsible for focusing the resources and activities of the University towards goals and activities to help humanity survive the new world. There were only so many people and resources to go around, and everyone seemed to have a different opinion on how those resources should be used and how the fate of the world now depended on it.

Agriculture was obviously critically important. The surviving humans needed the crops, animals, fiber for textiles, medicines, and other bio-products to keep things going. How did the new environment affect cultivation? Pollination? Animal reproduction?

They were, after all, in a new world, so the Biosciences were clearly going to be critical for survival, as well as Chemistry, Geosciences, and Environmental.

Would the strange Sun-Tube affect growth and life in general? What about Weather? Certainly, Psychology and Social Sciences were going to be critical. The trauma of Awakening Day and all that followed had shaken the survivors to their core. Aeronautical, Mechanical, and Civil Engineering were crucial to building the machines and structures needed for growth. The list was endless.

Then, the newly created Xenobiology department had real-life actual alien creatures to study, at least the bits and pieces of them. They were going to need huge amounts of resources just to create more clean rooms and procedures for safely handling and studying potentially infectious or otherwise dangerous alien fauna and flora – not to mention all the equipment, people, and resources to do the actual handling and studying.

And then, there was Dr. Leo Talib, the language expert. Dr. Nakamura was not an emotional or bellicose man. As an astronomer, he practiced a degree of discipline and patience that few could equal. Other than a certain French astronomer, who was most likely dead now, back on whatever remained of Earth, Dr. Nakamura had always found a way to work with his colleagues, no matter how difficult their personalities might be. He was universally regarded as being immensely fair and even-handed. That was one of the primary reasons he'd been drafted to become the University President. He got along, more or less well, with everyone.

Except for one man. Dr. Leo Talib. Nakamura usually dealt with people in such a subconscious and natural way that he rarely even thought about it. With Dr. Talib, however, it was different. Something about the man not only 'got to him,' it reached inside and twisted. Nakamura had never consciously been aware of hating any living soul, and he fought the unfamiliar feelings that clawed at him.

As Talib entered his office, Nakamura idly wondered if what he felt for the man really was hate or something else. Whatever it was, he bit down his self-control and maintained his calm, impassive expression. He would preserve courtesy and decorum.

He rose and stepped around the massive desk and reached to shake Talib's hand in the American fashion. Talib's response was a dry, perfunctory handshake, without the amusing play for strength dominance that some people tried.

Nakamura was lean, fit, and trim, and a 5th Degree Aikido black belt. His grip was as firm or soft as he wanted it to be. Dr. Talib seemed not to notice one way or another. Nakamura returned to his chair behind the desk, and Talib sat in one of the stuffed leather chairs in front of it.

Dr. Leo Talib studied Nakamura's face and appearance. As usual, the man's inexpensive suit was neat and clean, and his tie was uninspiring. His black and grey hair was neatly trimmed in a utilitarian and straightforward cut. Talib had come to realize that Nakamura seemed to have no awareness of fashion or style in himself or anyone else. *The man is so focused on his work. His wife must choose his clothes for him.*

Dr. Nakamura studied the young man in front of him, in turn. Dr. Talib, as always, looked like he had stepped out of an upscale men's fashion magazine. His brown hair was carefully styled, his clothing obviously expensive – possibly more so than the aging sub-compact car Nakamura drove. Talib was a Fop. Nakamura imagined Talib in some King's court in ages past, wearing a velvet coat and elaborate wig. The thought did not reach his expression, however.

"Dr. Talib, I expect that you wanted to see me because of the discovery on the military base?"

Straight to business, then. "Yes, Dr. Nakamura. As you know, the work studying the alien structure, the 'Spire' as it is now called, is being done by myself and a couple of research assistants. I'm working as hard as I can to make progress with a translation matrix, but my resources are limited as I realize everyone else's are. Now, we have a new site to study. We need to prioritize between the two sites, but dividing our focus will obviously impact our efforts."

Nakamura had been expecting demands for an entire staff and a more significant cut of the resources. It would not be the first time Talib had pushed for it. *So, you're trying a different tactic. Must be the influence of your diplomat parents.*

He leaned back in his chair, "Dr. Talib, the translation work you are doing is unique, and we are all fortunate to have someone with your native talent and skills here to focus on it. The problem is that you are just that. Unique. We really don't have people with sufficiently useful skills to help you with your task."

Talib's face very briefly flashed with anger and frustration before he could settle his mask. He started to speak, but Nakamura waved him off.

"Dr. Talib, I have consulted with others on how best to aid your efforts, but I want you to understand something. Your work is vital. So is the work being done to study the alien creatures. So is the work to study this world that we now live in. So is the work to make sure that our crops and food supply are maintained.... And that list goes on and on. We are all now in a life and death survival situation, and there are only so many people and resources available. You are not being ignored but assigning people to you who don't have the right skills, when those same people *could* be more productive elsewhere, is a problem."

Talib suppressed his growing frustration but latched onto the words 'assigning people to you' — that was promising. He nodded politely for Nakamura to continue.

"As I said, your work is truly vital. Because of that, I've reached out to see what other people and resources might be available to assist and enhance the quality and success of your efforts. I consulted with General Marcus's staff to see if they had any people with the right skills, or close enough to the right skills, to be useful."

Talib paled, and his lips tightened, "Dr. Nakamura, I...."

Nakamura waved him off again. "Please hear me out, Dr. I'd like for you to go and meet with Brigadier General Sabrina Chilton, formerly of the United Kingdom's Signal Brigade. General Chilton commanded units responsible for strategic and tactical communications for the Royal Army. She has a whole unit of people with her, including cryptologists and other specialties. I believe that with your guidance, her organization could be of great help to you, and can at the very least, help provide you with better basic support and organization. It also seems logical that if we humans are supposed to go off and fight these aliens, we'll encounter communications that are not so easy to translate and interpret. We have to understand their language before we'll be able to break any of their encryption and make sense of anything."

Talib sat very still, never taking his eyes off Nakamura. "Dr. Nakamura, may I ask what the working relationship will be?"

Nakamura nodded, "I assume you mean to say, who will be in charge? I know you're an ambitious man, Dr. Talib. I have no problem with ambition and drive. We clearly need that to survive here. In answer to your question, you are a civilian, and you are the universally recognized scientific expert on the alien language. We don't know exactly how things will be organized in the long run. However, you report to the University, not the Military, and they to their command. They will depend greatly upon you not only for your research but to teach them what they need to know. They simply will not be able to do their jobs without you."

Dr. Leo Talib leaned back in his own chair, considering Nakamura's plan to get Talib out of Nakamura's hair. *You've never liked me, and the feeling is mutual, Dr. Nakamura. I think I threaten your sense of bureaucratic order and control. And you're right that there is no one here at the University who can really help me. So be it. Let's find out if this General Chilton is any less of a stuffed shirt than you.*

While it was true that Nakamura was famous for his uncompromising attention to procedure and that his interpersonal skills were somewhat 'dry,' few realized that behind his stony gaze, he could focus his considerable intelligence on actual people when he wanted to. He never let it show, and it had served him well over the years to be underestimated and left to his own devices. Studying the relatively young man across the desk from him, Nakamura sensed the shift in Talib's ire. *Good, I have more important things to worry about.*

"One last thing, Dr. Talib, while I do not care to know *what* your vote is, I am told that you have not yet placed your vote on the plebiscite. I must urge you to place your vote, whatever it is, before tomorrow's deadline. There are those who believe that the fate of all of us may depend upon not only the result, but the degree of turnout the vote receives."

Talib restrained himself and managed not to show his frustration and bit back a retort that he had more important things to do. A small part of him wondered if the old man across the desk might actually have a point.

"Yes, Dr. Nakamura. I'll make sure I make the time to do that."

Sabrina Chilton

SigInt CIC: Joint Reserve Base
Day 12: 10:59 AM

Brigadier General Sabrina Chilton's expression did not change. She didn't rage, grimace, scowl, or even stiffen. With a herculean effort, she also resisted the overwhelming urge to pull her newly issued FNX-45 sidearm and use it to shoot Dr. Leo Talib squarely between the eyes. Or at least an arm or leg. The man was clearly brilliant but insufferable in the way that only such arrogant and, unfortunately, indispensable SME's (subject matter experts) sometimes were. The kind that knew their value and were determined to exploit their impunity and push the limits in every way.

Sabrina was well used to dealing with big egos and matching IQs. Those in uniform were challenging enough. For that matter, most civilian contractors and SME's tended to have the typical engineer or scientist personality types. She'd learned how to handle them more easily than most. Her father was a well-regarded geneticist, and her mother was a neurosurgeon. They'd never understood her choice of career, but Sabrina had pretty much imbibed dealing with brilliant people in her mother's milk.

Now, her face was an impassive mask as she stood nearly nose to nose with Dr. Talib, in the center of the still-under-construction 1st Signals and Electronic Warfare Combat Information Center. It had formerly been a series of handball courts in the same sports complex that held the basketball-court-turned Fort Brazos general Command Center. The walls between courts had been knocked down, and the far wall was lined with the largest big-screen TVs they'd been able to find, beg, borrow or perhaps steal. Rows of cafeteria tables and scrounged desks, and miscellaneous furniture were now arrayed opposite them. Still-unsecured cables and wiring crisscrossed and littered the floor and even hung from the ceiling rafters.

On the screens were live feeds from the alien spire in the Fort Brazos Town Square and, now, from the old dirigible hanger-turned junk warehouse that Sargent Ramirez and Corporal Dobson had discovered. There were views from all sides, including some drone footage, but the central focus was on the alien glyph characters displayed on the massive hanger doors. Thankfully, the ear-tearing accompanying screeching sounds were muted, although another set of screens showed audio waveforms and spectral analysis graphs.

Technicians and electricians scurried about, pulling cables and tinkering with equipment, most of them from the 29th Queen's Gurkha Signals Regiment that had been abducted from Earth along with Sabrina and her daughter Nicole. A full dozen of her top analysts intently hovered over a hodge-podge of laptop, desktop, and tablet computers.

Everyone in the room was tired and worried except for Dr. Talib. Ten minutes ago, four marine guards had delivered him, none too gently, into Sabrina's care. She stood impassively, unmovable before him, in her newly issued American-style ACU (Army Combat Uniform). However, she'd insisted upon keeping the black Queen's Gurkha Signals Regiment beret and insignia, now tucked under her shoulder epaulette, for her and those in her Command. General Marcus had liked the idea and ordered that similar efforts be made to preserve the heritage of the other absorbed international military forces.

The marine guards had been ordered to deliver Talib as expeditiously as possible. They'd arrive with Talib bracketed between them, with vice-like grips on his elbows and shoulders, his feet not quite touching the ground. Red-faced, Talib had shaken them off on arrival, straightened his bespoke Saville Row suit, and hastily smoothed his nearly movie-star quality hair. He'd wasted no time dressing Sabrina down. As he vented his frustrations, he gradually brought himself under control.

She'd stared calmly at him while he unloaded on her. She'd been initially amused and impressed at his creative choice of insult and turn of phrase, but her patience was evaporating quickly. Despite that, she let him expend his rage and, in her eyes, make a fool of himself.

Most of her command already knew something about her and her style, even if by reputation. She'd been terribly senior to all of them. She'd been in command of all of the Queen's Signals Brigade. She'd been passing through on inspection when all of them had been abducted by the Gardeners. Despite the lofty distance between her and the regiment, she'd been both respected and feared as a no-nonsense reformer and architect of many deadwood-cutting changes.

She pretended not to notice the widened eyes and twitches of grins and hidden smiles as everyone went about their business, waiting for her to drop a mountain on the self-important, overdressed man berating her and, by extension, themselves.

He seemed to be winding down, so she allowed herself a visible sigh, like a patient parent waiting for a child's tantrum to abate.

Dr. Leo Talib himself was more than livid. Two armed marines had snatched him from his campus office and bodily carried him, at a run, to a waiting military helicopter outside in the Quad, where he'd been tossed into the arms of two more marines like a sack of wheat. Now, as his heart had begun to slow, he thought that perhaps the marines had indeed bothered to say something to him when they'd grabbed him, but the suddenness and casual violence of it made it all just noise in his mind. The helicopter had been too loud to speak or hear anything, and when they'd landed at the military base, it was all he could manage to simply try and walk/run under his own power, instead of being carried like a child into the building.

When they'd grabbed him, the irrational part of his mind had feared that he was being kidnapped, or there was some other motive for malice or harm. When he'd realized that the men were not actually hurting him, anger scorched away the fear. When Nakamura had said he'd arranged for the military to help with analyzing the alien glyphs and language, Talib had never imagined that would include being shanghaied.

267

He was shaking, and the adrenaline was still slamming into his veins as he looked into the soft blue eyes of the tall, thin female military officer in front of him. Her gaze was solid and unwavering, despite the burning venom he'd poured upon her. He became aware of his surroundings as his tunnel vision subsided. Many people were in the room, all of whom were moving quietly and purposefully, yet he could feel all their eyes on him, and he paused.

Sabrina finished her sigh, glanced down at his suit, and looked back up at him, "Gilchrest & Hawthorne?"

Her crisp English accent caught him off guard. "I beg your pardon. What?"

She nodded at his suit, "Gilchrest & Hawthorne, Saville Row, yes? My late husband had several."

Talib took a half step backwards, "Ah, yes, it is. However, you have not answered my question. Why have I been abducted and brought here against my will!"

She turned away from him and faced the big screen monitors on the wall. "Dr. Talib, welcome to the Fort Brazos SigInt CIC. There has been a new alien incident. If you would kindly observe the monitors, we have a new subject for you to study."

Talib's eyes flared, and his lips tightened as he glared at her. He shook his head angrily, "What?" Then her words finally sank in. He grimaced and reluctantly turned to look up at the screens. He did a double-take as he saw the glyphs and groupings of glyphs slowly drifting across the surface of the tall hangar doors.

His fury ebbed as he absorbed the view. They were more complex. New. Different. His mind raced.

Sabrina smiled softly and reached out to take his limp hand from his side and shake it, "Thank you for coming so quickly, Dr. Talib. I was certain that you would have wanted to be here for this at the very beginning and not lose any time getting here. We are all looking forward to working with you."

Ignacio

Porterman Cotton Mill
Day 14: 2:12 PM

O n the outskirts of Fort Brazos, along State Highway 47 and an abandoned Missouri-Texas-Kansas rail line, sat a large and overgrown brick factory building. It had grown to be an essential Cotton Mill for the region many decades before, eventually employing hundreds of workers. Now, many of the tall windows had missing or broken panes. Over the years, the surviving equipment had gradually been scavenged for scrap, leaving a mostly empty and enormous wooden-floored factory area. There were signs and remnants of generations of graffiti, itinerant, drugs, and teenage use and abuse.

Now, the tall windows had mostly been covered or spray painted. The second-floor office area and roof had been subtly altered to conceal firing points and observation vantage points. Even though it was only a two-story structure, the factory ceiling was quite tall, giving the roof the height of a three or four-story building. Given the relative flatness of the surrounding landscape, it might as well have been a tower.

The building had no power. However, the main power line that had fed a nearby out-of-business gasoline station was still hot. The men who had turned the cotton mill into their headquarters had tapped the line but used the power sparingly. They had appropriated several small generators. However, they required regular refueling. No one in Fort Brazos had yet noticed the scouting and supply runs into town by groups of one or two or three men at a time, but none wanted to take the chance.

In total, there were 175 of them. Ethnically, at least visually, they blended well with the town's Hispanic population. Few questions were asked of them, even though their blend of Spanish was different than the predominantly Mexican flavor in Fort Brazos. As mercenaries, they were used to adapting. Many were from their home base in Columbia, but the rest were from all over South America, including Brazil, Peru, and a handful from other points around the globe. Still, even 175 disciplined mouths were a lot to feed. They needed a better understanding of what had happened to them and what their options were. Many wanted the group to strike out on their own, to leave the city, dominated by its arrogant white population. It appeared that this was a virgin world, ripe for the taking.

On the other hand, all 175 were young or at least relatively young. All were hardy and strong men, mostly Catholic. They had all joined the mercenary group to feed their families back home. Even if they had died doing it, their families would still receive death benefits.

They had liberated a few radios and TVs from empty houses to help keep up with the news from the city. The revelation of what had happened and the fate of their families... of all the peoples of the Earth had left them reeling.

To their credit, however, their discipline did not break. Regardless, they were vastly outnumbered strangers in a strange land. The idea of striking out on their own had been debated. However, without women, their future was bleak indeed. Even if their consciences could allow them to kidnap a few women, they realized that in order to have enough, the reaction from the American civilians and their military would likely be fierce, to say the least.

To survive, they needed information and a strategy. On Earth, their leader had led them through conflicts around the globe, from Yemen to Libya, to Nigeria, and more. They had both survived and prospered because of his careful planning and iron will. In the end, they would follow him anywhere.

Two dozen men were assigned to scout and observe the American military's movements and events in the city. Instead of their tactical radios, it had been decided to acquire and use disposable civilian cell phones, lest the Americans detect them and wonder who was sending encrypted radio messages.

The senior officers were gathered around a purloined flat-screen TV, which was hooked up to an old VCR with over-the-air rabbit-ear reception. There was no cable at the Cotton Mill. The TV announcer was breathlessly reporting on an encounter by the Americans with some kind of alien creature.

A few feet from the TV, maps were tacked to a hastily created plywood map-wall. A junior officer marked a location on the map along one of the main highways out of town.

A group of officers watched the TV news intently. One paused and reached into his pocket to retrieve his phone and answer a call. He spoke in quiet Spanish for a moment, then handed the phone to the oldest man in the group.

His name was Ignacio, and he was the founder namesake of the mercenary group. No one knew his actual age, and there were many different stories about his origins. Over the years, his tactical brilliance and loyalty to his men had saved them from bad situations, bad intelligence, and bad employers. The group itself was not widely known, and Ignacio had worked hard to keep it that way. He and his men did not seek glory or fame. They always let others, sometimes even other mercenary groups, take official credit for their work before disappearing into the mist. They were serious and well paid. Typical 3rd-world mercenaries were often paid a tenth of that paid to the big-name groups. The group simply known as 'Ignacio' or sometimes 'Ignacio's Legion' earned as much or more, and they'd paid for it in blood.

On Awakening Day, Ignacio and his men had awoken in a small compound on the outskirts of Fort Brazos. Confused and afraid of capture, they had quietly slipped away, with none the wiser. They had slowly kept moving and learning all they could for the first few weeks, being careful only to steal from empty/abandoned homes and businesses.

It had not taken long for them to discover that militaries from other countries had likewise been abducted. Ignacio's caution was vindicated when it quickly became apparent that *some* of those other military forces were being held captive, not that he could fault their logic about some, like the Iranians and North Koreans. The Americans would probably eventually integrate the Russians and

271

Chinese, who would likely be less problematic than those from some of the other nations.

Ignacio had deployed his best recon team to keep track of what happened at the base – and to those other forces. They had remained there in simple but devilishly effective blinds. The Americans had initiated heavy patrols around the base and city, but they were looking for aliens, not spies. Communications and resupply were tedious and time-consuming, but his men were veterans who been through much worse.

Later, as the main group had moved closer to the city, they'd found the abandoned Cotton Mill and decided to make it their base of operations. A few scouts moving around were much less noticeable than a large group of dangerous-looking men. Besides, they required fewer supplies this way.

It bought them time. Time to plan their next move. For days, they'd quietly talked about it. If they wanted to survive, they would need to find something valuable or become valuable enough to overcome the inevitable distrust that would follow any revelation of their existence. Something big enough and bold enough for the American military to treat them with respect. He didn't want his men to be absorbed. They wouldn't fit into a regular military, and they didn't want to give up their hard-won identity. Moreover, he didn't want to simply be allowed to continue as a unit under someone else's command. He, and his men, wanted independence and autonomy.

They couldn't stay out in the cold forever. The longer it took, the worse it would be when they revealed themselves. The American military and civilians would be correct and wise to ask just exactly what a foreign mercenary force had been doing all that time.

For now, they stayed quiet, watched and listened, searching for a solution.

Ignacio took the phone, looking the trusted officer in the eye and nodding. He spoke into the phone, "Si, que tienes reportar?"

Meanwhile, on the television, the reporting changed to coverage of the American plebiscite election on television, with projections for its outcome in bold graphics.

Captain Gwyneth Elliott, MD

Frederick F. Russel Medical Center:
Joint Military Reserve Base
Day 16: 9:00 AM

The Frederick Fuller Russell Medical Center, the "Russel Center," was the Fort Brazos Joint Military Reserve Base's main hospital. Named after the U.S. Army physician who perfected a typhoid vaccine in 1909, Russel Center was five stories tall. It had been expanded in 2006 to meet the growing size of the base's military personnel and dependents and the surrounding region's retired personnel and their family members. Russel Center was usually quite busy. However, since Awakening Day and the elimination of most medical conditions, it was now in transition. There was still an average of four or five babies being born each day, as well as emergency-room surgeries and treatment for injuries from training accidents and 'ordinary' injuries from falls, car accidents, and typical, day-to-day human-induced mayhem.

Most of the treatment rooms and hospital beds were now empty. The large pharmacy, built to dispense thousands of prescriptions per day, was now manned by a single, very bored pharmacist. The operating rooms were mostly silent and dark. Instead of treating patients, the staff was instead busy performing a careful and detailed inventory of all equipment and supplies -- which also served the purpose of keeping people and minds occupied. No one knew what might be needed in the future, and no more supply deliveries would be coming from factories and suppliers. For the foreseeable future, all they had was what was on hand.

Navy Captain Gwyneth Elliot, Russel Center's commanding officer, stood in the private bathroom of what she felt was her too-large and too-ostentatious office, in what amounted to a top-floor penthouse suite of command offices and cubicles. She studied her reflection in the mirror. She was dressed in her Service Dress Blues, which were very nearly black in color, complete with her service ribbons. She swallowed as she ran her fingers over the freshly added four gold-threaded stripes around her cuffs. The previous Commanding Officer, and the entire command staff, had been off-base at a conference on Awakening Day. She'd found herself catapulted to assume that role, along with the additional stripe.

She decided that she was satisfied with her makeup. Her pale complexion and dark red hair were similar to the patient she would momentarily receive, but the resemblance ended there. Gwyneth still managed a lot of time in the gym, but three years had passed since her last biathlon and more than a dozen since those heady days as an Olympian. Despite what David said, she knew she wasn't beautiful or even very pretty, but that had never worried or defined her. Her father, "the Colonel," had seen to that. Her eyes misted, and she straightened. *Dad would have cut you down to size for doubting your qualifications for this... unexpected command.*

She'd grown up an army brat, and dad had demanded much from his family. Her younger brother, Paul, his wife Michelle, and their four children had been in Seattle, close to her aging father. Gwyneth pushed the thought of them away as she reached for her new white peaked hat. The navy had phased out the old women's combination cap, with its rounded edges, and her new uniform included the updated headgear. She looked down and smoothed her trousers and scolded herself for the amount of deliberation it had taken to decide whether to wear the trousers or the skirt. That is until she realized that it had nothing at all to do with this meeting. It had a great deal more to do with her appointment, afterward, with a certain Dr. David Duncan. She pressed her palm against her still flat abdomen, inhaled sharply, and pushed those thoughts aside.

Pull yourself together, Gwyneth. Aside from a few biblical world-ending-and-beginning events, there's absolutely no good reason to be nervous. You've met Major Gail Finley several times. She shook her head. *Yeah, but you know this is different. Now, you're the senior uniformed medical officer.... In the world. Effectively you're the Surgeon General, and today's meeting is with the woman who everyone knows will shortly become Vice President Gail Finley.*

Gwyneth took a deep breath and turned to head out the door. Moments later, she arrived at the executive conference room and was greeted by Major Finley and her marine guard protection detail. Gail, at 5'9", was a full five inches taller than Gwyneth. She wore her Air Force dress blues, and the detail was in full combat gear. She and her detail saluted.

Gwyneth smiled and returned the salute. A Navy Captain outranked an Air Force Major, although she was very much aware that she would only outrank 'Major' Finley for a short time longer.

It had only been weeks since Awakening Day. So very much had happened. Gail, then a Captain, had rather severely fractured her tibia, along with significantly lacerating muscle tissue and other complications in the crash of her EA-18 that day. Saving the leg was almost a miracle. Gwyneth suppressed a frown. Finley was standing without any apparent discomfort in a walking cast and no crutches. It just wasn't possible, but there she was.

Gwyneth gestured towards the table, "Major."

Gail turned to the senior member of her detail, "Nate, I think I'm safe with the Captain. She's my doctor. If you boys would wait outside?"

Master Sargent Nate Hampton's expression did not change, but his eyes locked with Gail's just long enough to communicate his unhappiness. "Yes, Major." The four men were surprisingly quiet for all their gear and weapons as they left the conference room and softly closed the door behind them.

Gail sighed as she sat.

Gwyneth smiled. "That must be hard to get used to."

Gail closed her eyes and shook her head, "You have no idea." She hesitated, "It hasn't really sunk in yet, I think."

Gwyneth leaned back, studying her, "Not just the protection detail."

Gail shook her head.

Gwyneth reached across the table and lightly touched Gail's hand. "I'm your doctor. Who knows, it's possible we might even become friends. Regardless though, anything we discuss in this room is in confidence."

Gail sat rigidly, staring into the distance, consumed with her own thoughts.

Gwyneth let Gail have some time. The silence lingered.

Gwyneth finally broke the silence, "I'll tell you something I've not shared with others yet. Years ago, I had my tubes tied. I had a plan for my life, and children were never in it. My brother and his wife were popping out babies all the time, which was just with me. I was off the hook, baby-wise, so to speak. I had my tubes tied years ago. Then, Awakening Day happened, and I..., well, I commiserated with a friend, who had likewise, years ago, had had a vasectomy, and, now... Now I'm... pregnant."

"Wait, what?" Gail's head snapped back as she stared wide-eyed at Gwyneth, her mouth slightly ajar as she blinked in surprise. "How?"

"It seems our alien benefactors did not see fit to just 'rescue us.' You already know that they cured diseases and medical conditions. I've done some digging. What you don't yet know is that they also appear to have reversed infertility – everything from reversing tube-tying and vasectomies to restoring damaged sex organs and even undoing hysterectomies."

Gail blanched, "Shit! The goddamned Gardeners really do want us to build an army for them."

Gwyneth swallowed, "We are, all of us, still in various stages of shock." She smiled for a moment, "I suppose I should also mention that, apparently, although very few have openly admitted it, the Gardeners seem to have cured male erectile dysfunction. However, getting any statistics on whether that is 100% or not is unlikely to happen anytime soon."

Gail blinked and then stifled a grin, "No, I imagine that few men would want to admit that one way or the other. Maybe you could check on whether anyone is bothering to refill their little blue pill prescriptions?"

Gwyneth raised her eyebrows and then looked down at and jotted down a note on a legal pad. "That's a good idea." She paused, "It's a hell of a lot to get used to, isn't it. Everything, I mean. Bodyguards included."

Gail sat back in her chair and made a decision. "Doctor, I appreciate you trying to reach out to me... to talk to me. I'm not, well, I don't really have anyone I can talk to about... things. So, no, it's not just the protection detail. You're right. It's everything. The attack on Earth, Awakening Day, Aliens... the crash... being drafted into this damned election! It's like I've been fired from the Air Force." Her eyes softened for a moment. "There's also... something else." She pursed her lips, and her eyes blazed. "Dammit, I had plans! I wanted to fly!"

"Plans?"

Gail looked at her, and her shoulders slumped a little. "I know it's selfish and petty, in light of all that has happened...." She hesitated before reached inside her service uniform coat and withdrew an envelope. She clutched it for a moment, then handed it across the table to Gwyneth.

Gwyneth maintained eye contact while taking the envelope, then opened it. Her eyes widened as she read the letter inside. She carefully folded the letter, put it back in the envelope, and returned it to Gail. "Wow..."

Gail's eyes misted, and she cracked a smile for the first time. "Yeah, right? I had everything planned too."

Gwyneth smiled, "Slot Pilot in the Thunderbirds.... And I take it you haven't told anyone this."

Gail shook her head, "I don't know why. It's not like it matters anymore. It seems so vain and trivial, given everything that's happened."

Gwyneth nodded, "It does matter. All our lives, our destinies, are forever changed by what has happened. Despite everything that has happened, though, I must admit that you seem to be coping fairly well."

Gail quipped, "There hasn't been time for moping."

"Give yourself some credit. A little over two weeks ago, you woke up in an outside-in alien terrarium and nearly died trying to make sure your plane didn't hit a school. You suffered a severe compound fracture and complex tissue damage and damned near lost your leg, whether you want to admit it or not. You were immediately promoted and took a senior advisory role to the senior surviving human military commander in the universe, so far as we know. Since then, we've had attacks by alien creatures and found out Earth was invaded, and everyone you ever knew is probably dead or maybe even died of old age. Then you were shanghaied to become Vice President. Vice President. Oh, and for the foreseeable future, you have no private life at all."

Gail sighed, "Well, when you put it that way."

Gwyneth smiled, "Well, no offense, let's not make this just about you. I've talked to my... civilian counterpart. Prescriptions of anti-anxiety and similar medications are less than ten percent of what it was before Awakening Day. The truth is, everyone, the entire surviving population, is coping better than they should be."

Gail nodded slowly, "I confess that I've started to wonder about that. Why isn't there more panic? Why aren't people screaming, running down the street? More suicides or violence. People seem scared, but they, mostly, aren't losing control."

"We know that the Gardeners messed with us. They want us to be fruitful and multiply. So, they made us... healthier – both physically *and* mentally, as a whole. I've heard about a couple of agoraphobics who are now basically painting the town. As you said, people are scared, grieving, etc., but I've not heard of any survivors who are schizophrenic or bipolar or anyone still having medical imbalance issues. The Gardeners don't seem to care about us as individuals, given the thousands who didn't wake up, but they want the community as a whole to be healthy, *fertile*, and to grow."

Gail sighed, "And these creatures attacking us are training wheels, to teach us about what the Gardeners expect us to go out and fight."

Gwyneth nodded, "There's more. I noticed you are off your crutches. How is the pain?"

Gail hesitated, licking her lips, "No pain. It doesn't feel like I even need the cast." She swallowed, "and yes, I know that's not normal. I've avoided thinking about what that could mean."

"Like I said, the Gardeners changed us. I've looked at your recent X-Rays. Your bones look more like what they should look like in six to eight months." She paused to let it sink in.

Gail blinked, then swallowed. "I know. I've been hurt before, but this is… this has been… different. I feel…."

Gwyneth nodded, "You're not the only one with accelerated healing. Interestingly, the soft tissue damage is doing even better. I've also looked at other injury records. It's across the board. Wounds are healing anywhere from sixty to eighty percent faster than before. How's your appetite?"

Gail grimaced, "It's terrible. I've been eating like a pig."

"Thought so. That's also common. Your body is working much harder and faster to repair the damage, so your metabolism is jacked up. We're going to have to be careful about what happens as the healing is completed."

Gail shifted uncomfortably in her chair, "Or I'll turn into a… never mind."

"I'd like for you to start a daily log of intake and activity. Frankly, we're going to have to establish entirely new baselines. I want you to use one of those fitness tracker bands. We'll have someone take blood pressure and blood samples on a regular basis. We need to understand what is happening to you and watch out for, well, unexpected complications."

Gail slumped in her chair, "and hope the damned Gardeners knew what they were doing when they put us back together again."

Gwyneth sat up straighter in her chair, taking on a more formal posture, "One more thing, and I hate to have to ask, but have you been sexually active since Awakening Day?"

Gail flashed red with fleeting anger, caught herself, then closed her eyes and sighed, knowing she'd let her mask slip more than she was used to.

Gwyneth sat back in her chair. "Okay, Major. I obviously hit a raw nerve there. I'm your doctor, and you are not Vice President quite yet, so while I still outrank you, I'm ordering you to give. What was that about?"

Gail ground her teeth before answering, "It's just…. I'm sorry, for a moment, I thought you were one of those people."

Gwyneth waited, striving to put forth as calm and professional a face as she could manage.

Gail shook her head, giving up the fight. "For just a moment, I thought that you might be one of those people accusing... no, ASSUMING, that John and I....are...."

Gwyneth smiled softly, "Relax. Of course, I know what you mean. Do you think I haven't faced the same thing my whole career too? I know, Major. Like me, you fought your whole career against that kind of thing, especially anytime you got a promotion. Let me guess the rest. You feel your life has been taken away from you, and what remains of humanity, at least the male half of it, presume you are the weaker half of the Presidential ticket, and that of course, you are giving it up to the tall, gorgeous, and if I do say so, hunk of a male specimen? That you and he are, of course knocking boots between council meetings? Is that it?"

Gail's eyes flashed as the fury built within her. Her lips drew tight, and her expression darkened dangerously. Then, slowly, she calmed herself. After a long moment, she jerked an angry nod.

Gwyneth let the silence that followed stretch a bit while she studied Gail. "Well, I suppose it could be worse, he might have been dumb as a box of rocks too, but he isn't. Is he?"

Gail leaped to her feet in fury, ready to pour forth her anger, but stopped when she saw that the look in Gwyneth's eyes was not accusatory or haughty or even fearful of Gail's rage. It was an expression of understanding and sympathy. Gail ground her teeth and tottered for a moment since the cast made her legs be of unequal length.

She shook her head, slumped back into the chair, sighed hard, and deflated. She lowered her chin to her chest, and her hair fell to cover much of her face.

Gwyneth leaned forward and reached out to take Gail's hand and swallowed as Gail began to make a small noise, as though she might be crying. "Oh, Major... I...."

Gail looked up, and Gwyneth realized that she wasn't crying.

Well, she was crying, but she was also laughing.

Gwyneth smiled, and the corners of her own eyes misted.

Gail sat up straight and threw her head back, "Oh God, what are we doing? What am I doing?"

Gwyneth reached out and touched Gail's arm. "We're surviving, dear."

Gail sniffed and composed herself, swallowed, and sat back, "Well, Doctor, I suppose you meant to ask if, however crudely, that is there any way that I could have gotten myself knocked up like you?"

Gwyneth hesitated, "There is one more thing you should know. I'm beginning to suspect that prophylactics are much less effective than they were before Awakening Day. Also, and, well, it's difficult to say for certain, but it is becoming clear that significantly stronger libidos have accompanied the improvements in overall health." She smiled softly, "Right now, your body is fighting to repair itself. However, as you recover, you may start to feel other… effects."

Gail closed her eyes and shook her head sadly, "So, the Gardeners want their war rabbits to be horny and get busy. That may explain all the pairing-off I've seen going on. I'd chalked it up to a version of 'I'm going off to war' syndrome, but maybe you're right." She sniffed and paused before continuing, "And, no, to answer your question, there is not, there hasn't been, anyone for a long time. Unless the Gardeners have added immaculate conception to their bag of tricks, there is no way for me to have gotten pregnant."

Gwyneth raised her eyebrows and waited.

Gail gritted her teeth, "And yes… he isn't hard to look at, and I don't hate him as much as I did, but, no, nothing is going on." As she said it, the trouble was she wasn't entirely sure how much she believed it.

Gwyneth nodded, "Okay. I want you to think about something, though. Assuming you are indeed elected, you won't always be vice president unless you become a despot. Then we'll just have to shoot you, and then you won't have any more problems anyway." She grinned, "But I'm sure we don't have to worry about that. Hopefully, you and the rest of us will have lives after that. Who is to say that you couldn't return to the Air Force later?"

Gail's expression soured, "and by then, I'll be years older, with older reflexes."

Gwyneth leaned forward and reached out both hands to touch Gail's arm. "Major, there's an excellent chance that your eventual decrepitude won't happen nearly as quickly as you may think…."

Blanchard Shipping

Lucky Cat Truck Stop
Day 16: 2:15 PM

The Lucky Cat truck stop had always been busy. Fort Brazos was a regional focus of warehousing and distribution for that part of Texas and a natural waystation for long-haul trucking. There were several fast-food chains in a small food court inside, a convenience store, mini-offices for rent, and showers and fleet maintenance facilities. In the days after Awakening Day, it had grown into an encampment made up of stranded truckers and travelers, including Wayne and Sybil Blanchard.

Wayne and Sybil sat in a booth next to the food court, sipping coffee. Maintenance logbooks and various notepads, receipts, and papers were spread across the table. Wayne was bent over reading through the documents while Sybil sat with her back against the wall with her laptop balanced on her knees as she studied a spreadsheet, reading glasses balanced on the end of her nose. The room was full of people and noisy.

They did not notice the dark, ruddy-complexioned man in an army uniform work his way through the crowd to their table. He stopped short of the table and removed his service cap. His Tagalog accent was strong, but his English was practiced and clear, "Mr. and Mrs. Blanchard?"

Wayne and Sybil looked up at him, back at each other, and back again, before answering in unison, "Yes?"

The man extended his hand, "I am Colonel Cesar Salangsang, 1st Combat Engineers. May I speak with you?"

Sybil smiled sadly at the sight of him and moved the laptop aside. She sat up while Wayne reached out to shake his proffered hand, "Pull up a chair, Colonel."

Cesar looked around and snagged an empty chair, "Thank you."

Wayne waited for him to sit, "How can we help you, Colonel?"

"First, I'd like to thank you for your help after your encounter with the creature on the highway."

Wayne shrugged, "I just ran like hell while Sybil got off a few rounds at the thing."

"Yes, well, everyone was very impressed with how you two handled yourselves, and that's part of why I'm here."

Sybil smiled, "Thank you, Colonel. How can we help the, what was it, the 1st Combat Engineers?"

Cesar leaned back and smiled, "We want to offer you a job. We'd like for you to work with the army to provide freight transportation logistics as civilian contractors, a 'merchant marine' as it were, to support our, ah, building projects."

Wayne frowned, "So, you're going to set up agreements with all the drivers?"

Cesar cocked his head, "Ah, no, I see I am not being understood. No, we do not want to do it that way. We want you to manage it. The other drivers will need to work for you."

Sybil took her glasses off and set them slowly on the table, "This is very flattering, Colonel, but why are you coming to us? Surviving a creature attack doesn't automatically make us experts at anything more than running away."

Cesar smiled, "Yes, you are right, of course. It was what brought you both to my attention. You've shown that you can handle yourselves. However, I have access to your husband's service record. It seems that Wayne very effectively managed significant logistics resources during his U.S. Army deployments."

Wayne shook his head, "Several of the other drivers are also owner-operators and vets, and there are several existing trucking companies here in Fort Brazos. I'm not the only…"

Cesar raised his hand and shook his head. "The civilian population will still need support from the existing transportation and distribution infrastructure; however, you have experience under fire in wartime, and you already have experience managing military logistics operations. It was felt that you would better understand both the dangers and the urgencies involved – and you know how to work with the military. Picking you is also a way to avoid picking favorites from the existing trucking companies. You'll be tasked with making sure everyone gets their fair share of the work – and that they do it safely."

Wayne squirmed uncomfortably as he and Sybil looked at each other. "Am I being reactivated?"

Cesar shook his head, "You are not being called back to active duty. However, if you accept, you will be put on Reserve duty and promoted, so you would also receive Reserve pay and benefits."

Wayne swallowed, "Sybil and I will need to talk about this…."

"Look, you impressed General Marcus. He likes you. He gave me your file and ordered me to 'make it happen.' So, here I am." He shook his head, "You are both too modest, you know. Unless that is, you have a better offer?"

Sybil stared deeply at Cesar, then turned to Wayne. "Do it."

Wayne looked back at her, to be sure. She nodded, and they both burst out laughing.

"Well, if you put it like that, Colonel, welcome to the world headquarters of Blanchard Shipping."

An hour later, they had shaken hands, and Cesar had left. Wayne and Sybil refilled their coffees and sat in subdued silence. Then, they furiously plotted and planned strategies for another hour. Others had, of course, overheard the conversation with the Colonel, and soon a crowd gathered around. Everyone had been nervous about their collective futures. Many had not worked since Awakening Day, and nobody knew how long their "credit" would hold out. This news held the promise of work and a future, and the excitement in the air was thick.

Wayne sat back for a moment, drinking coffee, watching Sybil as she worked the room. Before Awakening Day, she had always been relatively quiet and reserved. Sybil was always friendly to people but never outgoing. Ever since the trauma of Awakening Day, however, she'd begun to change. She now seemed to have an almost uncanny gift for understanding and relating to people. Somehow, and he did not have a clue how it had happened, Sybil had managed to cement herself and Wayne in the very center of their little truck driver community. She'd become a leader in her own right and something of a mother confessor.

Suddenly, in the middle of a conversation, she was having with a small group of drivers, sweat broke out on her forehead. She gasped, swallowed hard, and clasped her stomach.

Wayne stood and came around the table, reaching for her, "What's wrong?"

Sybil's chest heaved, and she gasped again before clasping a hand across her mouth and bolting away from the table to the restroom. Somehow, the people in the room sensed something, and she was able to dash through them.

Being of relatively a large size and breadth, Wayne plowed through them rather easily in her wake.

Of course, everyone at the truck stop/encampment knew each other on a first-name basis by now. Several men gathered supportively around Wayne at the door to the restroom, while two of the other wives looked worriedly at Wayne while they followed Sybil inside to check on her.

Minutes later, one of the women returned, looked at Wayne, and put her hand on his beefy shoulder, "She'll be Okay, Wayne, but she's the third one this week."

Wayne looked pensively at her, "What?"

She smiled, "I think you two are going to need to find your own place soon. Someplace with room for a nursery." The other men crowded around laughing and slapping him on the back.

Wayne's mouth hung open, and he blinked absently, before his eyes widened and his jaw clamped shut.

The other woman exited with a sad smile, followed by Sybil, who looked worriedly into his eyes.

Wayne only took a moment to stare back before grabbing her off the ground, hugging her close, and spinning her around as though she were a small child, tears flowing down both their cheeks.

Their newly made friends gathered around, clapping and congratulating them.

Inauguration

Fort Brazos HS Stadium
Day 20: 12:00 PM

Several days passed, and the votes were tallied. The entire process was broadcast live. The voting had taken place over the course of a week, and all the ballot boxes were in one place. Excruciating care was taken to ensure that every step of the process was documented and recorded. Ballots were checked, double-checked, and triple-checked. No claims of fixing the vote would be credible. Everyone knew the Gardeners were watching as well.

After rancorous debate, it had been agreed that setting up Congressional districts and a Senate needed more thought and work. Ultimately, it was felt that the Gardeners were waiting for a decision on whether humanity would cooperate. Or not. Delaying the process to figure out Congress might make their alien 'hosts' unhappy. Everyone knew all too well the risks. A process and debate and subsequent elections for House and Senate were to be held in six months. In the meantime, the existing City Council would act as the temporary Congress. The vote on whether to accept the Gardener's demand and on a President and Vice President would proceed.

Fort Brazos County Judge Maria Gonzalez had presided over the plebiscite. Originally born in San Antonio, she'd been County Judge for 14 years. She and her husband Juan, and their only child Margaret, currently a grad-student at Bonham State University, survived Awakening Day. Unlike so many people who had been thrust into new jobs and responsibilities, Maria remained the senior officer of the judiciary in Fort Brazos. Now, however, the workload seemed to triple, as she was also the county's Director of Emergency Management and administered everything from county communications to veteran's services. Oh, and she also administered county elections.

The results were an anticlimax. With 92% participation, it was the highest percentage turnout of any vote in Fort Brazos history. 73% Agreed to accept the Gardener's demands. 86% agreed to the Constitutional Convention, 82% voted for John Austin and Gail Finley to become President and Vice President, and 61% agreed to accept mustered out New Arrival military personnel into the Fort Brazos civilian population.

It had been three days since she announced the results. She now stood on the stage at the podium in the football stadium. Tom Parker had spoken already and shared a prayer. General Marcus had also spoken, pledging his support and loyalty of himself and the military to the new government.

The stadium lights blazed like actinic stars below the cloudless crystal-clear sky. A cool gentle breeze softly rustled the surrounding trees as the standing-room-only crowd's applause faded.

Next to Maria stood a tall, slim, auburn-haired woman in a crisp dark suit, Vice President-Elect Gail Finley. Hers was a face that every surviving human being now knew. Her short-bobbed hair had grown a bit longer, and she walked with a slight limp.

Maria turned to Gail and smiled, "Please place your left hand on the bible."

Gail complied, her face somewhat pale.

Maria continued, "Thank you, Ms. Vice President Elect, please raise your right hand and repeat after me. I, Gail Anson Finley, do solemnly swear."

"I, Gail Anson Finley, do solemnly swear."

"That I will support and defend the people and the constitution."

Gail briefly paused, "That I will support and defend the people and the constitution."

"That I will bear true faith and allegiance to the same."

"That I will bear true faith and allegiance to the same."

Maria inhaled and swallowed, "Against all enemies, foreign or domestic, whether they be human or alien."

"Against all enemies, foreign or domestic, human or alien."

Maria smiled, "That I take this obligation freely."

Gail pursed her lips and answered, "That I take this obligation freely."

"Without any mental reservation or purpose of evasion."

"Without any mental reservation or purpose of evasion."

"And that I will well and faithfully discharge."

"And that I will well and faithfully discharge."

"The duties of the office on which I am about to enter."

"The duties of the office on which I am about to enter."

"So help me, God."

Gail stiffened and answered firmly, "So help me, God."

The crowd stirred, and the cheering and applause rocked the stadium as Maria stepped forward and shook Gail's hand, "Congratulations, Ms. Vice President!"

Vice President Gail Anson Finley turned to the crowd and stood rigidly, at attention. The applause swelled as her discomfort only served to endear her. Maria looked back to Tom, who stepped forward to Gail's other side. Gail startled as Maria and Tom each took one of her hands and raised them high, though Maria was six inches shorter than Gail. Gail blushed scarlet and swallowed hard.

Tom and Maria stepped back, leaving Gail at the podium. She dropped her hands to the sides of the podium and gripped it.

Gail paused as she surveyed the sea of faces before her. She'd flown many combat missions, but she'd never felt as apprehensive. *What the hell are you doing here, Major Finley?* She suppressed a frown at the loss of the rank, career, and life she'd worked so hard for. *No, not 'Major' anymore.* She had only held the rank of Major for three weeks, but they'd been the longest three weeks of her life. As a condition for accepting the nomination, she'd selfishly demanded that she keep the rank after the Presidency. If they were going to take her life away, she was owed a trifle of selfishness. She didn't want to have it later reduced back down to Captain because it had been a battlefield promotion or because she hadn't held it long enough to keep in retirement, presuming she didn't return to service after her term was over.

Hoots, whistles, and shouts joined the applause, which showed no signs of slowing down. She opened her mouth to speak, and the crowd responded by growing even louder. She blushed, shook her head, and a small, resigned smile finally broke loose. She'd been famously unable to hide her unhappiness at being shanghaied into office. In the few short weeks since, she'd earned a reputation for always being serious, even severe. Much to her dismay, this had only served to make her more popular.

The surrendered smile gave victory to the crowd, and they roared in approval. Gail blushed again fiercely, took a deep breath, let go of the podium, and held up her hands. The crowd loved it, but they gradually surrendered in turn, and a hush fell over the stadium and the rest of the world.

She set her jaw for a moment, then leaned forward into the microphone, her voice faltering. "Thank-you. I am... I confess I was not ready for this moment."

Laughter spilled over the crowd as she allowed another small smile.

"You know, ever since I was a little girl, all I ever wanted to do was fly." She swallowed and continued, "I started flying with my dad at age twelve, and I had my whole life planned by the time I was fourteen. I didn't simply daydream about it. I *knew* what I was going to do." She looked around the stadium. "And you know what? I did it. I had my license the day I turned 16, I graduated from the Air Force Academy, and I flew F15s and more."

She paused again and looked down, her nose wrinkling. "I wasn't going to do this...." She reached into her pocket and withdrew an envelope. The crowd grew quieter as she put it on the podium in front of her, smoothed it carefully, opened it, withdrew the official acceptance letter, and held it up. "Like I said, I had it all planned." Her voice threatened to break, "Before what we now call Awakening Day, back on Earth, God, it is so weird to say that, isn't it? Back on Earth, I had just been accepted into the Air Force Thunderbirds."

Soft applause began across the stadium, but she put the letter down and held up her hands to quell it. "No, I'm not, please, that's not why I'm saying this. I'm saying it because I'm not the only one who had plans. We, all of us, had lives and families and a whole world that Fort Brazos was only a tiny part of. None of us planned... *this*." She gestured upwards at the world-in-a-bottle they were inside.

"Many of you are students at the University, and you had plans that didn't include learning how to survive inside an alien world. Many of you are fellow military, and you never planned to have to learn to fight, of all things, aliens. Many of you had jobs and careers that don't mean anything here in this world. Not one of us ever really knew what the future held. Now, though, all of our lives and destinies have been swept away. There is no use in saying we didn't want it or that we didn't deserve it, or that it simply isn't fair."

"Winston Churchill once said that the price of greatness is responsibility…. I've known responsibility. As an Air Force officer, I took an oath very similar to the new one I just took. I was responsible for many things, not to mention expensive aircraft," she paused and blushed again, "Well, hell, I guess I didn't bat a thousand on that one. See, this is what happens when you go off-script."

The crowd erupted in laughter and cheers.

She swallowed and looked down at her feet for a moment before taking a deep breath and looking back up at the expectant crowd again. "The Air Force taught me many things, but until now… until this very moment, I don't think… I mean to say that until now, I was only responsible for the men and women I served with, and to defend them and my country, with my life if necessary. Now, standing here," She swallowed hard again, her voice growing husky as this time it did break. "I want everyone to know that as of now, my mission is no longer about my nation." She paused, "It's now about the entire human race."

The applause was vigorous, with an undertone of both anger and fear of the future.

"Getting back to Churchill, in the lead-up to World War Two, he came to the United States and spoke about the dangers to come. At the time, as a nation, I suppose it could be said that we were too self-absorbed in our own affairs to heed his warnings. We felt safe and protected with oceans between us and a far-away hypothetical danger. I expect that future historians will say that the peoples of earth felt protected by an ocean of space. That any outside enemy was the stuff of wild fiction, easily defeated by plucky heroes and an enemy's Achilles heel we would always discover in time to save the world."

Her voice rose in strength and tenor, "Well, from the depths of that ocean of space came an evil greater than even our own. Greater than any Hitler or terrorist." She swallowed, and her eyes shone wet, "The truth? The truth is that we never stood a chance. Not one. None. The Accipiters had the high ground of space and were untouchable. Our missiles couldn't reach them, and they had over sixty thousand starships. Sixty thousand. All they had to do was throw rocks down the gravity well and bomb us back into the stone age. And they did."

An angry, haunted silence fell over the crowd.

She waited a moment before continuing. "Our civilization was doomed. In our moment of defeat, five thousand years of recorded history were wiped from the face of our Earth. Every triumph, every discovery, every sacrifice, every birth, death, life, every friend or enemy, every joy, love and hate, every work of art and dance, every city and civilization, every language, every word and song and symphony, every god and demon, everything we were and did. Everything we as a people ever hoped or dreamed of was contemptuously erased. We were squashed like a bug by an arrogant evil. The Alien Apocolypse came, and everything that we as a race ever was or could be was destroyed. Erased."

She paused, letting the fear and sorrow and anger boil.

Her face set into a mask of stone. "They destroyed it all. They destroyed everything."

She looked out across the audience and seemed to swell with their growing fury. Then her voice turned to ice as she leaned into the microphone. Tears of rage began to stream down her alabaster cheeks. "They destroyed it all. Everything, that is, but us!"

Bellicose shouts of anger and determination rose. The security details shifted nervously, but Gail turned to them and motioned for them to relax. After a moment, Gail turned back to the crowd.

She wiped her cheeks, "So, here we are. The plebiscite is done. You…. No. *We* have spoken. We have chosen our path. We've chosen to remain. To not just exist, but to somehow, someway, fight back, to take that fight to the stars, and create a new destiny there for humankind."

An uncertain rumbling slowly spread.

She lowered her voice to a husky whisper, "They must be shaking in their boots."

For a moment, silence fell across the stadium. Then, they saw her small smile. It was not a happy smile. It was cold and hard. Resolute. Grumbling turned to grim laughter and light applause.

The smile vanished, and her voice grew soft and cold, "Well, maybe they aren't worried today. In fact, they hopefully don't even know we exist. They won't be worried tomorrow, either. But, someday." She paused again as a sigh flowed across the stadium. "Someday. Someday, I promise. I VOW. Someday they will wish that back when they had first come across our beautiful little blue planet, that they had instead chosen to tiptoe by. Someday, we shall repay our tears and sorrow and loss in spades. Someday they will remember us. Remember our name, and on that day, we shall wear their cursed feathers and dance on their graves, and their blood shall wash the foul pollution of their footsteps from the Earth!"

Dark peals of angry thunderous applause rolled across Fort Brazos for a full ten minutes.

Eventually, Gail limped back to her seat at the rear of the stage.

A half-hour later, after the crowd settled down, there were more short speeches and introductions for John Austin, followed by his swearing-in, using the same oath of office.

President John Hugo Austin stood at the podium. Instead of a suit, of which he owned several very nice ones, he wore pressed jeans, Lucchese boots, a bolo tie with a sterling silver-wrapped turquoise centerpiece, and a soft lambskin jacket. His choice had greatly dismayed the entire City Council, at least officially. There had actually been two meetings scheduled to discuss the inauguration dress code and agenda. He'd smiled, nodded his head, and promptly ignored them.

A detailed, to-the-minute script had been prepared, and no less than three speeches had been written for him. With proper solemnity, he'd chosen one of them and carried the notecards in his breast pocket. Its contents had been debated for days by a committee composed of representatives from the city government, the University, and General Marcus's staff. It was an excellent speech covering all the hot-button issues and had a well-crafted balance of hope, policy, strategy, and strength. He intended to carefully preserve for history the copy that had been made for him.

The crowd roared their applause again as he took the cards out and carefully placed them on the podium. He looked out at the crowd and then glanced back at Gail.

"You know, when I first met Gail Finley, and it was Captain Finley as I recall, it was amid the flaming wreckage of that airplane she lost track of…. I hear that her protection detail has given her the code name 'Pontiac.'"

Gail stared daggers at him, but her own self-deprecation on the matter dulled them considerably. The crowd, though, laughed heartily.

"It's okay, though. We all know that she very nearly gave her life to keep that plane from hitting the high school. Very. Nearly. When I found her, she was hanging from the ruins of that billboard, and her leg was shattered with bone sticking out. As I recall, she was really… very angry. I sometimes think that had it been me there, in her place, I'd have just been passed out cold. But not her. If she'd had more time, she probably would have beaten that billboard into submission." He smiled, and the crowd laughed.

Gail blinked and stared at him, trying to decide how she felt about all this… and him.

He paused and looked at her again, his voice growing soft, "I've never mentioned this before, but you know, the thing that I saw in those green eyes of hers was not just anger. Oh, she was quite livid, and, I'm sure, knowing her now, mad at herself, but there was much, much more. Something that stuck with me. Do you know what it was, Gail?"

Her eyes widened a little, and she shook her head sharply.

He turned back to the crowd, "What I saw was… wonder. She was looking up at a confused small-town sheriff, but she did her best to ignore me."

The crowd laughed.

"No, through the fog of her pain, what she was really looking at was the sky, up where she belonged, and beyond that sky was the suntube."

The laughter died softly.

"She was way ahead of me. The burning wreckage of her plane was nearby, roaring like a blast furnace. The heat was indescribable, and the billboard was shaking itself to pieces, threatening to kill us both. And there she was, bleeding and looking up at that impossible sky. As I was struggling to free her, I looked into her face. Some moments in your life are frozen in your mind. Thinking back, I could see her pain, anger, and incredible strength. The truth of this world and our future hadn't hit me yet, but I could see it in those jade green eyes that this was the end of the world as we knew it, and yet, at the same time, a horrible, impossible, terrifying, and an achingly beautiful new world had taken its place."

Gale stared at him and blinked as she whispered, "Who are you?" *Did I say that out loud?*

John glanced back at her and smiled before turning back to the crowd. He picked up the cards, looked at them briefly, then set them down again, face down. He glanced back at the council, University officials, General Marcus, and his staff. He grinned sheepishly as several of them began to frown. He tapped the cards with his forefinger.

"Lots of folks worked very hard to write a really nice, if somewhat long-winded speech. They did a really great job, and maybe I'll get around to giving it later. Sometime." He paused, "Or not. Right now, though, after listening to Gail, I just can't go there. My heart is in a different place. I agree with everything she said, but I'm asking myself, after all that we've lost, after, well, the damned alien apocalypse, what are we fighting for? This world?" He waved his hand to the upside-down sky.

Matti sat primly in her best Sunday Go-To-Church dress at the edge of the stage behind him, looking far older than her eight years. John reached out his arm towards her, beckoning. She smiled hugely and launched herself across the stage, and leaped into his waiting arm, knocking him back a step.

He hugged her tight before leaning towards the microphone, still holding her up. "I moved back to Fort Brazos to raise Matti. She was my world. Now, today, we are all, all of us, family. We. You. Us. This is what we are fighting for. Why we haven't given up. Why we won't give up."

"I'm not saying this as some simple, trite, 'we're all in this together' thing. Fort Brazos has always been a tight community. Some people think that's one of the reasons why the Gardeners chose us. I don't know about that. What I do know is that we are no longer children. We, the survivors of mankind, are now all one race. We are all one nation. One people. One Family."

"Our world is here. Now. Standing next to you and me, all around us. We will never forget that which was taken from us. We will never forget our murdered world. We are more than a lost tribe wandering the desert. We are a people, a family. I'm told there has been a wave of pregnancies and that we're in for a huge baby boom. Our family will be growing. Now, today, and forevermore, I will stand with, and hold dear, my brothers and sisters of man."

He paused and looked around the stadium as he took a breath, "Vice President Finley spoke of evil. Mankind has learned much about evil over the millennia. We have learned to visit evil upon our brothers. Sometimes for revenge. Sometimes for envy or profit or power. Sometimes, for ideals and noble causes, and sometimes, just for spite. Mankind has always known war, and war has served to advance both progress as well as great suffering. We've learned how to wage war. We've learned how to look for our enemy's weaknesses and how to strike them there. We've learned how to be ruthless and cruel. It's hard to admit, but mankind as a species has been forged in the crucible of war."

"We're told that Accipiter's have been wandering around the galaxy snuffing out civilizations like ours for God knows how long, dropping rocks from orbit, and sending their... monsters... to mop up what is left."

The wind sighed as he looked around the audience, "Well, I'll tell you, there's something else we brought with us here besides each other. We've brought five thousand years of recorded history, where we've turned war into an art."

"In World War Two, months after the attack on Pearl Harbor, Jimmy Doolittle led a group of B-25B bombers on an air raid on Tokyo, greatly surprising the enemy. We had no land bases close enough to launch the bombers from, and the B-25B was a land-based bomber. So, an audacious plan was made to launch them from aircraft carriers. When asked, President Roosevelt later said the raid originated from "Shangri-La."

John paused, looking around the crowd at the nods of understanding.

He waved his hands at the curved horizon and the other side of the world above them all. "My friends, we are *in* Shangri-La. The Gardeners have said that we will be given the means to take the fight to our enemy. Fort Brazos will be a hidden base in a land that doesn't exist. We will secret our families here, we will build our arsenal of revenge, we will remember the fallen, and we will sleep on Accipiter feather beds." The crowd growled their agreement, "And we shall paint the stars with their blood."

The crowd roared, and the council, General Marcus, and all the others behind him stood and joined him around the podium, joining the applause and clapping until the ground fairly shook.

Hardly anyone heard him say his next words, "And someday, we shall avenge the 5%."

Bits and Pieces

Council Chambers
Day 23: 1:23 PM

Three days later, the council, as well as John and Gail, gathered in the council chambers. Earlier in the televised portion of the session, Naomi Lamar had been sworn in as the new Police Chief. Her elevation from mere patrol officer had surprised many and upset more than a few. After the incident at Reinhardt Distributing, where she had successfully defused a potentially deadly standoff, John had asked Hector to find out more about her. The discovery that she'd served with distinction for 12 years in the U.S. Army Military Police and held a BA in Criminology from St. Edwards University had raised eyebrows. It turned out that she had left the service to return home to take care of a critically ill parent. She'd taken the patrol officer job to make ends meet. With a bit of persuasion from John, the City Council had appointed her to fill the vacant Police Chief role.

After Naomi, Hector Alonzo was sworn in as the new Sheriff. Hector had almost seemed surprised at the move. Almost. John knew that Hector was hugely more on the ball than he wanted people to think. Hector had found that being underestimated, and being generally brighter than those who did so, gave him advantages.

Later in the session, Gloria had announced a contest to formally name or accept names already widely adopted to the various prominent geographical features of the new world. Gloria had started bringing her 5-year old Rottweiler, 'Dennis,' with her everywhere she went. With all that had happened, no one had said a word to her about it. Dennis was utterly adept at staying out of people's way and always seemed to find a spot nearby where he could keep an eye on Gloria when he wasn't curled up around her feet like he was now.

Meanwhile, Tom had somberly announced the selection of land for the new national cemetery and a date for the formal interment of the thousands of dead from Awakening Day, who still lay in cold storage under 24-hour honor guard, in the warehouse district.

The room was cleared of spectators, and General Marcus, Doctor Nakamura, Doctor Sanches, and Doctor Becker entered from a side door.

Dr. Nakamura took the center chair and microphone opposite the council and plugged in his laptop, activating the projection screen. A series of images were displayed without a word, depicting various "pieces" of what remained of what was now being called a Wardog. The pieces and parts were shown next to rulers and measuring sticks. Mostly, the remains appeared to be armored exoskeleton with red metallic splotches.

He commented, "First of all, I want to emphasize that all of our findings are highly speculative and may very well be entirely wrong." He nodded to Marcus, "However, that said, the urgency of the situation is clear to everyone. So, I will summarize our very early thoughts and observations. The creature's exterior plating appears to be a dense matrix of carbon and metallic fibrils. It is much lighter than you would expect. However, the creature itself was quite large, so its overall mass was still significant. We're still working on an estimate of that. We have a long way to go to begin to understand its biochemistry, especially given that we lack a… complete specimen. Doctor's Becker and Sanches have become our lead researchers, so I wanted to introduce them to you today."

"Dr. Sanches, for example, has studied the surviving samples of bone and musculature and discussed them with the rest of the team. A basic model of how we believe the creature's internal structure was organized has been constructed. The results were quite baffling, although one hypothesis that seems to explain some of them is that the creature evolved, or, given that aliens are involved, that it was engineered for a heavier gravity world than our own."

"Some of Dr. Becker's work, and others, on its biochemistry, point to the hypothesis that it can survive in much lower oxygen-content air, but we're only scratching the surface."

He turned to Marcus, who nodded. Nakamura clicked a button, and a video began to play. Some of the video had been seen by almost everyone present, but for many, this was the first time to see the complete footage. It was helmet-cam video of the fight with the creature. Even with the sound off, several people visibly flinched and cringed at the sheer ferocity of the encounter. Sparks flew off its armored skin as bullet after bullet had little effect other than to enrage it more.

Gloria shuddered, and her eyes glistened as the hunting dog was swatted away and smashed by the creature's tail. She reached down to cup Dennis's head in her hand.

The video continued, though much was a blur of chaos, dirt, and blood. Suddenly, the massive 25mm tracer rounds from the Bradley Fighting Vehicle slammed into the creature, and it exploded in an angry splash of greasy fluids and offal.

Silence filled the room for long moments, then Nakamura added, "As you can see from the recording, it is clearly resistant to our soldier's hand-carried weapons. We have run many tests against samples of its outer layers, as have the military, looking for weaknesses. That work continues; however, I should add that we have also found that the creature appears to be highly resistant to heat and fire. Its skin and plating have proven to have profoundly effective heat dissipation characteristics that are, in some ways, comparable to those found in the heat tiles which were used on the American space shuttle."

He turned bleakly to Marcus, "General, we need more... examples of this creature to study, preferably more... intact ones. Perhaps there are ways to weaken it by other means, such as in the air that it breathes or in its diet."

Marcus nodded, "Dr. Nakamura if it can be killed, it can be captured." He frowned as he felt his cell phone vibrate. He reached in his pocket and answered. After a moment, he nodded, "I'm on my way."

Descent

The massive dirigible hanger was over 1,200 feet long, nearly 400 feet wide, and just under 225 feet tall at its peak. Constructed in early 1942, shortages of steel had resulted in a partially steel and wood structure. Later such hangers were mostly wood. While it wasn't quite nearly the size of the warehouse in the *Raiders of the Lost Ark* movie, many had joked, over the years, that there had to be some dark and serious secrets lost within. Decades of (in)valuable junk, was stuffed into every nook and cranny of the looming structure. Being assigned to inventory some portion of it was a genuinely dreaded punishment reserved for only the most deserving souls. Besides, who knew what might be found, or if those relegated to the duty would ever be heard from again?

Sabrina Chilton, her team, and Leo Talib had missed the election results and then missed the inauguration. It was all background noise. They'd worked around the clock trying to unlock the puzzle of the Hangar. Before sending for Dr. Talib, two engineers had driven a light armored vehicle to the edge of the... force field... protecting the Hangar. A wooden telephone pole had been affixed to the vehicle, with the idea that it was non-metallic, and perhaps it could be pushed through the field. The result had been... dramatic. The doctors said they were confident the engineers would make a full recovery. However, they were still in a comatose state after the vehicle had been propelled backward over a hundred yards in an energy wave that swatted away everything in the area not deeply attached to the ground.

After Talib had been 'delivered,' he'd insisted on going directly to the hanger, in-person. Instead, she had taken him out to see the shattered remains of the LAV and taken the additional step of bringing him to see the heavily bandaged men in the hospital. After that, Talib had tempered his indignation and attacked the problem with uncanny intensity. It had taken a week just to work the rough edges off, but the team had eventually come together at a new level of dedication and vitality that took Sabrina by surprise. Everyone in the room was gifted and talented in one way or another. Sabrina began to see herself as the conductor of a world-class orchestra with Talib as the 1st-chair genius violinist.

As the days passed, her biggest challenge was to keep Talib focused and out of the weeds. He was not used to working with others, so peeling off tasks and farming them out to the team was hard for him to adapt to. That, and getting him to do things like sleep or eat, sometimes very nearly at gunpoint.

That morning, she'd been sipping coffee, reading a report, and watching him sleep on the nearby cot – he'd accepted sleep only when she'd had a cot brought next to his workstation. While he slept, she'd noticed his hands twitching as he dreamed until he'd startled and snapped bolt upright, nearly falling off the cot in the process. He blinked, and then he met her gaze.

She set the coffee cup down and stood, "What?"

Talib blinked again, and the corners of his lips twitched.

General Marcus entered the room, and everyone but Talib came to attention. In his case, that was because he was dead sound asleep. Marcus took Sabrina aside while she dismissed her team to return to work. He nodded questioningly over his shoulder at Dr. Talib.

Sabrina smiled, "I think he's working out better than we'd hoped. We all knew he was brilliant, but it's more than that. I think you're going to need to declare him a vital asset. My people are very, very, good, but I don't know how long it would have taken us to crack this without him."

Marcus nodded, "He'll be thrilled to have his own detail, I'm sure."

Sabrina shook her head, "Handling him will be a challenge, and we need to make sure his detail doesn't become a punishment tour. Superficially, we can transfer his working knowledge, but he has a phenomenal gift with language and an intuition that is a dozen moves ahead."

"Better keep an eye on him. Sharp objects make good tools but handle them wrong, and someone gets hurt."

"Indeed so, General. However, I think it best we wake him up now. I shudder to think of the tantrum he'd pull if we opened the doors without him."

The small UAV flew to within a few feet of where the energy barrier, or force-field, or whatever it was had been. After Talib's breakthrough, a series of images and tones were played on a large screen mounted on the back of an open-bed Humvee, many yards from the edge of the barrier. All around the Hangar, a dome of energy had flashed purple, then vanished. After that, one of the sergeants had thrown a rock over the top of a sandbag barrier and quickly ducked down to avoid the recoiled stone. Instead, the rock had simply traveled a normal ballistic arc and bounced across the tarmac.

Through the former area of the barrier, the UAV flew forward and continued through without any resistance. In the command center, there was a collective sigh of relief. The video feed from the UAV was crisp and clear as the operator flew it around the perimeter of the Hanger. The windows were no longer opaque. The view inside was clear.

Gone were the enormous stacks and racks of dusty crates and aircraft parts. It was unclear just exactly what they were looking at, but there was clearly machinery with very human-looking yellow and black caution stripes on the floor and some sort of control room.

✪ ✪ ✪

General Marcus stood outside the Hanger's now open, massive doors, holding his phone to his ear. The sky was clear, and you could easily see the sparkling oceans and continents on the other side of the sun-tube.

"Yes, Mr. President, I'm sending an Osprey to pick you and the Vice President up. We've secured the area, and teams have swept the entire facility from top to bottom. It is clear that we're supposed to be here, now that we've passed the latest test from the Gardeners. You are going to want to see this as soon as possible. I suspect that they want to show us something new."

✪ ✪ ✪

Despite the area having been declared 'cleared,' President Austin, Vice President Finley, General Marcus, Captain Darryl Guevara, General Chilton, and Leo Talib were surrounded by personal security details as well as the special operations team that had remained in place after the clearance operation. John wore his signature pressed jeans, boots, and an open-collar long sleeve shirt with no jacket. Gail seemed uncomfortable in a civilian business suit.

The Hangar interior was brightly lit, and everything looked freshly machined and manufactured. The group paused just inside the entrance, taking it all in.

John craned his neck, "Everything looks very man-made. Very military-industrial. General, I don't see anything that looks, well, alien."

Marcus nodded, "That's our assessment as well."

Talib murmured, "Something we can fix."

Everyone turned to look at him, though his expression said that he wasn't really aware he'd spoken aloud.

Gail smiled, "I think you're right, Doctor, it seems the Gardeners either don't trust us with higher-tech, or they want us to be self-sufficient. Or both."

John kicked the flooring, "This doesn't look like original material, either."

Marcus shook his head, "You're right. That's high-density reinforced concrete. The kind used to support very heavy machinery or large aircraft."

Ahead of the group was a large area of the floor outlined in black and yellow caution striping. The square area reached across three-quarters of the width of the Hangar. There were yellow and black arrows emblazoned across its surface, pointing to sizeable recessed steel rings.

Marcus pointed to the edges, "It's 300 feet square. Anyone care to guess what it is?"

Gail gasped, "It's…"

Marcus smiled, "Yes, it is. I think."

John's eyes widened, "But it's… huge."

Gail added, "That's, like, five times the size of…."

Marcus added, "and there's another one at the other end of the Hangar."

Talib frowned, "What are you talking about? What is this place?"

Sabrina put her hand on his shoulder, "This is what you discovered for us, Dr. Talib. This is an elevator for moving large equipment, soldiers, and material. As the Vice President was about to say, it's five times the size of an aircraft carrier elevator."

"Okay… I can see that, but to where?"

Marcus grimaced, "Good question. We don't know. Yet. The control room is up ahead, the area with the large windows. It's full of computer monitors, computers and spaces for more computers and equipment. It is all very self-explanatory. We just have to activate the elevator to send it wherever it is that it goes. Lt. Garreth's Bradley platoon and support platoons are prepping right now to find out for us."

The group continued their tour past the elevator platform to the control room. As they did, a group of four Bradley Fighting Vehicles and Four Humvees entered the hanger and positioned themselves on the elevator. Other trucks followed, carrying sandbags and crates of equipment and supplies. For the next two hours, a stream of men muscled the sandbags and supplies into place. The supply trucks were positioned in the center of the elevator. The Bradleys, configured with 25mm chain-driven autocannons, and the up-armored Humvee's with .50 caliber M2 Browning machine guns, ringed the inside perimeter of the elevator just inside the sandbag emplacements. Positions were laid out with FIM-92 Stinger anti-aircraft launchers, FGM-148 Javelin antitank launchers, as well as four M1919 Browning .30 caliber machine guns for good measure.

In addition to the fighting vehicles, four Signal Corps trucks, a half dozen supply trucks, and another half dozen support and transport vehicles filled out the 90,000 square foot elevator surface, with enough food, supplies, and ammunition for a week's operations. They hoped.

In the control room, the monitors were organized into four groups. One group showed various angles of view of the elevator that Lt. Garreth's platoons were organizing. Another showed the empty elevator platform at the other end of the Hangar. The other two groups of monitors were blank. Cameras were set up and were recording, making sure that anything that happened was captured for later review.

John motioned to the blank monitors, "I take it we don't know how to turn those on?"

Marcus nodded, "And why we're cramming as much firepower onto that elevator as we can fit. We just don't know what they'll run into on the other side."

Talib furrowed his brow, "Ah, General, if I may, a thought occurs to me."

Marcus turned and raised his eyebrows, "Yes, Dr. Talib?"

"Yes General, well, it occurs to me that if these 'Gardeners' want us to fight aliens, and that those aliens are in space, and since we are on the inside surface of a hollow world, and this elevator, if it is vertical, would seem to be pointed towards the outside surface of this world… what happens if this elevator opens into… space?"

Marcus smiled, "Excellent question, Doctor, and yes, that did occur to us." He gestured towards the blank monitors, "Those are not blank or inoperable feeds. It's just dark on the other end. However, when we opened the interface, we also found that environmental conditions are displayed, including temperature and atmospheric pressure at the other end."

Talib shrugged off the answer, "I'm sure that's reassuring for your men."

Marcus nodded, "We're also sending oxygen masks and tanks with them, just in case, as well as a few man-launch-able UAVs for reconnaissance. They've all volunteered for this, and they've been briefed on all we know. We held nothing back."

A microphone was mounted next to a window overlooking the elevator area. There was a large button next to it. Marcus stepped to the microphone and pushed the button. His amplified voice boomed throughout the Hangar, "Thirty minutes, gentlemen. Make your final checks. You will disembark at 18:00 hours."

The entire group made their way back down to the Hangar floor. Lt. Garreth and the rest of the men finished their preparations and gathered together between the elevator and the control room. They saluted as John, Gail, and the generals and staff officers approached. They all mingled, shaking hands and chatting.

A circle slowly formed around John. He never knew whether it was an organic thing or organized, but a hush fell over the room as he realized what was happening. He studied their faces. Their young, strong, determined faces.

John shrugged and spoke with an over-exaggerated Texas Drawl, "Well folks, I reckon it'd be a good idea for me to say something all historic and good for the camera."

After the slightest pause, everyone chuckled, letting the tension drop.

"Seriously though, what could I possibly say right now that could equal all that has brought us here and all that we hope and pray for? What could I say after the loss of so many loved ones? Of our entire world? What would matter to you? To History? Well, to start, at least we still *have* history. The Gardeners tell us the Accipiters murdered our world. Maybe that's true."

He paused, looking around at their somber faces.

"Sooner or later, though, and I hope sooner, we need to see for ourselves. We, all of us, need to really know what has happened firsthand and if the truth is anything like what we're being told…." A low growl filled the hangar. "…If it is true, it's time to make a down payment on those feather beds!"

This time there was no hesitation, Lt. Garreth's men boomed, "Hoorah!"

Minutes later, back in the control room, it was quiet as Marcus nodded to the tech at a console, who touched an icon on the touch-screen monitor. A mechanical boom filled the Hangar as the elevator was released. The motion was smooth, though, and the platform itself did not shake as it dropped slowly out of sight. In moments, an identical but un-scuffed elevator pad slid into its place, covering the hole.

Two of the darkened monitor screens suddenly brightened. One now showed a view of the in-motion elevator platform with Lt. Garreth and his men. Walls and a roof had formed around the platform. The other screen displayed an image that startled everyone in the room.

John blinked. "My God, that's...."

Gail finished the sentence, "...the world."

The image displayed was a schematic. It was a diagram, a cutaway of the cylindrical world they had been deposited inside of. The outlines of the continents were easy to recognize on the interior surface. What was new was the revelation of what lay outside what they could already step outside and see. The world was a cylindrical planetoid or giant asteroid. They already knew the interior dimensions – it was almost 4,000 miles long. The "skin" was comparatively thin – perhaps a few hundred miles. An icon blinked on the interior surface, where Fort Brazos would be.

Darryl Guevara was closest. He turned to Marcus, who nodded. He touched the icon. The view zoomed in and showed a cross-section of the skin with the control room and elevator platform on the inside/bottom, a helical pathway towards the outside surface, and some kind of structure at the top/outside the elevator path ended at. Along the elevator pathway, several apparently large internal structures were depicted.

John wondered aloud, "I wonder if the helical path of the elevator is intended as a way to avoid a straight-line structural weakness in the... crust of the world?"

The elevator platform walls also had a row of display screens. One was obviously a view of the control room, and another appeared to show the same world diagram being displayed in the control room. The rest were darkened.

On the schematic screen, the progress of the elevator was indicated along the path. The indicator was moving slowly, with a series of time indexes.

Marcus leaned forward, "I'm assuming those time indexes correspond to the ETA at each of those stops along the way? The first one is obviously elapsed time, counting up, and the rest are counting down."

Darrel leaned closer to the screen, "The ones in the middle are a different shade of color... like a web link that's grayed out. I'm not sure, Sir, but I believe the elevator may be skipping to the end. ETA five hours, forty-three minutes."

On the elevator platform video feed/screen, Lt. Garreth touched something on the display. An indicator changed, and Lt. Garreth's image appeared in a window, "Hello, Sir? Can you hear me?"

Everyone had been so intent on looking at the elevator schematic screen that no one had been watching the other one. Everyone turned. Marcus stepped to the display and noticed a blinking icon, touched it, and it stopped blinking. Another window opened next to it. He grunted, "Huh, it looks kind of like Skype. Yes, Lieutenant, how's the ride?"

"Sir, the ride is smooth as silk and A-OK," he looked around at the other men behind him and exchanged glances, "but it, ah, reminds me of that Six-Flags ride that has that long drop? Like your stomach got left behind?"

Marcus smiled and nodded, "Watch your six, Lieutenant. We don't know for sure if you'll be making stops along the way or not, but if the Gardeners want to throw flaming space monkeys at you, I know you'll be ready. Make us proud."

"Yes Sir, roger that, Sir."

As Talib was staring at the world view diagram, his brows furrowed, and he cocked his head sideways, glanced at the elevator, and back at the image. He spoke so quietly that for a moment, no one noticed. "Ah, General?"

He cleared his throat and projected his voice with more authority, "General Marcus?"

This time everyone paused their side conversations, and Marcus looked over at him, "Yes, Dr. Talib?

Leo realized his head was canted sideways and that people were looking at him oddly. He straightened. "Yes, ah, General, it occurs to me from the diagram that where we are, on the inside surface of the hollow world, that we are, well, relative to anyone on the outer surface... upside down?"

Marcus blinked for a moment, then his eyes widened, and he inhaled sharply.

Gail shook her head and muttered, "Shit!"

John groaned, realization and everyone else's reactions were variations on the theme.

Marcus keyed the microphone, "Lieutenant?"

"Yes, Sir General?"

"Lieutenant, how much of your equipment has been tied down? We believe that your... vertical orientation will have to change before you reach the, ah..., surface."

Garreth's eyes bulged slightly as the idea sunk in, but he managed to keep a straight face. "Sir, yes, we strapped down some of the supplies, but not much else. With the General's permission, I'll get on that right now."

"Do that, Lieutenant, and keep the line open. Tell us if anything at all changes. We're watching."

"Yes Sir."

Marcus turned to Darryl, "I want at least two sets of eyes on each screen, at all times. Work out a watch schedule and keep everyone fresh."

Gail shook her head, "General, I find it hard to believe that the Gardeners would not have thought about the elevator orientation. They had to have figured that into the design somehow. Also... gravity simply has to be changing along the path of the elevator. We'd previously theorized that the gravity we experience here is partially rotational force and partially some kind of artificial gravity. However, that gravity would need to be different on the surface, or at least oriented in the opposite direction, and that somewhere between here and there has to be some kind of... flip."

Marcus nodded, "I pray you're right about that and that it won't flip our boys on their heads beneath their equipment. What really scares me is what else is there that we haven't thought about – that we *should* have."

John added, "General until we built airplanes, humans mostly thought in two physical dimensions. Even now, our frame of reference is firmly rooted on a

310

round planet that seems mostly flat because we're so small in comparison. When trains and cars were first invented, some wondered if the human body could survive such acceleration. Now, the evolution of our mindset is being pushed forward by our abductors. I'm sure we have no idea what new ideas and perceptional filters we're going to need in order to survive what is to come."

Marcus nodded, "I'm sure you're right. Now, Mr. President, Ms. Vice President, we found a briefing room next door, complete with duplicate display screens and workstations. I suggest that you might be more comfortable there. This control room is fairly cramped with all of us in here," he politely did not refer to the security details doing their best to line the walls invisibly.

John shook his head, "Look, General, after everything that has happened, I've got to see this!"

Gail grimaced and took his elbow in her hand. "The General is right. Mr. President, we need to give them room to work."

John flushed with anger and frustration, yanking his elbow lose. He started to object but saw the look in her eyes. Marcus was a study in practiced patience and neutrality. He sighed, "Okay. You're right, of course."

John, Gail, and their keepers filed out, and the room suddenly felt much more open. Everyone remaining behind relaxed just a little.

Marcus took a deep breath, "Okay. Somebody get coffee. Our boys are on an express elevator to God-knows-where. I want continuous analysis and options. This is going to take a while."

Bag Job

McCallen's Bottling Plant
Day 28: 5:16 PM

Ignacio's nostrils flared at the sweet molasses air inside McCallen's Original Bottling plant. The plant had never strayed from its 100% cane sugar legacy, and the pallets after pallets of brown paper bags lining the receiving dock told this story proudly. He leveled his eyes on the map he'd been handed: the shipping dock composed the entire eastern side of the plant with a large truck lot connected to the highway by a wide service road for shipments coming and going. He looked up from his map and over the edge of a receiving dock, padded for a reversing truck and extending down some four feet to the concrete ground.

He grinned as his low and dangerous voice inquired, "This will do nicely. I assume the plant has stayed unoccupied?"

Ramon Fuente was younger than Ignacio, if only in a milder face and crisp, commanding tenor, "Seems' the place had been shut down days before all this happened; went out of business. I suppose Americans don't appreciate the sweeter things in life."

The group of worn Colombians let out a burst of harsh laughter as Ramon opened a bottle and took a hearty swig. He patted his lips dry and beckoned, "What's the game plan, boss?"

Ignacio nodded and gestured out to the empty shipping containers in the lot. "Alfonso, have Jaime rig one of those with some sturdy piping from the mill. We're hunting big game; we need a nice big cage."

Alfonso nodded briskly without breaking his cross-armed immovable lean against the cinderblock wall.

"Ramon, I want a sentry on each entrance, a team inside the plant here at the loading gates, and a support team out in those containers, ready to surround the cage when El Perrito decides he is hungry."

Ignacio's men had been hunting El Perrito for days. From what recon teams had been able to deduce, the creatures had a particular hatred for big rigs along major roads. Usually, they bruise up the car and cabin a bit but leave the fast-moving hulk largely unharmed; a few days ago, however, Ignacio's scouts had found a truck ripped to shreds with an unusually vicious persistence. Their final and most important observation was that this truck, unlike the others, had only part of its cargo missing. The tail end of the truck's load had been a couple of pallets of cane sugar. Apparently, the creature had reacted strongly to it because while most of the load was intact, the shredded rags of the 50lb bags were scattered wildly. A shallow hole in the pavement had been dug only a few feet away, and the creature had passed out there. When Ignacio's men had approached, it had woken and trotted off into the bush almost drunkenly.

Finally, now with a method of luring it, Ignacio had devised an elegant if simple trap: baiting the creature with a trail of cane sugar to a reinforced shipping container wedged between the hard-concrete corners of a loading bay and a hastily built wall of concrete K-Rails. It had taken two days of welding to form the hardened steel frame inside the container, and nobody knew if it would manage to hold.

Buck fever could hardly hold a flame to the collective anticipation and anxiety of the elite Colombian mercenaries deployed to engage the over-sized rat trap that would ensnare the hulking beast which approached. The Wardog's hexapedal crawl carried a remarkable silence for its mammoth power and size.

Having been well encouraged by the samplings of rich sugar placed along the path to the plant, the creature tiptoed with an almost pompous gait as if emboldened by the anticipation of sweet reward.

As iron claws ever so quietly rapped on concrete, the platoon of Colombians sat in perfect and painful silence. The only motion among them was the slow and deliberate stroking of fingers along with the traditionally thick mustache of Ignacio as he observed the operation's progress from his concealed perch.

The Wardog moved without a hint of hesitation until it was greeted by the steel-edged frame of the massive cage prepared for it. The creature's sudden stop flung a wave of horror through every still un-flinching mercenary. It cocked its head and moved left and right to examine the outer edges of the container with skeptical interest alongside the pile of treasure awaiting within.

Ignacio's finger slithered onto the call function of his radio, readying him at an instant's notice to trigger the dangerous and risky backup plan that would likely leave many of his men dead. Still, his mind did not race. Instead, his calm and collected mind, weathered by many years of such moments, stood by with care and was poised to make the right call.

As the flinch of a muscle hinted along Ignacio's forearm, the Wardog flung its head around in a wild surrender to desire and launched itself into the cage to bathe in in sweet pleasure, gorging itself on the piles of refined sugar. But just as fast as it lunged forth, a row of strong Colombian men appeared from their hiding place and flung the edge of the gates closed with a securing bolt falling into place with a metallic thunk.

The men frantically rushed to ratchet the steel-threaded cables run through holes in the side of the container, pinning the other-worldly Gulliver into place. Before they could finish, a young soul misjudged his distance, and a violent snap of the creature's tail against the side of the container rocked it a half foot to the left and cracked the man's skull when he grew too near.

A deafening and entirely un-terrestrial howl rattled the teeth of the rushing captors and shook the sides of the reinforced container, but the strength of so many men and quality steel cables proved too much even for the beast, as the rattling of the cage dwindled despite the persistent wail. "And now, for the hard part," Ramon smiled as Ignacio approached to observe the success.

On the table

Hangar Briefing Room:
Joint Reserve Base
Day 28: 6:11 PM

As John and Gail entered the Briefing Room. John turned to the security detail and ordered darkly, "Give us the room, gentlemen."

After a moment's hesitation, the order was grudgingly obeyed.

The room's rows of seats faced down towards a small stage, arranged like an amphitheater. Large monitors duplicated the feeds from the control room. On the stage, John and Gail found themselves standing, hands-on-hips, staring at each other in the suddenly quiet room.

In recent days, the tension between John and Gail had ratcheted up. They did their best to hide it from others, but it was getting worse. John's lips were tight with frustration, and Gail's face was stern, her green eyes like flint.

John started, "Look, Gail, I don't know what's changed. We had been working well with each other for a while, but lately, it's starting to show."

John sighed, turned away, walked a few steps, then paced back. "We're going to have to learn to work together more… smoothly. I've never, I…," he swallowed, "Look, I'm doing the best I can, and I stopped before I said what I was about to say back there. Marcus is a good man. I give him credit for putting up with me. With everything."

Gail turned a dark shade of red, then shut her eyes and let out an exasperated sigh, "Oh God, there are times when I want to…."

"Slap me? Kick me? Or is it shoot me instead?"

She opened her eyes and blinked. Her shoulders slumped, and she shook her head, "Sometimes. Yes. But not now. What I was going to say was Scream. Don't you think I wanted to stay there too to see what happens firsthand? That's not our job now. We have to let them do theirs. Look, how much sleep have you had in the last few days?"

John blinked, "I ahh…. Shit. Probably as much as you've had." He closed his eyes and shook his head in frustration and bone weariness.

Gail nodded, letting her shoulders slump a little. "Yeah. I'm sorry too. World on our shoulders and all. Excuses, Excuses."

The silence dragged out for several long seconds before John looked down, shook his head, and laughed. He took a step closer and extended his hand. "Let's start over, shall we? Nice to meet you, Ms. Finley."

The corner of her mouth quivered slightly, and she relaxed before returning the gesture and shaking his hand. "Nice to meet you… John."

"Gail, then?"

She nodded, and they stepped back from each other. There were stackable chairs along the wall. They each retrieved one and sat down, facing each other.

Gail muttered, "This is insane."

"Which part?" He shook his head before she could answer, "I know. Look. I never wanted this."

She stared into his eyes, looking for vanity she didn't find. "I think I believe you now. I'm not sure I did before."

"I know lots of folks thought I had delusions of grandeur and somehow planned to end up…."

"King? They say you would have made a run for Governor and then for President like Bush did. So, when the opportunity to run for President of what is left of humanity came along, you jumped at the chance. It was your destiny."

He bristled and snapped back angrily, "What? Hell no!"

Then he looked closer at the tiny smile on her face and sighed, shaking his head. "Damn. It was bad enough when Gloria made up that shit back when I ran for Sheriff. You really pushed my button there. You are a dangerous woman. On the other hand, I'm sure you already know that."

317

She laughed a small laugh, "Me, Dangerous? Of course I am. I wanted to see how you would react."

"Well, you saw. Can we get that shit behind us? I never once thought that this was something you wanted, despite people putting you on a pedestal from day one."

She snorted, "What, you don't think people are saying things about me? God…. While some people seem to think I'm an angel, the rest think I'm General Marcus's lackey. Some whisper I'm sleeping with him, and the rest simply assume I'm sleeping with you. Others… others say I'm a soulless frigid dyke!"

John winced, blushed darkly, and sat back, grinding his teeth. "I… I have no idea what to say. I may have to pardon myself for killing some of them. Of course, I'm not sure if that is before or after I kill the people who conspired to put us in this situation. You and I should make a list." He swallowed, "That's bad enough, but if I were you, I'm not sure if I could handle half the things you're telling me people are saying. I mean, the way I was raised, I'd slug any man who said that kind of thing about a woman." He stopped himself before he continued that thought – that he'd slug anyone who said those things about a woman he… cared about.

Gail watched him closely, then sat back in her chair, crossing her slim legs. She closed her eyes for a moment, then looked at him, "Hell, I've heard worse. What do you think happens when a woman has the life I do?" She changed the pitch of her voice, quoting, "Oh, you want to be in the Air Force? Oh, you just want to look pretty in the uniform? Oh, isn't that cute how you learned how to fly? Who did you sleep with to pass your qualifier? Oh, and they let you fly combat missions?" And they're thinking, "Oh, like they would ever let a woman fly anywhere dangerous," or, "I hope she's not on her period when she's out there…." She paused, realizing for the first time that she was breathing hard and was suddenly self-conscious of emotionally dumping in front of this man and of how her eyes were suddenly just a little too wet.

He waited, giving her time.

She shook her head again, "We're tougher than you are, you know? Women? Professional women? Fucking combat pilot with eighty-nine missions? Oh, who did you sleep with to get in the Thunderbirds? It must have been affirmative action. I'm only telling you the relatively clean ones."

They sat in companionable silence for a while longer.

John pursed his lips, "How many people have you ever told these things to?"

Gail blinked. "I… I haven't. You don't. You just swallow the bile and work harder."

He grunted and grinned, "Did it feel good to say those things? Even a little?"

She looked down, "Maybe a little…."

"And now they all have to salute you."

She sniffed, and the edge of her mouth quivered again, "Yeah… I guess you're right."

"Good. Give 'em hell."

She inhaled deeply as she studied his face. "So, a Texan at Wharton? What was that like?"

He smiled, "A walk in the park, it sounds like."

Gail shook her head. "Yeah, right. I'm sure they accepted you as a peer and equal. I know their types, and I know what they think of Texans. I've known plenty of them over the years, but I have to ask. Why there?"

John sat back and thought for a moment, nodding to himself, "Pride. It was a time in my life when I felt I had a lot to prove. I had the money by then to do anything I wanted, but mostly, it was to prove a point. I'd been in too many meetings with self-important Ivy Leaguers who wrote off my success to luck. So, I went and proved that I was as smart or smarter than they were in their own backyard. Of course, I realize now that I was only proving it to myself. Nothing I could do or say would prove me different in *their* eyes. Not really."

She nodded, and they sat silently for a long time.

She shook her head and took a deep breath, "So, look, it is obvious to me that I don't know you at all, and I need to. Especially since so many people seem to think we are an item."

He raised his eyebrows and opened his mouth to speak, but she cut him off, "Oh, right, like you've been living in a cave, cowboy? I know you had to have heard the rumors. You're too smart not to know."

John sighed, "Yes, you're right. It just makes me mad."

She continued, "So, I don't mean to be insensitive, and I am aware of the circumstances of your wife's death but are you seeing anyone? Dating? Secretly gay?"

John stared at her for a moment, then chuckled, "No, I'm most definitely not gay, and no, I'm not seeing anyone. Folks have tried to "set me up" with someone, and Matti even tried to get me to date and even set me up on one of those dating sites." He shuddered.

"So, what happened?"

"I guess it boils down to… well, I don't know *how* to date. I'd been with Carolyn for so long, since High School. Women on those dating sites kept sending naked pictures, and some of them are people I actually know…. And the dates I got set up on by supposed friends were disasters."

Gail studied his face, "and you're something of a public figure. People think that they know you."

John raised his eyebrows, "Well, yeah, I think that's part of it. So, what about you?"

Gail shook her head and laughed, "No, there is no one in my life, although people always seem to think they know who I am from my reputation. They just assume things."

John laughed, "Yeah, well, I suppose the fact that your face could go on recruiting posters doesn't help?"

Gail smiled, "Ohhh, sneaking a compliment in there? Smooth."

They both chuckled, and she relaxed a little, "You'd know, wouldn't you? You should hear what the girls say about you."

"Don't worry, Matti keeps me humble."

Gail paused and tilted her head slightly, "Speaking of Matti, how is she coping with all this?"

John looked down, "You know, it scares me how well she is doing. I know that she hurts about everything that has happened. I sometimes wish she weren't as sharp… that maybe then she wouldn't… see as much as she does. It terrifies me how much she actually sees and understands. But, she is the brightest star in my sky right now, and she's what keeps me sane."

Gail smiled, "I like her. She's quite precocious."

John closed his eyes and shook his head, "You have no idea. A few months ago, all I thought I had to worry about was the day she would discover boys. Now? To be honest, she thinks the world of you. She thinks you walk on water."

Gail chuckled, "Ah, one of my angel followers then."

"Try not to give her too many bad ideas."

"From what I can see, I don't think she's going to take any bad advice. She's got her own identity, and it's quite strong. She won't be easily swayed."

"I know. She's a force of nature."

Gail frowned, "We're going to need more like her if the human race is going to survive."

John swallowed, "If anything were to happen to her… I don't think I would survive it."

Gail waited a long moment before answering, "You blame yourself for what happened."

John grimaced, "It was stupid and selfish, taking her with me like that…. What was I thinking?"

Gail reached out and touched his hand. She spoke softly, "You were thinking that you didn't trust anyone else to protect her. She was the most precious thing in the universe to you and with that universe turned upside down, you kept her close." She hesitated, "You couldn't protect her mother, and nothing was going to keep you from protecting your child. Carolyn's child. Not even the end of the world."

John flashed with anger ever so briefly, then looked into her green eyes, searching. When he spoke, his voice was husky and flat, "There are only a handful of people from the world before Awakening Day that I truly trusted, but this is a new world now, and we are creating a new arena that involves life and death decisions for our entire species… and a war we must somehow fight on a truly galactic scale. You and I both know there is a greater darkness to come. When it does, some will falter."

He looked down for a moment before continuing, "I've known you for a short time now, and in that time, I've come to see that you are physically brave and proud, but can I trust you? Gail. Not as Vice President. I mean you. Can I trust you, Gail Finley? Can I trust you with my life or Matti's? Can I trust you to be honest with me? To tell me when I'm being stupid or foolish and know the difference between when that is the right or wrong thing to do?" *I need you to say Yes, for so many reasons....*

Gail started to answer, but he held up his hand to stop her.

"You see... *President* and *Vice President* are the wrong words. We are not the political heads of state of one nation among many. We are... we are... we are the parents in charge of what is left of all of humanity. They are all looking to *us* to protect them. To lead them into the unknown, leading the lost last tribe of humanity in the desert of stars. Their faith in us won't be blind, and before long, the unity we see now will falter. Fear will become their leader, and they will question and challenge and go astray. Sooner or later, the knives will come out."

Gail sank back into the chair. *I keep underestimating this man.*

John continued, his voice low and measured, "My pride and hubris led me to risk my daughter's life. I know I'm not ready for this. I know my feet are made of clay, and to switch metaphors again, I'm no Moses in the desert, Gail, but I accepted this responsibility, and I will give everything I am to protect... our people. I need to know if I can trust you to have my back. I need to know because, in the days ahead, there may be no one that either of us can really talk to. Not until we begin to test the true measure of the people around us. I need to know." He leaned forward, searching, imploring, "Can I trust you, Gail Finley."

Gail's head was spinning as she mentally kicked herself. She knew that everything he'd said was true. She'd had many of those same thoughts herself, but so many things had been happening so fast that she hadn't gotten past her anger, her fury, to put all the pieces together and fully realize what was to come. In all of recorded history, mankind's behavior towards his fellow man has not really changed. Human nature. Damn, but if the cowboy wasn't right. Sooner or later, things would go to hell, and she didn't know who she could trust, truly trust, either.

She didn't really know where her answer came from, but it was immediate and emphatic, and her own eyes widened in surprise as she said it., and she knew in her heart that she trusted this man and that she suddenly, desperately needed him to trust her. And perhaps more. "Yes, on my life and honor, you and Matti can trust me... as I trust you with my own life. I have your six."

Then, as John started to answer, it was her turn to shush him. She gently put a finger to his lips, "Lincoln said we can't escape history and that we would be remembered in spite of ourselves. *No personal significance, or insignificance, can spare one or another of us. The fiery trial through which we pass, will light us down, in honor or dishonor, to the latest generation.* Let us both pray, John, that there will actually be more generations after us."

John sighed. "I need a drink."

Gail smiled, "You're buying. In the meantime, there is something I'd like to ask. With your permission, John, I think I should like to teach Matti how to fly."

Those who wait

Hoffman Family Dairy Farm
Day 28: 6:21 PM

Sandra Hoffman sat cross-legged, and her sisters Jordan, Hannah, and Elizabeth sat clustered next to her on the well-worn couch watching the Joint Reserve base's public access channel on the TV. Jordan bounced young Vicktor on her knee. An attractive female lieutenant was reporting on the progress of "the elevator." By now, everyone knew about the mysterious elevator and that a small group of volunteers was descending on it, to fates unknown.

Councilwoman Esmerelda Collins sat on the equally well worn but well taken-care-of armchair next to Sandra, holding her hand. Esmerelda was a long-time family friend of the Hoffman's. She was a cattlewoman, and the Hoffman's were dairy farmers. Historically, those didn't always mix well, but Fort Brazos was a different kind of place.

That two of the first alien attack survivors, Sandra and Lt. Garreth, had become romantically involved was hardly a secret. When Esmerelda had found out that Garreth was leading the volunteers, she'd made a beeline for the Hoffman place. Besides, Esmerelda had known Sandra since she was born and been there at her christening. Esmerelda's own son and daughter were grown and had moved to Dallas and Fort Worth. Now, Sandra and her siblings were dearer to her than she cared to think about.

Esmerelda's security detachment was outside, along with a more or less permanent squad of soldiers patrolling the vicinity of the first alien attack – just in case more ever showed up.

It was an ironclad rule at the Hoffman's that meals were only served at the kitchen table. No exceptions. Life at the Dairy Farm brought long hours and not much time for couch surfing.

On this day, no one gave the rules a second thought. Garreth had become a fixture around the farm – whenever he could get leave time – and all the girls simply adored him. Even Vicktor thought he was pretty special. No one was going to leave Sandra alone, in case something terrible happened. Esmerelda feared what would happen to them all emotionally if something dread did indeed occur.

There was no real news yet, and while general reports were being shared about what was happening, the military had put their foot down and simply refused to provide live video. Sandra hadn't decided if she was furious about that or relieved not to have to watch Garreth's face, minute by minute.

Sandra's plate sat untouched in her lap. Hanna nudged her, "Eat something, Sandy."

Sandra grudgingly complied, nibbling a fried chicken leg.

The Lieutenant on the TV looked up from a piece of paper handed to her, "…I'm being told that it is estimated that it may take another four or five hours or more for our men on The Elevator to reach their… destination."

Esmerelda watched Sandra's face as the news was read. Sandra's long golden blonde hair framed an ultra-fair face of Dutch descent, which suddenly turned a shade of green and her eyes widened as she clutched her stomach. Esmerelda deftly grabbed the plate before it could fly across the room as Sandra bolted from the couch and ran to the bathroom.

Her sisters all followed, with Esmerelda shortly behind them. Jordan handed Vicktor off to Elizabeth, and she and Hanna went into the bathroom to help Sandra, whom everyone could hear retching into the toilet.

Twenty minutes later, Sandra returned to the couch, face and hair clean and teeth brushed. All the food had already been moved to the kitchen, and the ceiling fan turned on to diminish the smell of food, lest it make Sandra sick.

Esmerelda wrapped an afghan blanket around her shoulders. Sandra looked up at her and swallowed as they traded looks. Esmerelda raised her eyebrows and glanced downward at Sandra's belly and back up again.

Sandra swallowed and nodded. Sandra's fear was not just about the safety and wellbeing of a young man that she cared about. It was for the father of their unborn child.

Esmerelda sighed inwardly but managed an outward smile of reassurance.

My God, she's only 17, but then it is the apocalypse after all. Besides, I hear there's apparently a lot of baby-making going on lately.

She realized that she wasn't, actually, very surprised at all and wondered if the sisters had figured it out yet. For a brief moment, she allowed herself the indulgence of wallowing in her own self-pity and loneliness and wistfully regretting that she herself was between husbands at the moment.

Enough of that! Sandy and the girls need you.

She sat down in the armchair next to Sandra, took her hand, and squeezed it.

"It's Okay, Sandy, girls, and Vicktor, it's going to be okay."

Special Delivery

Bonham State University
Parking Lot D. Reserved Parking
Day 28: 9:16 PM

E very living human being in Fort Brazos watched the same news feed as Sandra Hoffman, or on their phones, radios, or computers. No one was wandering around the large Bonham State University parking lot, especially the gold section, reserved for faculty.

No one heard or noticed the caravan of trucks and SUV's surrounding the semi-truck hauling an odd-looking shipping container, or the rough, dark, determined men who spilled out of those vehicles and proceeded to fasten class 120 steel chains to attachment points on the container and rapidly nail-gun them to the pavement. In less than 60 seconds, all but one of the vehicles had sped off into the night.

Ignacio stepped out of an idling, weather-beaten 1986 Ford Bronco and silently walked up to the back of the heavily chained, reinforced container. He paused for a moment, resting his left hand on the cool metal door, listening.

He whispered, "Tranquilo Perrito, duerme."

He wiped some of the dirt and dust away, and taped a note to the trailer door along with a bright red stick-on Christmas bow, then quietly walked back to the Bronco, got in, and slowly drove away while dialing a number on a disposable cell phone.

The female voice on the line was pleasant, but she sounded fatigued to Ignacio, "Fort Brazos Joint Reserve Base Emergency Response Center, what is the location of your emergency?"

"Yes, my dear, my name is Ignacio. I'd like to report a sighting of one of those fearsome alien creatures, like the one that attacked your soldiers on the highway."

The voice on the line suddenly perked up, and there were background noises that Ignacio assumed were intended to grab the attention of others, "Yes, Sir! Where is the sighting, and are you in immediate danger?"

"Why, thank you for your concern, my dear. No, there is no immediate danger to anyone. Your creature has been, ahh, captured and is currently sleeping. We've left it gift wrapped for you at the Bonham State University parking lot number D, in the reserved parking area. The beast is chained inside a reinforced container, but I honestly don't know how long that will keep it secure, so I do recommend extreme caution as well as haste. I'll call again, soon, to discuss matters of mutual interest."

He hung up and added to himself, *Buenas noches mi querido*, and tossed the burner phone out the window.

Topside

Day 28: 6:00 PM

O ther than the last, fading crackling sparks of the actinic St. Elmo's fire, the vast, subterranean vault was cold and silent. Soft light grew and filled the space, which was roofed with a network of graceful support arches that soared 6,500 feet overhead. They were interspersed with a filigree of raised relief structures that might have been art or device or both. The overall color was a powder blue with a tracing of white, gold, and silver. Underneath the roof lay a quiescent city of modern but ordinary-looking human towers, parks, and a massive central building complex.

Inside one of the towers, Vice Admiral Preston Milner III, Deputy Chief of United States Naval Operations, lay supine, fully dressed in his Navy Working Uniform, on a made-up bed with ornamental duvet covers. With a sharp gasp, he spasmed to life, jerking upright. He groaned in pain and broke into an instant sweat.

He shivered and blinked rapidly, looking around at the frigid, unfamiliar room. It was an apartment of some kind, with a balcony, but he could see nothing from where he sat. His stomach heaved, and he somehow managed to lever his legs over the side of the bed and find a vanity trash can to throw up into.

A bathroom was evident across the room, so he stood and picked up the trash can and stumbled weak-kneed to it to clean up.

Preston was not in the habit of getting drunk and waking up in strange places. In fact, the last time he'd been drunk was the night before he'd left home for the Naval Academy, and even then, he hadn't passed out.

He shivered and shook himself, blinking fast. All he could remember was some kind of weird dream that was fading fast.

Where the Hell am I, and how did I get here?

The bathroom was fully stocked, but he noticed that the soap and other toiletries were still in American-style western wrappers, like you would find in a hotel or a furnished rental apartment. There were no personal items evident. The electrical outlets were American style. He rinsed his mouth out and broke the seal on the mouthwash bottle before using it. He took a moment to run a hand through his thick but greying hair. Hair he'd thankfully inherited from his mother and not his prematurely bald father.

He left the bathroom and noticed there was no phone or clock on the nightstand. There was a TV on the wall with a nearby remote. He turned it on, but there were no working channels. On the other side of the room was a kitchen nook, complete with a refrigerator, cook surface, and a coffee machine. He checked the refrigerator, but it was empty except for a couple of dozen American-branded bottled waters.

Aside from a pungent ozone smell, everything seemed utterly ordinary. Everything in the room looked brand new, without a scratch or even other footprints on the carpet.

He blushed in anger. *Is this somebody's bad idea of a practical joke? Enough of this!*

He walked to the balcony door, jerked it open, and stormed outside. It was a long moment before he realized his jaw was hanging open as he stared wide-eyed at his surroundings. With an effort, he closed his jaw.

Nothing made sense. A cluster of identical office tower buildings surrounded him. No, they must be apartment buildings – they had balconies that looked like his own. Hundreds of men and women, some in Navy or Marine uniforms and some not, were emerging onto those balconies, pointing, talking excitedly, and staring around like he was.

It was apparent he wasn't anywhere near the naval base at New London, Connecticut anymore. The towers were not on the coast or in any city he'd ever seen. There was no sky. Overhead was an impossible, elegant, artificial sky-roof that was a least a mile high, like some kind of man-made underground cavern.

The roof was well lit, but it was clearly solid. Light came from somewhere, but it wasn't evident from where.

Looking down, there were streets or roads of some kind, but there were no cars or trucks – just a long line of what looked like golf carts.

For just a moment, he wondered if he'd been kidnapped to some underground North Korean city. *No, there's no way the North Koreans would have had the money and resources to build this place.* Also, there were no jackbooted soldiers waving Kalashnikovs around, and there were no giant posters of the great leader. No propaganda. No "minders." Besides, everything was too western, too nice.

He reached into a pocket and pulled out his secure cell phone. It had bars, so he dialed his wife, then his daughter, followed by a half-dozen other people. No one answered, including 911.

Scowling, he turned and headed to the apartment door. He made note of the number on the door and then made his way to the ground floor. None of the sailors, marines, or civilians he encountered along the way had any better ideas about what was going on.

Preston spotted a dark-haired Lieutenant who was studying a nearby two-seater golf cart. There seemed to be a variety of sizes available. "Lieutenant?"

The lieutenant startled briefly, turned, stiffened, and saluted, "Yes, Admiral?"

Preston looked at the Lieutenant's name tag and asked him, "Any idea what's going on, Lieutenant Marks?"

Marks stood at attention, "No Sir, Admiral. Begging your pardon, Sir, but I was hoping that you might know. Sir."

Preston smiled with a confidence he certainly didn't feel and nodded to the cart, "Well, what do you say we go find out."

The street had quickly filled with carts and pedestrians, and everyone had questions, wild speculation, and no answers. Every building, every cart, every visible item was new and fresh. There was no trash or dirt or debris anywhere.

The carts were all labeled in English. Theirs was "Cart # 1124", and the street signs were printed in plain English. The nearest read "47th Street."

As they made their way through the streets, others followed, perhaps hoping the man in the high-ranking uniform knew what was going on or that he would at least know what to do when he found out. There were empty cafes, shops, and ordinary-looking office buildings – none of which appeared to be occupied or had ever been occupied.

Eventually, they found their way to what had to be an administrative complex. The architecture had 'Government' written all over it, but like everything else, it looked immaculate and new – all freshly minted without a scratch or smudge anywhere.

The building was massive by any standard. At least 12 stories tall, the main entrance was faced with huge white colonnades and a glass dome that somehow managed to evoke both I.M. Pei and Frank Lloyd Wright. In front, a reflecting pool with fanciful fountains guarded the entrance, and beyond that lay an extensive park area with graceful lawns, groves of trees, and winding walking paths stretched into the distance. It was as though the Pentagon, the Palace of Versailles, and the National Gallery had a love child.

Admiral Milner, followed by Lt. Marks and a few thousand others, converged on the entrance.

Topside Elevator Control Room
Day 28: 11:40 PM

Lt. Garreth took a quick drink from his camelback and made one more inspection tour around the elevator. Hours earlier, they had only just finished hastily tying down the vehicles when everyone's stomach had lurched amid a wave of nausea as the elevator – and gravity had flipped. For a fleeting moment, they'd been in zero gravity, and then the moment passed.

A few people had thrown up. Sandbags had been jumbled around, and the machine guns mounted there fell over. A few people lost their footing, and lots of still unsecured small items fell or toppled, however, thankfully, amazingly, no one was injured and no equipment seriously damaged.

After the cleanup, he'd spent an hour on a 'conference call' explaining what had happened and making recommendations on preventing such problems in the future. Garreth made a mental note to recommend in his report the establishment of a role of "Space Elevator Loadmaster" … or some such thing to avoid these problems.

Now, the countdown to arrival clock was down to the final minutes, and everyone already had their oxygen-fed NBC gear at the ready, just in case.

The elevator platform was large. Everyone had short-range coms so that orders could be clearly heard. Garreth keyed his mic, "Okay, we've been over this a dozen times. Nobody knows what we're going to encounter on arrival, but I will remind you to hold fire unless fired upon. People, if we screw this up, the consequences could affect all that remains of humanity. So. Don't fuck up!"

Everyone on the platform was an experienced combat veteran. They were all professionals. As one, they replied, "Hoorah!"

As the counter silently ticked down to zero, the elevator's roof receded, and the walls retracted. The elevator smoothly slowed to a gentle stop that would not have spilled a coffee cup.

A few lights shone in their immediate area. Around them stood… the hangar. No, not the hangar, but very nearly its clone. They were in a large warehouse very similar to the hanger, complete with an identical control room. More lights came on in the warehouse, illuminating its differences. This facility was much larger, with very human-looking shipping and receiving areas, freight doors, forklifts, and all the typical sorts of items and equipment you would expect to see in a modern distribution center.

There were no people or aliens or any other living creatures evident.

With the walls receded, the video link back to the reserve base control center was gone. Garreth ordered a squad to scout the nearby control room and the

UAV operator to send up a small UAV to fly around and map the area around them.

When the squad gave the all-clear, Garreth went to the control room and checked it out himself. It was indeed a mirror of the one at the Reserve Base. He touched a blinking icon on one of the monitors, and they all came to life, including feeds showing Marcus and the others reacting to seeing their own blank monitors come to life, obviously relieved to see Garreth and his men alive and OK. Garreth touched another icon to open the video conference.

Garreth grinned, "General, Topside Base here, the Eagle has landed." He could see on the screens that the other control room was crowded with the General, President, Vice President, and many others.

Marcus grinned broadly, flashing a huge toothy smile, and Garreth could see that everyone around the General was clapping and cheering, "Roger that Lieutenant! We're all very relieved to hear from you. Tell us what you see. I take it you have not encountered any resistance?"

"General, no one is here but us. This appears to be the reciprocal of the control center facility where you are. It is a large warehouse or distribution center. We're scouting it now and have a UAV flying around inside to map and make sure it is clear. So far, it's very empty. There are a large number of loading dock entrances or loading bays like you would expect to find in a large warehouse, along with very ordinary-looking forklifts and equipment. There is nothing remotely, Uhm, alien, in sight, Sir."

Marcus nodded, "Okay, Lieutenant. I want you to secure that facility before moving on. The main group of the Signal Corps will stay and try and establish independent communications between your location and here. I don't like being dependent upon this thing. Secure all the entrances and leave an adequate defensive force behind before taking your scout command out. There must be more to that place than a warehouse. We can't fight space aliens with, ah, forklifts."

"Yes, Sir, General."

"And take the other Signals Corps people with you that have the translation equipment and long-range transmitters. You may need them."

"Yes, Sir, General."

After securing all the loading dock doors except what seemed to be one of the main ones, as well as all the other entrances they could find, Lieutenant Garreth rode in the third Humvee, with two of the Bradley's in the lead and Sergeant Garvesh Bahun's comm's trucks, formerly of the 29th Queen's Gurkha Signals Regiment, in the middle. They left two Bradley's behind as rear guard.

Outside, high above them, was the delicately patterned sky-blue artificial cavern roof. Next to the warehouse, there was a cluster of other oversized warehouses and industrial buildings on one side. On another side lay a long line of massive archways sealed with blast doors marked with prominent caution striping.

Running alongside the archways was an ordinary-looking wide road that led directly to the only open archway. Above it hung a titanic blast door, ready to drop in the event of some calamity. As their column of vehicles approached, they were able to see what lay beyond.

A city. A clean, new, pristine human city.

They stopped there, with the warehouse they'd left behind them still in sight, and launched a UAV. The stunning live video left Garreth and his men speechless. However, it was also being streamed back to the Reserve Base. Garreth was quickly bombarded with questions. Finally, Marcus put a stop to it and ordered Garreth to proceed.

The video from the UAV had shown people. Lots of them. Men, women, and even children. Humans. Many in U.S. Navy or Marine uniforms.

The city was organized into four main sections, with three of them encircling a fourth central zone. One of the surrounding areas appeared to be a collection of dozens of tall, multistory apartment buildings. The second section was an equally large group of office towers. The third seemed to be a stadium and entertainment area. In the center of it all was a massive, sprawling 12 story building surrounded by parks and lakes.

❈ ❈ ❈

It took nearly forty-five minutes to work their way through the crowded streets. Thousands of servicemen and women, and no small number of their on-base dependents and children, many in the ubiquitous golf carts, were wandering about, clamoring for answers.

No one they encountered had any idea what was going on, although the theories were sometimes wild and extravagant. Apparently, they'd only been awake for a few hours and had no idea about where they were or how they had gotten there. Their Awakening Day had apparently begun the moment Garreth's men had started their elevator journey.

Marcus had ordered Garreth to keep his men quiet and to find the senior ranking officer present. To accomplish this, Garreth assumed the best place to look was at the large central complex.

As they arrived at the massive building's marble steps, a vast crowd engulfed their vehicles. So far, there was no hint of violence, but with this many people, crowded in one place and more on the way, Garreth knew it was a potential powder keg waiting for the right bad news to light the fuse.

Amid the cacophony of questions and noise from the crowd, he climbed onto the hood of his Humvee and leaped across to the nearest Bradley Fighting Vehicle, and climbed atop of the turret. The Bradley's commander handed him the mic for the loudspeakers. His amplified voice boomed, "Everyone stand back! Stand clear!"

The crowd quieted a little, and some tried to move back, but more and more people were arriving behind them. "I repeat, STAND BACK! I need to talk to the senior officer present!"

Just then, he could see a small wedge of people making their way down the steps through the crowd. A group of marines surrounding a navy officer quickly and efficiently parted the human waters.

As the group neared Garreth's Bradley, he hopped down off the turret and to the pavement. As he landed, the Marines arrived and formed a semicircle around Garreth and Vice Admiral Preston Milner. Garreth saluted, and Preston returned the Salute.

Preston gave a worried smile, "Lieutenant, where did you come from, and do you know what's going on?"

Garreth stiffened, "Sir, Admiral, we're from Joint Reserve Base Fort Brazos, and what is going on, well Sir, that is a very long story. Sir."

Preston took a half step back, stunned, "Fort Brazos? Texas? How is that possible? What the hell is going on here?"

Garreth swallowed, "Sir, Admiral, my orders are to connect you to... higher, so they can debrief you and answer your questions."

Preston glared at Garreth, "Son, do you have any idea what's going on and what we've been going through here?"

Garreth nodded sadly, "Yes, Sir, I suspect I do, but I have my orders. If you will follow me, Sir, you can talk to people who can better explain things than I can."

Preston frowned, "Very well, Lieutenant, lead the way."

Preston entered the comms truck but had insisted that the door be left open so that the crowd could still see him. The video conference was a little shaky as they were quite some miles away from the relay, and there were many buildings in-between. As the conversation began, Preston was quite animated, demanding, and full of disbelief. The crowd could only hear snatches of the conversation. However, as the call dragged on, Preston became more and more subdued, and so did the crowd.

Preston disconnected from the call and slumped back an hour and a half later, sitting limply in the chair. He couldn't decide whether to curse, scream, pray or cry. In his heart, he knew he'd soon be doing all four, probably at the same time. At the moment, though, having learned that his planet and probably everyone he knew was dead and gone, his family, his wife, and daughter.... and aliens and a hollow world and, and, and, and....

Finally, the noise from the crowd outside shook him from his funk, and he stood and emerged pale and shaken from the truck. His legs were rubbery, and he stumbled as he stepped down the steps, and Garreth caught Preston's elbow to steady him. In that moment, Preston looked into Garreth's eyes and saw the truth of it. *He already knows all of this, but he's doing his duty.*

He winced before gritting his teeth and nodded to Garreth that he was OK. "Thank you, Lieutenant. I... I apologize for being angry with you earlier. I think that had I been in your shoes, I wouldn't have known how to tell me what has happened either, and, thank God there have been no alien attacks on our people here, but I'm grateful General Marcus is sending men and equipment to begin patrols, just in case."

Garreth nodded his gratitude, "Thank you, Sir, but we've had weeks to digest all that has happened, and even that was in bits and pieces over time. We at least had some time to begin to cope with it all." He glanced out to the crowd of anxious faces, "Sir... your people.... What will you tell them?"

Preston took a deep breath, collecting himself. He swallowed, "Lieutenant...."

Garreth waited. He could see the weight of their lost world suddenly thrust upon the Admiral's shoulders. The man seemed years older than when he'd entered the truck.

Preston blinked and looked out over the noisy, still-gathering crowd. He pursed his lips and swallowed, "First things first, Lieutenant. There is no food here that we've been able to find."

Garreth's eyes widened. He glanced out at the crowd. *And this will give people something else to think about, won't it?* "Yes Sir, I understand. We'll distribute what we have immediately and coordinate to bring up as much as possible, as fast as possible. May I ask if you intend to go down to Fort Brazos, Sir?"

"No, Lieutenant, I need to stay here and organize. I'm told a delegation will be coming here instead."

✪ ✪ ✪

Lucky Cat Truck Stop
Wayne & Sybil Blanchard's Sleeper Cab
Day 29: 2:12 AM

Wayne fumbled in the dark for his too-loudly ringing cell phone, his eyes not yet focusing on the painfully bright phone display in the darkened cab. "Ya.. yes?"

Sybil crawled into a corner of the cab. She wrapped a blanket around her shoulders, pulled her knees up to her chest, and yawned.

"Is this Wayne Blanchard, Blanchard Shipping?"

Wayne rubbed his eyes with his large fist and sat up groggily, "Yes, this is Wayne."

"Mr. Blanchard, I'm sorry to bother you at this hour, Sir. This is Corporal Jimenez. We have an emergency shipment we need your help with. We need a minimum of a hundred and four pallets or as many as can be managed within the next six hours of MREs and other supplies, picked up from the warehouse and driven to the base. After that, they will need to be… err… further transported for several hours to another destination."

Without even thinking about it, Wayne cleared his gravelly voice, "Uhm, you can fit 32 pallets on one forty-foot FCL container, so you'd need three full and one partial forty-foot containers, which means four trucks and crews, and then we need warehouse crew to load the containers. At this hour, will there be anyone at the warehouse to load?"

"Yes, Sir, we understand that. The warehouse will be fully staffed by the time you arrive. One more thing, Sir, we will need shipments of the same or larger size every day going forward."

Wayne blinked. "Okay, Corporal Jimenez, we'll get it done." He ended the call and turned to Sybil.

"Well, looks like we're in business, baby."

Sybil turned on the lights, "I heard. Do you know what's happening? Is everything okay?"

"He didn't say, but it is urgent, and we don't have a lot of time to get everything organized."

Sybil nodded. "Okay, I'll get the other drivers. You go run the checklist on our rig."

❂ ❂ ❂

Hangar Briefing Room -- Joint Reserve Base
Day 29: 7:00 AM

John Austin stood at the podium facing the cameras that now streamed live. He was flanked by Gail, Marcus, and the senior officers. Like everyone else on the stage, it was challenging to keep the combination of excitement, worry, apprehension, and fatigue from his face, but he tried. He wore his signature pressed jeans, lambskin jacket, and bolo tie.

"People of Fort Brazos and the Reserve Base. My friends and neighbors. I have two announcements to make. The first is that, overnight, as many of you have now heard, one of the creatures of the type that attacked our soldiers on the highway has been found. It was already trapped and is alive, chained inside a cargo container. It seems that some person or persons managed to capture the beast and left it for us to find on the University parking lot."

He shook his head, "We don't know who did this. So far, they're choosing to remain anonymous. When we know more about this situation, we'll pass it along. In the meantime, we now have a live specimen that can be better studied and tested. If we're to fight these things, we need to understand them."

John paused and reached for a glass of water on the podium. He took a drink and swallowed, gathering himself. "And now the second announcement. We have astounding news from our men on the elevator."

He looked around the room, gripping the podium in both hands. "My friends, we are not alone."

His voice became husky as the emotion welled up. "We have found more survivors! A lot more. It seems our abductors also kidnapped the active-duty personnel, civilian workforce, and many of the dependents who were stationed at the New London Naval Base. We don't have a count yet, but there may be as many as fifteen to twenty thousand people."

"The survivors have apparently only been awakened in the last few hours, coinciding with our discovery of the elevator. So, this is their Awakening Day. They're just like we were on Awakening Day – they don't have a clue what is going on. They do not yet know what you know, what we have all learned over the last few weeks."

John paused again and lowered his voice slightly, "Now, I know that a natural question that many of you will ask is, does this mean there may be even more survivors we don't know about yet, maybe whole other cities? This is something we all desperately hoped for in the early days after Awakening Day as we first began to explore the interior of this world, only to find we were alone. I understand. At this point in time, I'd like you all to think about this from our abductor's point of view. They said in their announcement that they had specifically saved Fort Brazos and selected other military units from around Earth. We saw that many combat units from other countries were deposited on the outskirts of the Joint Reserve Base. Now, we've discovered more survivors and this time from a Naval Base. Logically, it seems like our abductors have selected the Fort Brazos city as the foundation for a civilian population and experienced combat soldiers for on-the-ground future fighting...."

"Several people have pointed out that we can't exactly fight space aliens with tanks and rifles. There had to be more that we haven't seen yet. Well, now we've found Navy personnel. Why Navy? Not because we need ships in the water, but because we'll need ships in space, and our navy is the closest analog of that experience that we have. I think this is a big missing piece of the puzzle."

"So, you might ask, could there be other specialists or communities still waiting to be revived that we have not yet discovered? Possibly. At this point, though, I have to say that I doubt it. Based on what our abductors, these Gardeners as some call them, have told us so far, I regret to say that I will be surprised to find more. It breaks my heart to have to say these words, but I have an obligation to tell you what I think."

He paused to take another drink of water and gather his thoughts.

"Also, I should tell you that we've only just begun to explore this new area that the elevator leads to. However, as many of you already know, we've discovered an entire city as well as industrial infrastructure. The other thing we've learned is that our abductors apparently saw fit to leave no food for the New London survivors. They have running water but no food we've been able to find, so a relief operation is underway to ensure they have what they need to survive. Now we know one reason why the Gardeners expanded our warehouses so much, including those at the reserve base. We have ample supplies of military MREs for the foreseeable future. I'm sure that we can start working out other arrangements for fresh food as soon as possible. There is no shortage of supplies."

"I'm sure many of you will ask what all of this means in the long run. The truth is, we simply don't know. This is a developing situation, and we'll share more information as it becomes available, including a list of the names of these new survivors."

✪ ✪ ✪

Elevator: The Hangar
Joint Reserve Base
Day 29: 7:49 AM

Looking for all the world like Landing Signal Officer's on the deck of an aircraft carrier, waving their coned flashlights, several soldiers carefully guided the semi-trucks being driven by Wayne and the other drivers onto the desired spots on the elevator pad. This elevator pad had slid into place immediately after Lt. Garreth's team had departed, so no one knew how many pads there actually were. Someone had stenciled a large "2" in block lettering on one corner.

No sooner had engines been cut before a swarm of men tied the trucks down. During the loading process at the supply warehouse, the pallets had been securely lashed down and together inside the 40-foot containers. While the trucks were positioned, Wayne, Sybil, and the other drivers had been taken aside and briefed on the task before them and what to expect. Thousands of hungry people were waiting for them.

No Pressure, Wayne had thought to himself. From the expressions of the other drivers, it was a shared sentiment.

At 300-foot square, the elevator pad was truly massive. The four semi-trucks and trailers left plenty of room for other vehicles and supplies, including another Bradley platoon, but these had already been assembled and secured to the pad by the time the trucks had arrived.

The last to arrive was the VIP delegation, including President Austin and Vice President Finley. The question of who would be included in the delegation had been hotly debated. When it was clear that both John and Gail felt they should go, the debate had shifted to trying to talk at least one of them into staying behind. Everyone else seemed shocked when John and Gail had joined forces and abruptly shut down the debate entirely, and commanded General Marcus to stay behind and deal with the captured alien creature and to 'watch the fort.'

Now, John and Gail sat together, along with a marine driver, in a borrowed Suburban, bracketed by their security details in a collection of Humvees.

While waiting for the last of the preparations to be completed, they finished a conference call with Dr. Nakamura about the preliminary observations about the captured alien creature. "Mr. President, Ms. Vice President, before we get disconnected, I wanted to mention an observation made by Dr. Lee, our sociologist. Our community here, Fort Brazos, and the newly found survivors from New London have a direct connection via this elevator. However, they are still separated by the physical distance between them and, from a practical perspective, by the amount of time it takes to travel between them. In fact, the travel time is not very different from how long it took to fly from Los Angeles to, say, New York. So, while we may collectively be the last survivors of humanity, these two population centers will likely remain very distinctly different from each other. We should, as a society, be prepared for the perceived isolation many may feel now that Fort Brazos isn't the *only* human community. Now that there is another, people will be reminded even more of how much has been lost."

John and Gail looked worriedly at each other. John whistled, "Wow, Doctor, you're just a ray of sunshine today."

If Dr. Nakamura took offense, he didn't indicate it on the call.

Gail shook her head, "Doctor, you have a point, and I hadn't considered the ramifications... I think that we've all been so overwhelmed at the positive aspect of the news of survivors that we hadn't thought that far ahead."

John followed up, "I'm sorry, Doctor, I didn't intend to seem harsh. Did your sociologist have any suggestions on how to deal with this?"

Dr. Nakamura continued smoothly, "Oh, I do understand. To be honest, I had much the same reaction as you did when Dr. Lee mentioned it. While we are not in front of a crowd, I just thought that would be a good time to discuss this with you privately. When the emotional high from this discovery fades, some people may have... issues. Other than trying to make sure that the populous feels confident that there is a plan for moving forward and establishing trust in their leaders, that is, you, I have no idea what to suggest."

Destiny

The caravan of trucks, Bradley's, and the VIP delegation drove out of the warehouse and headed towards the city. In the suburban, audio from the tactical radio channel played on the speakers, but John and Gail were lost in a debate about just exactly how much information they should "dump" on the New London survivors.

The caravan slowed to a stop as someone asked on the radio, "Vic 2, this is Lead Vic. I thought there was only supposed to be one door; what's this other here?"

All of the caravan except the Bradley's were quickly herded back to the warehouse. The Bradley's drove towards the newly opened blast doors to investigate.

John, Gail, and Dr. Nakamura made their way to the control room to see the live video feed. Since the attack on the highway, all military vehicles had been fitted with cameras sending live feeds back to their operating base.

The Bradley's had stopped a short distance away from the blast door entrance, and Lt. Pendleton's squad was on foot, reporting via radio.

"Godfather, this is Roughneck, everything looks clear here, but we've got a large... device here. A large object of some kind, over."

"Copy that Roughneck, advise, "device?" over."

Pendleton's exasperation was unconcealable, "Godfather, Area, looks like a super-large hangar with lots of equipment surrounding some sort of very big, very large piece of equipment; Roughneck recommends you see for yourself. No clue what this is, over."

"Copy that Roughneck, Tincan-1 this is Godfather, get us a live feed of what Roughneck's seeing over."

Another voice within a now moving Bradley called in reply, "Godfather, Tincan-1 wilco out."

Moments later, the feed from the Bradley's changed perspective as they approached the entrance. The light coming from the other side seemed harsher, more actinic. The space beyond was indeed quite large. The floors and walls seemed to be entirely made of some kind of dull metal. Caution-striped lift trucks, gantries, and cranes littered the vaulted room. As the vehicles passed underneath the colossal blast door, the field of view widened, and a large construction came into focus.

Gail whispered, "Is that…?"

John nodded, "I think that's the other shoe."

Marcus ordered, watching the scene from the Joint Reserve Base, "Roughneck, proceed with your team to search the area. In the meantime, I suspect it is safe to send the food and support personnel on to the city. In the meantime, Godfather, contact Lt. Garreth and have him bring Admiral Milner immediately. I imagine this is why the Gardeners wanted him in this mess too."

There were supposed to be protocols for how a President is first introduced to his top military officers. For one thing, there was a formal election cycle, an inauguration, and the auspices of the Oval Office to help cement both the legality and the perception of power and authority. Even in those tragic instances of a President dying in office, the transfer of power to the Vice President has been a deliberate, careful process that was both understood and expected.

In the hours and days after Awakening Day, the distrust and friction between the city government of Fort Brazos and General Marcus and been potentially explosive. However, there had at least been *some* time for the parties to get to know each other, begin to absorb the enormity of their circumstances and develop a tenuous agreement on how to move forward.

Vice Admiral Preston Milner III was afforded none of this. For him, it was a fait accompli. All he had was an hour and a half conference call that had left everyone he knew and loved raped and murdered, and his world chewed up and spat out.

Everyone had gathered in the parklike area around the fountains and reflecting pool. What food Lt. Garreth's men had brought did not go far, but to everyone's credit, it had all gone to children. Preston had been impressed when he saw Garreth's men even volunteer the power bars and what food or snacks they had on their persons to the children. Garreth, in particular, seemed particularly concerned about the children and women with babies and had radioed back an urgent request for baby food and supplies. However, Preston knew that this was not uncommon with Marines and soldiers Garreth's age.

When the call came for Preston to immediately leave and go to the warehouse area, he'd been about to refuse angrily. Even though he'd only been visiting New London, somehow their common circumstances with him, and him being senior, made them *his people*. He wouldn't leave them.

His emotions raged. Some small-town sheriff now claimed to be President, and a woman who weeks before only been an Air Force *Captain* was now Vice President!? Intellectually he understood the circumstances, but the rest of him screamed Junta or Coup or God-knew what. And to be held hostage with *food?* And now, to be summoned by them was just too much to take.

"Sir? Admiral?" Lt. Garreth had been talking to him or trying to, but he hadn't been listening. Garreth motioned that he would like to speak with him away from the crowd.

Preston ground his teeth, hesitated, then nodded, and followed the Lieutenant.

When they were a discreet distance from the noisy crowd and playing children, Garreth asked, "Sir, permission to speak freely, Sir."

Preston sighed and nodded curtly.

Garreth's expression was sympathetic, "Sir, like I said earlier, the rest of us have had weeks to digest everything that has happened, but if I may, I'd like to tell you what I've observed about the current... leadership," he looked furtively around him, "but I will deny ever saying any of this. Sir."

Preston's eyes widened, his brow furrowed, and he nodded, "Okay, Lieutenant, I did not hear what you are about to say."

Garreth took a deep breath, "Sir, I'd never met General Marcus, President Austin, or Vice President Finley before all this happened, and when it did happen, well sir, things very nearly went to hell. The General had just taken command a few days before, and on Awakening Day, in addition to waking up... here... forces from 19 other countries were also deposited on the base, and we almost had a small war. General Marcus defused that situation, and then we found out that the aliens had killed thousands of civilians in the city, in Fort Brazos, and General Marcus took it hard. When the city government realized that we were basically all alone, they were afraid that General Marcus would roll in and take over and that he wouldn't be willing to take orders from a small city government."

Preston shook his head, "I suppose that's understandable, in a way... from both sides."

"Sir, nobody, trusted each other, and the city was piled high with bodies. I know, I was first on scene."

"You were?"

"Yes, Sir, a flyover the city had shown us that an alien structure had been placed in the middle of town, and there were reports on the radio of chaos. General Marcus feared that there was an attack taking place."

"I see."

"Sir, the city leaders somehow kept their cool, for the most part. They met with General Marcus and, well, I think they realized that they needed to figure out how to go forward, and that's when they drafted Sheriff Austin and Major Finley."

Preston blinked, "Drafted?"

Garreth nodded, "Yes, Sir, kicking and screaming. It was a compromise. Under the circumstances and with the population imbalance, they decided that one person from the civilian government and someone from the military would be elected. That and the alien ultimatum."

Preston took a step back, "What? What ultimatum?"

Garreth sighed, "Sir! There's so much you don't know yet. The aliens did this big light show where they showed a video of the earth being attacked and told us that we either needed to accept our fate and go to war with the Accipiters, or they would find someone else to do it."

Preston's face fell as his eyes gazed into a void, and he shrunk back, "My God."

"Yes, Sir, so we had an election and voted to go along with the ultimatum and elect Austin and Finley and to have a constitutional convention in a few months. Sir, if I may, please cut us some slack. We've all got a gun to our heads and, well, I have to say that I've really come to admire the General as well as President Austin and Vice President Finley. I know that I sure as hell would not have held up as well as they have if I were in their shoes. Sir. Oh, and Austin was the first person to kill an alien."

"He what?" Preston cocked his head,

"Yes, Sir, Sheriff Austin gunned down one of the alien creatures. It's all on video…. Sir, he personally killed the alien who killed one of my men, several civilians, and nearly killed me. Sir… he saved my life. Also, apparently, he was already quite popular before the Aliens came. People are saying he would have run for Governor and won."

Despite the cool temperature, Garreth was sweating.

Preston swallowed and began to reevaluate Garreth and many other things. "Thank you for your candor, Lieutenant…."

Garreth waited pensively.

"It's too bad I never heard you say it."

Garreth closed his eyes briefly and sighed. "Thank you, Sir."

✪ ✪ ✪

Vice Admiral Preston Milner III exited the Humvee outside the warehouse/control center and unconsciously straightened his uniform jacket before walking to the entrance where President Austin, Vice President Finley, and an assortment of officers and neutral-faced security details waited. Rather than wait, as protocol demanded, John stepped forward and met him halfway, extending his hand with a smile. Not only that, the man was wearing jeans, a leather jacket and of all things, a bolo tie! He could also see that the man was armed with what looked like a 1911 in a holster on his hip under his jacket.

Preston stopped and took John's hand. At 5'11", he was a full three inches shorter than John, and he took the handshake firmly. He was surprised there was no contest of wills, no test of whose grip was stronger. It was simply a handshake.

John reached around and put a hand on Preston's shoulder. "Admiral Milner, I'm delighted to meet you. Look, I know all of this is all a lot to take in, believe me. All of us are still in various stages of shock ourselves, but you and your people are all a miracle! We had no idea there were more survivors. Please know that we'll make sure your people are taken care of. Anything you need. A convoy of food and supplies passed you on your way here."

Preston warily nodded, "Thank you, Mr. President, that is greatly needed. We're still in the process of organizing and figuring out who is here and exploring the city."

John sensed Preston's hesitation and took the opportunity to move to introduce him to Gail, "And I'd like to introduce you to the other member of the Presidential shotgun wedding, Vice President Gail Finley."

Gail, still wearing the permanently borrowed business suit, moved with her usual fighter pilot's jaunty grace, her limp almost gone. She shot John a blistering look, then turned to shake Preston's hand, "Admiral, don't worry, you'll get used to him. Eventually, and, I'll second our commitment to providing whatever your people up here need."

Preston was taken aback by the energy, both positive and negative, between the pair and could not imagine a less… Politic… combination. "Thank you, Ms. Vice President, although I'm beginning to wonder what I'm supposed to be Admiral of… at this point. A war with Aliens? The country, our planet, gone?" His voice broke, "My wife and daughter, gone?" He swallowed, "Also, if I may, I thought we were all going to meet in the city somewhere and address the people there?"

John and Gail exchanged looks.

Gail lowered her voice, "Believe me, Admiral, we understand how you feel. The damned aliens killed five percent of the civilian population just to make a point, just to make sure we thoroughly and completely understood that the sharp jabbing sensation on the back of our heads was the barrel of their gun."

Preston looked at Gail, then John, and back at Gail. He swallowed and nodded.

John added, "Look, Admiral, you didn't get a chance to think about all this and absorb it over time like the rest of us." He paused, "And you didn't get a chance to vote in the Plebiscite to indicate whether you would go along with the alien demands or to go along with the election of Gail and myself, an election we did not want or ask for, mind you. You're being thrown into this without time to think or emotionally deal with any of it."

"Yes… Mr. President."

Gail picked up the conversation, "So, we're not going to ask for your vote right now. We're going to make sure you and your people are Okay, and then we're going to answer everyone's questions and give you some time to think. After that, you and everyone else up here will have to decide what they want to do."

John continued, "Down the elevator is an entire virgin world. Your people will be free to immigrate to Fort Brazos or go off and explore the wilderness. Those who want to stay will need to pledge an oath to the new government and to accept the alien terms."

Preston unconsciously rubbed his chin, "I see. Sir. Maam. And what are we supposed to be doing if we stay?"

Behind them, a unit radio crackled, and the group could overhear Lt. Pendleton's voice call out, "Godfather, this is Roughneck, all clear in here, but this room has got a least a few hundred meters on each side, over."

John and Gail looked at each other, and Gail answered, "And that, Admiral, is what I suspect will answer the question of what you will be Admiral of and what you and your people will be doing."

Lt. Garreth's platoon escorted Admiral Milner, John, Gail, and their details to the hangar bay entrance on foot, where Lt. Pendleton and his men waited. It had been decided that they wanted to see everything on foot and that the vehicles would follow behind them, providing video coverage and, if needed, support or evacuation.

The entire far end of the bay was an enormous caution-striped blast door. In the middle of the bay stood what could only be a spacecraft.

The outer shell of the craft appeared to be seven or eight hundred feet tall with a very alien and vaguely blue-green organic appearance to the elliptical rings wrapped around internal mechanisms of some kind, and a dark cylindrical object in the center with a large rectangular section attached to the front of it that did not look original. A central spindle impaled the whole thing.

John muttered, "It's like a misshapen Christmas ornament…., the kind with a cage around an object inside. What *is* that thing inside it? Is that…?"

Preston stopped and stared. "I don't know about that thing tacked on the front of it, but, my God, it looks like… maybe the Montana with her propulsion section missing." He heaved a sigh, "That's why the aliens picked New London!"

John raised his eyebrows, and Gail answered, "New London is, or was, a nuclear submarine base in Connecticut."

John objected, "A submarine? What? Why a submarine? Why not the ISS or something?"

Gale shook her head, "Of course! It would be the logical thing for us to do if we were to try and merge our technology base with a working alien propulsion drive. A submarine is a closed environment that already has a life support system. It already is a warship, and it is designed to operate without resupply for months or longer underwater. The ISS is paper-thin and fragile and can only carry a handful of people, and it's not a warship. The gardeners have merged our technology with something obviously alien to us to create a hybrid ship with systems we can understand. It's… training wheels."

Preston turned to John, "And the Navy has the training and traditions for operating independently a long way from home for extended periods of time."

He nodded to Gail, "And no offense to the Air Force, but Air Force missions are generally measured in hours and operate from fixed locations."

Gail smiled, "No offense taken, Admiral. It appears that the Gardeners have studied us more closely than I had imagined."

The hangar bay was too large for an echo and seemed to swallow the noise from their conversations. Even the noise from the Bradley's seemed muted.

John turned to Gail and Preston, "You noticed how strange it sounds in here?"

Gail thought for a moment, exchanged knowing looks with Preston, and smiled, "Flight decks can be brutally loud. You need hearing protection. I suspect that when things get busy in here, the noise would be deafening, so the Gardeners have some sort of active noise abatement going on."

John nodded, "That's what I was thinking. On an oil rig the noise can make it hard to communicate, and that can lead to accidents."

As they approached the base of the ship, Gail smiled, "It reminds me of those concept designs NASA did a while back of what a warp drive ship might look like."

John asked Preston, "Admiral, is there anything else you can deduce from looking at the submarine portion of this thing, and what's on the front of it?"

Preston nodded, "From here, it looks like the engine room and propulsion sections are gone, but I believe the reactor section is still there, assuming that's what is still inside. Maybe they want us to use our own power systems and keep them separate from the... external alien part? As for that large, squared-off section on the front, where the sonar dome section would have begun, I would guess that that would be a new control center to navigate and operate the spacecraft portion of the vessel."

John nodded, "I suppose that keeping as much of our own technology intact means there is less complexity to deal with, and we already know how to use and maintain those systems."

John stopped in front of one of the blue-green rings. The surface was glassy and smooth. He reached out and touched the cold and nearly frictionless surface. He swallowed and ground his teeth for a moment.

He looked up at the vessel that towered above him and whispered,

"Though much is taken, much abides; and though
We are not now that strength which in old days
Moved earth and heaven, that which we are, we are;
One equal temper of heroic hearts,
Made weak by time and fate, but strong in will
To strive, to seek, to find, and not to yield."

Gail looked at John in surprise. *Who are you?*

Preston stopped and reached out to touch the ring himself, "One of my earliest memories was my dad taking me to see the ship he commanded at the time. It seemed so vast, and I was so small I had to be carried across the gangplank lest I fall into the water…. I wanted to see everything, but I was so small he had to carry me everywhere so that I could see…."

Gail traced her hand across the surface of the ring, not even leaving a smudge. She swallowed and let her arms fall to her sides, her hands clenching into fists. Her lips tightened as she gazed up and up at the craft. She took several steps back until both John and Preston were in front of her.

Her eyes glinted as her anger grew, "Admiral, John, I believe we should name this ship the Blood Phoenix…. She is risen from the pyres of our dead… of our dead world."

Preston's eyes widened, and he slowly nodded.

John smiled thinly, "And may her flight be terrible and true."

The End

BOOKS IN THIS SERIES

Accipiter War # 1: A military town "awakens" to familiar surroundings but soon discover that they are not in Texas, or even Earth, anymore. The current-day city of Fort Brazos, Texas, and the nearby Joint Reserve Base have been abducted — scooped up whole and deposited inside a vast artificial hollow world, nearly 4000 miles long. Thousands are dead. Who has done this and why? Are the humans to be lab rats? Slaves? Or is there some other, terrible purpose... or a greater destiny? Accipiter War emphasizes hope and the endurance of the human spirit in the face of unthinkable tragedy.

Stealing Fire: Accipiter War # 2: The citizens of New London and Fort Brazos awakened to find themselves in a hollow world. Accipiter War # 2: Stealing Fire follows their journey of discovery and what promises to be a generational war against an ancient and galaxy-spanning enemy. Now they must race against time and conspiracy to launch the hybrid starship. The window of opportunity to strike a crucial blow against the enemy is closing fast, and they must somehow put their differences aside long enough to work together. If they don't, the Gardeners, the mysterious race that abducted them in the first place, might well decide the human race isn't worth saving after all.

The Forge: Accipiter War #3: After the harrowing raid on occupied Earth, the survivors struggle to cope with what they have learned and to devise a strategy. The Accipiter empire spans the galaxy, and while the remaining humans are safe, for now, the clock is ticking. The Accipiters are turning over every leaf to find them – and they have the millions of ships to do it with. The humans have one cobbled together hybrid. Secrets are revealed and desperate work begins to build defenses. Meanwhile, the true conspirators behind the homegrown attack remain at large. All the while, mysterious craters and fires begin to erupt closer and closer to town, and Phoenix is sent off on a secretive mission to parts unknown.

McKendree Cylinder
(SPOILERS)

I've long been inspired by Larry Niven's Ringworld (Okay, it was bigger at 997,000 miles wide), Arthur C. Clark's Rama (just 31 miles long) and especially, Gerald O'Neil's Cylinder Worlds. Babylon 5 (oh how we miss you) was merely 5 miles long. The world of Fort Brazos is inspired by these dramatic visions and is closer to a McKendree Cylinder. The world Fort Brazos wakes up inside is nearly 4,000 miles long, with a surface area almost twice that of the moon and about half that of Mars.

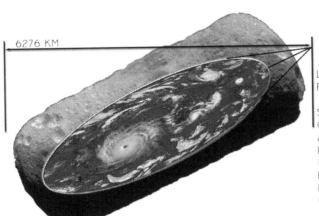

6276 KM

LENGTH: 6,270 KM
RADIUS: 1,448 KM

SA: 70,274,160 SQ KM
ORIGIN: UNKNOWN
AGE: UNKNOWN
LOCATION: UNKNOWN
INHABITANTS: UNKNOWN
PURPOSE: UKNOWN
ENVIRONMENT: EARTHLIKE
OTHER LIFE: HOSTILE

About the Authors

Patrick Seaman is the principal author. He created the concept and drives the storyline for the Fort Brazos series. He crafted concept art and managed creative development for Fort Brazos. Patrick is an entrepreneur, consultant, Internet pioneer, former publisher, editor, and author. In addition, Patrick is a lifelong shooting enthusiast and former rifle and pistol instructor.

Since helping launch broadcast.com in the early days of online digital media, Patrick has launched, advised, and served in many startups around the globe in C-Level positions or their boards.

You can follow Patrick at:

http://www.amazon.com/author/patrickseaman
https://twitter.com/PatrickSeaman
http://www.linkedin.com/in/patrickseaman
http://AccipiterWar.com
http://patrickseaman.com

Blake Seaman is an Information Technology executive, author, and classical composer. His music is available on all major streaming platforms. He is a proud resident of the State of Texas, where he celebrated the birth of his first child with his wife 6 months before the publication of this book; he dedicates his work on this project to them, and hopes to raise part of a new generation of Science Fiction fans. Blake is also an avid sports shooter and Tea aficionado.

https://BlakeSeaman.com
https://open.spotify.com/artist/3aK0vHFZEJ7YLq6a9CV9Yw
http://www.amazon.com/author/blakeseaman
http://www.cdbaby.com/Artist/BlakeSeaman
https://itunes.apple.com/us/album/fort-brazos/id961266753

6755e109-67f4-41d7-8366-8a3073f3ec5dR01